AZORA'S RIFT

Elaia Crowe

CONTENTS

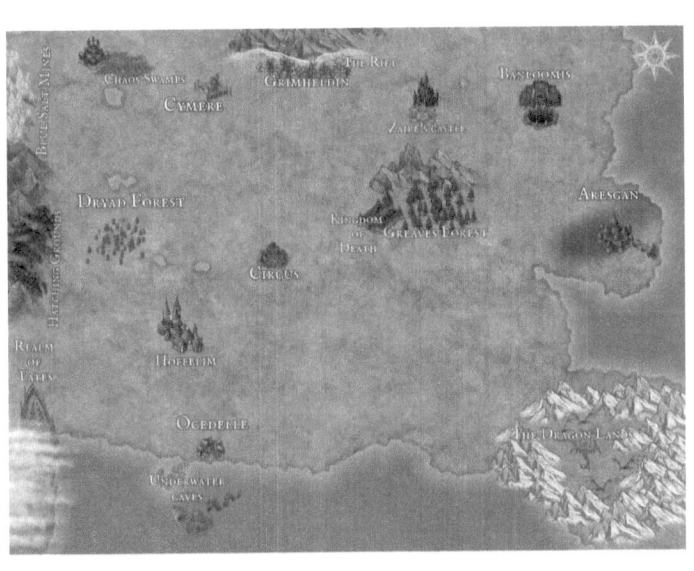

CHAPTER ONE
VISITOR
Azora

"You've angered dragons." The woman shoved something into my hand and glanced behind me. "Can I come in, so we can talk?" The woman with white bobbed hair and amethyst eyes stared at me with a blank expression. Her porcelain skin reddened around her cheeks and gave her a natural glow.

I clutched my dagger tighter in my hand but kept it concealed behind my front door. "Which dragons?"

"All of them."

My tracker sense knew the woman who stood unexpectedly on my porch in the middle of the night, but not strong enough to conjure who she was. My seer sense allowed me to find objects and people I had a connection to. It filed everything and everyone I'd ever interacted with into compartments in my brain, and when I came across something again, I could search my mind for where the connection originated.

Most of my memories had been stolen and returned two weeks ago, and it was taking me a while to recall everything. There were most likely many things I had no clue I didn't remember. Finally, the short memory of her rushed back. I'd met her at a circus and hadn't seen her since.

I stared at the gold parchment that looked made of dragon scales. "Why would I let you in my house?" The main reason I gripped the dagger in my hand tighter was the protection of my reaper, Alcaius. Fear constantly tormented me that his location would be discovered, and the authorities would drag him to his execution as punishment for killing another reaper. A transgression he'd committed to keep the one he'd killed from collecting my soul.

"Do you always make visitors stand out in the rain?"

"When they arrive uninvited and I don't know their intentions, I do."

She jerked her pointy chin to the odd paper. "Read the note."

I undid the red seal and read the contents. "The dragons have requested my presence in their valley. I am to come alone to answer for my crimes against them and pay penance for an enormous problem I've caused their kind." After reading the instructions two more times, I glanced up and laughed. "This is serious?"

"Yes, they are aware of your capabilities. Can't you connect with the note and see its truth? That's what they told me you could do."

I closed my eyes and tugged at the part of my brain that housed my seer sense. It opened up into images of angry dragons condemning my name and demanding I make amends.

The woman shivered and held a cloak over her head to block out the endless rain my hometown of Aresgan thrived on.

I opened the door wider and spread my arm behind me. "Come in out of the rain."

My house didn't have a ton of room in it, but the seating in front of the small stone fireplace would warm her enough. She took the worn blue chair closest to the flames, and I took the couch after making her some warm tea in my tiny kitchen that held a counter, chill box, and stove. The rest of the area had little to it in the way of decor. Only a few framed cross-stitch pieces, that my sister Raya and my mother had made, hung on the walls.

I handed her the teacup and saucer and set mine down on a little end table. "So you speak for dragons. I'm Azora, in case the dragons didn't tell you. Do you have a name?"

"Dagny. I guess I should have introduced myself when we met at the circus."

"Things were a little intense then," I said.

"Yes, that whole thing was intense, but I volunteered to bring you the letter because I wanted to thank you for freeing my dragon. That was the entire reason I was stuck there because I couldn't free him. Phyrix, the dragon you released, has been defending you against the dragons who are angry with you."

"Which is apparently all but him?"

She gave a single nod. "Correct."

"They're most likely mad about the dragons I harmed during jobs and on the quest, and that doesn't make me exactly want to go meet with them. Angry beasts much larger than me, all bunched in the same spot and vengeful, doesn't sound like an ideal venture for me."

"The problem is, dragons are stubborn, and it's not just those things you mentioned. There is another matter they are cross with you about, and they believe you owe them to fix it." She set her teacup on its saucer that rested on a little table with a lamp. "It's not a simple matter to let it go, either. They will most likely attack your city and force you to their valley if you choose to not willingly comply."

"What is this grave error I have committed against them?"

She glanced around the room as though looking for eavesdroppers. "That's something I'm not allowed to discuss outside of the valley, but you are welcome to connect with me to see I speak the truth." She held out her hand and waited for me to accept.

She had blocks up in certain areas of her mind, which was common for people familiar with seer magic. It allowed them privacy, but I could weave around it and find what they wanted me to see. Through a sense different than vision, I saw dragons lined up in a beautiful valley full of enormous flowers and exotic trees. The entire place seemed like a paradise, and it was a rare treat to see because, according to all texts I'd read, the location of the valley was hidden from most species outside dragon kind. Through Dagny, the dragons' anger toward me poured stronger than even the note had conveyed. Desperation hung around all of them, but the reason was masked in her mental blocks.

She sat back down in her chair and took another sip of the tea, giving me a few minutes to process the visions. "Part of the reason I am involved is my bond with Phyrix, the dragon you freed at the circus. As you might know, dragon and human bonds are rare, but I am one of the lucky few. They believe it puts me at a unique advantage to speak on their behalf to another human. Transparency seems best here, so I'd also like you to know that I, like you, have a seer sense. This way it will seem less like manipulation, hopefully. I used my sense to tell your motivations, and they have agreed to terms I told them would most likely make you go to the valley and do as they wish."

"A motivation seer. And what do you think I want?"

She glanced down the hall. "I'm guessing your reaper is staying here?" She sidestepped my question by asking her own. "Since those probably don't belong to you." She nodded to the large black boots at the door.

My hands curled around my blade. "Maybe I have big feet. You make a lot of assumptions."

She stared at where my hand clutched my dagger handle. "Protective of him you are, but no need to stab me. His location won't be told to anyone by me, but honestly it's not the boots. I saw him stepping out for a stroll about twenty minutes ago. It's how I knew it would be a good time to speak with you. It's not surprising he's gotten himself into this mess."

"Why is that?"

"He has a temper. I went to school with him, and he was never someone anyone wanted to mess with because he's cold, impulsive, and explosive."

"Alcaius is harmless, gentle, and kind."

She snorted a laugh and stopped when she caught my face. "He's only soft toward you, dear, but he has created quite the stir in the kingdom of late. The Accounters have placed a high bounty on his head."

"The Accounters?"

"Yes, the council directly above the Determiners. They are the ones in charge of reaper affairs, and they keep the Determiners accountable as well as many other things."

"Alcaius says the Determiners have no accountability. That they are allowed to place any soul they want on the fate fabric to be reaped in the name of universal balance," I said.

"A reaper would think that because they are commanded to obey their assignments with no questions, but it's more complex than that. Back to your motivations. When you were at the circus, and I fixed your hair, I read you at the ringmaster's request." She stopped and nodded. "Yes, I committed a violation. I think you may understand better than your face is telling me you do. Seers often use their sense without thought of mental ethics and privacy, but in my case, Onyx, the ringmaster, had my dragon. You are motivated by Alcaius's safety. Even then I saw that, and as I confirmed while you were reading me, you want his name cleared."

"You read me?" I sighed and shook my head. "Of course you did, but it doesn't take a motivation seer to figure out I'd want that. Not only do I love my reaper, but it's my fault he's in the mess in the first place. He saved my life. Broke one of the highest laws to keep my soul from an early afterlife."

"Yes, that's true, but not only do the dragons have a way for you to clear his name and protect everyone you love from an incoming threat, but they will sweeten the deal by giving your fairy back her wisping abilities."

I narrowed my eyes. "My fairy? What are you talking about?"

"Bryony. I sensed that as a high motivation for you at the circus."

"I don't know what you're talking about."

Confusion spread across her face in an expression that probably matched mine. "Well, just the same. Would you come to see the dragons to clear Alcaius and get the bounty off his head, as well as take care of a threat that could harm your family?" She stood up and moved to the door. "The dragons are allowing you a week to decide before they take more drastic measures. It'll give you time to put your affairs in order and ditch the reaper. That's one of the requirements. Alcaius isn't allowed to come with you. You are to come alone, except the fairy you seem to not want to acknowledge. If you decide to, she can come with."

"I don't know any fairy."

"Okay." She put her hands up in surrender. "A week for you to decide, and then there might be dragons knocking down your door." She saw herself out into the night.

I sat contemplating everything she'd said. Was there any choice but to go? There seemed to be none, but I needed to get things together first, and somehow figure out how to travel to the dragon valley without Alcaius. The only way that could possibly happen was if he didn't know anything about it.

I rubbed the ache in my shoulder that caused me to miss Alcaius. His fang marks on my skin drew attention to my addiction to reaper venom, but it wasn't enough most days. He often took us close to a permanent bond, only to pull back before it was solidified. I wondered if making me his mate would increase the addiction or finally soothe it enough to not constantly crave it. We'd decided to take things slowly, but I was human. Alcaius bonding with me would break another high law of his people. A fierce protectiveness swept over me for him, and I knew I'd see the dragons.

About an hour later, he stepped through the door. He strode quickly over to me, and yanked me up from the couch, drawing out a slow kiss that coursed desire through me. Never had a greeting created such security in me, showing me how loved and desired I was. He led me back to the bedroom.

He drew me down with him on the bed, kissing my neck. "I've missed you."

"You're the one who went on a walk without me."

"A walk? Yeah, that's what I was doing."

I pulled back from his kiss. "Your tone doesn't sound suspicious at all."

"Good." He unbuttoned my shirt after removing his own.

"You're trying to distract me." I gasped as his mouth moved between my thighs. The distraction definitely worked.

Chapter Two
Thirst
Alcaius

I kissed a sleeping Azora, as I slipped out of our bed, and left to stalk the midnight streets for my prey. Her scent lingered on my clothes, mixing with the smoke from barrel fires and the stench of spoiling food in rubbish bins. I snuffed out the other aromas with my reaper nose, but let her smell of rain-washed cedar and honeysuckle propel me through her city. As a fugitive, portal jumps were too dangerous, but a reaper had to reap and soothe his blood lust. The desire to kill had devoured me for weeks.

I followed the man who beat his wife and children daily in a drunken rage and completely sober. No state of his gave them any reprieve, but that ended tonight. As long as I didn't use my scythe to collect his soul, I wouldn't be caught by the fate fabric watchers. I had a different fate in mind for him than delivering him to the executioners. The binding thread buzzed in my pocket and urged me forward. He stumbled into the alley on his way to the tavern to numb himself after leaving his wife bloodied on the kitchen floor with their children in their beds.

Anticipation tingled in my fists as I stepped into the light in full reaper form. My scythe crackled on my back, willing me to use it, but I remained in control by not reaching for it. The blade had a temper, but it had no choice but to accept my decisions. A tabby cat jumped off a trash bin, and the man kicked it across the alley. The cat hissed and limped away.

"You should pick on someone who can hit you back, or are you that much of a coward?" I lunged toward him, itching to energize myself with his fear.

He stumbled over air before catching himself on the brick wall. "R-reaper, it's not my time."

"That's not really something you get to decide. The gods are tired of your violent hands."

People telling me I had their death date wrong was the number one response humans gave me as a reason not to kill them. They seemed to think they could convince me of a misunderstanding that would spare their lives.

He stuck his palms up. "I ain't hurtin' nobody who ain't deserve it."

"You see, that's my motto, and it's pretty accurate because it's how you ended up on my list. What exactly did your wife do to end up bloody on your kitchen floor?"

He tossed his hand to the side. "Burnt my dinner too many times."

A crack broke up the silent night as my knuckles met his cheek, and his back slammed into the wall as he crumpled to the ground.

I took five steps until I stood over him. "And what did your children do to earn your brutality?"

His depraved yellow eyes met mine. "They were born."

My boot slammed his head into the wall and didn't stop until his life left him. I removed the binding thread from my pocket, lured his newly released soul into it, and slipped onto the streets. I'd done it all fast enough that his soul hadn't alerted a collector, and he'd stay trapped in the thread until I could place souls into my scythe to take to the executioners. The executioners decided where souls went after death and sent them down different lava channels with unknown destinations. Only they knew the places they sent souls.

Satisfaction washed over me as taking a life fulfilled a deep purpose bound to my soul. The destiny stitched for me made killing something meaningful, and while I relished everything that went with it, a part of me knew to enjoy slaying meant I'd damned myself by perhaps no other measure than my conscience. The addiction I fed came at the cost of my peace, and the only consultation was slaughtering people who harmed in the cruelest ways.

Fresh paint burned away any other scents in the quaint house where I'd hidden away for the last two weeks, ignoring that life waited outside its walls.

Azora bit her lip as she stared at the newly turned blue wall. "I think he'll like it. It's his favorite color. The color of the sky and Lowan's eyes, not that Alexios thinks about those things when he sees the color. It's more like I feel Lowan still lives every time I see blue." Lowan was her youngest brother who'd died as a child a couple of years ago.

"It's a nice way to remember him," I said.

Together we'd added a room onto her house to give her other brother, Alexios, his own room as he used to sleep in the living area at the front of the small cottage. He'd turned eleven a week ago and was currently gone to school.

I threw Azora over my shoulder and smacked her ass. "Hard work deserves a reward."

She squealed as I spun her around and ran to the next room. "I should show you how grateful I am for your help on the room."

I plopped her on the bed and hovered over her. "Or I could show you how grateful I am for you letting me stay here."

She shrugged. "What can I say? You provide well."

I kissed her stomach, loving the way she arched into me. "Time to show you exactly how well I provide." I kissed down her belly and moved downward, and my tongue licked between her legs until she moaned. I nibbled on her thighs and returned to her clit. She shuddered beneath me, and I turned her over, positioning my cock at her entrance and slamming inside her.

I took my time but chuckled when she bucked back for me to pick up speed. "Patience, love."

"Mark me." She gasped and gripped the sheets at my deep thrusts.

"You're getting addicted."

"Like you mind."

"Maybe I want you to want me for my personality."

"You'll be waiting for eons there." Her smile lit up her voice in a teasing manner.

I slowed down my movements, savoring how she clenched around my length. She tried to not let go until I gave her something more. "Alcaius," she whispered my name like a desperate prayer.

My fangs sank into her neck, and I enjoyed the sweet taste of her blood as I released my venom into her. It sent pleasure pulsing through her, and she squeezed my dick hard. I grunted as her blood zipped through me in an intense connection—an almost fusion of our souls. So often, I'd taken us to the edge of a forbidden mate bond, and sometimes the control felt impossible to keep. I wanted her for more than the physical, and the bond would connect us in every way either of us needed. My people would riot that the prince of Death had mated himself to a mortal.

We rode out the waves of euphoria that the brief, unstable connection brought us. I rammed into her until her clamping against my dick dragged everything from me, and I rolled out of her, pulling her on top of me.

I kissed the top of her head and ran my fingers over her spine. "I love you."

She hummed and snuggled closer. "You're becoming addicted."

"That happened ages ago."

"I love you too."

Her breathing slowed to the perfect rhythm of sleep that showed she trusted me, and I kissed her temple, wishing time could not rip us to any other event. Time, however, was greedy in its devouring of existence.

I awoke to the smell of something seasoned and smiled as Azora carried in a tray of food. "You're spoiling me too much," I said.

"Like you have for me for the last five meals. It was my turn." She set the tray on a little table next to the small round bed we'd been sharing over the last few weeks.

I plucked a red grape from its stem and placed it on her lips before accepting the one she offered me. Indulging in a simple life with her had made a complex life of reaping and royalty seem insane. If only killing didn't pull me like a stick caught in a tumultuous current.

I crept around the brick wall to the alley to watch as the man took his latest funds to the bank. The signed note in his hand transferred money from his elderly aunt to him. He accomplished the task by keeping her captive in a small room and gaining her signature for the promise of food and water. If she refused at all, he left her without any for hours and even days. I'd gotten the tip in my favorite place to find my targets, which was the pub. His housekeeper had spoken about it during a drunken rant that had led me to follow him and confirm the rumors over the last couple of days.

He skipped out of the bank and into the stone streets, heading toward the market with his newfound coin as he did each week. The sun had nearly set with only a sliver of orange competing with the appearing stars for light. A covered bridge appeared ahead, and when he slipped under it, I pounced. The thud of his body against the tunnel wall resounded with a crack, and I followed the shove with a punch to his jaw. He raised his arms to block me, and I kneed his gut.

He buckled and slid to the ground. "Please! I have money. Lots of it. Please! Just take it!"

"It's how you got that money that's the problem. Isn't it?"

"W-what do y-you mean?"

My flesh retreated into bone, and I raised my scythe. "Time to pay for the coins in your pocket. The coins that should weigh too heavy for you to frolic to the market with. The guilt should press you into the grey streets."

"It can't be my time! It can't be! There's so much more to do."

I brought my scythe across his throat, and blood splattered onto the brick wall as I severed his jugular. It'd been months since I'd killed with my blade, but it was driving me more and more mad with its complaints. It took great effort to not activate its magic when I used it for violence. The minute magic crackled from it when I killed was the moment it would alert the fabric watchers. For this reason, I controlled every thought and action carefully to keep its power dormant.

"Alcaius!"

I froze at the beautiful, shocked voice behind me and spun around. "Azora? What are you doing here?"

"I woke up to an empty bed and grew terrified when I sensed you in the city. I thought they found you because there's no way you'd risk going into the middle of Aresgan. Did this man try to capture you?" She stared at my target, who clawed at his throat.

He went limp, and I had no choice but to watch his eyes go vacant. The high flowed through me, giving me new life, and I needed to indulge in it before I could address things with the gorgeous woman next to me. I removed the binding thread from my pocket and bound his soul to it. It went into the pack next to my scythe for safekeeping. The pleasurable tingling tiptoeing across my arms eased, and I pressed against the wall to absorb the last bit of the energy into my nerves.

"Alcaius!" Azora stood over the body like she wanted to confirm he'd actually died. "What happened?"

"Not here. We have to get out of here before someone catches me." I grabbed her hand and slipped out the opposite end, taking back streets all the way to her house.

Azora had me sit on a chair while she scrubbed the blood from my face and hands. "What happened back there?"

"I killed a man."

"Yes, I know, but why?"

I avoided her eyes as the enjoyment of killing bled into shame. "He was evil, and it needed to be done."

"He was evil? That's why you killed him?"

"Yes."

I explained to her my unquenchable thirst for slaughter, and her eyes grew in disappointment with each new word I spoke.

I forced my gaze to hers. "You're looking at me the way all of them do."

She tossed the bloody rags into a bin. "How's that?"

"Like I'm a monster. Like you see me differently now."

She washed her hands in the sink and pulled away when I grabbed her wrist. "Why would I see you differently when you have warned me countless times about what you are? That's not exactly my problem here, though saying I wasn't disturbed would be a lie. Lying to you isn't something I'd take to well."

"Good. I'd never want you not to be honest with me, even for my sake. If it's not what I did to the man, what is the problem here between us?"

She handed me a towel and stepped toward the door. "That you risked execution, and that it seems you will continue to do it."

"It's who I am. Without reaping I will waste away, so the only way to remedy it with my conscience is to kill in a manner that seems just. What I was created to be leaves me no peace."

She closed her eyes and nodded. "What will become of the aunt?"

"I restored what he stole and paid for her future care out of my own funds."

Her eyes flew open. "That's kind."

"But it doesn't lessen what I did. Does it?"

"I don't know. How often have you done this, and why didn't you tell me?"

I stood up but didn't step closer as I watched for any indication of what she thought. "Because it's not something I'm proud of, but I should have told you."

She studied me for a moment before leaving.

CHAPTER THREE
LEAVING THE SIMPLE
Azora

I sat on the small bench that backed up to my bedroom window and alternated between watching the sunrise and Alcaius. He slept on his stomach, sprawled out, taking up lots of space like he did most places. When Alcaius entered a room, you didn't miss him. People often said reapers carried dread with them like they leaked woe from all the pores in their bodies. I never sensed that with Alcaius, and I was too smitten with him to feel anything but affection for him when he entered the room. However, what I'd witnessed under the bridge disturbed me. Despite his actions making sense, it wasn't clear to me that his reasons justified what he'd done.

My genuine doubt gave me room to tell him I needed a break so I could go to the dragons. Either way, that needed to happen because we couldn't keep living with the fear of his potential trial and execution. I couldn't, anyway. If the dragons had some way to get his name cleared so he could go back to reaping, that seemed better than him playing judge and executioner. He'd made it clear he needed to reap, but I worried about so many things with his current method.

After the sun made it into the sky, he stirred and sat up, smiling at me. "Hey, beautiful."

"Hey."

His smile dropped, and he studied the patchwork quilt over him. "Are we okay?"

"There's not much okay about our situation. You're a reaper and need to do what every instinct in your body is telling you to do. The drive you diminish with your form of justice probably seems unquenchable. It's your nature. Something created for a purpose that is now stolen from you."

"Your understanding comes with a rebuttal."

I got under the covers next to him and crawled onto his lap when he tugged me over. "There are still many things unresolved that I think need to be fixed before we can relax into a simple life."

He played with my hair and kissed down my neck. "Why can't we live in this place with no enormous responsibilities? I clean up the streets of Aresgan and make it a safer place for you and Alexios."

"Prince of Death can't possibly find fulfillment in that. Can he?"

"He finds fulfillment in this." He cupped my face, moving his lips over mine in a slow, sensual manner.

I returned the kiss, and our tongues entangled, competing for dominance in a pleasurable way. We slid onto our sides as his fingers lowered. I moaned into his mouth, which encouraged his enthusiasm. His bulge pressed against me, and I freed it from his pants. He eased inside, taking things slowly as we matched the rhythm with the speed of our mouths. We took our time, and I burned the feel of him inside me deep into memory, afraid someone might steal it from me again.

Emotions and his thrusting overwhelmed me, and my body convulsed, taking me over the edge by the deep bond I felt with him. It was an orgasm, both physical and emotional. Tears trickled down my cheeks, and he kissed them while still moving inside me. I came two more times before he finally joined me on the last. Maybe it was because I knew this was a sort of goodbye that created the intensity of it all. I sobbed into his chest, and he held me, not speaking. Maybe because he also knew something differed from all the dozens of other times we'd slept together over the last several weeks.

He left and brought in breakfast like he had nearly every morning. "Alexios is still asleep."

"His season break starts soon. I'm thinking about taking him to see Raya."

"You're going to Greaves? Right next to my father's castle."

"Yes, and I know you can't come with me, but you're welcome to stay here or it might be good to visit Zaire again." I spread strawberry jam over my toast and took a crunchy bite.

He stopped buttering his toast and studied me. "This is about what happened under the bridge."

"What you did is a lot to take in, and I realize that if I'm going to be with a reaper, I have to accept taking lives is a big part of who you are. What about the reapers who only collect or the women who don't reap at all? I still think that's sexist, by the way, but how do they quench their thirst to kill?"

"For one, my drive is higher as the son of Death. As proven by all the heirs before me, they have a powerful instinct for slaughter. It's believed this is placed into us by the gods to fulfill our duty without question. Not all reapers are activated in the same way. Some have their powers dormant. My brother Myik can never be a reaper and therefore has no desire to kill."

"Why can't he?"

"He has a rare condition that is causing his heart to slowly turn to glass."

I finished my latest bite of toast and set it next to my strawberries. "Is there a cure?"

"No." He pushed his food around with his fork as though his mind left the room.

We both contemplated things for a while, and the entire conversation reaffirmed my need to get to the dragons and see what they had to offer to save Alcaius.

"Do you remember a fairy named Bryony?"

He dropped his spoon back into his fruit bowl. "Yeah, you say that like you don't. I thought you had all your memories back."

"I did too, but I'm not sure now."

He set his tray next to him and reached out his hand. "Can you connect to me to find Bryony?"

"I would imagine so if you knew her well enough." I accepted his invitation and concentrated as he thought of the fairy.

Flashes of images poured into my mind, and I saw a lot of Alcaius's memories of the tiny fairy without wings. After I gathered enough, I sat back against the headboard and concentrated on bringing my memories of the wisp forward. Slowly they trickled back in like I'd buried them so deep they had to push through several feet of desert ground. Sadness and regret followed the revelation that I'd abandoned one of my dearest friends. "I have to go to her and keep my promise to her."

"What promise is that?"

"To help her find a curse breaker and get her wisping abilities back, and then she can return to her people."

"We can go to Zaire's castle first, and I'll stay put while you take Alexios to see Raya and then help Bryony."

I nodded, knowing I'd be doing a lot more than that, but he couldn't know until I was well into the dragon valley.

Zaire's castle rose with what must have been a hundred silver turrets. Small cubed spaces connected the dozens of towers. Red roof tiles contrasted the silver stone walls well. Apparently, being a fate watcher paid well. That was what Alcaius told me his best friend did. Zaire had once been a Mothman, a creature who warned of pending doom and then caused the doom.

The Determiners who ruled over reapers, Mothmen, executioners, and fate watchers fired him because of forbidden love. He'd fallen in love with someone who was supposed to die in one of his cases, but he'd saved her instead. Through time, he'd worked his way back to good standing and earned the position of fate watcher. As a fate watcher, he watched the fate fabric for any discrepancies with the souls stitched into it—the souls fated to die by hand of the reapers.

The grand hall rose into a painted dome with tiny angels flying amongst fluffy clouds, with their bows poised to fire. The smooth blue marble floor contrasted with the golden accents on the walls. Voices echoed across the room, as it was empty of all but a few paintings and several closed doors. It was like the isolation of the room was to lend appreciation to its architecture.

I tapped my fingers on my thigh as I waited for Zaire to fetch Bryony. Tears brimmed in my eyes at the thought of her rejecting my apology, which she'd have every right to do. Alcaius wrapped his arms around me and kissed the top of my head, rubbing my arm and releasing a lot of tension from my body. With Alcaius, it was the still moments when we could just exist together that tipped my feelings for him into something more tangible.

"I'm hungry!" Alexios looked around the room like he might spot a snack.

I straightened the collar on his shirt. "You just ate three entire muffins."

He crossed his arms in protest. "It wasn't enough."

Alcaius tousled my little brother's hair. "We'll have dinner here in a minute."

A little fairy zipped into the room, and I squinted at the pink sparkling wings fluttering on her back. I worried my memory had failed me again, but it insisted her wings had been clipped.

She twirled in the air and created little patterns with dips and circles. "Azora! Azora! You're here! Do you remember me? Zaire says you remember me."

"I do, and you have some pretty wings. I love them," I said.

She turned to give me a full view of her flapping appendages. "They're great. Zaire helped me find a mage that could stitch on new ones for me. They're created from troll magic for durability. They have a lot of limitations, but I can enjoy them for small amounts of time." She wrapped her small arms around as much of my neck as she could. "I'm so happy you remember me. The grief of your loss was almost the same degree as losing my wisping abilities."

I placed my hand over her to return her hug the best I could. "All the promises I broke, and the pain caused by me to you, make my heart ache. How I could ever forget you isn't something I understand."

"It wasn't your fault. So many terrible things happened to you. I should have stayed by your side and not left for a second."

"You are as loyal as a friend could ever be. Please never doubt that."

My neck dampened with her tears, and I wanted so badly to tell her I had a possible solution to getting back her wisping abilities that were stolen from her when she was taken for the market. Not being able to float as a mystical orb to attract prey and repel threats kept her from being able to return to her people. If the visions and Dagny held any truth, hope lived with the dragons.

Zaire cleared his throat, running his fingers through his black hair. His almond eyes appeared brass under the bright chandelier light. "My servants have prepared dinner. If you'd come this way."

Zaire led us down a long hallway with decorative floral paintings and enormous leafy plants tucked into the corners beside grand pillars. Two large mahogany doors rose to the ceiling. Two men with silver swords pushed them open for us. The dining hall table extended across a grand room, appearing to have the capacity to hold dozens. The chairs had high backs and pearly white cushions. Zaire took the only red cushioned chair at the end of the table, and we sat in the seats next to him. A tiny chair sat close to my spot with a miniature table, plates, and utensils.

Bryony zipped into her seat. "Zaire has been so considerate of my needs. He's built me a tiny world here."

"You're welcome here anytime, Bryony. We've enjoyed your company." Zaire snapped his fingers and whispered something to the servant who rushed over.

Food was brought in, and we listened to stories of when Alcaius and Zaire were boys and all the mischief they caused the realm. It was a good evening spent in laughter. After we'd nearly cleaned our plates, a black-cloaked figure rushed into the room and leaned over to speak with Zaire.

His eyes widened, and he nodded, turning to Alcaius. "Azora, Bryony, if you would excuse Alcaius and me, we have an urgent meeting to attend."

The men left, and I wanted to follow them to eavesdrop, but thought better of it. Alcaius would most likely fill me in when I saw him again.

I glanced around the room at the abundant servants. "Is there somewhere we can go where we will have complete privacy?"

Bryony zipped into the air. "Yes, my room. It's practically an entire city, but there is a large bed I nearly get lost in that can accommodate you."

I leaned over to Alexios. "Time for bed."

He chomped on a honey biscuit and rushed the bite. "No fair. The sun has barely set!"

"And we have to leave early to see Raya, so to bed with you."

He grumbled and grabbed three more biscuits to take to his room. After tucking my brother in bed, I followed Bryony after telling one of the guards to give the message to Zaire of my whereabouts.

Byony's description was accurate on fairy scale. Tiny buildings, probably around a foot in height, formed a circle around a small flower garden maze. The curving pathways were palm-width. I sat on the oak bed she had mentioned, and she climbed onto the top of two stacked pillows. She snuggled into my arm, and I rubbed her back with my finger. Once we settled in, I told her all about the dragons and my secret meeting.

Bryony yawned and rested back on the pillow. "That's a lot and scary. I fear what the dragons want with you."

"It is a lot, and I get it if you don't want to go with. Part of me prefers that for your safety, but it's a choice you must make. It's a chance to get your wisping abilities back and from what I could tell, Dagny speaks the truth, but all I could sense was what she let me. She had some blocks, but what I saw looked like the truth."

"Where you go, I'll go." She closed her eyes and curled up on her side.

"You're not afraid of dragons?"

She gave a sleepy shrug. "I'm more afraid of being without you again."

I sank next to her and drifted to sleep. Tomorrow we'd go to the dragons.

Chapter Four
Reunion
Azora

Alcaius had slipped into bed sometime in the night, smelling of burnt cedar. He'd pulled me close, and I snuggled into his chest, drifting back into sleep easily. The sun illuminated the horizon with sparse light when we rose to leave.

Alcaius kissed me slowly, like he wanted to draw the kiss out so long I'd change my mind about leaving. "Be cautious. I don't want to come out of hiding to burn a city to the ground to find you."

I gave him one last quick kiss. "You're so dramatic."

"Your safety is everything."

"It shouldn't cause mass loss to everything you touch."

"Stay safe, and it won't."

I rolled my eyes as I savored the tight hug we fell into. "You do nothing foolish to get caught either. I care just as much about you."

"I'll keep him in line," Zaire said behind me. He spread his arm toward the half-circle portal that rippled with what looked like water held in by an invisible barrier. "The portal is ready. It'll get you pretty close to Greaves."

I stepped through the portal with Bryony on my shoulder and my brother at my side, instantly recognizing the purple lightning that zipped from one tree branch to the next. The violet electricity only struck the thick green summer leaves and avoided living things. Tiny jars hidden in the branches caught the crackling energy, and wisps fed it into crystals to fuel lights for forest dwellings. The wisps appeared in better shape than the last time I'd seen them. The jars they resided in were larger, with tiny houses where the fairy could escape for privacy.

Bryony gasped and covered her mouth. "The lids are off."

I inspected to see if she was right. "It appears they now have a choice to work."

Bryony zipped into one of the jars, and I waited for her to finish her conversation.

Alexios fidgeted next to me. "Why can't I go with you to see the dragons?"

I froze and spun around to face my little brother. "What are you talking about?"

"I heard you talking to that lady who came to our house in the middle night. She had white hair like Myik."

"You know better than to eavesdrop! You never should have heard any of that."

He shrugged. "Not like I care about what I should. I'd rather go with you to see dragons than be stuck in a stuffy cottage with Raya."

"If you heard my conversation, then you know very well that they are angry with me. I am taking you nowhere close to furious dragons."

"They're angry with you. Not me."

"It's out of the question. Besides, I'm sure Myik will let you visit some of his if you ask nicely enough."

He crossed his arms and shook his head. "It's not the same as seeing wild dragons no one has before."

"Exactly. Wild dragons equal unpredictable."

Bryony emerged from the jar and interrupted my brother's whining. "Twila, that's the wisp I talked to, said Granill has improved living conditions at his apprentice's insistence."

"That would be my sister. Certainly sounds like her."

We continued past the dangling jars. Not as many were full as the last time I'd arrived, and I wondered if it diminished the electrical enough that Granill regretted his decision to listen to my sister. Raya lived in a little cottage that was behind the massive tree that housed her walker mentor.

The goat man held a walking stick in his black hook fingers as he approached us. "Good to see you again, Azora." White fur covered every inch of his skin, and he had two sets of curving horns that sat on the top sides of his ram's head. "Raya told me to let you in her cottage if you arrive before she returns."

"Thank you. That's much appreciated. It's good to see you again as well."

He let us into the small stone house where we found sandwiches and a note from Raya telling us to enjoy the meal while we waited. Everything except the washroom area was contained in one room. The small kitchen, sitting area, and bed allowed little space to move around, but it seemed suitable for one person. The blue curtains in the window had delicate wildflowers stitched throughout them. My sister's skill with a needle was unmatched by anyone I'd ever met.

Alexios devoured three sandwiches before moving on to the scones, washing all of them down with two glasses of milk from Raya's chill box. Bryony found a thimble in Raya's sewing supplies and washed it at the sink to drink her tea with. I nibbled on a sandwich while sipping the tea and thinking about what Alcaius would do when he found out I went to see dragons without telling him. Ultimately, it wasn't something I'd hide from him in the end. If he didn't find out before I returned, then I would tell him myself if I survived whatever it was the dragons wanted from me.

The door burst open, and Raya rushed at me. My sister's bright red hair flew around me as she crashed into my outstretched arms. "I've missed you!"

I squeezed her and stepped back to look at her. "You look amazing."

"Happiness and love will do that to a girl." She let go of me and tousled Alexios's hair before hugging him. "We should have some fun. Myik says you can help him with the dragons."

He crossed his arms. "I'd much rather see the wild ones Azora is going to see."

I sent my brother a glare. "Alexios!"

Raya glanced between us. "Wild dragons? I thought you were taking Bryony to get her wisping abilities back. That's not exactly in the direction wild dragons are."

I didn't much care for lying, not to anyone I cared about. With reluctance, I told her my entire plan. "You can't tell Myik. If he even thinks about telling Alcaius, it'll ruin everything, and I'll lose him. The dragons were clear on that."

Raya placed her palm over her chest. "No one will know it. I swear. You'd do the same for me if I needed to save Myik, but the issue is this one." She lifted an eyebrow in Alexios's direction.

"Fine! I won't tell, but only if you promise to bring me back a real dragon scale from a wild dragon. Something rare, like from a shadow shifter."

"I'll see what I can do," I said.

We sent Alexios for a bath in the washroom and plopped onto Raya's red couch to talk.

I lifted Bryony onto the back of the couch and turned my attention to my sister. "You never told me about Myik."

"What are you talking about? Of course, I told you about Myik."

"No, about his heart."

Her eyes widened and relaxed so quickly that it was almost unnoticeable. "It's not something he likes people knowing. They treat him differently once they do. Alcaius is the only one who never has. It's one of Myik's favorite things about his brother."

"I thought it was odd that Alcaius never told me either until recently."

"I think maybe it's because he sees his brother first and the heart condition as only one personal fact about him."

"How long does he have?"

Raya shrugged and looked at the wall like it was a window into the forest. "It's difficult to know. The mages have a potion that slows it down, but eventually, it'll stop working. No one knows when because it varies for unknown reasons."

"I'm sorry, Raya."

"Don't be. The time I've had with him has been abundant, and I will take more of that for as long as I can have it." A sadness sat in her eyes as she said it, but sincerity rested in her small smile.

Alexios came out from the washroom, and Raya pulled on a spot on her floor, lifting a hatch that revealed a wooden staircase. "This will be your room while you're here."

"I get my own fort! This is better than I thought it would be!" Alexious grabbed his things and headed into the underground room.

After we each got a bath, Raya and I climbed under the covers of her bed and talked long into the night about everything we'd missed in each other's lives since we'd parted weeks ago.

A knock on the door startled me awake. The closed curtains made it difficult to tell the time, but the air had an eerie feel to it. I concentrated on the door and felt a connection to whoever stood on the other side, but no image of who they were developed in my mind.

I had my dagger clenched in my hand as Raya stumbled out of bed to get to her door. "I should be the one to open it."

She continued as though she hadn't heard me. "My house. You don't get to rule here."

Raya swung open the door to reveal a figure in a royal blue cloak with intricate silver stitching throughout. "Kerensa!" Raya looked around the figure. "It's raining. We could have come to you." She stepped aside, allowing her visitor inside.

As soon as the woman removed the cloak, I knew who she was. While I'd never met her and only seen her from afar once, I knew all about her. Alcaius's mother sat in one of the wooden chairs by the small fireplace and warmed her hands. Her white hair looked like a bunch of feathers attached all over her head. They suited her beautiful round face and defined cheekbones. She had the same hair color as her son Myik, but the golden eyes were all Alcaius in shape and color. A crown of short black vines wrapped around her head, and a large purple gemstone rested in the middle, directly in line with her straight, small nose.

Raya went over to the stove and put on the teapot, grabbing cups from an upper cupboard. "Is Myik okay?"

"Yes, if something had happened to him, servants would have knocked on your door as I would not have been sound to deliver the news myself." The Queen of Death's eyes landed on me. "I'm here to see you, Azora."

I sat in the chair across from her and bowed my head briefly in a show of respect. "Me?"

"Yes, I know my son has been with you for the last several weeks. It's quite clear to me where you are, he is."

"It is strange that Samael didn't guess Alcaius would be with me as well."

"He did, but my guess is someone has been warding your house from anyone who has ill intent for him. Myik told me you were coming to visit Raya, and I knew there was no way Alcaius could be this close to his father's castle. Not even he is good enough to ward ground in his father's kingdom. I've come to see how he is."

"He's doing okay at the moment. He's stay—"

She held her hand up. "Don't tell me where he's staying. There are ears in this forest that do my husband's bidding. They can't listen in here, but they may catch my scattered thoughts on my way out. We must keep this as brief as possible." She held out her hand to me. "If you are okay with it, I would like you to connect me to your seer sense. If you are ever in need of help, find me, and I will help you for all you've done for my son."

"I'm the reason your son is even on the run in the first place."

She smiled, but her eyes remained sad. "My son is the reason he is on the run."

I took her hand and concentrated on forming a connection that would act as a thread to her in the future. The tangible lifeline would help my tracker sense locate her in the future. It was something I could have attempted through my bond with Alcaius, but a direct link to what I wanted to track was always more accurate.

Raya waited until I was done to hand the queen the blue teacup. "Something to warm yourself with. I'm sorry I don't have anything other than plain black tea."

The queen accepted and took a sip. "This is perfect, my dear. Your hospitality is always so welcoming."

"You showed me that warmth first."

They smiled at each other in a way that told me they'd probably had many heart-to-hearts that had made them close. I envied it as I'd wanted to get to know the woman Alcaius talked so fondly of while at the same moment cursing his father. His opinions of his parents existed extremely opposite of each other.

The conversation turned to simple things as the queen sipped her tea.

A question nagged at me that I had wanted to ask since Alcaius first told me something about reapers.

I cleared my throat to work up the nerve to follow through. "There is something my curiosity won't leave alone, but I'm dying to ask you."

"Go ahead, dear. I'm not easily offended and rather you speak your mind than have your curiosity waste my son's sacrifice."

I laughed at her way of putting me at ease. "Does it bother you that female reapers can't reap?"

"No, it's a relief, to be honest. Leave the murder to the men. There are much better duties to attend to that don't require bloodshed."

"It doesn't bother you that they don't give you the choice?"

"I think it's that they are afraid of us having the same power as them. They suppress us because they know anything given to a woman is given back to them tenfold. What they don't realize is that if we wanted to, we could take that power from them. Look at the power you hold over my son."

"That's not one-sided."

She set her empty teacup down, and her eyes flashed with something that made her look cunning in a way that maybe should have startled me. "Yes, that's why I like you, and our sweet Raya." She reached over and squeezed my sister's hand. "You both love my sons. That much I can tell. For that reason, I still don't need to play the part of reaper." She stood up and concealed her face in her hood before abruptly disappearing into the night.

Chapter Five
Warning
Alcaius

Zaire led me through his palace to whatever meeting we needed to attend. Azora looked at me curiously as I left the dining hall, but I didn't have the slightest idea who could be meeting us. We'd surprised Zaire with our sudden arrival, as I hadn't trusted correspondence. We turned down a long hall and walked halfway down it when Zaire slipped into a room to our left. Inside was a long table with several thrones around it. The room held no space for anything else, and the bulky man at the end of the table had a difficult time sliding between the chairs and the wall to reach us.

One of my closest friends, Rook, wrapped his muscular arms around me and lifted me from the ground. His thick brown beard and hair made him resemble a bear, as only his large hook nose and hooded green eyes could be seen on his face.

He set me on the ground and looked me over. "You look no worse for wear."

"The facial hair is a nice addition. It's even harder to tell you apart from the beasts than it previously was."

He gave my cheeks a couple of pats. "Better than the baby face you got going."

"Yes, because babies have trimmed beards."

"That's more like a bit of stubble." He jabbed me with his elbow as his broad shoulders bobbed up and down.

"Azora doesn't complain."

"Her opinion is all that matters now, then, is it?"

I arched a brow. "Absolutely."

Zaire took a spot at the table and gestured for us both to do the same. "What is this urgent news you came all this way to tell us?"

Zaire rarely jested about anything as he took most things seriously, unlike Rook, who saw the humor in almost everything. A lot of Zaire's issues stemmed from the intense nature of being created a Mothman, and while he rarely shifted out of his human form anymore, he held his oath to duty above all else. However, Rook was the son of Chaos and thrived on bringing mayhem to the order Zaire valued.

Rook twirled his finger on the table, creating a small tornado that he kept spinning in place. "Belphagor has been spotted in the chaos swamps, and rumors said he's looking for you." His eyes landed on me.

I tossed a hand up in a casual shrug. "If Belphagor wanted to find me, he would."

"Yes, that's true. He can find anyone. Even me, and he did. He gave me a letter to give you and demanded I hand deliver it to you. He said it had to be delivered by me or it would be intercepted, and you'd be executed. If I open it or chose not to deliver it, all the realms would end. Seemed a ridiculous thing, but given he's an Oblivion, the consequences seemed big, and I'd been wondering about you, anyway."

I took the letter from him and retrieved the small knife from my pocket, using it to cut open the envelope. The paper had a charred scent, like someone had bathed it in ashes and cedar. "He wants me to meet at the rift in two nights. I'm to come alone, and he'll make sure my path is clear."

Zaire shifted in his chair and shook his head. "That's unwise. It's best to let him come to you on ground that doesn't belong to him."

"He says if I don't follow the instructions precisely, my worst fear will be realized. Not sure if that's a threat that he will cause or a warning he sees with his time ability."

"You can't really be considering it. It's best to stay here in my castle like I've told you for weeks until enough outrage has cooled about your actions that we can ask for a private hearing." Zaire held out his hand and took the note from me, reading it for himself. "This sits poorly with me."

"I owe Belphagor twice over for Azora's life, and he's not exactly an enemy. More like an acquaintance."

"Yes, you two pummeling each other on the academy front lawn makes him merely an acquaintance." Rook twirled the tiny tornado into a rain cloud that he snuffed out at Zaire's stern expression.

"We settled that a while ago. The rift is a potential threat, and my worst fear is losing Azora. If he needs my help with it, then I don't think I should ignore that request," I said.

Zaire folded back up the letter and slid it my way. "It does seem too big a thing to mess with, but it seems risky. You can use my portal, and I'll try to get you as close to Grimheldin as possible."

"Two days will be good. Azora will be away visiting her sister because there's no way she'd be okay with me venturing by myself back to the rift."

"You're not going to tell her?"

"It's best I don't. She'll cancel her trip to see her sister and restore Bryony's wisping abilities. It's best to let her think I'm safe here."

Rook waved his hand over the table, drying it from the rain he'd created. "You're treading dangerous waters, keeping things from her."

"It's only temporary. It's best to explain after the fact and plead with her to pardon me than have her want to go with."

As different as my two best friends were from each other, they had a similar look of doubt on their faces. Belphagor had never caused me any trouble, and he was an Oblivion, which meant he could see pathways in time. He'd most likely seen something terrible he wanted my help with, and that meant I wouldn't be caught because if he needed my help, he'd make sure everything lined up in our favor.

We wrapped up the conversation, and I slipped into bed with a sleeping Azora. My chest ached at the thought of being away from her, especially with things not completely resolved between us. The break would give her time to process watching me kill, but that brought its own sense of fear. I couldn't lose her, but if she couldn't accept that I had to reap, we were possibly doomed already. I kissed her forehead, and she snuggled into my chest. I stayed awake for a while longer to savor the feel of her in my arms.

Azora had left two days ago, and I probably wouldn't hear from her until she returned. We couldn't risk magical communication methods. If my father hadn't thought to punish me in every way possible, I could have summoned my personal crow to send messages back and forth between Azora and me. Father had locked up my bird at unknown location, so I couldn't access him. A crow messenger wasn't something I could just buy in a market or borrow. Crows only delivered messages to and from their masters, and it required hand raising one for its loyalty to remain tied to you. I stood in the portal room with Zaire. The room had a large archway that opened to other realms and kingdoms. The rest of the room was empty of all but the grey stone that absorbed any loose power.

Zaire opened the portal and studied the blue ripples that danced in front of us. "Be careful. Belphagor is still the son of your father's enemy."

"An enemy I killed easily enough."

"Yes, because maybe he wasn't ever the real threat. Maybe that terror belongs to his son."

"Perhaps." I rushed up the stone steps and into the portal.

I arrived in a dead forest. The air pressed a deep woe on my shoulders—the unmistakable sorrow of Grimheldin. Everything that lived in the area breathed despair, and often, phantoms bound to the border of the trees wandered and attacked. Belphagor's family owned the forest, and he'd cleared my way to meet him. Not that I couldn't take on a few phantoms, but avoiding the annoyance was welcomed.

My reaper eyes saw well in the low light and could soak up even the smallest illumination to use it to aid my steps. That became unneeded as soon as I arrived at the marble, glowing rift that flowed like a glimmering river. It rested among stony banks that looked like a crack of gemstones cut open into the earth. It swirled every color and stuck out among the black stone around it.

The rift was a divide between our world and a netherworld. A place that held the vilest of entities that owned the shadows and spread darkness on anything it touched. Azora had a second seer sense that allowed her to unlock things, and Belphagor's father, Belial, had wanted to use Azora to unlock the rift and unleash a dark army upon our realms. Since the original key had been lost to time, he saw Azora as the only means to carry out his plan. Azora had almost done as he wished in exchange for having her life put the way she wanted, but a vision showed her the damage it would cost so many. She gave up her life to stop the plan, but Belphagor had returned her soul to her body at my request. I still didn't know entirely why.

Belphagor stood nearly as shimmering as the rift with his shiny bronze skin. Eternal flames rose from each of his broad shoulders. He wore a blue cloak and had the hood down to show his bold square jaw and triangular nose. His eyes mimicked the flames on his shoulders, giving him a constantly fierce expression.

After a glance my way, he kept his back to me. "Alcaius, it's good to see you again. Indeed, it is."

"You've never been one for formalities. What did you ask me here for?"

"Silverie was the most beautiful woman I'd ever seen. From the moment I first saw her, she had my heart, though I couldn't admit it for a long time. I was a monster. Not like you, where you at least don't look like one. You're attractive to many, and they don't know your secrets unless you reveal them. But Silverie somehow saw past all my ugly and loved me. It gave me hope I could do something more than expected of me." He kept his eyes pointed at the rift like it would return his dead wife to him.

"I'm sorry about Silverie. That's something I never got to tell you."

He laughed a cutting cackle. "Yes, that will bring her back. Everyone being sorry. Not everyone was; that was my problem all along. The ones who should have been sorry never were."

"I can't imagine your pa—"

"You're not one for platitudes, Alcaius. Never have been, so don't start now. And you're right. You can't imagine my pain, but you did get a sliver of it when you lost Azora twice. So let that grow inside you because I need you to imagine what that would actually feel like and mean. To lose her forever."

I took a step closer to him. "Are you going to help with that? Is that the point you're trying to make?" My scythe crackled on my back at a potential threat against my woman.

"It's a warning that if you don't allow something, losing her will be your fate."

"What exactly am I supposed to allow?"

He turned halfway and extended his hand to the rift. "I need to take her in there without your interference."

"In what realm would that ever happen?"

He turned his back on me again. "If I had known the last time was the end, I would have opened my eyes wider and taken Silverie into my soul. I would have let myself remember exactly how she moved, and the way her eyes smiled at me like she saw the man beneath the monster. She saw what no one else did. Azora is that for you. You're so blind, Alcaius. Just as I was. Your obsession with protecting her will be your downfall and her end."

"Is that the truth of an Oblivion or the lies of a demon who wants to use her?"

"It isn't the dragons you should fear, but the reaper inside. Or one day you'll wake up and wish you'd known that the last time with her was the end."

"Touch her, and I'll destroy everything to get to you."

"I'd have to have something to lose for that to scare me."

"Fear isn't needed. Only pain. On some level, you must fear me or you wouldn't be standing here, trying to convince me to let you take the person I love most into the abyss."

"Or this conversation is needed for another purpose. I'd destroy things for her, too. She's meant everything to me since her first breath.

From the first moment, I saw what she could do. You're not any less of a monster than I am," he said.

I moved beside him in swift strides. "We're both monsters. The difference between you and me is that you'd burn cities to use her for your twisted advantage. I'd burn cities to stop her pain. I'd destroy everything for her because there's no world in which the sun can rise with Azora not in it."

"Just know this, Alcaius. When Azora goes with me, it will be of her own free will. That's something not even you can stop."

"That would never happen unless you coerced her." My fingers tingled to grab my blade and end him where he stood.

"It will be easier than you think." He raised his finger in a way I knew signaled he was about to teleport. "Right now, you should be more concerned about the dragons

"Wait. Why would I fear dragons?" His words finally caught up to me. "You said earlier I shouldn't fear them."

"A little slow there. Caution around dragons is always advised. Azora is headed to the dragon lands to see them. Not that I would stop that if I were you. Lady Fate might have something to say about that if you do." He snapped himself away, not allowing me to ask anything further.

Chapter Six
Chill
Alcaius

I f Belphagor thought I'd ever give him my blessing to take Azora into a sinister abyss, he'd never paid attention to who I was.

Zaire watched me pace across his bedroom with rage barreling through my muscles with nowhere to put it. "Why would Azora go to the dragon valley? No one that I know has ever made it into the valley without being incinerated. They're territorial because of humans and elementals kidnapping them and placing control collars on them for slavery."

"Belphagor didn't say why, but I can't think of any reason she'd actually be going to see them." I shoved more clothes into my bag.

Rook moved from the doorway to a large hooded chair beside Zaire's bed. "You can't go after her. For one, you don't even know for sure she is going there, and you can't track her. Belphagor could want to lure you to be caught. He is the son of your father's enemy."

"He hated his father and considered me killing him a favor." I zipped up the bag and flung it over my shoulder. "If he wanted to trap me, he could have done it at the meeting."

Zaire watered a small red plant that rested on an end table next to his closet. He specialized in plants and loved tending to them throughout his land. "Rook is correct. The best place for you to be is here."

"And what? Stay here for the rest of my life, moping in self-pity. I need to resolve my situation one way or the other, but first I need to check on Azora."

Rook moved between me and the door. "We can figure out a solution to your issue, but we all need a little more time to do so. Besides, if you want to send someone who will protect her at all costs. You should employ Fennec. That boy's a crazy one."

"I don't need to unleash my brother's psychopathy on the world. And while he may be more mad than our father, I won't send my younger brother to handle my business."

Fennec was my youngest brother and was as mentally stable as a ball balancing on a fence. He'd bypassed any sanity my mother had handed out to Myik and me. His reaper genes had been activated only five years ago when he'd turned thirteen. He loved every minute of reaping, and one never knew what exactly he'd do.

I stepped around Rook and went straight to Zaire's portal room. They both followed close behind, trying to talk me out of what they already knew I was set on doing.

Zaire gave in and opened the portal to Greaves. "This is a terrible plan, but if I don't give you access to my portal, you'll be walking to Azora. The shorter the journey, the better." He tossed me a small brass cylinder. "A return key if you can find a portal somewhere. It'll break through the wards I have cast on my portals."

I stuck the piece in my bag. "Thank you."

"Alcaius, I'll continue to work on a solution for your predicament."

I nodded and stepped through the portal.

Greaves had so much energy firing from tree to tree. The air crackled as though alive and trying to talk while burning. Lightning sizzled, zipping from tree to tree and making it difficult to hear any message the trees might be saying. The woods of Greaves were where I spent boyhood by digging out forts and hunting small creatures in anticipation of becoming a reaper. My instinct to kill wasn't as strong then, and I always released them after the hunt.

Fennec's instincts for slaughter were always strong, like he'd been born with the impulse and didn't need magic or a scythe for it to live inside him. He embodied what everyone wanted the next Death to be, but my youngest brother was more complex than that. While he had the traits of a natural-born reaper, he wasn't without other layers. I often caught him slipping extra food to the lower servants, but sending him on a quest for Azora didn't seem like the wisest solution. His lack of self-control had the potential to cause issues, and protecting Azora was my job.

Though she did very well at protect herself, too many things lurked to harm her, including Belphagor. My old classmate created a challenge for all of us with his time abilities. He could see across time and manipulate events how he saw fit. He used to do so for his father, but with his father gone, it gave room for his own agendas.

I knocked on the door of the small cabin where Azora's sister, Raya, lived, hoping to catch Azora before she moved on to the next part of her quest. The redhead opened the door with her hair pulled back into a braid. She had similar cheekbones to Azora, but their eyes looked significantly different. Raya had round, bright green eyes while Azora's were more upturned and silver.

She opened the door wider and looked over my shoulder. "No guards chasing you?"

"Not yet." I stepped inside and immediately smelled my woman had been there. I closed my eyes to take in her scent and missed her in my chest. "Where is she?"

"Who?" She laughed.

I raised an eyebrow. "The woman I love more than reaping."

"If you love her more than reaping, you wouldn't put yourself in danger with the task."

"She told you?"

"Yes, we debated the entire thing, much like we do all our problems."

I sat down in a large chair and waited for Raya to move to the kitchen. "Tell me she's coming back."

"Eventually, I'm sure she will be, but she left some time ago."

"Where was she going?"

She turned on her stove and placed a blue teapot on the burner. "Where did she tell you she was going?"

"That's not answering my question."

She pulled down a couple of cups from an upper cupboard, stretching on her tiptoes. "She didn't entirely tell me. Only that she needed me to watch our brother, and she didn't know how long she would be away for."

"I've been told she's going to the dragon valley."

"The dragon valley? That's insanity. There's no point to it. Anyone with business there best avoid it if they don't enjoy being roasted by dragon's breath. Myik is obsessed with the place as a dragon keeper. It's not anywhere Azora would want to go, and I'm sure she knows that. My sister is well versed in the dangers of the land from previous employment opportunities."

"Danger doesn't stop Azora if she concludes the quest is beneficial to her."

Raya handed me a saucer with a steaming teacup on top. "Yes, look how quickly she agreed to go with the son of Death on a quest."

"That probably does seem foolish to most people." I took a sip of the hot liquid, letting it burn down my throat almost pleasantly.

"It still makes no sense. She said she wanted to get Bryony's wisping abilities back. There's no need to go to the dragons for that. It's something a lot of mages could do. She might have to travel to a magic city, but dragons aren't needed for it."

"Look, I have no clue why she would go to the dragons, but I have it from a reliable source that's where she's going," I said.

"It must be pretty reliable for you to risk everything to come out of hiding to go after her. Why else would you risk hurting my sister with your loss?"

I drank the last of the tea and set the cup on the small table next to me, giving myself a moment to reflect on her words. "Staying hidden forever isn't an option. Eventually, I'm going to have to face the consequences of my crime. My crime that kept her with us all. If anyone understands the pain she'd bear without me, it's me. If she felt even a fraction of what I did, it would be torture. But for us to have any kind of life, I need to get everything in order."

"You admit your loss equals torment for her, but you will risk execution anyway. All in the name of a possible life together."

"Yes, because her peace of mind long term is much better than her living the rest of our lives in constant fear of my execution."

Her eyes moved over to a portrait of my brother, Myik. It looked strangely lifelike for being sketched with charcoal. "You know as well as I do, I'm going to lose Myik long before I should. Every day I live in fear of that truth. It makes time precious. Don't take time with you from her."

"My father used to constantly threaten me with Myik taking my place. In fact, he did right before I left with Azora on our quest together. He brought him to the throne room and had him stand next to him as he told me Myik would take my place as heir if I failed."

"Myik could never be the next Death. Why would he do that?"

"It was a message to me. One he thought would cut deep. That my broken brother, who couldn't even reap, would make a better heir than his first-born son, who kept failing him. The truth is Myik, with his strong conscience and gentle spirit, would rule far better than any of us. My brother may have a body that's failing him, but most of the time, he's the only one around the castle with any sense. All unless it comes to you. You make him lose his mind a little."

She smiled and nodded. "Yes, his madness is why we are together. I will not complain about it."

I chuckled, remembering how my brother had first seen Raya through a looking globe and became smitten with her. So much so that he sought her out and convinced her to come to Greaves with him.

I stood up and took my cup and saucer to her sink, where I washed and dried them, placing them back in the cupboard. "The fastest way to beat Azora to the dragons is to use my father's portals."

"You can't be serious. What if your source is wrong? You'll be headed right into the lion's den for nothing."

"My source isn't wrong. They may be deceiving me, but I can't take any chances when it comes to Azora."

"You're taking so many chances, and maybe you should trust my sister to take care of herself."

"I trust her, but not the dragons." I moved toward the door and stopped when she called my name.

"Is there anything I can say to convince you to return to Zaire's castle?"

"No. I'll be fine. I know lots of secret ways to my father's portals."
I slipped out the door and into the forest, scanning the ground for
mushroom rings.

I spotted a cluster of red mushrooms with white spots and drove the
staff of my scythe into the middle of them. It lit up a blue ring around
them and the grass withered outward until a hole broke up the forest
ground. I dropped into the tunnel system and within minutes, grass
and dirt once again covered the hole.

Glow worms inched in and out of small crevices in the rocky wall.
Father kept them to light the tunnels rather than artificial light to make
the tunnels look insignificant and naturally formed should someone
stumble across them by accident. Most wouldn't make it beyond the
wards as trespassers not matching a certain aura would be burned by
the magic chargers closer to the castle. With Grim blood, I could pass
through quickly.

Thick black roots hung from the ceiling, flickering with a blue pulse
that made the castle a living entity. It held all the rotting things my
father loved within its life force. The most decaying of them all was the
Grim Reaper himself. I'd tried endlessly to follow my father's wishes
for as long as I'd breathed, but in reality, my father never found satisfaction in my accomplishments, only disappointment and disgust.

Three doorways pressed into the dirt that would take me to various places in my father's castle. The markings, written in ancient
reaper dialect, explained one was to the kitchen, the second to servants'
quarters, and the third to outside the grand hall. I chose the servant
quarters, as most who caught me there would say nothing and do what
I asked. I pushed open the door, and the striking scent of manure and
hay led me into the rundown corridor. Neglect from Father reeked
from the ever crumbling corner of the wing that housed his most loyal
servants.

From there, I found a door in the lower areas of the castle until I made it to my quarters. The air had a sense of gloom to it that showed my father had recently invaded the space. I dug through several cupboards, trying to remember where I'd placed the looking globe attached to Azora. After we'd gone on our quest, I'd locked it away since I thought my days of spying on her had ended. I flung open drawers and moved everything around in my closet. Finally, I located it under a box on a corner shelf. The globe lit up blue as my palm tossed it into the air.

My jaw clenched as Azora appeared behind the glass. She stood in front of dragons with a bold stance. The massive reptilian beasts towered in a crescent formation around her. As a child, I'd collected dragon carvings and studied my encyclopedia of dragon types. Myik's heart condition had sent him on a different path, and Father named him the dragon keeper, which had ignited jealousy in me. As heir, I owned our dragons, but Myik commanded them. My dragon obsession led to me learning all the known types, but several we found on our quest had never been classified. If they hadn't been standing in front of my love, looking ready to set her on fire, I'd have combusted from the excitement of finding new dragons to add to the royal collection to classify and tame.

I lunged for the sphere and slid it into my leather satchel as a chill that spread inside my boots flooded the room. My fingers itched to grab my scythe as I spun around to greet the skeletal figure—my father, the king of decay. Death himself waltzed into the room, gliding across the floor with an unexpected calm. The last time we'd seen each other, I'd left him to the fate he bestowed upon others. I'd left him to be reaped by one of his underlings. Somehow he'd survived.

"Were you uninformed there is a bounty on your head?" Icy mist rolled from his mouth, and he needed only to touch anything living to destroy it with a frosty bite. Death held frigid, stiff nothingness in his grasp.

"I was, but I needed a few things here before I'm no longer a problem for you."

He took two steps forward and flung his scythe toward me, only stopping millimeters from my throat. "You will always be my problem. You had so much potential and now all you do is reek of disappointment and shame."

"It's a good thing I long ago learned not to care what you thought of my actions."

He slid the hooked blade around the side of my neck. "I need only tug to end you right here"

I leaned into his weapon. "Do it then."

"That would be too easy. I had a visitor this morning, and he told me the way to restore everything you've screwed up is to allow you to follow your whore into the Realm of Fates."

"Call her whore again, and I'll kill you with your own blade."

His ivory teeth slid into a grin. "Do you forget it is me who is poised to behead you in the kingdom I own?"

I kept my golden eyes pinned on his hollow ones. "I'm waiting."

"You will go to the Realm of Fates and find the box you failed at retrieving. My visitor assured me it is there, as well as an object that would tip your fate away from execution and return you as my heir."

"Why would you want me to be your heir still? Not only did I leave Death for dead, but by your mouth, I breathe disappointment."

"Yes, to write out all your failures, I'd need a large wall." More ice chilled the room as he spoke. "Follow the seer woman into the Realm of Fates. She will know how to track the box, and it's already been arranged for her to want this task. Retrieve the box and clear our name to the Determiners. Don't force me to start writing on a second wall."

"Wouldn't dream of it, Father." My eyes followed his exit from my room.

Decades ago, Belphagor's father put pieces of my father's essence into four objects. If the objects were used, my father would lose a specific part of his essence—his line, kingdom, power, or soul. Azora and I had collected all the objects, but they couldn't be destroyed safely without a specific magic box. Without even talking to her, I knew Azora would track the box for the sole purpose of destroying the object that, in the wrong hands, would end my father's heirs. She'd tracked the box to save me alone, but something had happened that had made her unable to locate it. It appeared my father thought that had recently changed.

I packed a few things that would come in handy on a long journey, keeping my focus on multipliers that would allow me to carry extra supplies within the limited space of a travel pack. I grabbed my secondary scythe from where it hung on my wall and tucked it behind my back, so that it crossed over my main weapon. One of the weapons held great power and was bonded to me, while the other could simply slice and maim.

I stepped into the cold hallways with more confidence than when I arrived. My father would have cleared my way to his portal since his will guided my mission.

My youngest brother, Fennec, emerged from a shadowy hall. "Let's do this, shall we?"

CHAPTER SEVEN
TRIAL
Azora

I dreamt of Death, frigid and made of bones that creaked just enough to reveal he lurked in the shadows. His abnormally long fingers wrapped around my wrist and yanked me to him as ice rolled from a fleshless nose. Flowers occasionally sprouted between cracks in his ivory skull. Death fertilized life, strengthening it—the irony of despair giving rise to hope. The real Death embodied no beauty, so I knew my mind had conjured him, trying to paint a picture that lessened the Grim Reaper's power. That was what I thought until his eyes met mine, and I realized, while he looked erroneous, his soul had somehow found my subconscious.

I slid my wrist away from his grasp, which in my dream happened by my arm twisting shape for easy release. "What do you want?"

"You always were such a disrespectful little wretch. You tempt me to eat your soul on my toast with my eggs and potatoes. Being unsure it would have flavor is about all that holds me back."

"Or maybe you're worried I'd possess and end you."

His teeth parted in a way that might have been a smirk if he had flesh to complete the expression. "Little ant, I don't even fear you holding the object that is connected to my soul. You owe me a fifth object. The box to destroy the other four without ending me." He plucked a tiny daisy growing from his elbow and flicked it at me.

"And if I refuse?"

"My son will pay the price." My dream faded into nothing, and I slept the rest of the night undisturbed.

When morning arrived, it took me a moment to realize why I rested under an unfamiliar canopy of trees. Branches dangled with wispy purple leaves far from my reach. Blue like a robin's egg speckled the deep brown of the tree bark. An earthy sweet scent like mud wrapped in baking cake carried throughout the dense forest of the unusually tall yet thin trees. As my senses woke with me, I remembered I had to confront the dragons to find out their demands and hopefully the grave transgression they insisted I'd committed against them.

Though it didn't matter at this point if I had guilt or not. If it spared Alcaius, it would be done. The dream of Death made me shiver. Not from fear, but from the memory of his icy hands on my skin. The dream had felt in between sleep and awake, leaving little doubt that it was the Grim Reaper plaguing me with a strange proposition. If the dragons had made a deal with Death, then they'd prove more of an enemy than I'd originally guessed.

Bryony fluttered onto the log across from where I sat on a mossy tree stump. "We discussed how important sleep was before meeting the scaly massive beasts, yet you look like you stayed wide awake all night."

"No, I slept, but it was disturbed. My mind will sharpen as soon as I'm surrounded by the beasts, so there is no need to worry." I unzipped my bag and grabbed the thimble I used as a tiny fairy cup and filled it with water from my canteen, handing it to my friend.

She took a quick sip and looked toward a group of brown ground birds. "How much farther is it to the valley?"

"My tracker sense isn't overly precise when measuring distances, but I can stretch out the path in my mind and give a guess. It's usually longer than I estimate."

"Why don't you add on some time, then?"

I shrugged. "It's usually something I expect, but in this case, we should reach the entrance by noon."

"So maybe by dinner, then?" She gulped down the rest of her drink and handed me back the thimble. "It'll be exhausting to travel that much more, but the companionship makes it tolerable."

"Exhausting how? You sleep in my pack most of the way."

"I attempt to, but the jostling isn't a soft lull to slumber through."

"I will try to be more careful with my steps to accommodate your laziness." I tossed Bryony some bread before packing all my supplies.

The fairy loved food more than most things and quickly devoured two morsels that dripped with honey. We packed up our camp and started the journey for the day. The forest with the unique trees shifted into hot sand, and I insisted Bryony stay cool in my bag, away from the scorching temperatures. She complained about needing to keep me company for a little while before she accepted my explanation of the sun harming her smaller size faster. Doubt lingered in her eyes, but she seemed to reason I'd never led her astray before.

The dragons rumbled under my skin, fueled by my seer sense pulling me to them. Tracking wasn't seeing or hearing and was closer to feeling. It became difficult to explain to people how I could translate feelings into clear visuals. Legend told how seer senses developed from mages so experienced with magic that it infused into their essence and became something natural to pass on to their descendants.

Other myths said that some divine entity placed the magic in a few people to create guardians for the children they'd created. One of the few concrete seer facts was that it followed a line of the wealthy and royal. In theory, it was possible that centuries ago, the gifted were elevated to prestigious positions, and the line followed across generations.

I grew up neither royal nor rich because my seer father had hidden his gift for reasons I never got to ask him before he died in my arms. The pain of it sat next to my sorrow for Lowan and manifested at random times, reminding me neither still lived. Grief liked to forget death had occurred, but it always returned with brutal reminders at the worst of times.

I followed the rumble toward a massive wall of roots, like a dam constructed by thousands of beavers over several decades. The gnarly branches had shimmering silver pasted between them so that a solid wall was created without even a small hole to peek through to the other side. No doors or windows appeared no matter how far we walked, and on both sides, the twisted root fortress ended at the start of mountains that towered far into a blanket of grey clouds that appeared to create a sky barrier. My tracker sense knew hundreds of dragons lived on the other side.

"Not exactly polite to invite guests to a party with no clear place to knock." I poked at the shimmering silver to find it as solid as quartz.

Bryony poked her head out of my bag. "There has to be a way in somewhere."

I sat down on a boulder and pulled out the sandwiches Raya had made us for the journey, breaking off a fairy-sized piece and handing it to Bryony. "If they wanted me here so badly, they should have given better instructions."

Wood creaking and snapping turned my attention to my right where the roots parted, and three cloaked figures stood in front of the open curtain.

The tallest one held the opening by pushing each side with his large palms. "If you don't mind, hurry yourself up," a husky voice said through clenched teeth.

My first guess was a group of reapers had greeted us with their deep blue hooded robes. Normally, the skeletal beings wore black to signify the death they brought, but not always. I stepped into a rock valley, and the roots sealed behind me as though they'd grown untouched for centuries. The thunderous rush of dozens of waterfalls flowing over grey rocky walls played all around us. They led into smaller channels that flowed into a large body of water that shimmered in the distance.

Oak trees grew sporadically among rich green grass, with a few weeping willows mixed in. Orange, pink, and blue flowers decorated the terrain in random spots along with gaping holes in the rocks that appeared to be caves. Dragons crept just out of sight, but within reach of my seer abilities. My previous connection to Dagny's dragon allowed me to weave threads to the others.

Our three greeters walked toward the lake but banked left to head toward a cave. White clusters of flowers grew on each side of us to create a pathway that smelled of roses and honey. The natural perfume made me take a deep breath to take the aroma deeper into my memory. Scents often worked as a paste for the bonds I'd make to find them later, and I had a feeling enchantments placed on this place would make it harder to track after I left.

A silver dragon with lava currents flowing between his scales emerged from a cave to our right. Dagny's bonded dragon, Phyrix, stretched his webbed wings out before tucking them against his back. His irises shifted between hues of yellow and orange, giving them the appearance of a flame that flickered based on how the light hit his eyes. He lowered his head in a bow to give a clearer view of the two spiraled black horns that rested at the back of his skull and were larger versions of the spikes that ran along his spine to the bottom of his tail that had a cluster of barbs. His height towered double that of the oak trees.

"We meet again, but this time it is me who must save you. I welcome the opportunity," he said with growls sharpening each word.

I kept my head bowed for a few seconds as a sign of respect. "Yes, that's what I heard. Though no list of my crimes has been announced."

"That will be given to you shortly. It's all a matter of formalities with dragonkind. If you would follow me, we can get started on your trial and sentencing." He lumbered toward a cave to the left of the one he'd arrived from.

"Hold on. Trial and sentencing imply I've already been found guilty. If I am guaranteed sentencing, what is the point of the trial? Have I no chance to defend myself before a verdict is placed?"

"We do not operate as humans do, and the dragon assembly has already proven your guilt. The trial is to explain the punishment."

"I am not a part of dragon society and should not have to abide by its rules."

He stopped walking and glanced at me. "Normally that is true, but for one, humans do not leave us to our ways, so why should we them? Second, this case is severe enough that you are a frightening exception."

I wanted to grumble more about the injustice of the entire thing, but protecting Alcaius at all costs held priority, and so I followed Phyrix into the cave, zipping closed my bag to protect Bryony more. Only a small slit in the zipper left her exposed to provide oxygen exchange. At first, simple brown, slimy walls surrounded us as we walked through an arched tunnel, but it soon opened into a massive cavern of smooth purple and green rock that covered everything but the floors that remained the brown of the rest of the enclosure. The ceiling appeared to extend the height of a mountain and gave plenty of room for the twenty or so dragons in front of us.

Many of the dragons had traditional forms with colorful scales, black horns, and webbed wings, but many had unique appearances. One of them floated with a smooth opal hide and tiny wings that fluttered like a butterfly. Another looked made of rich blue water with a shimmering translucent appearance. A few resembled the rocky cave walls with stony grey skin and ruby eyes.

The strangest and most stunning of them all stomped forward, shaking the ground with each massive step from his four paws. His purple and blue metallic skin glowed at his belly and wings. Thin feathered spikes shot out from his skull, almost making hooks. The spikes carried down his back, and his wings had thin feathers that all joined to create a beautiful luminescent blue blanket. Golden cracks wove randomly over his otherwise smooth body and matched his claws, that curled to the floor.

The rare beast lowered his head until his blue glowing eyes stared directly at my level. "Azora of the humans! I am Dysom Balohar." Heat brewed in his breath and blasted across my face to singe my cheeks. "We have waited much too long for you to arrive in our presence. You will join us at our table where will discuss your trial and punishment."

I wanted to protest the same as I had with Phyrix, but the terms needed to be discussed and gotten over with. Dysom swung around, and I ducked to miss his tail barbs that nearly impaled me. The enormous table gave me the unique perspective that Bryony faced every day she walked among humans. Phyrix scooped me up, wrapping his claws around me like bars in a cage, and set me on the table that held a human-sized table and chairs. Both sets of furniture were grey with bluish swirls mixed in. Carvings of crows, flowers, and ancient writing decorated the chairs.

Twelve dragons climbed onto their massive thrones and seemed to represent different tribes of dragons by the markings on their chair that matched their armored breastplate. Dysom put his armor on and took his place at the head of the table. The three cloaked figures sat at the smaller table with me and removed their hoods. Two men and a woman stared back at me with intense gazes, and I knew they weren't human. Their energy shifted differently under my skin, but I couldn't place what they were. They had a similarity to Alcaius, but each had a distinct feeling that told me they were three different races that all looked human.

The first had a bald head with painted stars that replaced hair. The top of a sun tattoo poked out from his robe, covering his collarbone and part of his throat. His blue eyes matched Dysom's in their hue and brightness. They stood brighter against his ebony skin. His towering, bulky frame and sharp facial features would have gotten him chosen for an intense arena fight.

The other man had an ivory complexion with freckled, ruddy cheeks, copper curly hair, and a matching trimmed beard. He tossed a set of dice in the air and caught it without looking as he leaned back in his chair.

The woman's lavender hair hung in various sized braids with metallic beads and flowers woven into many of the strands. Her marshy green eyes looked endless, like I could view an entire universe by peering into their vivid irises. They contrasted her olive skin. She had an eerie beauty to her that caused me to shudder and turn away from her gaze.

Dysom whipped his head to the side. "Seal the chamber. We are about to begin the trial. The new creature at our table is Azora of the humans."

Growls rumbled through the room and dozens of reptilian eyes landed on me as though I'd committed unforgivable war crimes against their people.

"Silence!" Dysom roared. "She is here to make amends, and while we have a low tolerance for transgressions of her magnitude, the procedure will be followed or punishments will be dealt." He waited for the room to calm before continuing. "We are the dragon council that represents all the twelve realms of our kind." He went through and named each of the dragons and where they were from. His eyes landed on my table. "Across from you, Azora, is Moderatus, son of Balance. On his right is Ashern, son of Luck, and on the left is Moirai, Lady Fate, daughter of Destiny. They represent three of the twelve unified elements and their people."

"The unified elements are mere legend." I quickly closed my mouth when my words darkened his eyes, and smoke whipped from his mouth.

"You will not speak unless asked to! You say that while in love with one of them."

"Reapers? How are they one of the unified elements?"

"Do you not listen? Do not speak until spoken to. All the unified elements balance each other by nature. Safety checks given by the gods to ensure not one element is allowed to take too much. Death and Life, Existence and Oblivion, Luck and Fate, Order and Chaos, Morality and Corruption. And finally Nightmares and Dreams. All keep our universe in balance as the balance oracles ensure." He nodded at Moderatus. "His father has a very important job. However, these are all things your accompanying elements can tutor you on during your journey. Now to your grave crime. Phyrix, as her defender, read them."

Phyrix straightened himself in his chair before clearing his throat and sparking out a crackling sound. "Azora, human and seer, you are hereby found guilty of causing damage to our hatching grounds that are killing all our hatchlings while they sleep in their eggs. Our offspring can only hatch once every thousand years, so if these are lost, it will most likely mean the end for our kind."

"How could I possibly be responsible for that?"

"The Rift you did not close properly is leaking and damaging our eggs."

"I never opened it," I said.

"You did, and now we are running out of time. The open spots have grown too big. The only way to spare our children is for you to travel to the Realm of Fates and ask the forgiveness of the Celestial elders, so they may give you what we need to seal it before our babies become ashes."

"You expect me to do that?"

"Yes, you will be equipped to fix your mistakes. It will only require you to sacrifice your fate."

Chapter Eight
Knowledge
Azora

I shook my head and thought about walking out of the meeting. "If I opened the rift, why are there not armies of evil forces destroying the kingdom? That's what I saw would happen if I opened the rift, and it's why I didn't."

Dysom stretched his head to put his face inches from mine. "It is leaking. You messed with the balance of it, which created cracks. We know this to be true from our investigation, and it doesn't matter if you were aware you did something so grave. Our children are still dying because of your actions, and you must therefore fix it. Long have humans and other races oppressed our people, and we are tired of it. The final straw before we destroy your kind is losing our hatchlings, our future!"

"You're putting the whole of the realm on my shoulders? That's no pressure whatsoever."

"You threatened them with your selfishness. We know why you wanted to open the portal, and it was for your own advantage. There is no other reason for you to have wanted to do so. Our motivation seer has explained the reason you would have done such a thing, because no human would have desired to venture into the rift."

My cheeks warmed with shame that I quickly suppressed because it would do nothing for me. The dragon leader wasn't wrong. I'd started opening the rift because Belial, the person forcing me to make a choice, had promised me a simple life for my siblings and me, along with a sort of vengeance for Lowan by taking out the people who decided who would die. While some deaths were accidents, the rest were fated by a group called the Determiners, and I wanted someone to pay for the sudden passing of my youngest brother.

When I'd started to open it, I saw the dark armies destroying all of mankind. It was why I'd stopped, but my secondary seer ability that allowed me to open it was rusty. I hadn't known I was a key seer and had potentially caused leaks when I'd almost opened the rift. Guilt hit stronger than shame, though they worked as sister emotions, guilt always struck me more brutally than shame.

I closed my eyes for a moment and nodded. "Yes, I will save your hatchlings and own my portion of fault in the rift. However, I want the things promised to me honored as well. Redemption from a death sentence for the reaper Alcaius and wisping abilities returned to my fairy."

"While we owe you nothing for you to carry out this task, we will for extra motivation. Moirai, the daughter of Destiny, will make sure you get an audience with her mother and the elders who will be able to grant you all you request. We also demand your fairy stay behind as assurance of your return."

"No, that's not an option. She is with me in all things."

Around us, ogre servants brought drinks to me and the others at the table. They gripped delicate porcelain cups in their enormous green hands.

"We will not give the things promised unless the fairy is here to ensure you help our hatchlings after sealing the rift. This is because Alcaius will be saved the moment you make an agreement with the Fates."

"The Fates? We have the Determiners, the Accounters, and now the Fates." I took a sip of my steaming tea to not be rude and let it burn down my throat intolerably.

He sighed a rumble that shook the table. "Yes, must I explain it all to you? It would be better to send you to our library to learn, but I haven't the time for that. The Determiners determine things on a smaller level. They carry out the will of the Fates who decide fates. The Accounters keep the Determiners and lesser races accountable. What they do is all in their names."

"So the Fates are the bosses of the Determiners?"

"Yes, and the Accounters make sure the bosses are followed."

"Got it," I said.

"Are you sure? Or do we need more history lessons?"

I shrugged with a toss of my hand. "You could explain how Alcaius will be saved as soon as I make it to the Fates and strike a deal."

The dragon clenched his eyes like my questions pained him. "I will let your guides explain more as you go, but the Fates are the only ones who can get those under them to change a reaper's sentence, especially a sentence that was handed out because of such a grave crime as Alcaius has committed. They will require a great sacrifice as payment."

"What could I possibly have to give them? Are you sending me with anything?"

"What you will be asked to give is something they will know you can give, but it won't be any a simple thing to let go of. That's all I know. There will be many things to pay along the way, but they will be things you don't expect but always have." He hopped down from his chair, shattering our porcelain cups from the force. "That is all we have to say about this. You are guilty, and your sentence is to visit the Fates to retrieve the magic only they can provide to seal the rift. If you do not save our eggs, we will squash your fairy into pixie dust to fuel our lanterns for a day."

Moirai stood and waved me forward as she walked toward the edge of the dragon table. "We have much to do to prepare. Come now. I will show you to journey preparations." Her braids created a melody as she walked, as though the decor in her hair had been placed to create a symphony.

The hall we went down sparkled with jewels, creating pictures of dragons in various environments. The glittery tunnel turned into rooms with the same shiny walls that carried through two more halls that we traveled down. Every area was extensive enough for dragons to roam, and the intricate details put into the surroundings appeared to confirm the rumor that dragons loved anything that glimmered.

Moirai waved her hand over two brass dragon head doorknobs, and two towering doors scraped open. "Welcome to the hoard."

The room appeared as a typical dragon hoard mentioned in most books, with hills of gold coins and rocky ledges covered in many treasures. Golden soldiers lined the wall, making me wonder if magic would bring them alive to defend their surroundings. Incense provided a sharp jasmine aroma as it burned in copper bowls between the metallic soldiers.

I lowered my head to study several black goblets that had fairies etched into them. "Are we here to gather payment for the Fates? Why don't you just save me the trouble of visiting your people since you are Lady Fate herself?"

"Dysom is right that you clearly need a history lesson. Humans are kept so to themselves that they hardly know how things work outside their own affairs."

"You have to waste time insulting my race rather than answering a simple question."

She stepped behind the tallest pile of gold and waited until I caught up. "How do you know your question is simple? I am not part of the Fates Council. That would be my mother, who has any sort of weight in decisions. I am here to guide you to my kingdom because I care about dragons more than pretty much anything else."

"So you're my guide?"

"I am one of them, but I am not here for your benefit. This is your mess that I will help you clean up to avoid disaster for the creatures I love. We are not friends."

"Understood. Good thing I don't need any of those."

She let out a quick snicker and continued her journey through a doorway only beings our size or smaller could fit through. The new room had supplies that would come in handy for any lengthy travel. It reminded me of the room where I'd chosen survival items before leaving on my quest with Alcaius right after we'd met. I'd hated him then and had pictured what items would bludgeon him with the most success. If someone had told me I'd fall for him in the end, I might have considered bludgeoning myself instead.

"What if I was to tell you the reaper is not your fate?"

"I would tell you to screw destiny."

She pursed her lips as she looked through a bin. "Just because you feel so inclined to spread your legs to the reaper at every whim doesn't mean you should."

"But he fits so nicely between them." I batted my eyelashes.

Her upper lip twitched. "Are you the least bit curious about what you are meant to truly be?" She handed me a bag. "You get only this. Choose wisely."

"This must be a common practice. Death sent me off this same way."

"It's a practical way to send anyone off on a quest."

"True. And no, I'm not curious what any force or entity has decided I should be doing. My choices are mine, and if they defy what is expected, the more fun they become." I searched each shelf, being careful to select only essential items. Anything that was a mere convenience got overlooked for something to keep me alive.

"You're a fool. Only bad things come from ignoring what those much wiser than you have decided is your right path to create balance for you and those around you."

"Balance can burn by dragon's fire if it means I lose my life with Alcaius."

She clicked her tongue and moved over to a glass box. Music flowed from it while a tiny archer spun in a circle. "This once belonged to a woman who rebelled against her fate."

"What happened to her?"

"Probably nothing good."

"You don't know?"

She closed the box and turned back toward me. "I'm better at seeing what fates should be, not what they should've been. That belongs to a different type of Fates. Discord will follow you all the days you are with the son of Samael the Lord of Death."

"It's a good thing he will one day be the lord himself."

"So you say."

I put an extra filled canteen in the front pocket of the bag and made sure I'd accounted for all basic needs. My continual weapon of choice, daggers, went into my boots and several pockets. After swinging the bag over my shoulder, I stepped closer to Moirai. "I believe I am ready."

"Are you sure? You will not be permitted another chance to choose."

"I'm sure."

"Very well. We will get you to your room to relax for the night. Tomorrow, we embark."

The damp chill of my room made it difficult to sleep, and I climbed out from under the thin blanket that provided the only source of warmth. The doorknob turned easily, with no lock. I stepped into the dark, empty hallway. Blue light lit up the sides of the path in both directions, and I went left since Moirai had dropped me off from the other direction. It led away from the fancy jeweled hallways and into ones that stayed the natural brown and grey of the cave. Closed, red doors broke up the dullness every so often.

At the end of the long corridor, two blue doors that reached the ceiling stood slightly open, and I slipped between them, gasping at the sight of endless books. Light spread across the room with each step I took forward. Large podiums held books the same as the hundreds of shelves. The podiums looked like the right height for a dragon to read from. The aged paper and leather scents clung to the air as I moved through the vast library. A small section, several rows in, had chairs and a table that would serve any human well.

The room opened up to blue tiles that surrounded a yellow sun. The points of the vibrant star led to symbols I couldn't interpret and always had two images between each point. I walked around the circle and counted twelve groups. A skull was carved between the same two-star points as a tree with a golden scale, and two balanced bowls shared a section with a demonic red creature with horns and a forked tail.

I studied each symbol and wondered at their meaning. An ornate clock paired with a black circle held speckles of purple and a red. A dripping moon shared space with a bright yellow orb complemented by the white clouds around it. The last two pairs were two hands attached to the same thread and a pair of dice, as well as a tornado next to a circle with a bunch of interlocking spheres inside.

"Those are the twelve elemental races."

I jumped at the gruff voice behind me and spun around to see the silver dragon, who nearly reached the top of the massive bookshelves. "Phyrix, you startled me."

"Yes, but I could see no way to prevent that from how engrossed you were in your studies."

I moved around the circle slower. "Why are they a focal point for a dragon library if dragons hate other races so much?"

"We do not hate them. Only the ones who harm us. We have no room at our table for those that treat us as lesser." For his massive size, he maneuvered like a cat as he wove around obstacles to join me in the open space.

"That makes sense."

"It's where we come from. The gods created the dragon races with the elementals in mind. They created balance by making tribes of people who balanced out things the universe needed. Life needs death as much as chance needs fate. Anything given too much power causes things to bend and twist until all are destroyed."

"That's why dragons are divided into twelve groups as well?"

"Yes." His snout twitched as he seemed to snarl out the word. "It has long been forgotten by anyone but dragons. Others wish to forget the old ways to keep their power and enslave us through magic that diminishes our strength and power. We do not wish to forget where we came from."

"No, that is a good thing to keep with you forever. Let's see if I can remember them all. Life and death." I pointed to each symbol as I spoke. "Order and chaos, dreams and nightmares, corruption and morality, chance and fate. What was the last one again?"

"You listened well to Dysom to almost remember them all. It's existence and oblivion. They are time shifters, and many can see branches of blurred possibilities. However, the ruler of those people can see the branches clearly, and it makes it easy for them to manipulate time to gain power as most Existence elemental rulers do."

"They're like seers?"

"Where do you think seers came from?"

"Seers are human," I said.

"With elemental blood as some portion of their makeup."

"Reapers are elementals according to this and Dysom. Samael is the King of Death, but reapers are never seers."

"Yet, they have magic, just as seers do. It's just a different type, and it all comes from the same source. The Celestial lake in which all life is created and molded to fit what the divine see as their purpose."

"They place traits into them that they can't shake. Like reapers needing to kill."

"Yes, and no conscience. Reapers can't have empathy or a conscience to do what they do. They are lacking most emotions for this reason and can't grasp what others feel. Anger is usually the thing they will feel most, if anything at all."

I froze and let his words sink in. "That's impossible. Alcaius has a conscience. It's why he's in trouble in the first place. He feels so much more than anger and has even cried when he thought I died."

A rumbled hum escaped the dragon. "That is abnormal and interesting, but maybe he has learned to fake all of that well."

"Or something is different about him," I said.

"Different. Yes, but maybe not a good different as it has cost him much. If all goes well with your quest and we restore the hatchlings, I'm sure you will be welcomed back to explore this library as you wish, but for now, I must ask you to go to bed before the night guard catches you."

"Is that why you came in here? To tell me that."

"No, I saw a light on and then heard small footsteps. It's abnormal for anyone to be wandering around at night." He turned his head and picked up something from his back, dropping it at my feet.

A grey stone rolled to me, and I scooped it up. "What's this?"

"It's a god stone, and it will protect you. Anyone with it on their person can't be stabbed through the heart."

"They can be stabbed elsewhere?"

"It does not make one immortal, only less vulnerable," he said.

I slipped it into my pocket. "Thank you."

"You might also consider choosing two books to take with you. The journey will be tedious with nothing to occupy your time."

I moved away from the circle and toward a bookshelf. "Where would I even begin? Maybe something that explains elemental history better?"

"Yes, there are some over here." He stretched his neck over several shelves, moving it around until he found something he liked. He held the tome between his front teeth and delicately placed it at my feet. "This might be good."

I picked up the blue leather-bound book. "History of the gods and Celestials? This may not be exactly what I meant."

"It is. It'll detail their creation, too."

"Thank you. I will squish it into my bag somehow."

"Climb on my back and lie flat between my wings. I will get you back safely to your room without incident." He lowered his head, and I did as he asked.

Boots stomped down the hall, but the soldiers didn't question Phyrix. Most people probably preferred not to disturb a dragon.

He deposited me in my room. "My people are angry with you, but I owe you an immense debt. The reason I owe this debt is that you're a good human, and I know that even if none of my kin do. You will go with my good thoughts for a prosperous journey."

"Thank you. I am happy to know you made it home."

"Home is never really a place, is it?"

I thought of Alcaius, Raya, and Alexios, and knew he was right.

CHAPTER NINE
FATE THREADS
Azora

Moirai came and fetched me for breakfast after what felt like barely any sleeping time. My mind had refused to shut down for the night as it mulled through the tasks ahead. I'd gotten defensive when Moirai had suggested I wasn't meant to be with Alcaius because a lot of me knew it was true. At the same time, I'd never been one to listen to what I should do. His blood lust bothered me and conflicted with my morals, but what did I expect with a reaper? It seemed ridiculous to think that he would have no pull to the point of his creation.

After sharing a forced and tearful goodbye with Bryony, I was taken to the wall at a location different from where I'd entered. The dragons crowded in a semicircle to see us off. Many growled as I walked past and heat rolled across my skin as they puffed steam at me, showing their deep disdain. Many most likely wanted to roast me but were held back by orders from the dragon council. A few shouted their distaste to ensure I understood their stance on my existence.

Moderatus was the first to join us. The markings on his forehead glowed, and I wondered at their meaning. Perhaps, all balance elementals had them. He wore green leather armor which accented his built body much more than the robe had. Moirai matched him with a blue set covering her much smaller frame. Their third friend joined them in red. A rainbow would follow me, and while the colors were dulled in intensity, my black armor blended me with nature much better than their outfit choices did them. They didn't seem to need stealth.

No one moved, and I tapped my foot. "Are we going to get going? Getting this over with is a top priority."

Moirai rolled her eyes, adding a head shake. "As it is for us."

"We have one more companion we must wait to accompany us." Moderatus's deep voice matched his colossal size, sounding like he had giant blood.

Ashern adjusted the blue hat resting over his wild red hair and tossed gold dice in the air. "We could just wing this entire thing without the fifth member. When have we ever needed anyone else on a quest?" He eyed me with a mischievous grin he seemed to wear as his signature. "We could handle this all without her even."

"Yes, we could, but this is about her taking responsibility for her actions. It is imperative she come with and rectify her mistake. The only one who should pay a price is her." Moirai used her thumb to pick at her pointer finger. "It is aggravating this newest member is late. The sun is already several degrees over from what it should be for our departure."

"You're the one who always says things will work out the way they should," Ashern said.

She chewed on her lip as she studied the sun. "Sometimes we must assure fate is moving in the right direction."

"How do we not know it is?"

"Because I assure you things are displaced."

Moderatus watched his two companions argue with his jaw looking like it might snap off from the tension. "Fate isn't all that matters on our journey."

Moirai crossed her arms. "It should be."

"Balance is much more important than one weight being heavier than the other."

My spine tingled because I knew the essence of the person approaching. I turned around to find a man with stunning blue eyes approaching us. "You?"

Elisha, the man who'd wiped my memories then returned them, bowed his head. "Azora, it's nice to see you again."

"I'm unsure if I feel the same."

Elisha was a mystery I'd wanted to solve. He was a memory seer and a reaper, which was said to be an impossible combination. Somehow, he was both things, and Phyrix's explanation of seers and elementals was a thread to possibly solving Elisha. He still seemed an odd case to me, and it continually messed with me that I should look more into who he actually was. What I did know about him was that he was the reaper who had reaped Lowan. All of me wanted to hate him when I'd first found out but later realized he had nothing to do with my brother's death and was only keeping his soul safe. Gratitude probably should have been the dominant emotion I felt about him, but my stubbornness called that too far.

Moderatus waved his hand over the dragon wall, brought both hands together, and spread them apart, splitting open an exit for us to step back into the scorching desert. Sand and rocks flew in all directions as a vibrant blue dragon landed in front of us. She had four purple spiral horns at the back of her head that matched her claws. Her deep green eyes blinked, making her diamond pupils constrict each time.

She dipped her head onto the ground. "I am Taza, and I will take you as far as the Realm of Fates. That is all."

Ashern tossed his dice in the air. "Should we ride the dragon or walk?"

Moirai used the scales to anchor herself all the way up the dragon's head until she could grab onto a horn to pull her all the way onto the beast's back. "If your dice tell you to walk, we'll be leaving you."

Elisha, Moderatus, and I all followed her and chose one of the eight cushioned spots that each had two holding bars and a bin. We deposited our items inside the bin and latched it closed.

Ashern joined us last. "Lucky for you, the dice agree with this action."

"You're not going to be doing this the entire time. It'll be a waste of energy as we are not leaving decision making up to chance," Moirai said.

Taza shot into the air, and I had to scramble to grab my bar as she zoomed straight into the sky for some distance before leveling into a soar.

I relaxed my grip and settled into the cushions like the others. The wind whipped my hair around as we broke into the clouds. Blue skies spanned over the white fluffy veil beneath us. "Does anyone know how long the journey to the gate will be? We can't exactly sleep."

Ashern, who sat directly next to me on my right, lifted something next to one of his poles and pulled out a rope attachment. "These will strap your arms in and keep you on to sleep. I see you've never ridden a dragon before."

"I have not. I've climbed on their back before, but this is the first time I've flown with one."

"To answer your question, it'll be about two days' journey."

"Can the dragon last that long without rest?"

"Yes, a well rested dragon can fly straight on for a week. They have good stores for energy." He rifled through his bag and held out a piece of jerky. "Would you like some?"

"No, keep it for yourself in case you run low."

He shrugged and tossed the dried meat into his mouth. "You and Alcaius are together? I heard rumors of that truth."

"Does everyone know Alcaius? It seems they do wherever I go."

"The son of Death is well known. Many feared him in the elemental academy. That's where I know him from."

I laughed and recalled Dagny had said something similar about my reaper. "It's strange to me that everyone sees him as hostile. Yes, he has violent tendencies, but only toward those that deserve it."

"He followed his own moral code, which makes him more dangerous than he seems. He will do what he sees as right, whether or not it is. His temper got him in trouble many times when we were classmates."

"Morals are subjective and change based on perspective. Only some things are universally seen as right and wrong."

"True, but that's what makes Alcaius's temper an issue. His morals change based on his feelings and not well thought out principles."

"Is that how you conduct your life? With well thought out principles."

He tossed his dice in the air and caught them in his palm that he extended to me. "These guide most of my choices, but I do have rules I keep that I've decided are right. I'm mainly surprised you stay with him. He has to be intense."

"Only on Ferris wheels and certain other places."

Ashern raised an eyebrow and smirked. "I'm not sure I want that explained."

"You don't."

We rode most of the day in silence, keeping busy with small tasks. All of us read except for Ashern, who drew in a leather book. I saw bits and pieces of his drawing, and they looked well enough done that I wanted to see the final result but left him to his privacy. When the stars emerged into the sky, we strapped our arms to the poles and pulled out the blankets that we attached to the pole using clips that snapped tightly to the fabric. Taza said she'd keep watch, but that not much bothered the sky.

"Hello, Azora, it's so nice to finally meet you," a voice whispered as a blur of black swished across my vision. The brief interaction chilled me and only when I opened my eyes did I realize it occurred in my sleep again. Death hadn't been the whisperer. Somehow, I knew that but didn't understand how, other than when most people dreamed, they knew most things without explanation.

The cool air made me pull my blanket with me as I sat up to take in the clear night sky full of shimmering stars and a half-moon. Clouds crept along underneath us, leaving no visibility on the ground far below.

Ashern propped himself up on his elbow. "Everything alright?"

"Yeah, just taking in the stars."

"I have an extra blanket if you need it." He pulled a brown roll from his pack and held it out.

"It's okay. I'm fine, but thank you for the offer."

"Sure. Offer stands at any point." He put the item back in his bag and joined me in looking at the sky.

"Could you two quit having a conversation while the rest of us are trying to sleep?" Moirai glared at us before turning over.

I slid back down and pulled my cover to my chin. "She doesn't like me much," I whispered to Ashern.

"She doesn't like something you have." He winked and settled back into sleep.

We flew through the next two nights with little to do other than
to read. I'd learned quite a lot about the entities who claimed to have
created everything, and within that creation, had developed a system
to keep everything balanced in the hopes all they made would thrive.
The elementals were given magic by the gods based on what element
they were responsible for.

Reapers, being the most well-known and obvious, could take life
and hoard souls, as well as several other things. Oblivions had an
interesting set of powers. They could see through time and change
size as their main abilities. Their corresponding elemental, Existence,
could move between timelines but couldn't see what would happen
if they did. They could also change the shape of matter to create new
things.

Everything around me shook with a great earthquake until I opened
my eyes to see Ashern above me. Dark shadows interrupted my sleep
frequently, making the journey exhausting, despite only riding on
Taka's back. I dozed and tried to make sure I kept at least one wrist
strapped to the poles.

Ashern narrowed his eyes. "You dozed again. It takes some getting
used to traveling this way, but you will if you do so often enough."

"I don't think I will, since the dragons are pretty much done with
me. Even if I restore the hatching grounds, dragon grudges are said to
last centuries."

Taza turned her head back to meet my gaze. "Some of us will forgive
swifter than others endure in their anger. We are about at the gate. The
landing may get bumpy."

"That's what I was waking you about," Ashern said.

"Thank you. You should probably get yourself settled now." I
pointed to his spot to emphasize my point.

He retreated to his pad and strapped his wrist to the pole. It was nice that the ropes were long enough to allow us to sit up and move with little restriction, though standing would have been an issue. The drop happened so quickly that I flew into the air and plopped back on my butt with a thud that might have fractured my tailbone had I not had a cushion under me. It still shot pain up my spine to my shoulders. Taza flew straight down like an arrow toward the ground, and I gripped the bars for extra stability. My palms burned as they almost dislodged from my anchor.

We lurched forward as the dragon leveled herself out and sat down somewhat gracefully. She stretched her wings into the air, blocking any view of our surroundings, and all I could see was the blue glow making an outline around her head.

The dragon turned, jerking her head forward. "Gather your be-longings and exit my back. You have fate keepers to speak with."

I packed up my things quickly, rolled my blanket small enough to hook to my pack, and slid down the bowed dragon's neck after the others.

A blue curtain shimmered between a rock wall that extended far out of sight on both sides. It looked like all the portals I'd ever stepped through but on a much larger scale. It felt like the massive portal might lead to another world instead of places around our kingdom. The possibility of other worlds was a concept I'd read in a book once, but as the possibility stood in front of me, it seemed insane. However, many insane things had happened to me since I'd met my reaper.

We moved toward the gateway, but before we could get close enough to jump through, five translucent beings stepped out. They had a silver tinge to their skin that occasionally shifted to white and pink, almost as though they were made of sheer opals. Their three black eyes created a triangle on their otherwise featureless face, and the irises appeared to have stars streaming through them with dazzling dances.

The tallest among them raised his long arms and fingers in a wave. "We welcome you to the Realm of Fates. You may not pass without sacrifice. We require a price from you." He reached into his chest and pulled out a silver ball that shined when his gaze hit it. "You will store one of your fates in one of these for us to feed from."

I took a couple of steps forward but stopped when the two flung their hands at me. "We are to give you one of our destinies to feed you? How does that work?"

"All who live have threads that establish the pathways they are meant to walk. Things given to them by those who impose universal balance upon all those who live. Some are good and others are bad. You must choose one of three good fates to give us. Energy flows along your fate thread to each pathway. One will wilt and die to sustain us."

"We get to see all three?"

"Yes."

Moirai started forward to the gate and three of them created a barrier by stretching in front of her trajectory. "I am the daughter of Fate and can pass through this realm with no sacrifice."

"Not this time. Since you are on this quest, our instructions are that you must abide by the same rules as the others." The tall being lowered his hand until his friends returned to normal size.

Moirai crossed her arms. "This is ridiculous. We can't give up things meant for us. It's unnatural. I should be given a pass as I normally am to travel through. My mother never would have agreed to this."

"The orders are straight from her. She said you must face the consequences of your choices."

Moirai flung her hand toward him. "Get it over with, then!"

The being took the silver ball he'd removed from his chest and plopped it into her hand. She stared off with vacant eyes that widened the longer she held the object. When it glowed as blue as the gate, he took it from her, and she stumbled back.

Moderatus caught her. "I have a hold of you. I am here."

A tear trickled off her chin, and she blinked. "This is terribly unfair."

Elisha went next and made no sign of emotion as he paid the gatekeepers. His stoic demeanor followed him everywhere. Ashern laughed about whatever he saw in his vision, and Moderatus clenched his teeth. After each person took their turn, the silver being shoved a newly blue orb back into his chest and yanked out another silver. I turned my palm up, and he started my turn.

I sighed as I rested against Alcaius's chest. "I love you. This is the most wonderful life with you. Never would want anything more than this life with you."

He played with my hair and kissed the top of my head. "I'd give up a thousand kingdoms to have this with you."

I clenched my eyes and grabbed a rock next to me to deal with the jarring flood of being ripped to a new destiny. Alcaius scooped up a shiny red stone and held it out to a small boy with golden eyes.

The child ran to me and held out the rock. "Look, Mommy."

Alcaius smiled. "An anniversary present for our hundredth year together."

Before I could tell them, it made no sense that we'd lived a hundred years together and had such a young child, the scenery changed to me standing in the middle of a platform with a crowd below. Alcaius held my hand and lifted it into the air. "I present to you, my queen. Azora of Aresgan."

The crowd cheered and not a single soul rejected me.

"Choose now," the entity yelled from overhead.

"I don't have enough information to choose between any of these. These can't be real. It's not even possible for me to live another hundred years, let alone bear a child at that age. I am human." I crinkled my nose. "I don't even want children."

"Children are not fated to you anytime soon. As you saw, it is decades in the future, and many things change in that time. I can't tell you how the threads become permanent stitches, only that, these are threads to possible destinies. You have many of them, but the one you choose will no longer be a possibility. No matter your actions."

"None of them make sense. Alcaius's people would never accept me. Only the first one has any sort of possibility, and that even seems shaky now."

"Choose or you can't enter our gate and fulfill your quest."

"Would it mean these fates couldn't be fulfilled in any sort of way at all? Like if I choose the first, I will never have simple moments with Alcaius again. The second means no children for us, not even in a hundred years. The third means I will never be his queen, or at least not accepted by his people?"

"Yes, you gain knowledge and interpretation quickly."

I definitely didn't want to be the Queen of Death, and it seemed farfetched, but if I chose that, would I have any sort of chance with Alcaius? Did I even want children? I wasn't even sure I did, and if I did, it would be far into the future. The first one didn't even make the debate. I wanted the possibility of simple moments with him forever.

I steadied my breathing, shutting out the shouting of the being rushing me to a decision. "The second isn't even possible for many reasons. I will choose it."

"Are you sure?"

"Yes, the second."

He balled his fist, and something peeled from my skin. Just as I opened my mouth to scream from the agony, I stood in front of the gate and a heaviness close to remorse settled in my chest.

It wasn't possible anyway, and therefore, not a big deal, I reminded myself. My tears darkened the black soil at my feet in disagreement.

Chapter Ten
Pursuit
Alcaius

F ennec led me through the tunnels until we reached the southern wing of the castle where Myik lived. His chambers faced the rock valley where my father's dragons were kept, as he was the royal keeper of the beasts. He had his own small palace attached to our father's castle, and I'd once heard servants saying it was to keep my brother far from his sight. I thought maybe that had been the goal at first, but Myik frequented the throne room and was never asked to leave. Samael, King of Death, hated imperfections, but it seemed my brother, heart condition and all, had grown on him.

Fennec knocked on the steel door with golden flower patterns carved into it. "That woman has given him the strangest taste in decor. You both crumble at the word of women."

"Love does that sometimes."

"Weakness does." Fennec's tone rarely fluctuated. He had the normal blight of a reaper to feel little to no emotions. He didn't even house the immense rage of our father.

My wide range of emotions was highly abnormal for my kind, and it made sense why my father often threatened to have Myik take over in my place, even with a weak heart. He saw that as preferable to my emotional range. He didn't know Myik felt much deeper than I did because Myik was much better at holding it inside until it burst from him in solitude. Whereas my impulse left me unable to contain what I felt and a big part of me didn't care who saw the display. That made me more broken than Myik.

Myik opened the door and rubbed his eye, adding a yawn. "What time is it?"

Fennec pushed his way in and glanced at Myik's enormous cedar bed that could fit five grown men. "Hello, Raya. We are about to have a meeting if you could give us a moment."

Raya slipped under the covers, and Myik punched Fennec in the shoulder. "Don't look at her in my bed! Out in the hall!"

Fennec smirked, but his eyes remained hollow. "As I said, weakness is bred in this family. That's what Father gets for cheating."

"Cheating his way to power or not, Father still has the power of the Grim Reaper. It changed little."

Fennec snorted. "The weakness showed up in his loins."

Myik shoved Fennec into a room across the hall. "If feeling is a weakness, then I'd rather not know strength."

"And this is why Father will ultimately hand rule to me."

I took the large black throne in the corner. "We have a favor to ask."

"That couldn't wait until morning?" Myik chose the end of the small bed that looked out of place in the large room.

"Do you think I have even hours with Azora heading to the dragon valley? Would you wait if it were Raya?"

"No," he grumbled.

"We need supplies. Things to take down dragons if needed."

"It's one thing to confront a wild dragon, but thousands in their territory is insane. Even with the best weapons, you wouldn't win if they all greet you."

I shrugged. "Give us your best. I have a theory they won't kill me."

"You know nothing of angry dragons, but no, that would not stop me if it were Raya, either. Let's go to my armory. I have a few things that might get their attention enough to annoy them. If you can survive their aggravation, you might stand a chance."

We hiked across Myik's house, passing beautiful paintings and tapestries that looked like he'd consulted our mother for decorating advice. Anywhere worth viewing in the main castle had my mother's hand involved. My brother's once lifeless abode had changed around the time he'd first met Raya. He often spent much time giving her pretty things.

Cool air brushed through my hair that landed just below my ears as we stepped outside. I pushed it back with my fingers and balanced on the thin stone wall that led to the dragon barns. The structure loomed nearly as tall as the black mountains behind it. Snow covered the roof on only the southern side due to the way the wind had blown the frosty touch from the jagged cliffs that met the purple sky. My boots did well to grip the ice, but the chilled layer looked like glass protected the ground from intrusion. Ice shards flew from the first barn window, landing icicles like daggers at our feet. The last one nipped my leg.

Myik pulled a small horn from his pocket and blew into it. "Bylur! That's enough!"

A massive spear jabbed Fennec in the thigh, and he quickly levitated the frozen weapon back at the beast. A white, scaly head emerged from the building and blue mist rolled from his mouth. Bylur belonged to Myik as his bonded personal dragon, but he grew testy around strangers. Myik let the dragon out after a stern warning not to freeze us. The beast grumbled his blue breath our way to frost our arms, but my armor and gloves fended off his attempt to tiptoe around obedience.

Myik glared at Bylur and went to work searching bins and shelves in the room with the dragon-sized ceiling. "He is stubborn despite years put into his training."

"Probably doesn't like slavery," I said.

"He is no more a slave than the sun is cold. Bylur is free to leave my presence any moment he chooses." He climbed a wooden ladder, brought down a marble cylinder, and slid over to a shelf across the room to find a blue wooden stick. "When you strike these two things together, it'll create a fire that burns through dragon barriers. There's not much else that does. Any water dragon can extinguish it, but it'll be enough to gather their attention."

"That's all we need since I'm told we will either be scorched on sight or ignored. Burning us won't be easy while we're in reaper form."

He put them in a silver box, followed by a leather bag. The last thing he put in was several sleeping arrows and two bows. "One last thing that will let you get close to them." He opened a white wardrobe with ivy and tiny purple flowers painted all over it. "Dragons see on a special spectrum, but when you put these cloaks on, they can't see you. Other people and things still can. It'll allow you to see each other but sneak up on them easier if a fortune dragon isn't paying attention." He handed us each a black cloak with golden stitching. "That's about all I can give you."

"It's better than what we started with." I swung the bag over my shoulder.

Fennec stared at the bag with mischief almost gleaming in his deadpan. "We can burn the whole wall down if we run with what you gave us."

Myik started toward the exit. "Alcaius better hang on to it all. We don't need a dragon war because we set a psychopathic reaper loose on them."

"You say that as though that's not what a reaper should be."

I patted the bag and caught up to Myik. "Safe with me. He won't be touching them."

"All it would be is a little fun," Fennec said.

"Can you feel fun?"

"No, but I like the concept of it and the closest I think I get to it is watching the light exit someone's eyes. You know the moment they go dull and that energy pulses through my scythe. That's the most alive I ever feel. The closest I get to understanding what the rest of the living calls emotions."

"The gods made reapers addicted to only that. It's an intoxication unmatched." I glanced away wistfully as I pictured it.

Myik gawked at us both and shook his head. "Hearing you two talk makes me glad I never endured the ceremony. It's abnormal to crave ending life."

"It's as natural as breathing, but it's not without its guilt and pain."

Fennec stared at the mountain. "Reaping was the only thing I desired long before any ceremony. You two are the broken ones." Our youngest brother walked back toward Myik's house.

The portal got us close to the dragon valley, but not so close it would notify any scaly monsters guarding the territory. We shifted into our skeletal forms and put on our cloaks before trekking in the way the map told us. Walking skeletons were all we became with our ivory bones hidden in clothes, but our skulls were harder to conceal because even in hoods the light would give away our monster status under the right circumstances. I removed the orb from my bag and threw it in the air for the third time, and once again, nothing happened. At first, it sparked to life and once I even thought I spotted a glimpse of Azora.

I flung it into a tree. "Bastard orb!"

"Hey, that inanimate object probably has more of a father than we do." Fennec's tone almost held amusement, and he had an odd sense of humor to go with his muted emotions.

The grass and dirt slowly disappeared into blowing sand that leaked into my cloak and poured between my rib cage. An unnatural root system wound around itself, blocking our path.

Fennec chuckled dryly as he peered at the barrier. "We get to burn this to the ground."

"For the sake of peace, we should at least attempt to do this amicably."

"Screw that!" He pulled the black cylinder and blue stick from his pocket and struck them together.

I gaped and checked my bag to see if he'd stolen another set, but mine had disappeared from my possession. "How did you get that?"

"One never tells secrets that may benefit them later for keeping." He threw the inferno and landed it between two roots, but it stopped at a grey rock that covered any spaces in the wood. Anything the blue fire touched crumbled, including the roots and the grey filler clay.

Roars struck our ears moments before the orange fire swallowed us in its flames.

Three dragons dropped behind us.

An emerald dragon with shimmering scales and jagged horns tossed his head around like my father's whip correcting an obstinate horse or son. "Where is the threat?"

A slate one with purple eyes stepped forward. "They are here, but magic shields them. My singed tongue is clear." He stuck out his lengthy forked tongue to taste the air like a cobra ready to devour skittish mice.

The third one appeared made of suspended turquoise liquid, swishing around in the air. "We burn everywhere, and they will be ashes."

I removed my hood. "We don't want trouble."

"The hole in our wall says otherwise, reaper," the emerald one snarled.

"That was to gain your attention. We request an audience with your council."

"Our council does not meet with those who steal from us and enslave our kind." He growled each word with his teeth chomping aggressively.

"Then I fear we must burn down your wall." Fennec struck the stone and stick together until a fire lit, and he ran with it along the wall.

The dragons roared. "We'll just devour you then!" the water one said moments before sending his energy into destroying my idiot brother's actions.

Fennec didn't hesitate as he shot several arrows in quick succession into each of the beasts. "Want to talk now?"

"He's poisoned us," the slate one mumbled, collapsing to the ground.

"Moron!" I grabbed his hand and took off toward the trees.

He shook my hand loose. "Looks like it got us an audience."

I followed his gaze above our heads, but all I saw was a massive open mouth before the jowls closed around me. Our flesh couldn't be pierced, but our bones could crunch. Damp heat steamed around me in the dark prison, held together by teeth and skin. It was a good time to be made of only bones as I bounced around in the organic cavern.

"You fool! That was about the dumbest thing you could have done." I felt around in the dark to find my brother and shove him down the dragon's throat.

"I got us to the council."

"You got us eaten!" Energy buzzed through my fingers as my scythe crackled on my back, also enraged by Fennec's actions.

"If we are eaten, why are we still in the mouth? Swallowing is required for that because being eaten means exiting the wrong direction."

"You're about to do just that!" I followed his voice and kicked him with my boot. "I can't afford to fuck this up! The only thing that makes my life worth anything is on the line here!"

He grunted. "Yes, because killing me in here will help things, and you wonder why you have so many issues when your emotions endlessly get you in trouble. You wonder why reapers were made to have none."

"Except anger, right? Because anger makes us more brutal. We were taught to kill on impulse, but rage-filled killers all the better."

"Less than half feel anger, and the fact father is filled with it points to it being a weakness. A mutation not originally meant for reapers, but they left it because anger has advantages coinciding with violence."

"Father is the most powerful reaper of all. The Grim Reaper himself, so how could you possibly see it leans toward weakness and unintention from the gods?"

He laughed, but it remained cold, like everything about him. "You really don't know how father cheated his way to power? Have you never even cared about why Father's soul, line, power, and kingdom are all in objects that can be destroyed with the wrong magic placed upon them?"

"No, Father would never tell me why, and I never cared enough to search out an answer."

"You never cared enough with your soul on the line?"

"Until recent events, he never even admitted the rumors were true. After we had them secure, I guess I had too many other things going on to worry much about it."

"Like thinking with your dick," he said.

"That used to be the case with women, but it no longer is. My heart is what I use now."

"That makes no sense. There's an entire kingdom of harlots you could have your pick of. All wanting to get close to the son of Death for prestige. My bed is never empty unless I want it to be."

"It's something you'll never understand with a heart more stone than our brother's. Tell me then, why did Father allow his highest possessions to be placed into objects? It's always a willing choice. Impossible for essences of the living to be stolen."

The dragon spit us out on brown rock as my curiosity for answers about my father grew. Torches lit cave walls and spread light over around ten dragons that snarled in our direction. Rook thought my brother's mania would help us, but it'd only cooked us. The scent of herby roasting meat seemed to emphasize our pending fate. Fennec stood next to me, and I narrowed an eye at him to warn him not to screw this up more than he already had.

"We don't take lightly to attacks on our territory." A dragon who looked made of rubies swiped his claws at my face, keeping mere inches from mauling my skull. It would have done little, but it seemed only a tactic born of anger.

I stepped toward him as my bones heated. "And I don't take likely to dragons coercing my woman into quests."

"Yes, you are Alcaius, son of Death. We forced nothing upon your human. We only gave her but a deal."

"Let me see her, and then we will all be on our way together."

He grumbled steam from his nostrils and slipped farther from the shadows. "You are in no position to demand deals from us, and she is not even here."

"Let's kill him. Both of them!" a black dragon on the left shouted.

Several other dragons joined his chant, but the ruby one shook his snout. "That we cannot do. It will break the deal we made with his human, and she will not follow through with what we need her to."

"You are to let them go to the Realm of Fates after Azora." Belphagor entered the room with the flames on his shoulders burning especially bright in the low lighting.

"You said he wasn't to go!"

"Yet. He wasn't to go yet, and now he is. It's why I sent him here to align it all up."

Belphagor always played chess with what he saw in his visions, and if I went after Azora, I'd play right into his game. But no part of me could stay idle while she ventured into unknown territory at the will and instructions of scaly monsters who cared nothing for humans. Azora had died twice in my arms, and her soul didn't have the strength to last a third revival. The image of her dead sped my heart to panic, and I knew I'd play into Belphagor's plot if it got me to her as quickly as possible.

Desperation beat against wisdom until I ignored any discernment that attempted to persuade me against pursuing the woman I loved across any land. The horrific emptiness of losing her again bred a visceral impulse to keep her safe, so I never had to endure the deepest pain of a shattered heart again.

Belphagor held out his hand. "Let me see your orb."

I crossed my arms. "What orb?"

"Let me fix it, so you don't wander for years. It's not doing you much good as is."

I handed it to him, knowing he couldn't render it any more useless than it already was.

He removed a pouch from his pockets and covered it in blue dust, rubbing it all over the smooth marble until it glowed to life. "You will be able to follow her with this now."

It sat uneasily with me how much he desired me to follow her, but once again, I didn't care how I got to her as long as I did.

The ruby dragon filled the room with more steam, which fogged up his polished gem skin. "We will let the reapers go, but they will get no help with transportation from us."

Belphagor returned the orb to me. "That's okay. I have something in mind for that."

CHAPTER ELEVEN
CHAOS
Azora

The Realm of Fates looked unexpectedly ordinary with its plain, rolling hills. We traveled on a dirt path with thick grass and red wildflowers on both sides. Oak trees made an occasional appearance, and more wildflowers dotted the background. The only thing off was the sky that kept a lavender tint with orange streaks running through it, much like the purple lightning that surged through Greaves forest.

No structures, people, or animals broke up the scenery, and toward what seemed like midday, we stopped at a small stream to fill any water jugs we'd depleted. Ashern babbled about random things most of the time, and the rest of us added a few thoughts. For the most part, we let him carry on about a plethora of topics.

When the nearly one-sided conversation lulled, I brought up some things I'd learned while reading. "Out of the six elemental pairs, all of them balance each other as opposites."

Moirai shook her head and clicked her tongue as she threw a few of her braids over her shoulder. "Yes, we are all aware of all of that. We rehearsed all those facts in school so many times."

"Well, I wasn't in your school and knew nothing about it until a few days ago."

"Do you have to tell us all about it?"

Moderatus gave a single slow nod. "I, for one, do not mind being reminded my people are above all the other elementals. We have no opposite pair because we are balance itself. We cut off anyone trying to gain unfair power."

I tucked my book back into my sack. "It's not that yours are superior from my understanding. You regulate their jobs."

Ashern snorted. "Simple regulators is all you Balancers are, so much so you aren't important enough to be listed as elementals in most texts and artwork. All glorified and smug until a human humbles you."

Moirai stared at me. "At least Moderatus and his people get to have elemental powers when some are just descendants." She smirked and stood up from where she stooped over the stream.

Elisha, who sat underneath a tree writing, had said little the entire journey, but he paused his pen to look at us. "Many seers are stronger than elementals. The powers passed down did not diminish in most cases, but rather increased. Look at how Azora's power is the entire reason we are even on this quest."

Elisha's words both bothered me and made me proud. My ability had caused a chain of events that harmed dragon hatchlings to such a great degree the entire species faced extinction, but to have the seer reaper acknowledge I belonged with the group made me return Moirai's smirk with my own.

I packed everything up and joined Ashern, who'd already started down the dirt path toward another grassy hill. "How long do we have to walk until we get to the Fates?"

He glanced behind him at Moirai. "She could answer that a lot better than me, but she doesn't seem to want to help you."

"Why is that? You said she wants something I have."

"Yes, she definitely does." He shot me a toothy grin that confused me even more. "To answer your question the best I can, days maybe if we're lucky. Possibly weeks."

"Weeks? That's not going to work."

"It'll have to. The kingdoms we must walk through are unpredictable. Moirai's mother is the leader of the Fates, but she won't give us an easy path. She says we have to walk the same journey all others with a Fates request have."

A howl ripped apart the air as though the wind wailed in fury. The sky turned dark, dimming everything instantly into night, and a loud crash of thunder shook the ground as it joined the howl in a horrific symphony.

"Point your eyes toward the ground and remove yourselves from the path!" Moderatus ran for Moirai, throwing his oversized robe over her body to protect her.

My cheeks stung like a poisoned Jusper tree leaf touched them, but before I could grasp the pain, shock rocked me as my armor sizzled. Cloth went over my head, and Elisha shoved me off the path. Any exposed skin touched by the raindrops boiled, and I struggled to gain composure through the excruciating melting of my body. Elisha had morphed into his skeletal form to protect himself. We rolled into a ditch, and he kept himself over me as a storm raged around us. The thunder and wind joined forces to deafen me, and I covered my ears, screaming as my skin continued to burn. The agony intensified until my vision went black.

"Humans are so weak. A few rain burns, and they wilt and take forever to heal. It's pathetic really," Moirai said from somewhere close.

I kept my eyes shut and gritted my teeth at the lingering pain.

"Rather, you are lucky that you aren't suffering as she is. She has greater strength because she is enduring through it, instead of having it quickly relieved." Elisha sounded right next to me, and it was nice to hear him defend me when he didn't even know I was listening.

Things grew quiet, and I opened my eyes to see a blue canvas ceiling flutter in a calmer wind. The natural force still had a slight wail to it, but it had chilled enough not to take out the tent. Rain pattered but didn't devour our protection, so either the water had turned normal, or the material magically shielded us.

Elisha raised his hand as I stood up. "Rest. We need your wounds to heal before we can move on. I will make you some tea to help you sleep again."

"What happened?" I groaned and shut my eyes.

"We got caught in a chaos storm. They run naturally through this territory and are unpredictable. That's what makes them chaotic."

I lifted my arms and looked at my bandages. "The rain ate me."

"Yes, it seems that it did, but thankfully I brought elvish mint leaves to help repair you faster, but they will drain a lot of your energy as they work. You need to rest." He placed a blue teacup on a grey stone, sprinkling in herbs and various leaves. Once he stirred it and let it cool for a short time, he helped me sip it until I fell back into slumber.

Consciousness greeted me occasionally, and Elisha always insisted I return to sleeping to properly heal. Time lost any substance as I drifted, but as much as I tried, I couldn't resist the darkness as I'd hoped.

"What I always found fascinating was how Alcaius knew you were special without really knowing it." A tall bronze man with blazing shoulders stood under the light of a pulsing streetlamp.

I whipped my head around to gather my location, but nothing familiar stuck out, and when I went to use my seer sense, only blurry images appeared. "What's going on?"

"You're dreaming."

"This is too real."

"Because another soul has entered your dream. That magnifies the dream. Do you know who I am?"

I glanced around at the hazy air to realize the only thing real around me was him. "I don't recognize you, and my seer sense is useless here."

He stepped closer, and a chill seeped into my muscles like when Death had visited me, but it also felt different, as though it didn't cut quite as deep into my bones. His fingers grazed my cheek. "You are so beautiful. It's no wonder the Prince of Death is fascinated with you. I found you intriguing long before him. A tracker seer and a key seer as the same person is a terribly wonderful combination."

I jerked my cheek away from his hand and put space between us. "What do you want? Why do you and your master insist on disturbing my sleep?"

"I have no master except myself. Your reaper killed the only being to ever have any sort of control over me. Alcaius gave me a substantial gift the day he slaughtered my father, Belial, for me."

"You're Belphagor. You saved me twice."

"You were the price of my revenge, and ironically, you are my salvation."

"How could I possibly save you?"

"In time, we will discuss that, but we're being disturbed." He glanced at the grey sky churning and disappeared.

"Azora!" a voice called me from above, where Belphagor's gaze had fallen. "Azora! Wake up!"

I groaned and shoved open my eyelids, blinking them rapidly a few times. "What?"

"I hate to bother you while you're healing, but another storm is on the horizon. This one will rip us apart." Ashern pointed to my right.

Several vortexes swirled in our direction, and a few had touched the ground to form gigantic tornadoes.

I gaped for the three seconds it took me to get to my feet and take off running. Ashern grabbed my hand and yanked me faster than my barely roused feet could run. Moderatus and Moirai were already far ahead.

I squinted to see if our fourth member was even farther ahead. "Where's Elisha?"

"Behind us. He's using his magic to hold the funnels off long enough for me to get you awake and out of here," Ashern said.

"What? He'll be killed!"

"He will figure it out. Your safety is top priority to all of us." He gave me another fierce tug to urge me on.

My calves burned and collapse seemed imminent, but I had no choice but to push forward. "Not all of you. Moirai wants nothing more than for the tornadoes to carry me far away."

"Maybe only after we get you to turn around the dragons' fate."

"Where are we running to?"

"The wind caves. The hills aren't what they seem here." His declaration appeared to fuel his speed more, and he dragged me with him.

We trudged up the hill as my hair tore from its bun and flew frantically upward like it was bonded to the sky and needed to reach it. My feet lifted from the ground, and I curled my toes into the soil to anchor myself while I squirmed my palm free from Ashern to latch onto the root of the oak tree next to me. Ashern stomped on the ground, slamming his boots hard into the dirt. The rattling ground and forceful wind beat at me, and unlike Ashern, I could barely hold on for my life. The earth gave under his feet, and he dropped an unknown distance. I tracked him in my mind to find him standing on a solid surface, but he scaled up instead of remaining in his sanctuary.

I crawled along the root, and my body lifted in the air as my hair whipped across my vision. The clouds darkened, further lowering visibility. Everything around me wanted to rip apart my life, but I refused to let it. All that mattered was meeting Ashern at his created tunnel. Bark scraped my fingers until raw pain shot through to my wrist, loosening my grip on the roots. I shoved through the pain and blasting wind.

Ashern popped above the hole and extended his hand. "Azora! Come on. I thought it was clear to follow me."

"I got the message, but the wind doesn't seem to want me to respond to it." The wind screeching made it difficult for our words to carry, and I turned my focus on making it to him.

I crawled to the edge of the roots and tried to reach him. Our fingers brushed, but the wind caught me, throwing me into the air. One of the daggers sheathed at my side fought me to stay caught, and I tugged at another until it gave, allowing me to slam it into the tree trunk. The rain made the blade slippery, and I stabbed another next, swinging my feet to a low-hanging branch. My back slammed against the trunk as I dangled from the tree limb. A gust scooped me from my hold at the same time a cloak wrapped around me to throw me under its protection. Mud softened the blow to my knees, and I sunk deeper into the mush. The storm raged its fury around me with thunderous roars and violent demands. The cloak held me secure through it all.

When all went quiet, Elisha released me from the suffocating prison that spared me. Muscle and tissue covered exposed ivory, knitting him back into a human. "Are you hurt? More than you already were?"

"I'm fine. The bruises will show tomorrow, but they will not be a new thing to get used to."

"Your rain burns are healing as well. More time resting would have helped, but I believe the scarring will be minimal." He pulled out a jar with blue ointment. "May I?"

I nodded, and he patted the chilled salve on each wound. It smelled of mint and ginger, freezing each area it touched.

Ashern stuck his head out of the hole. "We might want to consider traveling the chaos lands in these tunnels. Two storms this close together is an aggravation. It's battering our human too much."

I sent him a scowl because I was too far to shove him into his self-made pit. "I've handled worse."

"Doesn't look like that's the case."

Elisha closed the ointment and returned it to his bag. "Humans break easily, but they fight their way back with the same enthusiasm."

"The tunnels are still the best way."

"Chaos happens just as easily underground," Elisha said.

"Yes, but we at least don't have to worry about Azora becoming windmill blades." Ashern turned around to study the horizon. "Where did Moirai and Moderatus get off to?"

I walked over to Ashern and looked down the dark, curved tunnel below him. "Probably decided they could do it without me."

"That's doubtful. Moirai is all about justice and the rules because they are all about what should be. She fully believes you need punished for your sins."

"Right. How are we even going to see down in the tunnel?"

He held onto a rock jutting out from the grass and searched through his bag until he located a stick that he beat until it lit up. "Didn't you bring any light sources?"

"Yes, but I didn't want to use them up first thing."

He tossed me his stick and threw another to Elisha. "Let's go underground. It's not like we can really lose the others with a top-level tracker seer on our side."

I closed my eyes and concentrated on Moirai and Moderatus. Both took a few seconds to pull to the surface because I'd met them but connected with neither. "They're underground too. Everyone apparently knows you can stomp holes in the hills here. That would have been a nice thing to let me know, too. For guides, you keep a lot to yourselves."

"We're your guides, which means you don't have to know."

"What if I'm separated from all of you? Even though I can find you, the separation might be too far, or I can't reach you. Information is survival in unknown lands."

He held out his hand. "Come on down, and I'll tell you what I know as we travel. The first thing is that the wind is the most unpredictable thing in the chaos lands. Only the chaos wielders can control it, and some still struggle. Copy where I put my hands and feet the best you can." He put his light in his mouth and descended into the tunnel.

I followed him and did my best to copy his path and switched to my tracker sense for better accuracy. Occasionally, I pushed my thoughts to Elisha to make sure he kept up. He controlled memory and death, and those wouldn't help him with directions. At a few points, Ashern slowed down, and the sound of scraping rocks rumbled. It became clear he punched out our tunnel as he went.

He looked up at me. "Azora, I seem to have issues finding one of the caverns. Can you point me in the right direction? I'm sensing there may be one here with the way the temp fluctuates between here and slightly lower, but I'd rather not continue to punch through solid clay if it's unneeded."

"I've never been here before, so I can't be precise, but I can sense where things are different enough to probably tell if there is a cavern."

"That will work. Right now, it's all endless rock."

"Are Luck Drawers super strong or is it soft land here?" I closed my eyes to feel the way the land sat.

"A little of both. You could do this easily with the right tool. It's interesting because the land is sturdy enough to hold significant weight, but bends and crumbles when a being wills it to. Normal laws don't apply in the chaos lands."

Something in my mind opened behind me. "To your right. If you turn around, there is what I think is an open space that extends for a great distance."

He slid around and positioned his fist on the brown, chalky wall. "Here?"

"Slightly left." I waited until he lined up just right with it. "Yes, there. That's it."

He brought his arm back, jabbing my thigh with his elbow and slamming his fist into the spot I'd told him. The wall shattered into a grey rock cave. Red, glowing creatures hanging from the ceiling screeched and flew away in a quickly formed horde. One got lost and came at me. A quick slap corrected its mistake, and it caught up to the others as it hissed at my actions. Blue Crystals stuck out of random spots on all the surfaces, and smoke rose from pockets in the rocks, leaving a sulfur stench behind.

We all dropped to the ground and headed after the red-winged creatures. When we came to a fork in the path, Ashern took his dice out and whispered into them before tossing them into the air. He studied them and nodded. "Right, we go."

"I could just track for us."

"Branches in paths are best left to luck if we don't want misfortune to follow us."

"You just went on about how helpful my tracker sense is, only to abandon it immediately."

He shrugged and kept walking, not stopping to check on Elisha. I appeared to be the only one to want to keep track of the reaper seer. It seemed every man for himself except me. Everyone agreed they needed to keep me alive so I could suffer for my transgressions. A chill set in that the steam traps eased every time we passed one. The downside was the awful rotten egg smell that went along with it.

Ashern whistled and studied the blue crystals like each one wasn't the same. "How is your reaper doing without you?"

I squinted at his odd question. "How would I know?"

"I would have thought with how close you are to him, you would track him constantly to see him. Isn't that how your tracker sense works? The more connected you are to a person, the more you can see them and the things they are connected to?"

"It is, but I've been starting to feel like he answers me back. There's been a few times I've felt our connection is so strong I accidentally sent him feedback, and I can't risk him knowing I'm on this quest. He'd risk everything to come after me."

He removed his glove and placed his hand on one of the crystals. "Where does he think you are?"

"Taking my fairy to get her wisping abilities back. We needed a break anyway." I caught Elisha freeze at my words.

"Trouble in bliss?" Ashern picked at the crystal with his fingernail and frowned.

"Some fundamental beliefs we are having trouble agreeing on."

He punched the blue rock where he'd picked at it and put the loosened piece in his bag. "Can't you agree that it's okay to think differently?"

"We do, but I'm not sure I can stay with him because of the belief."

"I see. The quest away from him is a good time to sort that out."

We continued walking, and Ashern went back to trusting my seer sense. He claimed the first branch was the most important, but I believed it was really the two times that we reached a dead end that changed his mind. The farther we trudged, the more I thought about Alcaius and the more I missed him. Maybe one quick peek wouldn't hurt anything.

I gasped as he quickly pushed forward through my seer sense. "No way!" I whispered. Fear and anger seeped into my chest with nowhere to escape.

Chapter Twelve

Transportation

Alcaius

The lush green and blue mountains, along with the perfect temperature and purple skies, made the dragon land somewhere enviable to live. It was no wonder the creatures put in immense effort to keep their lands hidden.

Belpahgor had led us out of the cave and down a path to pastures where strange, tall creatures pecked the ground. "Here's your ride."

I glowered at Belphagor as I took in the wide birds with elongated necks and tiny heads. Their oversized beaks looked as ridiculous as their stick legs and flat three-toed feet. "Flight tends to be faster, but they look clunky."

"They don't fly." The flames on his shoulders bounced over his shimmering bronze skin as he laughed. "They'll get you there in sufficient time."

"I can walk faster than they can sprint."

"You're basing this on what facts? Have you ever seen a washicoo before?"

"No, but those legs will break with a small rodent on their back. There's no way they can hold us." I leaned in to look at the bird closer. "How do their bulging eyes not roll to the ground? There's barely a face to hold them in."

"They will hold you and get you there quickly." He threw a black saddle on the back of a black one with purple-tipped feathers. "This is Gymoere. He is under my orders to obey you. Give him a chance. Time will align exactly right if you do."

"It's not like I should even trust you. You want the love of my life for some nefarious purpose."

"You should trust me because if it weren't for me, dragons would have eaten you already."

Fennec leaped onto the back of a blue-tipped one, and it took off, sending him flying to the ground. He darted after it, but it vanished in a spewing dust cloud. Belphagor hadn't lied about the birds' speed, but that didn't mean they could handle people and packs. Fennec tried to catch another by hooking it around the neck and holding on. The washicoo squawked and bucked violently, trying to rid my brother from its back. Fennec held tight, and the bird's squawks muffled to a choking gasp.

He stood over the defeated fowl in victory, nudging it with his black leather boot. "This is mine. I ride nothing I don't claim."

Belphagor carried a brown saddle to the fallen bird. "One Grim brother has reaper genes, after all. His name is Spinute. Once I resuscitate him, he's yours."

I rolled my eyes and shoved my brother into the wooden fence. "Must you impulsively put on a show wherever we go?"

"It only looks impulsive because your thoughts occur at the speed of an inland ogre," Fennec said.

"Rather, your thoughts don't process at all."

"They process, and I agree with my first conclusion."

I climbed onto Gymoere. "Are they the same commands as a horse?"

Belphagor attached a pack to my bird and then Fennec's. "Yes, only tap gently or they will take off at a speed your skin can't keep up with."

"Maybe I should shift."

"Sure. If you want to alert everyone on your journey, that reapers ride to the fate gate."

Belphagor made a decent point. I could hide in my cloak, but certain races could sense the darkness of my people when we were only made of bones. In our human form, it became difficult for most to see us as anything unusual. He led us to the root wall, where dragons of all colors growled and hissed at us. Their snout twitches showed how much most wanted to gnaw on our bones, but dragons stayed loyal to their clan. The dragon king had demanded obedience, and they complied with his wishes without question.

Belpahgor split the barrier with the wave of his hand, and we stepped through. The looking globe floated through the air and flickered to life. Azora slept on the back of a dragon, and I liked that I'd be able to see her on our journey to know that she was safe. The wall closed, leaving Fennec and me alone with the moronic birds.

The globe led us toward Azora, and I often watched her instead of the journey. The birds turned out to be much faster than anticipated and their stick leg strength seemed supernatural. Gymoere often tipped his head back, and it took me several times of him doing it, then squawking to realize he wanted to be scratched just below his tiny ear hole. The logical course of action would have been to trade the birds for horses at the next village, but horse sales needed recorded and had the potential to alert someone to my whereabouts. Stealing them risked much as well. My father wanted me on the quest, but the farther we traveled from his kingdom, the more I risked getting caught.

"We need to talk about your impulsive behavior." I watched Azora laughing at the heir of Luck and seethed.

"Or we could talk about how your jealousy is irrationally seeping from every inch of your skin."

"There's no jealousy here, only murderous thoughts toward Ashern touching what's mine."

Fennec's eyebrow raised the slightest bit to show the strongest form of amusement he could muster. "That's the same thing. Emotions only impede rational action."

"They lead to my fist in his face and that leads to him backing away from Azora."

"Yes, but emotions make you kill him without thought and that leads to you being caught and having another bounty placed on your head. Killing is not your problem. It's what the gods bred you for. By nature, you are to reap souls, many times through violence. To deny that is the deny the fabric of what makes a reaper. What worsens it is thinking the rules don't apply to you."

"And they apply to you? It doesn't seem like it when you're burning down dragon walls."

"They do because it allows me all the violence I could ever crave, but within the constraints that have no one stopping me. There is a time to obey rules and a time to annihilate them. It's a matter of which choice most benefits you."

"We agree, but on what the times are, we will never be in accord."

Fennec had little emotions, and it made him rely on his logical brain for most decisions. Somehow, even with using reasoning, he made foolish choices that I'd cleaned up his entire life. My choices depended on what was right for me at the moment. That could change based on the circumstances and had always worked well for me until recently.

We followed the globe through the next day and night, not stopping even to sleep. Reapers could avoid sleep much longer than many other races. Since I'd met Azora, I'd slept more than I ever had to be close to her while she did. The thought brought an ache to my throat, and I swallowed, missing her in my arms.

We avoided towns, relying on our lessened physical needs and the supplies the dragons had reluctantly given us due to Belphagor's insistence. I'd gone to the elemental academy with Belphagor, and everyone had expected our fathers' rivalry to carry through to us, but we'd mainly stayed indifferent toward each other. He'd never struck me as someone who I should worry about being my enemy.

All of that had changed the minute he brought Azora into his games, and it made me question everything he'd done to save her. When she went limp in my arms, I'd pleaded with him to not take her as the reaper sent to collect her soul, and he'd spared her. Reapers both knew how to give life and take it. However, if we had any sort of connection to a person, we couldn't return their soul. That had left Belphagor as my only hope.

We rode for the next several days, and I kept a close watch on Azora through the globe. It seemed uneventful until her party arrived at the fate gate, and she had to cut a thread of a fate owed to her. She didn't cry often, but when the keeper released her, tears fell from her eyes as she stared off. What had she given up?

Fennec stared at the globe. "What if she gave you up? Seems that was a slight loss to her."

I kicked his knee to send him off balance just enough that he had to grab onto his bird's neck. "She would never."

"Whatever you say."

She wiped her tears and moved forward through the gate, and the orb went black, dropping onto the ground.

I hopped off Gymoere and picked up the obsidian ball, trying to get it to reactivate. It gave me nothing. "Damn it!"

"You really thought it could send images across realms?"

"Silence!"

"You sound like Father when you shout one-word demands."

I brought my boot up to kick him hard, and he grabbed my foot, knocking me to the ground. In one quick move, I landed on my heels and flung myself forward, throwing him off his beast. I stepped on his chest. "Never compare me to Father!"

"Yet, you make it so easy with your violence."

I returned my boot to the ground and jerked him up with a toss toward his bird. "You say that while your first-year reaper count surpassed mine in my first five years combined."

"Reaping isn't violence, Alcaius. It's order in the universe."

"How is you taking life on an assignment different from me choosing who I take? Choosing those who deserve it more."

"Assignments tell you who is due to die for universal balance. It's a noble profession that you slander by thinking your conscience knows better than those who have spent eons learning the fate fabric and the needs of the universe. Your violence is born of arrogance. Mine is born of duty."

"Yours is abhorrent and mindless with no question to whether the system is just to all the living forced to endure it."

He cackled, but it held no more life than an empty scythe. "Ironic. You, of all people talking about justice."

I took a step toward him. "What does that even mean?"

"Again. You are set to be executed once caught because you think you are an executioner. The irony is that in you thinking you know just ways is that you will endure the damnation of justice for yourself."

I climbed back on Gymoere and forced Fennec's words away from taking root under my skull. My baby brother knew nothing of anything he spoke about. No thought was given to the assignments he took. He carried them out whether infant or elderly, good or evil.

Those I killed deserved it by every moral measurement. Basic ethics told anyone that.

I pushed Gymoere forward and gripped his feathers. The bird didn't squawk or nip and seemed okay with my tight hold. If he hadn't, I'd have probably abandoned him to the forest terrain we'd entered. Pine needles covered giant red trees with twisted branches that rose far above. A house could easily fit under the height the branches started. Snow covered the ground in patches, and with it had brought a cold that felt welcoming. Reapers preferred cold to most things, and my only exception was Azora's warmth pressed against me. For some reason, I craved the heat she brought more than I loved the cold. It was something unnatural that I embraced and didn't question.

Fennec removed his cloak and strolled over to a pile of snow that he patted over his black stubble to create a frosty beard. He stuffed some under his shirt and closed his eyes like he could actually enjoy something. "It's been much too hot on this journey. Questing is so barbaric."

"Why did you even come?"

"Rook convinced me."

"I told him to leave you out of this."

"You're easy to ignore. Ask Father." He flung some snow at me. "You need chilled a great deal."

I raised my scythe and commanded electricity to shake a branch until it covered my brother with white fluff.

He broke free with vigorous shaking. "Thank you. That was exactly what I needed."

I increased the electrical intensity until all the snow on the branch plopped on his head. He charged me, and we tumbled to the ground, rolling and throwing snow at each other. I got him into a headlock, and he morphed his shape to twist out of my hold.

"Now. Now. What do we have here? Grim boys acting like savages. Not exactly a surprise." Dagny, my old classmate, stood above us, shaking her head.

"My brother shouldn't be such a hollow skull, and he wouldn't find himself receiving my wrath." I stood up and walked back to Gymoere.

"Your wrath gets you in a lot of trouble. "

"So I've been told."

"Belphagor says you are too slow and thought getting to Azora would have left you more motivated. I'm here to speed things along." She turned and waved for us to follow her.

"He's the one who gave us these silly beasts and insisted they could go faster."

We trekked through the wintry ground until we reached an open field where a silver dragon nearly blended with the white landscape.

Dagny ran toward the dragon and leaped onto his leg while using his scales to climb to his spine. "Phyrix is the only dragon who agreed to transport you."

Fennec stroked his Washicoo's wing. "What do we do with our birds?"

"Leave them. They know the way home."

I moved toward the dragon without hesitation, but my brother strangely lingered, as though it bothered him to leave the creature. Affection was a rarity for reapers, and Fennec was as typical as they came.

"We can't take the birds? They should fit on his back. Azora's entire questing party fit on the back of their dragon," Fennec said.

Phyrix growled a low murmur. "They cannot pass through the fate gate, so you would have to leave them, anyway."

Fennec nodded and joined us on Phyrix.

We rode for another night, and I used the time to catch up on the little sleep I needed, so I could devote my time to Azora once we found her. The energy from the fate gate surged through me hours before we reached it. The large portal magnetized elementals to it as though calling us home to our origins. Anything divine lived on the other side, and the gate seemed to declare that fact to anyone who held ethereal pieces inside of them.

The entrance to the next realm looked more like a wall than a gate as it rippled blue, like a luminescent waterfall. Without even so much as a goodbye, Dagny and Phyrix dropped us at the entrance and rose back into the sky.

Silver liquid creatures emerged. Only my textbooks had taught me they were fate finders and responsible for screening anyone who wanted to enter sacred realms.

The tallest stepped forward and held out his hand while wiggling his fingers up and down. "To enter here, you must give up a fate."

Fennec whipped out his scythe and stuck it into the fate finder. "Or we could take some."

The being screeched, and Fennec sent electricity through him until he dissolved into a slimy puddle at our feet. The other two charged him, and he ended them both.

I braced myself for hordes of them to climb out of the portal. "What in Hades did you just do?"

He dug through the mucky remains and pulled out small glowing balls he stuck in his bag. "Don't you remember anything about fate finders?"

"Yeah, of course."

"Apparently not enough. They're connected to everything, and the minute they got inside your head, we would have been given away to the Determiners. I expected you to strike first. I thought that was your sure plan."

"You could have discussed that with me." I cautiously approached the gate and stuck my hand through.

No pain or barrier hit it, so I stepped through the rest of the way. Once on the other side, I tossed the orb in the air and watched it bring Azora back to my sight. She was underground and so close I could feel her as though I was the one with a tracker sense. Whether the sensations of her presence were created in my mind or not, they made me miss her and pressed me with urgency. Fennec joined me in the new realm, and I charged toward my woman.

Fennec and I traveled most of the morning and stopped on the edge of a stream to gather water. The air tingled to indicate a chaos storm brewed, waiting to pounce with no other warning. Most beings missed the signs my reaper bones could pick up on.

I shifted to a reaper and stuck my dry bony finger in the air to get a better feel. "We need to take cover somewhere or risk the wind ripping our bones from their joints." I placed the globe into a pocket in my pack for safekeeping, not wanting the storm to steal my way to Azora.

Fennec watched the violently blowing tree branches. "Might be too late."

"No, the reshin trees should hold us in their hollow trunks until the storm passes. I learned about them at the academy." I jogged toward a cluster of trees on top of the hill in front of us and used my scythe to slice a hole in the black, brittle trunk of the widest tree in the group.

The wind roared as it picked up Fennec, and I stabbed my staff into the ground while leaping up and grabbing him before flinging him into the hollow tree. The wind gust slammed into my stomach, so I rose into the air, hunched and gasping. My scythe crackled blue and used its electricity to fight against the storm. It gave me time to grab my weapon's staff and slide into the tree, dislodging my scythe to bring it inside safely. We moved away from the hole and tucked into the sides to let nature rage its fury.

When everything calmed, Fennec left the trunk before I could move. He grunted, and I rushed after him, only to have brown feathered wings lock me into place. The crunch of the chisel breaking into my collarbone struck as quickly as the poison seeping into my marrow to paralyze me. I shifted to rid the poison from my system, but a sharp pain halted my transformation.

"I wouldn't shift, or I will drain the marrow from you. Instant death for a reaper that would be," said the owner of the wings around me.

The wings retreated, and black bands snapped on my wrists to contain my magic and weaken me. Four Valkyries stood in front of us with massive brown wings and blonde hair wrapped around their heads in intricate braids. A leather corset met their short black skirts. Swords blazed at their sides, but it was their onyx-speckled blue eyes that captivated my attention.

"You have damaged one of our most sacred trees and must be punished," one said.

"When they were teaching you about the trees at the academy, did they mention that part?" Fennec smirked and twisted his wrists to escape his confinement but couldn't shake loose the black cuffs containing his power.

A Valkyrie lifted me into the clouds.

CHAPTER THIRTEEN
CLIMB
Azora

"He's on his way here." I sat on a stalagmite that had its point cut off, and it was large enough to make a nice chair.

Ashern stopped advancing. "Who is?"

"Alcaius. I didn't track him for the reason I told you earlier, but you asking me about it made me want to see him. He knows where I am and is on his way here. There's a floating globe, and he can see me through it."

Elisha leaned against the brown wall next to me. "There was no way he wouldn't follow once he knew what you were doing."

"He should have trusted me."

"You deceived him on your whereabouts. Whether or not for a good reason, he probably wants to know why."

I closed my eyes and checked one more time to take in the scene of Alcaius stalking me. "If someone told him I left, he most likely knows the reason."

"Not necessarily."

"Is there any way to take out a looking globe? The dragons insisted he couldn't come with, and it'll ruin everything. Here I am trying to protect him from everything, and I have to protect him from himself."

Elisha pulled a small green vial from his bag. "Normally smash them, but this might soften the obsidian enough from a distance for it to work. The globe is connected to you, so with a strand of your hair, I can mix a potion to kill anything connected to you in the way the globe is."

"We can't complete the mission with him. The dragons said he was not to come."

Ashern tucked his legs under him as he sat on the ground. "How would they even know at this point?"

"I can't afford to be wrong and void the agreement. The main reason I'm on this quest is to clear his name. His safety is my priority."

Ashern laughed and rolled a small rock between his fingers. "You both have the same priority but disagree the other should have it."

"We need to do something to throw him off our path." I stormed forward like I could actually outrun Alcaius. The path dipped suddenly in several places before slanting upward. Rocky obstacles and wet spots slowed me down, but I pushed myself to keep going for the sake of my reaper. Twice, I nearly tripped and landed in a sulfur pit, and it made me close my eyes to allow only my tracking abilities to guide me. After running through the cave system for several turns, my chest burned from the effort. The fear and determination urged me to not give in to my physical limitations.

Ashern jogged next to me and Elisha hovered, as reapers often did. It was a skill I envied because it would get me anywhere faster with little effort.

He floated in front of me and put his hand up. "Azora, perhaps, it would be better to let Alcaius reach you and explain to him you won't be safe if he comes with you."

I thought about darting around him a minute before my lungs spasmed, and I limped over to a boulder to rest. "He's stubborn and won't listen."

"We really should rest for the night. You're not completely healed, and if you overdo things, it won't matter where Alcaius is because your mission will fail."

Ashern set his black leather bag on the ground and pulled out a rolled green canvas. He pressed a black button on the side, and it burst into a fully formed tent. The tent held magical properties that allowed extremely large ones to fold into tiny travel sizes. Alcaius had used one on our quest together, and it was one of the first things that forced us closer when we wanted little to do with each other. Things had changed. I still wanted far from his presence, but love and not hate fueled my actions.

Ashern held the tent flap open and bowed. "You first."

I thought it over a couple of seconds before accepting his invite, and Elisha went in last.

Elisha searched his bag and pulled out the ointment. "About three more applications, and you should be set."

"Can you try to damage the looking globe while we sleep?" I arranged my sleeping area and glanced up at Elisha to see if he'd heard me.

He set a few items from his bag in front of him. "I will try."

"That's all I can ask. If we can end his fake tracking, then I can maneuver us successfully away from him."

With all the worry on my mind, I'd have guessed sleep would flee. Sleep surrounded me as easily as closing my eyes.

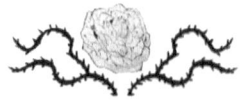

Belphagor returned to my dream, standing on a blue crystal platform to peer at me far below. "Let Alcaius catch up with you."

"I can't. The dragons said he couldn't come, and it'll mess up the
entire mission if he does." I ran my fingers through the fog drifting
through the black abyss around me.

"I can see timelines, and I'm telling you to let him catch up if you
want to succeed at your mission. The dragons will be fine with it, and
you needed only to delay him following you."

"How does that make sense?"

He jumped off the boulder and landed with ease a few feet from me.
"He needed to stay behind to get a companion and talk to his father.
Those things have been fulfilled. Now you need him with you."

I chewed on my lip and thought it all through. "If he follows me
and something terrible happens to him because of it, I will find you
and gut you."

"If only your fiery spirit could. If you want to save him, allow him to
catch up. This is a direct message that has the blessing of the dragons."

"They should have told me before I left that I only needed to delay
him catching me."

"All things happen as they should," he said.

"Yes, because you manipulate them, so they happen the way your
gift shows is an advantage to you."

The entire scene faded until I opened my eyes and sat up in the
tent. Belphagor clearly had his own motives, and it was unclear if they
aligned with mine.

Ashern turned on the light, blinding us all. "You're a restless sleeper.
We probably should get going if we want to outrun your reaper."

I packed up my bag and decided I didn't trust Belphagor. "Yes,
we need to get a move on." I concentrated on Alcaius and saw him

sleeping. I planned to keep checking to see if Elisha's spell on the globe had worked.

We packed everything up and continued through the tunnels. Moirai and Moderatus remained underground as well, but far ahead of us. They had no way of knowing if we were alive or how to get to us, and I figured after they stopped moving, they'd finally let me track my way to them.

I kept my eyes closed as we hiked, and the other two kept their eyes out for any threats around us. I'd sense certain things before they approached, but tracking sense was more accurate with anything in my forward path. That meant anything to our sides or behind had the potential to sneak up on me. We stopped to have lunch. Ashern left to take care of some business out of sight.

I screeched and jumped up from where I chewed on bread as a fuzzy large insect ran over my feet. "Gross!"

Elisha set a cup of tea next to me that he'd brewed using magic. "Romel flies. Harmless."

"Would rather them stay harmless somewhere else."

He laughed and poured himself a drink. "I didn't think a woman who could take down dragons would be bothered by such small creatures."

"Dragons can't crawl in your ears or up your pant legs."

He sipped his tea and glanced around the cave. "My brother and I used to explore caves a lot when we were kids. They were good places to hide from the other children in our city."

"Why did you need to hide from other children?"

He pointed at where the pest had disappeared into a crack in the wall. "There he's gone. You can sit again. I was unwelcome. My mother hid her affair with a reaper for a long time. Not even her husband, my brother's father, knew."

I sat back down after scanning everywhere for more insects. "That's how you are both. I was told that wasn't possible to be both a reaper and a seer."

"It's rare, but not impossible." He waved his hand over his body. "I'm proof of that, but I shifted for the first time in the schoolyard when a classmate shoved a girl, and I stepped in to stop him. He'd gotten me to the ground and pummeled me until I grew angry and shifted. After that, we were unwelcomed. Our family stayed for a while until it became too much. My mother's husband left her, and she took us into the poor parts of a distant city to hide from anyone who knew our secrets."

"I'm sorry. That's awful. It's terrible people would judge a child so harshly."

"The elites are one of the biggest groups who do."

"You have royal blood? Or at least noble? I know most seers do," I said.

"Yes, it didn't matter how strong that blood was either in the end. Even being a sister to the king didn't save my mother from being ostracized."

"No wonder your seer sense is so strong. You're not only an elemental, but your seer sense flows right from the source."

He smiled, but his eyes looked distant. "Yes, my family line has always had strong seer senses. Almost as though we are elementals ourselves and not descended from them. Though I don't know which category we'd be."

"Maybe one long lost to history."

"Perhaps."

After Ashern returned and ate, we packed up, and I tracked Alcaius again, hoping Elisha had found success.

"Just great!" I kicked a stalagmite.

"Probably good not to piss off the locals by damaging property," Ashern said.

"Alcaius is in a cage, swinging over a massive fire pit with winged women all around him. His brother is with him. I hadn't seen him before, but I recognized him from a painting in Samael's castle. The white streaks in his hair are memorable."

"Winged women? What color are their wings?"

I closed my eyes tighter and concentrated. "It's difficult to tell, but they look dark. Black or brown maybe. They're wearing leather shirts and armor."

"Valkyries. They have cities in the sky to keep them above all the chaos storms. It also keeps most enemies out."

"How do we get to them? I have to save a reaper once again."

Elisha brought a yellowed parchment over to us and unfolded it into a map. "There is access to the clouds in the Greock Mountains, beyond the sleeping forest."

"Do either of you know the way there? I can track Alcaius, but my sense may get confused with trying to find a way into the clouds. There needs to be no time wasted on uncertainty. If you allow me to access your mind, I can form the best pathway based on your experience with it."

Ashern offered me his wrist. "I've been there twice. It's a great party city. Lots of reckless fun available."

"Yes, hanging people above fires in cages like they are going to be roasted alive sounds like such fun."

"I said it was reckless fun. It's not without risk. They love to take males as slaves. If you aren't careful, they'll illegally tag you to keep or sell you in their market. Well, they wouldn't you, but if you were male, they would want to."

I took Ashern's wrist and closed my eyes. "Think about the way to the sky city and the city itself. It won't be as clear as if I'd been there myself, but since you probably know the way, you could steer me if I get it wrong."

"Why don't I just steer us? Or you could use Elisha's map."

"Maps don't show all the details, and I don't trust you not to leave our fate to chance, and if I get separated from you like Moirai and Moderatus, I will have a way to get to Alcaius all on my own."

He closed his eyes. "Alright. On it."

I searched Ashern's mind, looking for threads to the Valkyrie sky cities. He didn't have many guards up, which made it take longer and gave me too much information about him. The Luck needed to protect his mind better. He also had many amusing things about him, like a love for elf shoe making and basilisk riding. Few had the guts to tame the massive sea monsters, but he'd won three championships. Finally, I located the thread leading to information about the Valkyries and siphoned all of it I could.

I released Ashern's wrist and took a few more minutes to connect as much of the pathway as I could with what I'd already tracked in the area. "I have several ways we can go."

"Choose the one that gets us there the fastest. You took a lot of time figuring that out." Ashern rubbed his temple, probably getting a headache from my excessive prying.

"If you didn't have such an open mind, it would have been much easier for me to find what I needed quicker. You need better guards in place. A basic seer could learn everything about you."

"Not all of us have secrets we need to guard."

"Nice elf shoes. I particularly liked the ones with the obnoxious bells that gave me a headache."

"Those weren't even the best ones. I once made a pair that sum-moned mice wherever the wearer went."

I crinkled my nose. "What a terrible hobby."

"It has its uses."

Ashern warned that storms still raged above us, and it seemed best to stay surrounded by the safety of rock as long as possible. It added time to the journey but was better than not making it at all because of a tornado ripping us apart.

Ashern stopped at a branch and repeatedly tossed his dice into the air as he looked at our newest choices. "I think maybe one of us should find Moderatus and Moirai to let them know what's going on. We might also need backup."

Elisha tucked his map back in his bag. "I will go since I can figure out the way as long as you watch over Azora."

"We all have the same goal here."

"That is unlikely."

I waved my hands around. "Hello, I'm right here and perfectly capable of watching over myself. I did many dangerous things with no one to watch my back for years." I asked Elisha to take his map back out, and I marked where Moirai and Moderatus were.

Elisha left, and I tracked our way underground beyond the sleeping forest. Ashern told me legends of it as we walked, and that the area was a feeding ground for the King of Nightmares. Elementals mostly had immunity to his tricks, but a mortal like myself had vulnerabilities it would expose.

I didn't fear any nightmares, as the worst one I could have lived involved watching my little brother be swallowed by the ground and suffocated. There seemed little worse than that, though I didn't want to test that theory. The dullness of the cave continued with the brown, slimy rock surrounding us, broken up only by the occasional jagged crystal or mediocre stalagmite or column.

The ground steeped upward, and I often had to hold onto the walls, using dented places in the rock to pull me upward. Ashern walked normally, and nothing humbled my mortal limitations like hanging around the elementals. Bright sunlight burst through the darkness, and we put our lights away. We exited between a foggy forest and massive blue mountain peaks.

The air chilled enough I had to fetch my cloak from my bag before we started climbing the mountain to reach the cloud cities. My tracker sense led me along the quickest path, but that didn't always make it the safest. In several spots, we had to use metal hooks to catch our rope and allow us to use it to climb across gaps or up tricky slants in the mountain. After around the tenth time of having to cross a gorge with rope, my hands cramped and slipped from my hold.

Ashern caught me by the wrist and swung me onto a small ledge. "Careful now. I promised the reaper seer I'd keep you from meeting your lover's people."

"What do you know about Elisha?"

"What do you know?" He slid to a different ledge and packed up the rope after studying the path above us.

"I asked you first. Are you obligated to keep secrets for him?"

"No, but do you want me to repeat what you might already know?"

"Yes, I'd like to see if your knowledge of him aligns with mine. He's had several curious things about him since I first met him."

"I know hardly anything about him. Only that he signed up for this quest to make sure your best interests were served."

"My best interests?"

"Yes, he seemed very interested in assuring you stayed safe and weren't taken advantage of. I don't know why." He kept his eyes pinned above us. "Your tracker sense can tell me if I'm wrong, but I believe we've reached the top?"

I concentrated on the best trajectory and saw level pathways above us. "Yes, we're pretty close."

"Can you handle climbing straight up or should I go first and toss down the rope?"

"I can handle it. It's not that steep now."

"Yes, but the ground is just as far below." He started up instead of waiting for me, and I liked how he took my capabilities at my word.

I found good footholds and easily made it to the top of the mountain. We trekked the narrow peak, and it thinned so much in some places that it required us to balance like on a rope. The cliff dropped sharply to jagged rocks below, and one misstep spelled impalement.

"Why are you even on this quest?" The silence had grown so thick that I needed to quench my curiosity to stave off the boredom.

"I told you why I am on this quest. We're all here to protect you and make you pay for your sins while saving the dragons. They're very important to us. My people have long had bonds with water dragons. The sea is unpredictable, the same as chance."

"Yes, I read that each elemental group has a different dragon tribe attached to them."

"That is true, but most have lost touch with that part of their past," Ashern said.

"And the people of luck haven't?"

"No, we hold the traditions with our people in high regard."

"I read in your mind that you can tame sea monsters. That must be your kinship to them."

He fiddled with a strap on his bag as he stared at the ground, taking a little bit to respond. "Yes, it gives me an advantage. I can communicate mentally with any that come close to me."

"So you want to save water dragons, but when I was in your head, your motives seemed very personal."

He stopped walking and rubbed his temple. "As I told you, I have no secrets. Most of the time we bond with a dragon. It's more common with my kind than most others. The bond is deep and unbreakable. It's an intertwining of souls. But water dragons have been diminishing and leaving us with less to bond with. Most royals need a dragon to realize their full power."

"But you don't have one, and you're meant to be king."

"That's true, because I have a connection to all water dragons. Not a soul bond, but they all feed my power." He steadied himself on a boulder as he slid sideways down a small hill. "But yes, I am here for a more personal reason than saving all my dragons. When our dragons laid their eggs, before they were taken to the hatching grounds, the dragons worked with our elders to assign the eggs and bond the dragons to our people before they even hatched. This formed an early bond and the Lucks who bonded can sense their dragon and even talk to it. My little sister falling ill was our first sign something was wrong."

I took in a shuddered breath. "People are ill because the hatching grounds are dying? Your own sister..."

"Is dying. We can only hope you succeed."

"You must hate me."

He stopped walking and smiled tensely, trying to hide the sadness in his eyes. "No, because you had no idea what you were doing. Once you had the smallest inclining that your actions would bring evil, you tried to stop it. While I think you need to help, the blame is not mainly on your shoulders."

"We'll save her. I promise."

"Best not make promises you cannot guarantee any more than you can guarantee the stability of your powers." He winked at me, returning to the playful smirk that accompanied him most places.

Guilt and determination twisted in my gut until I resolved to go to any length to restore what my key sense had damaged.

Misty clouds gradually dipped into the pathway, lowering visibility to only a few steps in front of us, and I closed my eyes as they became more and more useless. Ashern stopping made me open my eyes to see him tossing his dice in the air and staring at the large pit my tracker sense had picked up moments earlier.

He stepped closer to the edge. "The gap looks too big to use the rope. Even if we had an extra long rope, there's not really anywhere on the other side to anchor to."

"Let me see what our options are." After focusing on all possible pathways, I found grooves in the pit's side that looked like good foot holds and places to grip.

Ashern squinted one eye when I explained the plan. "You can't be serious. Those tiny dents in the rock won't hardly give us anything to work with."

"It's the best solution."

He tossed his dice in the air, not seeming to care about the drops on either side where his dice could easily tumble. "I think it's time to leave this to chance." They landed perfectly in his hand. "Well, isn't that nice?"

"What? What do they say?"

"They say your way is best. Two out of three." He tossed them in the air again.

"You could also trust my tracker sense. It thinks it's the best solution."

He tossed the dice three more times, and it landed on my choice each time. "Someone has to be tampering with these."

"That or chance agrees with me." I lowered myself into the hole and slowly selected each movement that inched me closer to the other side. It went well until a few feet from the other side when the ground shaking dislodged me from the side. Ashern held onto a ledge with one hand while trying to catch me with the other, but he missed. He pushed off the wall and fell with me.

CHAPTER FOURTEEN
BIDS
Azora

I 'd never fallen in the pit in the Valkyrie mountains before, and therefore, had no connection to track the bottom. Objects and barriers showed up a little stronger than a gut feeling, but only within a short range. This made it tricky for me to find something to break my fall. A shadowy form broke through the open air, and I stretched out my hand to reach for it. My fingers burned as they scraped against the jutted pieces of rock, and I kept tumbling past. It took three more times to study the sensations to grab hold of a rock and halt my descent. Quickly, I shifted my thoughts to Ashern and grabbed his wrist as he spiraled by.

The force of him falling jerked me downward, and my other hand started to slip as I swung him against the wall. He slipped and scraped along the side, finally catching a root as I pulled myself onto the thin ledge. Slow movements allowed me to remove the rope from my bag without tumbling off the edge. I tied one end to a solid blue crystal and dropped the rest to Ashern. He pulled himself up next to me, and we studied the way back up to make sure we had a good understanding of the layout. It took some creativity to maneuver around some spots, and we looked out for each other as we moved out of the pit and onto the other side to continue our journey.

The farther we walked, the more the mist thickened and turned into a solid white surface. The fluffy ground dipped a little with each of our steps, but it seemed stable. Smoke hit my nose long before silver buildings poked through the fog. Black dots covered the sky, zooming around the slender, shiny buildings of a bustling metropolis. Alcaius didn't feel far, and our connection was so strong that my sense seemed to yearn for him as it yanked me toward him. It almost felt as though I could stop walking, and my sense would transport me to my reaper.

We stopped at the edge of town as the mist cleared and made us more visible to Valkyrie who zoomed in and out of doors carved into buildings far above the ground. No one seemed to use the streets, leaving the black smooth surface bare. Platforms wrapped around each building that the inhabitants used to rest on and access the entrances. I tightened my cloak and put my hood over my head to fend off the chill growing in the air.

Shadows in my mind gave me a rough idea of the city's pattern that all spiraled inward to where Alcaius rested in a cage. I couldn't see everything going on around him, but I could tell he was alive and still dangling above an extreme heat source. The harder I concentrated, the more I could pick up. Sounds streamed into my vision and a crowd cheered as metal clanged together.

"It's an arena," I whispered.

"What is?" Ashern whipped his head about, trying to determine what I referenced.

"Where they have Alcaius. They have him in an arena. I wasn't sure at first."

"The son of Death shouldn't have too many issues with that."

"I'm not going to bet on that with him in a cage. He has strange cuffs on, and I think maybe they're stopping his power. We need to hurry. He doesn't have his scythe." I kept toward the side of the building and dashed past any open spots.

"How exactly are we going to take on an arena full of Valkyries?"

I stopped behind a pillar and peeked around it. "We aren't taking on anyone. If we can get to the cage, I can unlock it, as well as his restraints. It'll be an easy thing."

"Are you sure? Your key sense didn't work out well the last time you used it in a big way."

I resisted the urge to roll my eyes and focused on making it to the side of the next building. "It's most likely a simple lock and won't take much effort to unlock."

Spaces between the buildings grew larger, and the risk of running between them increased extensively. We made it to the enormous round structure that had pillars wrapping around out of sight. It appeared the tallest landmark in the area and had open archways between the pillars. As with everywhere else in the city, it had no ground-level entrances. Crowds flew onto platforms, leaving us baffled about how we'd join the event. Neither of us possessed wings to blend in with the crowd. I closed my eyes to see if there was an easier way to Alcaius, but none appeared. We made it under the platform and stared up at our dilemma.

I removed my glove and ran my hand along the side of the building. "How are we going to scale this with no issues?"

Ashern kept his eyes planted on the platform. "We could wait until the event starts and then hook rope to those beams and crawl over to the edge."

"You don't think they have people watching things from the sky?"

"Probably, but what else are we going to do?"

I turned my head to take in the metal beams under the platform, as well as the small gap between each section. "What if we walked around and looked for the least busy spot? A shadow is made every time someone passes close. If we could find an unlikely spot, we could make it up with little notice."

"But as you pointed out, they're probably still watching from the sky."

I walked to my left, being careful to hurry past the gaps. As I jogged, I monitored the gaps to watch how busy each one appeared.

When I spotted no darkening of one section, I slowed. "This might be our best bet."

Ashern studied it for a moment before nodding. "Better than not trying."

"You have such confidence in me. Have you any better ideas?"

"We could abandon the reaper and proceed with the mission. Silently slink back into the shadows and out of the clouds." He cringed at my glare. "Yeah, I didn't think that'd be an option for you. Putting it out there anyway."

"You're welcome to leave."

"Not really. Not with you wanting to stay. Did you not notice how important this mission is to me?"

I grabbed a rope from my bag and launched the metal hook end at a lower beam. The magnetic hook stuck to the beam, and I tugged to make sure it had fastened well. "You take that love you have for your sister and think about what you would do if she were the one in a cage."

"Right. Alright. Let's do this insane thing, but there's something you should know that I should have mentioned earlier."

I paused, climbing the rope to give him my full attention. "That's never a good thing."

"You're going to have to pretend I'm your slave."

"What? The Prince of Chance, a slave?"

"I explained before how males are treated here. The Valkyrie are different. They believe males of all races and species are inferior, and females dominate their society."

I leaped into the air and grabbed the rope to climb. "Not a bad way to live."

"Yeah, probably the wiser way, but if you don't pretend you own me, they will think I'm free to be given to someone."

"This should be fun." I angled my head so he could see my mischievous grin and continued my climb to the beams.

Before I'd gone on the quest with Alcaius, I'd often done paid missions to provide for my family. They involved a lot of physically challenging tasks, and as I climbed several stories, I became grateful for that endurance practice. Once I made it to the end of the rope, I rolled onto one of the beams and waited for Ashern. He had an advantage in that he could somewhat propel himself into the air magically. He would give himself a boost with his hovering abilities, then hang onto the rope to rest before repeating the cycle until he made it to the top.

"Using magic to boost you seems like cheating," I said.

He pulled himself up next to me. "I didn't know it was a game. Besides, you expect these muscles to get me this far?" He flexed his average-sized arms that had almost defined muscles. "Never been a very impressive prince, like your Lord of Death."

"I didn't know it was a competition."

"To some it is. Mainly your reaper. He likes to be the best at everything. Have all the best. It's why he picked you."

I crinkled my face. "A charmer you are, underneath all the humor."

He shrugged. "A bit of one, but not in first place there, either."

"You're easily in the top five."

"Who's using flattery now? But it's true. I can see why Alcaius pursued you."

"I am taken."

"Maybe. If Alcaius is sold as a sex slave, you may need someone to move on with."

"And that should be you?"

"Maybe a quick fling. Let us get lucky," he said.

"If that happened, I would slaughter Alcaius's Valkyrie master in a blind rage and not be anywhere near you."

"I'd be near to watch that happen."

We crawled along the beams that were wide enough for our knees if we kept them very close together. It made it challenging to maneuver to the end, but we succeeded after much longer than I'd anticipated. I held onto a rod connected at the top of the platform to help roll onto my back and slide to the edge where I could peek onto the main level outside the arena. Most of the Valkyries had gone inside while only a handful of stragglers loitered or hurried inside. I waited until all the remaining ones seemed occupied to pull myself onto the floor.

Ashern followed and handed me the rolled-up rope. "Leaving something behind?"

"I figured you could get to practicing being my slave." I winked at him and started toward the door, hoping either the winged women didn't mind visitors or they would think I hid my wings underneath my cloak.

The coliseum pillars had intricate markings and pictures carved into them of Valkyries in battle and in between each scene were words written in a language I couldn't interpret. Underneath massive archways, blue wooden doors rose nearly to the stone ceiling that protected the outside part of the entrance. Women with brown feathered wings, wearing black leather skirts and armor, put their hands on their sheathed swords as we approached.

The one put her palm out to us. "What business do you have? Are you here for entertainment or for the sale?"

I took a couple more steps forward but stopped when she pulled out her sword. "We're here to watch the show." I lifted the blue velvet pouch on my hip. "We have coin to purchase entry."

"We're full up for outsiders. Best return where you came from if you aren't here to sell or purchase property."

The other nodded her chin toward Ashern. "Is he your personal slave or have you brought him to sell?"

"He is mine, but I wouldn't mind purchasing another. I guess if we can't watch the show, I will look at your stock."

The first Valkyrie pointed with her thumb to the left. "Sales are around the side. They won't sell you tickets to watch the show, but you can barter there any day or sign up to fight."

"Thank you. We'll do that." I walked in the direction she'd said, but it was farther from Alcaius.

We needed to find a way inside because it was becoming increasingly clear that Alcaius would either be bait for monsters in the show or be sold. It took some time to round the curve of the building and find the line where Valkyries and a few other races stood outside, waiting to be let in for sale.

Several had slaves with them, and every one of the servants was male. Savory smoke rose from stone pits where men roasted meat by turning a wooden handle to rotate the skinned animal to cook all sides evenly. Several Valkyries stood around talking and drinking. While we waited, I read the signs posted with the rules. One could sign up to buy slaves the owners had agreed to put up for general sale or they could win them in the arena.

"Some slaves have to be fought for." I pointed to the sign I'd been studying.

"Yeah, didn't you know that?"

I narrowed my eyes. "Is there any other vital information about our mission that you have assumed I know? When did you expect me to be versed in the Valkyrie slave market?"

"I thought it was common knowledge."

I closed my eyes and rubbed the bridge of my nose. "Assume I know nothing about Valkyrie from now on and give me all the details you feel pertinent to our current dilemma."

"Okay. Deal."

I circled my hand. "Continue with the information."

"Oh, right. I'm not an expert on it, but what I do know is that a female of any race, except ogres, I believe, can sign up for any slaves designated for that type of sale."

"Let's hope, Prince, that your specialty kicks in and we are fortunate to get to buy Alcaius outright. Avoiding the arena is the best possibility."

"I am the prince of Luck. It means I am lord of all types of luck."

"Sprinkle around some good for us."

He took his dice from his pocket and tossed them in the air. "I can give you instantly the probability that Alcaius is for sale for money."

"Not needed. I will cross my fingers and hope your kind sees favorably upon me."

"It's not really my kind choosing to grant or deny your wish. We don't have a say with the force of luck. We can only somewhat manipulate it for ourselves, tell probability, and use dice to show us the most likely successful road to what we want. It's still not a hundred percent. Even things with the highest odds are never a hundred percent."

We inched our way up the line, and I paid attention to those who went before us and how they worded things. Everyone was given either a blue ticket and sent through a door to the right, whereas those with a red ticket went left. As we almost made it to the front, a Valkyrie in a white robe became easier to hear.

She looked up from writing on the parchment to acknowledge the shiny silver siren in front of her. "Are you here to look in the saleroom or sign up for a more exotic slave in the arena?"

The siren leaned in, causing her blue hair to fall forward and making me have to strain to hear her. "I heard you have two reapers. Real reapers to play with and suck the marrow from."

The Valkyrie shook her head and handed the woman a blue ticket. "Everyone here today has heard about and wants the reapers. They are a rare find, and one shouldn't expect to easily gain them. Good luck with your attempt."

Ashern stared at the siren and tossed his dice in the air, taking in whatever answer it just gave him. "She's vicious but not much competition."

"Your dice told you that?"

"Sort of. Sirens are known to be cruelly aggressive, but her odds of winning are extremely low because their tempers don't do well in fights that have multiple people involved. They get too focused on one target."

I leaned my chin onto Ashern's shoulder, so he could hear my whisper around the noisy crowd. "This may be more difficult than expected. She said reapers were rare for the slave market. I could see that being true."

"It's mainly human males they bring here because they are considered weak and that makes them worthy of being enslaved."

"Are there no male Valkyries?"

He blinked at me long enough I wanted to punch him for making it awkward. "No, all female. The gods create them and there are only females. They sometimes sleep with males of various races, but by nature of who they are, can't reproduce. Though it is rumored a few have."

Our turn arrived, and I'd already determined based on what I'd overheard that Alcaius was in the arena to be fought for. "How much to be added into the queue to fight?" I asked the Valkyrie at the entry table.

She stared at me, similar to how Ashern had moments earlier. "You look very human."

I put several gold pieces on the table. "Yes, I am. Now how much to fight and claim a slave or two?"

She laughed boisterously enough that it caught the attention of nearly everyone, and the surrounding chatter quieted. "You won't stand a chance. Humans are the weakest here."

"Then this will be easy profit for your kingdom."

She snorted a snicker and handed me a blue ticket after she took ten of my coins. "True. Have fun dying today."

"Thank you. Your well wishes will make this all the more fun for me."

She frowned and shooed me out of the way. "Next!"

We made it to the door for the blue tickets, and I handed it to the Valkyrie in charge of that entrance.

She marked the numbers from the ticket onto her scroll. "Name and race, please."

"Azora of Aresgan. Human."

She stopped writing and giggled. "This should be a quick thing."

"My demise, I suppose."

"Yes, fool. Go along now, but make sure your slave's hands are bound before you enter the fighter's wing. There is rope at the entrance, and tie him well. He'll be inspected. Remember, if you die, he is given back into the market." Her nostrils twitched as she stared at Ashern.

"Yes, he will be properly restrained, so you may easily take custody of him at my downfall." I led Ashern over to the fighting wing door and grabbed a red rope from the bin, tying it into several knots until the entrance guard nodded her approval and let us in.

The Valkyries in charge directed me down a long slender hallway and ordered me to put Ashern in a small metal cage with a bucket and chair. They handed me a white claim ticket and attached the same numbers to his collar.

"Sorry," I whispered as I sealed him in.

He grinned. "I get to be lazy while also contributing to the quest. It works out."

I returned his smile and moved on to the next step toward the arena and Alcaius. The entire arena would burn if that's what it took to free him.

CHAPTER FIFTEEN
LOW ODDS
Azora

A Valkyrie in green leather with a bow and quiver of arrows on her back led me down stone hallways. More scenes of glorious battles were displayed in each area we strolled through. Men locked in tiny cages curled into corners, looking defeated, while other males of various species cleaned the floors and moved items from one room to the other.

My guide stopped in front of double silver doors. "Would you like to see the slaves for sale before deciding if you'd like to enter for sure? The entry fee is not refundable, but you'll be able to escape with your life."

"I didn't come here as a coward." I waved my hand at the door. "Proceed."

"You may want to reconsider. As a human, you have inferior strength and wits."

"For being of lesser intelligence, I'm not the one making assumptions about someone I have never seen fight."

She opened the left door. "Be Death's guest, then."

"I have been a guest of Death, and it no longer even gives me a twinge of anxiety." I stepped into a cold damp stable with greenish-yellow hay covering the stone floor.

In wooden stalls, chained male humans, elves, centaurs, and others all waited in their enclosure. Some paced while others slept or stared at the wooden walls. I concentrated on Alcaius and knew he wasn't among anyone here.

I stopped at the last stall and looked at the cedar door that led to Alcaius. "There are rumors that you have two reapers for sale."

My guide didn't look up from a paper pinned to an enclosure. "It's not like you'd stand a chance fighting for either. They're highly sought after, and the one already has fifty fighters bidding for him. The other has thirty."

"Bidding?"

She drew out a sigh. "Bids are fighters who have said they want to fight for a specific slave. You're wanting to participate in a tournament you don't even know the basics for."

"You're telling me to get both reapers, I have to fight eighty people?"

She stuck her chin in the air. "You most likely won't make it beyond the first round."

"Let me worry about how well I fit your prejudice. How do I place my bid for both reapers?"

"The crowd does like to see a bloody defeat. Might as well entertain them with the way you become a corpse."

"Been one twice before, so not a big deal anymore."

Her entire face narrowed in confusion and disgust. "You're strange."

"I thought I was so familiar you could predict exactly how I'd fight."

"Your strength and reasoning abilities are familiar. Valkyries train their entire lives for fighting and are built stronger and faster."

"Yes, but do they have a lychan and the son of Death as their sparring partners? Have they taken down dragons?" I choked back a laugh at the disbelief on her face. "Where can I place my foolish bids?"

She opened the door, and the rush of Alcaius's presence flooded me. I gripped my chest as the overwhelming sensations stole my breath. I wanted to run to him and tell him how much I missed him. I wanted to promise him we'd work out the differences between us. I wanted more simple moments like the fate keeper showed me I was owed. They showed me that potential future that I craved more than any other.

A long black table spread across an open grassy area, and on the table were jars with numbers on them. Cages swung from the branches of a massive oak tree, and I knew which ones held exactly who I'd come for. I concentrated and got the number on Alcaius and Fennec's cages.

My guide pointed to two jars on the end. "Those are the ones you're wanting for the reapers. Put forty coins in each of those, and the barters will give you a band that matches the number to claim them if you're alive and still have your band at the end."

She had pointed me to the wrong jars, and I searched the others until I found the ones I needed. "These will do."

She gaped as I walked up to the barter Valkyrie with the right jar numbers and handed her the required forty gold coins for each of them. My guide's jaw dropped at my selection.

The barterer in front of me took the coins. "You really should just bid on one. Not that I guess you'll be needing money anymore."

"The only thing I need is hanging in your cages."

She tied a leather band to each of my wrists, and one represented Alcaius and the other Fennec. "You know the rules?"

"I could use a refresher."

"Wait until the number is called and then you will line up on the edge of the arena. You will win only if you are the last one wearing a band and alive. Participants may only take bands from the dead, unconscious, or surrendered. You can't steal a band, and if you do, you will be caught by the watchers and disqualified. Everyone may render someone unconscious or dead. Then you may take their band."

"Do I have to collect all the bands and turn them in?"

"No, as some will be eaten whole, it's deemed unnecessary. You only need to be the last one standing to win the slave." She handed me a white flag with a shimmering golden circle. "If you wish to give up, wave this and a Valkyrie will swoop down and remove you from the field. You can only hope they will make it to you before another opponent takes advantage of your weakness and slaughters you."

"That's not against the rule? To kill an opponent who has clearly given up."

"Sometimes in the thrill of battle, things like waving flags aren't paid attention to. The gold circle helps some, but we don't discourage displays of violence as it's the main thing that brings the crowd back every time." She spread her hand toward where hundreds of bystanders sat on benches that rose many rows to the top of the coliseum. "You are free to leave if that intimidates you."

"Your lack of morals doesn't scare me in the least. What are we allowed to bring into the arena?"

"Anything goes, but you are only allowed to use it on other opponents. Any use of weapons on the watchers or bystanders will result in disqualification and instant death courtesy of our skilled archers." She pointed to Valkyries aiming arrows from the top of the coliseum.

"Will we have a place to securely store our things?"

"Yes, I will send a servant to help you with that shortly. For now, head to the tunnel that matches your number. Ask the door monitors for which of your slave battles is first."

"So what is the point of removing the bands if we don't have to collect them?"

"It's mainly helpful for the unconscious. Once a person is knocked out and their band removed, they are disqualified. It encourages more violent attacks than if you could remove them from the conscious. Also, some people like keeping the bands as trophies, and you have to have yours on your wrist to win. If you surrender, it's removed before you leave the arena."

I went to the waiting area, being careful not to come into the view of Alcaius or Fennec. It would do no good for Alcaius to see me and try to break free to cause drama that I could handle better without him angering every Valkyrie in all the sky cities. Most likely he was unable to break free on his own, or he would have before I arrived. However, if he saw I could be in potential danger, he'd raise a ruckus, whether it helped him or not.

All around the circular structure were inner tunnels that had numbers above them that corresponded to the bracelet. A worker let me know the fight for Fennec took place first.

A Valkyrie with black braids and three bands curled her fingers around the handle of her sword and looked me over. "Where's your weapon?"

"I thought I'd freehand this one." I kept my face straight ahead to not give her any indication of where all my daggers hid around my body.

A small troll boy lowered his egg head as he approached me. "Can I show you where the bins are to place your things?" His pointed, large ears twitched on each side of his head.

I removed my cloak and wrapped it around my pack. "That would be helpful."

He showed me some black chests and lifted one to reveal the metal locks that corresponded to the chest under it. I took the key from the lock and slid it into my pocket. Though I wouldn't need it with my key seer abilities, it would keep someone else from accessing my things. I tested the lock on the bin before feeling confident enough to place my possessions inside.

I grabbed a few more daggers and hid them in several of the hidden pockets I'd created in all my pairs of pants. They concealed the small weapons completely, but opened easily when I inserted my hand into them in a precise way that few would have guessed. This made it so only I could retrieve them.

During my paid quests, I'd taken on many monsters and come out ahead. I only needed to connect for a moment to any enemy to know everything I needed to. The ability needed to be saved for whatever was said to swallow fighters whole. For all the other opponents, I could turn on my tracker sense, which would help me expect their movements faster than typical reflexes.

Several battles took place before ours, and I sat in the corner of my tunnel to rest up for the pending exertion. A centaur and two Valkyries stood close by in a circle, talking about the upcoming fight.

The centaur clawed at the ground with her front hoof. "This is the first time there's ever been reapers in the mix. Can you imagine getting one of them?"

"I heard reaper marrow is a delicacy," one of the Valkyries said.

The centaur crinkled her nose. "You're going to eat them if you win?"

"Any Valkyrie here would drug the reapers immediately because they would know the danger they hold. They can't be allowed to keep their scythe but can't live long without it. Might as well enjoy what you can out of them."

The other Valkyrie glanced at the swinging cages. "I heard they're both stunningly beautiful. Might as well enjoy a few rides before they die."

The centaur backed away from them slowly and disappeared into the crowd of waiting opponents. The only one riding my reaper was me, and none of them would sure as the sun goddess be eating him. Hungry looks in the eyes of all the nearby Valkyrie took on a whole other meaning.

After what must have been hours, they told us to line up. Once a whistle sounded, everyone was to run into the arena and find a place to hide or take a stand. No one could kill or hurt until a second whistle announced the true start of the battle. The first signal screeched through the air, and everyone bolted into the dirt arena. Blood and body parts ruined several places where the servants had run out of time to clean. Part of me believed they left all of it to scare some of us from the fight. People-sized barrels and large opaque globes served as hiding places randomly strewn about the fighting area.

The crowd stomped the ground to add deafening noise to the anticipation, and on the opposite side of the arena, monsters growled and swiped at the bars holding them in. They were what I wanted. If I knew how to do anything, it was how to climb up the back of swift-moving beasts. I'd done the task on many of my paid quests, and it would be my strategy to let the other contestants and the monsters take out as many as possible before I expended the energy I desperately needed to defeat the best of the participants.

I ran toward the cages while everyone else hid inside the barrels and globes. Someone called me an idiot as they slipped into a globe I knew would roll easily at the swipe of a massive paw. The hiding spots were an illusion, and the Valkyries telling us hiding was the purpose made many believe it. Valkyries choosing beams to hide themselves further proved my theory, as they'd probably grown up watching these battles and knew the best strategy. It gave them an advantage, but I had some of my own.

The second whistle screeched, and the clanging of chains hitting the iron doors as they rose warned me to get ready. I kept my back pressed against the chilled stone wall with only a decorative engraving keeping me slightly concealed. The first monster thrashed its bulky frame and roared its extra wide mouth, lifting its dozen or so horns into the air.

Spikes covered its grey-furred back, and it stomped its tree trunk legs into the arena where it used its horn to send several hiding globes and barrels flying, smashing them against the wall to shatter. The people inside collapsed from the impact, most likely dead or severely injured. Most did not move and quickly had their bands removed. That reduced the amount I had to fight significantly. Three more monsters entered the ring, and one matched the first monster, while the second was a green wyvern that hopped on its back legs and spread its wing arms back.

The last was the most magnificent of them all and became my target. A gorgeous ruby dragon stomped forward. Its black wings and horns glistened under in the sunlight, and as stunning as they were, it was his amethyst eyes that stole attention. I'd never seen such a beautiful dragon, and something drew me to him. He whipped his tail at fleeing women until they collapsed with fatal wounds. The beast was a beautifully deadly force. I forced myself to break the trance he held over me. Never had I felt connected to anyone or anything I'd never met before. Especially to the degree the bond pulsed through my blood. What was happening? It felt like something significant had taken over my senses, and more than ever, I needed to get closer to the dragon to annihilate most of my competition.

Two Valkyries rose into the air and impaled the first monster in the head until it collapsed. They moved on to a second similar one and succeeded. I waited until the red dragon became occupied with eating a troll woman and crept along the side, keeping my seer sense heightened for anything that might approach from behind.

I leaped onto the dragon's back and used its spine humps to climb to its neck. I removed my glove with my teeth and placed my hand on his back to form a connection so I could make a deal with him but something else flowed through me, making me dizzy and reminding me of when Alcaius came close to sealing a mate bond. It was close, but a different type, not sensual or romantic, but fierce and strong.

He whipped his head back, and I was paralyzed, unable to break free from the potent connection surging through my body. His enormous teeth shot at me, and dread mixed with regret. I expected terrible pain followed by unconsciousness, but he nipped my skin and warmth flooded me, both blissful and terrible. His fangs dug deeper, but his nip had numbed me. He buried his teeth into my side, and it seemed a sure thing I'd die from how far he penetrated my abdomen.

My skin burned out from my wound through the rest of my body, and that's when the pain hit. His purple eyes flashed to blue-grey like mine for a moment before returning to purple, and then he finally let me flop onto his back to shake and bleed. He licked my side, and the bleeding stopped as my side wound sealed up, leaving a shimmering opal mark behind. They looked like scales with no texture. I ran my fingers over them to find my skin smooth, like nothing had disturbed it.

"Mine!" he growled.

My body trembled as he soared back into the air and spiraled toward the crowd. He plucked a Valkyrie from the air and bit her in two, flinging her to two opposite corners. He continued his rampage until three Valkyries joined me on his back. The dragon whipped its head toward us, and my newly formed connection gave enough of a warning to dodge his teeth and give him access to snatch up one of the intruders and violently toss her into a screaming crowd. Her journey halted when her back slammed into a beam, and she fell with her body twisted at weird angles.

I jumped up and took a fighting stance while locking my boots under one of his scales. My knees trembled from the dragon's venom still coursing into me and attaching me to him. Both enemies lunged, and I shoved the first one to the side while sending a message to my new monster friend. He grabbed her and swallowed her whole, causing his neck to hit against my back as he swallowed. The last opponent flipped me onto my spine, and I reached by my ankle, bringing my dagger into her side. Her leather held strong.

She laughed and stood, holding me down with her boot while lifting her sword to strike. I punched the back of her knee, and she wobbled enough for me to wiggle free and flip her. A small piece of skin peeked out from where her neck armor ended, and I threw my dagger, landing it on target. Her eyes widened, and I ripped the blade from her neck and sliced it open more until her blood blended with the crimson scales of my new beast. The dragon and I ended all others who sought to procure Fennec as property. My vision blurred as the venom wrapped around my heart and I rolled into his wing joint.

"What did you do to me?" I gasped.

"Bonded, human. Catch up!" Each word rumbled warmth.

"I'm dragon bonded?"

"Yes, I said it quite slowly but can draw out the words more."

I heaved and desperately clung to consciousness as he flew me to the winner's circle to free Fennec.

The dragon lowered his head. "Remove yourself from my back and finish your quest to get the other reaper. I must go rest to make sure our bond takes."

"You bonded me without permission."

His diamond pupils constricted into circles for a brief moment before returning to their normal state. "Dragons choose who they want. It's how it's done."

"Maybe you should rethink your laws."

He blinked slowly and clenched his eyes for a moment. "Regardless, what's done is done, and we are intertwined as long as our hearts both beat."

"And you're just going to leave me?"

"Yes, I have to sleep so the bond takes," he said.

"And I don't have to sleep at all?"

"No, you are much smaller, and my venom is much more powerful."

"When will you be back? And what's your name?"

"I am Eiro, an Oblivion dragon." He took to the air, dodging every arrow the Valkyrie shot at him.

Eiro had never truly been captured.

Chapter Sixteen
Ownership
Azora

My legs wobbled as I made my way to the long winner's table and showed them the band on my wrist that matched the number for Fennec.

The Valkyries had several check it and searched the field for any standing participants. When they located none, they reluctantly declared me the winner. The crowd cheered, not caring who their champion was. They'd bathed in the mass bloodshed and gained pleasure from it.

Two men brought in a bound Fennec, and he met my eyes, displaying no emotion at his sale. I was unsure if he even knew who I was. Something in the way he gazed at me told me complex plots formed in his head. He had similar features to Alcaius. They had the same strong jawline, but Fennec's dark hair had a streaks of white running through the sides.

A troll stepped closer to me. "Would you like us to place your new servant with your other?"

"Yes, that would be appreciated." I turned back to the table. "Where is the tunnel for my next fight?"

The Valkyrie looked at my wrist and then at her scroll. "Hmmm... Tunnel forty-five. That would be to your left, about ten tunnels down. Are you sure you don't want to be done and off with the one servant you won today?"

"No, I need the other as well." I needed him more than anything.

"Greed will be your downfall. Exhaustion is all over your face."

"Good thing I work best sleep-deprived." I hurried toward door forty-five to wait for the entire reason I'd even come there.

My body ached in every muscle and blended with exhaustion to make me wonder if I could really defeat everyone around me. The amount of competitors had grown, which I'd hoped the opposite would happen since many of the ones fighting for Alcaius were taken out fighting for Fennec, but that clearly wasn't the case. The same strategy seemed best, and I didn't think any other beast could bond with me now that I had a dragon bond.

The first whistle blew, and we filed into the arena, and more of the day's massacre had been left behind. A woman next to me stared at a severed head, threw up, and ran back to the tunnel, reminding me everyone fighting had fully volunteered to either die, be seriously injured, or take my reaper as a slave. It put my focus back on my true goal, and I'd fight for it with all I had.

More body parts created obstacles to hop over, and the tangy metallic scent of blood tinged the air. Most of the fighters chose the barrels and globes, and I said nothing because their lack of reasoning gave me an advantage.

I crept over to the beast's gate and hid behind a pillar until the second whistle screeched through the silence. Three women marched right for me as the door containing the monsters loudly lifted. I lodged a dagger in the middle of one's chest, choosing her for her lack of armor. It stuck just right to send her to the ground immediately. I leaped up against the pillar and scaled, pressing my hands and feet into grooves in the wood. A woman grabbed my ankle, and I rammed my boot into her head. She continued to tug until four more swift kicks knocked her unconscious. I climbed faster, reaching the wooden archway that went over the monster entrance.

The third woman followed me, and I scooted sideways across the thin beam that had a width slightly less than my shoes so that my toes stuck off the end. I made it to the middle where the platform stuck out farther to give me better stability. It also had a nailed on metal sign I could grab onto to stabilize myself more. The woman was facing out toward the arena too, but she attempted to swipe her sword at my side. I dodged the first few, both of us nearly toppling from our high ground. I threw a dagger into her neck.

She screamed and struck my leg with her blade. Blood gushed from my thigh, and I cursed the strength of her weapon being able to cut through my leathers. She must have known little about wounds as she ripped the dagger from her neck, allowing rivers of blood to pour from her veins and anointing the monster doorway like a sacrifice to the gods. I used the distraction to remove my belt and tie it around a cloth to keep pressure against my bleeding leg.

The woman fell onto a goblin running by, and the small green creature screeched and clawed its way out, caught sight of me, and hissed. It removed a tiny arrow from the quiver on its back to fire at me. I crept across the beam and carefully bent down to retrieve the dagger removed from my opponent's neck and dropped it on the goblin. It fired its arrow, and it landed in my arm.

Immediately, the burning alerted me to the poison. I yanked the arrow out to stop as much poison as possible. My armor had stopped it some, and I didn't bleed out like the foolish woman. I leaped to the ground, stabbed the arrow into the goblin several times, and the last time drove it into the creature's temple. The warmth of the poison spread up my arm and raced into my chest, leaving me dizzy. I blinked as I tried to push it out of my head.

I closed my eyes and relied on my tracker sense to tell me the best route to the furry horned beast that had exited the doorway first. Everything around me had a rainbow translucent aura, and the only thing that kept me on track was that my tracker sense stayed the only thing stable, but it was fading too. I needed to get to the beast and climb its back. I concentrated with all my remaining strength and collapsed onto something furry and warm, sinking down into the grayish softness around me. A sharp stench like burning wood irritated my nostrils, waking me some. I sat up and blinked as I tried to figure out how I'd ended up on the beast's back.

The temptation to fall asleep in his fur yanked hard on me, but I had to push through or Alcaius would die. I sucked on my arm where the arrow had punctured my armor and skin just enough to deliver the poison. My head cleared some after a few minutes, but the dizziness and slight disorientation remained. My thoughts cleared enough to think things through, and I crawled to the neck of the monster and peeked over one of his black horns at the base of his skull.

Melee and monsters ripping apart opponents happened all around, and it looked like we'd lost over half of the participants. I rolled onto my back and sunk into the fur. The main challenge was to not give in to the pull to sleep. All of me wanted to surrender to the bliss of unconsciousness. I pushed through the feeling while gripping the fur as the monster rampaged. I sucked on my arm some more until it felt like I'd cleared the poison and could think clearly. I waited a while longer for as many fighters to be eliminated as possible.

When the beast flopped on his side, I rolled onto the ground as the wind fled my lungs and left me gasping. Two Valkyrie had stabbed the beast through the head until the blade pierced through his chin.

I jumped up as they turned their attention to me and flew into the sky and dropped as blurs to carry out the oldest trick in the Valkyrie book. I leaped off the fallen monster and ran for his other side, tucking myself under his front limb.

The first attacker rounded the creature's leg and jumped onto the other opponent's back, slitting her throat. The injured one flipped her attacker with the last of her strength as she grabbed her throat and plopped on the ground. The other drove their sword at me, and I dodged, yanking a dagger from my pocket. She cried out as it grazed her ear, and her cheeks grew red with fury. I tossed another dagger straight into her thumb, and she yelped, dropping her weapon with a clang on a rock.

Her face twisted, and she shot forward, gritting her teeth. I slammed my head into hers, but she put both hands on my throat, ripping away my access to oxygen. I gasped and wiggled my hand free as I stabbed against her armor, trying to find any weak points. My vision blackened, and I rammed my head into hers again. She grunted and loosened her hold enough for me to bring my knee into her stomach and flip her off me. Without hesitating, I jumped on top of her and punched her temple over and over. She grabbed my hair and yanked it half out of its bun.

My neck tingled, and I jumped out of the way quick enough for the arrow intended for my back to land in her throat. She grabbed one of my discarded daggers and threw it at the new attacker, missing them by a good foot. The new woman leaped at her, ripping the arrow out of the other woman's neck. The attacker stabbed the arrow through her victim's neck, and I flung a dagger into the base of the attacker's skull. She dropped onto the other still woman. I used the beast's body to hide behind and gain a better view of who was still in play. Most had been wiped out, and a few people limped toward the exit without bands.

I took the bow and arrows off the woman I'd killed, and while I wasn't the best at them, they could possibly come in handy. The beast provided protection as I watched everyone but one person destroy each other. A Valkyrie with pinned-up black hair and white-speckled brown wings raised her hands in triumph. She thought she owned my reaper, and I chose that moment to send an arrow at her and missed by several feet. The Valkyrie gawked at it, and I bolted across the field. She spun around and lifted her sword, and I threw a dagger into her thigh. It bounced off her armor, and she laughed. I landed another small blade in her hand, and it ceased her cackling.

The Valkyrie charged me with her sword, looking ready to decapitate me, but I dodged her swipes and blows. She growled in frustration and took to the air to free fall into me, but I'd seen the trick too many times and easily rolled out of the way. Her upper lip twitched, and she looked ready to maim my entire body. I removed as many daggers as I could hold in one hand and launched them one after the other. She deflected them with her sword. Another presence tingled the back of my neck where my tracker sense liked to warn me. I turned just enough to see something moving out of my peripheral and flung a dagger using only my tracking ability for aim. A cry and thud sounded behind me, but I kept my eyes on the Valkyrie.

She marched toward me, whipping her sword in the air, and I could only duck and jump backward. I slid my hand into one of my secret thigh pockets and curled my fingers around the leather handle.

She kicked me to the ground and stood over me. "Stupid human. Thinking you're worthy of a reaper slave."

"My lover is no one's slave!" I grabbed her ankle out from under her, twisted around, and stabbed my last dagger into her side where her top armor had ridden up.

It pierced her skin with little effort, and she screamed. "I'll kill you!"

She tried to sit up, and I kicked her back to the ground and kicked again until she didn't move. The dizziness returned as I scanned the field to see all the destruction. Some I'd contributed to, and even though it was to save Alcaius and protect myself, it all seemed senseless. All the participants volunteered and could have left at any moment. All of them were fighting to enslave the love of my life, but the bloodshed made me queasy in a way nothing ever had before. I stumbled over to an upright barrel and leaned against it to regain composure. The world still spun when I finally calmed enough to limp back to the winner's table.

The Valkyrie at the table stared at me with wide eyes and a twitching nose. "How did you do that a second time?"

"Strategy. I let most of them take each other out to save energy."

She shook her head and wrote my name on the winner's certificate that proclaimed I owned Alcaius. My nerves tumbled at the thought of seeing him again. I both craved and dreaded it. I wanted nothing more than to find my way to his arms, but he wasn't going to be happy with me for not telling him my true plan. I entered the stables and gave my certificates and Ashern's claim ticket to the troll manager.

His stubby fingers held the paper and searched through his record book. "Are you wanting them all now, or are you staying? We can feed them and give them bedding for the night."

"I want them now. We will be on our way." Getting away from the sky cities and back on our mission was my highest priority.

Alcaius rounded a corner with his head down and hands bound behind him, but he soon jerked his head up and stared at me. His lips parted, and I shook my head, passing a message for his silence.

I turned back to the troll manager. "Where are my reapers' scythes and other possessions? I need them at once, since the weapons are necessary for the survival of my slaves."

He opened his book to the back half and ran his finger down the side. "Yes, they do come with scythes. Good thing for you to know."

Reapers needing scythes to live was burned into my memory from the time I'd almost lost Alcaius when his father had separated him from his weapon. The troll had two other servants fetch the items, and then he asked me to sign off on all the possessions. "You are to keep the weapons until you exit our border, as no slaves are allowed any weapons here."

I nodded as I took the scythes and nearly toppled from the weight. "This is going to be an issue." I dropped them on the ground.

The troll tapped his chin. "You could purchase a cart."

"How much?"

"Thirty gold."

I opened my coin purse. "Fine. It's done."

He had someone fetch me one, and I paid for it. His staff placed the scythes and bags in the cart, and I put my stuff in to free me up more. I pulled the rope since all the men had bound hands, and I led our group out of the arena.

The moment Alcaius thought we were far enough away from on-lookers, he turned his hands to me. "Untie me."

I put down the rope and went to my bag to find extra daggers since I'd lost all the ones on me in the fight. I located one at the bottom and cut his hands free. He pulled me against his chest and rested his chin on my head. I wrapped my arms around his waist and sighed as his scent reached me.

"Damn! I missed you!" He kissed my forehead.

I squeezed him tighter and wanted nothing more than to fall into a bed somewhere with him and sleep away the pain and exhaustion overwhelming my mind and body. "I missed you so much."

He lifted my chin with his thumb and finger, kissing me until his tongue and lips left me unsure if the floating feeling in my body was from him or the lingering arrow poison.

"We would like to be untied, too." Fennec broke through our reunion.

Ashern cleared his throat. "If you could finish all of that after we're in separate tents, that would be appreciated."

I pulled away from Alcaius and felt him stiffen. He grabbed my hand and held on until I wiggled it free to cut the others loose. Alcaius and Fennec strapped their scythes to their backs, followed by their bags.

Alcaius swung mine over his shoulder. "We have a lot to talk about."

"Yes, like how I can carry my bag perfectly fine as I have on this entire quest." I tugged it away from him.

"You're limping. If my hands had been free, I would have thrown you over my shoulder the moment I saw it."

"How romantic for you to just assume I wanted to be carried like a barbarian's wife."

"You never complained about it on the way to the bedroom." He sent me his crooked grin that always made me hold in a gasp. He couldn't know he had that power over me with a single look.

"Just the same. I'll carry my bag."

"Obstinate woman."

"Controlling reaper." I took out my rope and walked to the edge of the platform. I swung half my body over the side to tie the rope to some metal beams.

Hands held onto my feet as I worked so close to the ledge, and I knew without looking back they belonged to the overprotective reaper I'd missed more than expected. I shoved the cart off the side because it was either risking it breaking or leaving it behind. I'd paid for it and refused to give it back to the Valkyrie. It landed roughly on the ground but stayed in one piece.

Alcaius insisted on going first to catch me if I fell, and I decided not to kick his ego immediately by showing him his ownership paperwork. I went second, then Fennec, and lastly Ashern. The clouds dipped a little lower than before with each step we took. The more we walked, the heavier my muscles became, and my vision dimmed like the Valkyrie had her hands on my neck again.

I stumbled forward, and Alcaius had me before I hit the clouds. His reflexes and concern for me didn't care if the ground was soft. He scooped me up, and his worry was the last thing I saw.

Chapter Seventeen
Cost
Alcaius

Azora, limp in my arms, brought back all the agony of the last two times I'd watched her die.

I placed her on the cart, searching her for injury, and realized she'd used her cloak to conceal a cut on her thigh. "What happened to her, Ashern?"

He stepped over to examine her with me. "She fought the Valkyries for you."

"Yes, I know." My jaw clenched at the thought of her in an arena fight where most didn't walk away. She'd always been an impressive fighter, but surviving two Valkyrie coliseum battles was another level.

Fennec grabbed his bag and pulled out a needle and thread. "Raya has taught me how to sew some. I think I can transfer that skill to skin."

I undid the belt and poured whiskey over her wound. "Work quickly and be careful!"

"Maybe you shouldn't make such forceful demands from someone who is helping you for free."

"Just get it done with!"

He stopped for a moment, like my frustration changed his mind about the task. "If you'll control your tongue, I might not mutilate her due to you distracting my inexperience."

My eyes only moved from Fennec's fingers stitching her up to study her breathing. I moved back and forth between her wound and signs she still lived. I gripped my hair, wishing I'd done a better job of getting to her sooner. Wishing I'd paid attention better to the Valkyries dropping from the sky to capture me.

Fennec cut the string and tied a band of cloth around her leg. "We should probably find some elixirs soon to prevent infection. She has a cut on her arm too, but I won't be able to stitch the one up. It's probably the real reason she's unconscious."

"Why can't you stitch it up?" I moved closer to inspect the place he pointed to.

"There are black vein marks around it. Probably a poison arrow but seems most of the poison was sucked out or it's slow-moving. Should buy us some time to get her somewhere for a cure."

"Elisha is with us. He has quite a few health potions with him." Ashern moved all the items to the right side of the wagon and arranged a few blankets and pillows on the other side. "Set her here."

I picked her up and cradled her to my chest, kissing the top of her head. "I have her."

"There's no reason for you to waste strength when we have a cart for her to ride in, Grim."

"I said. I have her. Let's go."

Ashern rolled his eyes and grabbed the rope to pull the cart. We'd been in a lot of the same classes in school but had never interacted much. A slight awkwardness always sat in the air when we were around each other, and I could never place why. The awkwardness had morphed into brewing disdain for how close he put himself to my woman during instances I'd seen in the looking globe.

Fennec hopped into the ride and put his hands behind his head as he stretched out and crossed his feet at his ankles. "Leaves more room for me."

I caught up next to Ashern. "How far is Elisha?"

"I don't know. He went to get Moirai and Moderatus."

Every muscle in my body locked up, and I froze. "Moirai is on this quest?"

He laughed a little too vigorously for my taste. "Yeah, is that going to be a problem? Create some temptation?"

"Was she ever that for me?"

"Moirai likes to think so."

I adjusted Azora in my arms and closed my eyes to say a prayer to the gods to keep her with me. "Why didn't I see Moirai in the looking globe if she's been with you? I sure saw a lot of you."

"I don't know exactly how your looking globe works. Moirai understandably doesn't like Azora and stays as far from her as possible. She doesn't like people who take things that are hers."

"Why the Hades is she on this quest?"

"It's complicated." He nodded to Azora. "She needs to tell you what's going on."

"She needs to wake up first, and that means she needs help."

"Too bad you had a falling out with Rook, or we could walk north to his castle," Ashern said.

"We made amends, but he doesn't live there anymore, and if I show up at his father's castle, I'll be turned in."

"The other option is the witch in the sleeping forest, but that's not without risk."

We dropped into the Greock mountains, and we had to abandon the cart. Regretfully, I had to hand Azora to Ashern on the steeper areas and drops. I always took her back possessively, but with gentle care. With reluctant teamwork, we made it to the bottom of the grey rock mountains. Little vegetation and trees grew on them, and they were more like the boulders of giants. At the bottom, trees flourished into a forest of green oaks and red maples that broke up the usual woodsy look with a pop of color.

Ashern stopped at the wide strip of grass that ran between the rocky mountains and the dense forest. "There's the Chaos castle on that hill. That means we still need to walk east then north. It'll be out of the trees, so we shouldn't have to worry about sandmen."

Sandmen dragged anyone who stepped into the forest to their doom. It took most of the day of walking the border between safety and darkness to spot the rising smoke that we followed to a large stone cottage. A woman in a white robe raked sand into complex shapes next to a garden held in by a short, black metallic fence. Two weeping willow trees nearly concealed a white wooden bench, and in front of them, was a small pond where dragonflies zipped in and out of the water. A light fog settled around the cabin as we approached the bright red door.

Ashern knocked, and his hand flung back. "Damn!" He shook his hand. "That has a bite."

Fennec walked over to the woman in the white robe. "Are you the witch?"

"No." She continued raking without glancing up from her task.

"Can we speak with her?"

She shrugged.

The door flew open and a woman with a massive pile of frizzy straw hair burst out of the cabin, knocking Ashern on the ground. "What do you want?" Her purple pointed hat and matching robes showed she was probably the witch.

I stepped closer to her and lifted Azora toward her. "She needs help. Poisoned wound."

"Bring her inside, but be warned, if your visit has other intent than helping her, you will be killed at the doorway."

I followed her inside and laid Azora on a couch where she told me. The stone cottage had black wooden floors and shelves covered with potions, books, and various trinkets. The shelves wrapped around the room, and the two sides met at a fireplace where a green pot boiled. A cooking savory aroma intermingled with the scents of sharp spice and mud.

The woman looked down at Azora. "Where is the poisoned wound?"

"On her left arm, near the shoulder."

She stared at me for a moment. "You're her lover? A reaper with a human lover. Interesting."

I narrowed my eyes as I realized she was no normal witch. "Yes."

"Remove her shirt," she commanded.

I grunted and stared at Ashern. "Not with them here."

She turned back to Fennec and Ashern. "You two can go get yourselves situated in your rooms. This is going to take a few days. You." She pointed to Fennec. "Take the third room on the left. It has a washroom inside. Dinner will be served later. If you enter any other room, you will receive punishment. And you." She pointed to Ashern. "Fourth door on the right. Stay in there until you are asked to come to dinner."

Ashern obeyed immediately, but Fennec stood firm, staring at something on a shelf. He looked up and opened his mouth, but I sent him a stern look that seemed to do the trick as he said nothing and went down the hall beyond the large kitchen full of strange devices.

I carefully removed Azora's armor by bringing her against my chest and undoing the back. This took her down to her white cotton undergarments that covered her breasts. It left from her stomach to her hips exposed. Her arm wound was around the length of a fingertip and looked shallow and insignificant, but the concern stemmed from the spider web of twisted black veins that mapped the upper portion of her arm.

I rubbed the back of my neck as I stared at it. "Can you help her?"

"Give me a minute to see."

"You can tell everything you can about me and her right away, but not if you can heal a wound?"

"Is there a reason you're questioning the person you're asking for help?"

"No, sorry. I can't lose her."

A stool scraped across the floor as she pulled it to Azora's side. "I will work. You go sit in that chair. I'd banish you to your room as well, but I know it won't do much good with her here. Not even a reasonable threat will persuade you to leave her."

"You know a lot about me." I sunk into the enormous red cushioned chair, and it reminded me of the one Azora had in her living area that she used to read by her front window. Hers was tattered and old, while this one looked brand new. I made a note to shop for a new one whenever we made it back to Aresgan.

"Yes, I think I know this poison." She moved over to her shelves and searched for a few minutes before pulling down a jar of yellow powder and a blue liquid that she mixed in a red bowl. She patted them onto Azora's wound and placed green thin leaves in rows until they entirely covered the injury and black veins. "Take her to bed. Second door on the right. She should wake soon, but she needs rest."

"Thank you." I picked Azora up from the couch. "How much do I owe you?"

"We can discuss that in the morning. Get her warm in a bed for now. I advise you to remain here a couple of days until her strength returns." She cleaned up her mess and put the leftover powder and liquid back in their place.

"I have one more request. We need to find some of our friends. Is there a way to locate them and get a message to them?"

"Do you have anything that belongs to them?"

"I don't, but Ashern, the man with red hair with us, he may have something."

"Very well. I'll ask him about it then and add it to your tally."

"That works." I carried Azora to the bedroom the witch had indicated.

It was a fairly small room with a circular bed in the middle against a wall next to the only window. An open door showed the washroom. I turned on the oil lamp on a wooden stand and shut the door. A bookshelf across the room had a few books, several small statues, and candles.

Azora groaned. "Alcaius."

My entire body relaxed at her calling my name. "Yes, my love."

"Where are we?"

"A witch's house. Outside the sleeping forest. She says you need to rest in bed."

She wiggled free from my arms but flopped to the ground. "I need a bath first. Is there one here?"

"Yes, do you want some help with it?"

"I can't stand well, and you need one too."

I picked her back up and kissed her. "Do I now?"

"Definitely. You smell of barn animal, and I can only imagine what I brought back from the arena,"

I set her on the toilet and started the bath, checking the temperature to make sure it was the level she liked. I preferred it much cooler, but I'd bake to have her skin against mine. Once it was filled to the needed level, I searched through the cabinet where soaps and perfumes were generally kept. Jasmine and lavender seemed the best choices. I spread them through the water and put a bar of aloe and rose on the ledge of the tub.

My attention turned to the shivering woman on the toilet who was leaning to the side, washing her hands in the sink. We couldn't have her remain cold.

When she finished, I dropped to my knees, kissing her neck. "Are you ready?" I whispered in her ear.

She turned my face, so our lips stood millimeters apart. "More than." She rested her forehead on mine.

I undid the back of her undergarments and freed her breasts. "You're injured on your arm. The witch has treated it, and you'll have to keep it above the water."

I lifted her to slide the rest of her clothes off. "Not much can be done about your thigh. I'll re-bandage that after you bathe."

I placed her in the water, and she moaned, closing her eyes and sinking against the tub. I stayed on my knees as I lathered a cloth and washed all the dirt and blood that had stained her skin fighting for me in a death arena. Pride swelled in my chest, even though I hated she had gone through that. She was mine. At least I still hoped so.

She drained the bath and refilled it. "I know we have much to discuss."

"Not tonight."

"Not tonight," she agreed. "Join me?"

I removed my clothes and got in behind her in the fresh, steaming water. She removed all aversion I had to the heat because being next to her trumped everything. She poured soapy water over my arms and moved on the scrubbing my legs. We drained and refilled the bath a second time after washing each other clean. She fell asleep as we soaked and didn't wake again after I dried her and carried her to bed.

My bag had bandages and ointments that I used to patch her leg back up while also making sure she stayed warm under the blanket. The last few things I did were braid her hair and climb in next to her to pull her close and gain the best sleep I'd had in days.

The sunlight danced across Azora's face from the small slit in the blue curtains next to the bed. She looked blanched and almost grey, but her breathing assured me she'd survived the night thanks to the witch. I snuck out of bed, hovering off the ground to not hit any creaking boards and wake her. Roasting meat and potent herbal tea greeted me as I walked into the kitchen.

Ashern and Fennec sat on the small square table with four crooked chairs. Sausage, toast, boiled eggs, and several unknown dishes filled their plates.

The witch sat in her black chair, sipping a cup and reading from a red leather book. "Good morning, reaper. How is your woman?"

"She's alive, and I took your advice on her needing sleep seriously. Would you mind if I took breakfast to her?"

"Not at all. Take whatever you need from the kitchen. For yourself and her. Are you ready to discuss payment?"

I took a plate from a stack next to the food. "Yes. What do you believe is reasonable?" I'd have given her all my possessions had she asked the night before when I needed Azora to live. There was no price too big she could ask from me.

"I want your woman to unlock a box."

I nearly dropped the spoon full of eggs. "Excuse me?"

"Your key seer who I saved. I need her to open a box for me."

"I can offer you a lot of gold." My heart slammed against my chest. Very few people knew about Azora's second seer sense, and it was best kept that way, as many would seek to abuse her unusual and powerful ability.

"I have no use for gold."

"What evil will be unleashed if she does?"

"That's for her to figure out when she touches it." She grinned, showing off the gaps where her fangs should have been. "We all know she has no trouble opening things she shouldn't for the right price."

I reminded myself the hunched-over old woman had saved Azora's life and controlled my growing irritation. "Whatever you think you know about her, you don't. She has a high moral code. Is there anything else you will take?"

"No, I want the box opened for the price of saving her life and accommodations until she's recovered. Lack of payment will result in stopping treatment and curses."

"You'll have to talk to her. That's not something I can decide for her." I buttered her toast and finished it with strawberry jam.

"I suggest you persuade her." She smiled like she'd just told me she loved the weather we were having.

I gave her a single nod and carried the plates back to the room. It wasn't surprising that a wood witch would ask for a questionable price, but I hadn't thought she would use Azora's powers for personal gain. Objects, and especially boxes, could hold essences that delivered swift and terrible consequences when opened or destroyed.

Azora stared out the window and smiled when she noticed me. "Morning."

"Morning. Brought you breakfast. Do you feel strong enough to sit up?"

She pushed herself up and leaned against the cedar headboard in response. "Thank you for the food. We need to talk. Don't we?"

"We do, but let's get you better first." I cut up the sausage and brought the fork to her mouth.

"We can't avoid it forever."

"It shouldn't take you forever to get better." I cut up the rest of her food and fed her each bite.

Part of me knew she was right, and I was avoiding the subject of what we'd both done and what it meant for our relationship.

Chapter Eighteen
Recovery
Azora

O ver the next couple of days in the witch's cabin, I recovered from the poison, and Alcaius hovered over me like one of his relatives would soon collect me for the afterlife. On the third morning, I woke up before Alcaius and slipped out of bed to meet the witch. Since my reaper brought everything to me, I hadn't even seen a glimpse of her.

She sat at the fireplace, stirring a green cauldron with her purple pointed hat bobbing above her black hair. All the locks of her hair had an organized chaos to them. Her robe matched her hat, and she kept her back to me. "Good morning, Azora. I was wondering when I'd finally get to meet the dragon slayer."

"That's not a good title for me. I always try to temporarily disable and not kill them."

"Yet here you are, about to wipe them all out."

"I'm also trying to remedy that." I glanced around the room and studied all the strange jars and items on her shelves. One shelf overflowed with cloth dolls that had button eyes. Each looked unique and patterned after someone with extreme detail devoted to each doll.

"I make those of all my visitors."

I coughed and took a second to regain composure. "Oh. Is there one of me yet?"

"Not yet. Has your lover spoken to you about the price of your care?"

I moved closer to the doll shelf to study them closer. Something about them intrigued me. "He didn't, but he doesn't like to bother me with such things."

"This is something that only you can fulfill."

"That intrigues me." I frowned at the small doll with the red hair clutching a needle and thread sitting next to one with white hair holding a baby dragon. They reminded me of Raya and Myik.

"I need you to open a box that I long ago lost the key to. If you can do that, it's all the payment I need."

"I'm not the best at my key seer abilities. They are still fairly new to me, but I can see what I can do. You wouldn't rather gold?"

"No, the box will be payment enough. Let me go get it." She walked down her hall and was gone for several minutes while I inspected more of her shelves. When she returned, she had a plain box that looked aged with chips in the brown paint. "Here it is." She handed it to me.

I turned it over in my hand and stared at the brass clasp that didn't budge when I tried to lift it. Nothing extraordinary stuck out as I held it, so I closed my eyes to gain information I couldn't see. At first, nothing pulled forward, and I thought it had a block on it. Foggy images of a woman running through the rain, clutching the box close to her heart, streamed through my mind. The woman ran into the forest as she glanced behind her, as though she were fleeing a dangerous monster. She buried the box in the woods, using a stick to dig through the mud. A sense of fear and desperation washed over me, but when I thought of the box, only a strong sense of love remained.

"What's going on?" Alcaius broke my concentration.

I blinked a few times to shake myself back to the present. "You didn't tell me that the..." I glanced at the witch. "You didn't tell me your name."

"Mistral. My name is Mistral," she said.

"Mistral needs a box open as payment for helping us."

Alcaius's eyes bounced between her, the box, and me. "It wasn't something for you to worry about during your recovery, and I thought you might not be interested."

"Why would you think that? Even if it were true, you should have asked." An irritation bubbled under my rib cage as I stared at his defiant face. "You were going to ask me?"

"Like you asked me if you should confront dragons and travel in the Realm of Fates without me."

"That's different."

"You're right. One is a lot less dangerous. At least I'm assuming." He threw his hand toward the box. "Maybe this opens a portal to the netherworld as well."

"We'll discuss this later. Let me get back to our task, so we are no longer indebted to Mistral."

I caught in his eyes the desire to stop me, but instead, he spun around and stormed back down the hall. The anger he'd hidden toward me the last few days had simmered at the surface, and we were headed toward the biggest feud we'd ever had. I shook it away from my thoughts for the moment and concentrated back on the box, letting it tell me its story. I willed it to open, and at first, it resisted. "Mistral has missed you so very much," I whispered into the keyhole.

The box popped open, and a burst of blue energy swirled into a tornado that bounced around the room, knocking over bottles and dishes. It calmed at Mistral's feet and formed into a glowing grey cat with a blue aura around its body.

Mistral scooped up the cat and squeezed it tight. "Thank you! Thank you so much! So long have I tried many things to free Amir from his prison. Nothing has ever worked with all my spells and powers. You're a gift from the gods, Azora. A true gift with a kind stubborn heart." Tears rolled from her cheeks onto her familiar as he rubbed his face against her and purred.

"I never knew about the wars against magic and mages. I'm sorry they imprisoned Amir."

"Yes, it was a terrible time, and I escaped with the box they'd stored him in but could never find the key. It was rumored they were destroyed when the castle of King Rilin crumbled."

"Are there others?"

"Yes, but they are in the middle of the sleeping forest. No one dares venture into it. Amir is why I live so close because I'd buried him in the woods since the box needed to be close to the forest to keep him alive. It was a trap put on all the familiar boxes, so no one could leave. I knew this because they had told us so we would not try to take them, and when I got him back, I tried to flee far from here. I could sense him inside. When I got a certain distance from here, I felt him dying. That's why I buried him until I could come back. After the war ended, I returned, but the same thing happened, stepping too far from the sleeping forest started to kill him. I hired some help and built my house on the edge of the woods, but nothing opened the box to free him."

"Is he still bound to here now that he's free?"

"I'm not sure. I will take a walk with him and see." She closed her eyes and gave him another squeeze.

"You say there are others still in the woods?"

"Yes, but it's controlled now by Strix son of Ralil. Strix is the new Lord of Nightmares."

I studied the books on her shelf. "Do you have any books on the war?"

"No, I'm sure there are some in a library somewhere, but I can answer any questions you might have on the subject."

"The Nightmare King controls the source? With that, it has bound all the familiars to the forest. Probably even if they are freed."

"Yes, but there are many witches and mages who miss their familiars greatly. Most moved on without them, but it is a hollow life. Our bond is so potent that they follow us into the afterlife. You know something about that don't you?" Her eyes stopped on where the dragon had bitten me.

"I can't say that I do. There was a weird experience in the arena, but the dragon left, and I've heard nothing from him since."

"He's sleeping to seal your bond," she said.

"That is what he said as well, but I feel no different."

"You will, and then he will be your companion to the end of all the realms." She tickled Amir's chin and smiled.

"I'd rather not have a stalker dragon. I've been fine alone for a very long time."

"You have learned to survive alone. But your bold attempt to save the reaper shows maybe you're not as fine as you believe."

I studied the direction Alcaius had left through. "He's complicated. Without him things are simple, but..." I let my voice trail off as I thought about it.

"There's a hole that lingers always in your chest that randomly stirs sadness and longing."

"Yes, it's not like I can't be alone, or that Alcaius has made it so I can no longer enjoy solitude because I certainly can. It's more like now when I've sat in my darkness too long. When I've sat in anything too long, heaviness reminds me I don't have him next to me to experience it with. That's what builds the loneliness, not that the void needs filled by just anyone, but that all of it needs experienced with him."

"That's what it feels like to find the person you are to experience lifetimes with." Mistral kissed Amir's nose. "I have missed you, dear friend."

The cat purred in response, and the witch looked joyful and not the solemn woman I'd first met only a short time ago.

The more I watched them interact, the more I wanted to do something to help the trapped familiars and their masters. "I could unlock the boxes and talk to the Nightmare King about lowering the barrier that keeps them attached to the forest."

She moved to the kitchen and put a teapot on the stove. "It wouldn't be something simple to do. The Nightmare King has frightening abilities, and the familiars would probably be difficult to locate."

"Do you know where they are? If you'd allow it, I could connect with you, and it would help me form a map in my head to them."

"You're a tracker seer too?" She tapped her chin. "I missed that one." She held out her hand. "I can show you what I do know, and you make your own choices."

I took her hand and searched through the things she allowed me to see. In the middle of the sleeping forests was a shed with rows and rows of plain boxes like the one Amir had emerged from. Even through the vision, I could sense the energy radiating from the boxes. It was only a short hike from the cabin and could be carried out without much delay. Talking to the Nightmare King would be another thing altogether. I sipped tea with Mistral for a bit not to be rude then excused myself to talk to Alcaius about my new plan.

He was back in our room, holding his glowing scythe and taking the energy he needed from it. "Did you give payment?"

"Yes, everything is settled. There is a lot we need to talk about."

He leaned his scythe against the wall. "Yes, there is like you telling me you were visiting your sister and getting Bryony her wisping abilities back."

"Both those things were on the agenda."

"But you left out a big part of this. You left out the most dangerous part that you were headed to see dragons. All of the dragons were also furious with you. That seems pretty big details to leave out."

"It's not like I have to ask your permission for anything I do. My choices are still mine, and I didn't like you implying I had to ask you earlier."

He crossed his arms and stared at me for several seconds, as though calculating his words with great effort. "I didn't mean it that way. How are we supposed to work if we can't communicate with each other?"

I sat on the end of the bed and nodded. "They told me not to tell you. That I had to come alone, or they wouldn't make a deal with me."

"A deal for what?"

"To save you. To clear your name. It's what they promised me, and I couldn't tell you or it would be ruined. There was no way I'd take a chance on your life."

He marched across the room until he was so close his anger became tangible, burning my seer sense and making me slide away from him. "That's not for you to worry about clearing my name. That's something for me to worry about. It's my problem."

I scooted to the side and stood up. "It's both of our problem or does what happen to you not affect me?"

"You should have told me!"

"And would you have just sat around Zaire's castle, like all was well while I went to visit dragons? I think not since you are so angry about me doing what I knew was best."

"You made a decision about my life without any input from me."

"Because I was told I couldn't, you hypocrite!"

"Hypocrite?"

I paced across the room, trying to calm my growing anger. "Yes, you're a hypocrite! How long did you go into the night killing without telling me? You came home with blood-stained hands and then held me with them like nothing had happened."

He stared at his palms like he could see the blood I spoke of. "I never once held you without washing them first."

"Blood doesn't wash from the soul!"

He blinked like the blow had taken too much life from him. "So that's it. You see me as irredeemable all while claiming to go on a dangerous quest to save a monster."

"I love you! That's something that doesn't die with your actions. It burns so fiercely that the conflict I feel at your reaping grieves me at a level I can't explain. It is my love for you that deepens my sorrow for your deeds."

"Then maybe we should break whatever this is so who I am created to be doesn't cause you such great mourning. You can go back to Aresgan and not worry about clearing my name."

"What are you saying?"

"I'm saying I think we're over. My name and life aren't something you have to worry about any longer."

"Yes, because at your word my love for you will flee my body and destroy my will to save you. It really works that way!"

"It should! We're nothing to each other now."

The warmth of my tears nipped my chilled cheeks. "You're an idiot. Stupid reaper."

"A fool I've always been. You were just blind to it as you were the moment you took on this quest to spare my life. Something I already had handled."

"You had it so handled. Yes, such a great plan to clear your name. Maybe you could remind me what it was."

"You call me a hypocrite while you killed in the arena."

"Nice changing the subject because you are proving you had no real plan. I killed out of necessity because it was the only way to save you, and all of them had signed up to die. They could have left at any time."

"That's what you don't see. You don't see that killing is a necessity for me. It's my design. Something I can't shake from my bones. It eats me alive if I try to fight it. I'm a reaper for Hade's sake! This is why we can't be together. You can't see who I am."

"I have always seen who you are, Alcaius. Always, and I love who you are, but I have to question the impulsiveness of your choices and your willingness to risk everything for your blood lust."

"Every kill I make is methodically planned. Down to the morality of who meets my scythe."

"Is it for you to play a god?"

"Yes, because they gave me this power and forced this desperate hunger on me."

Ashern popped his head in the room, reminding me I'd forgotten to close the door. "Is everything alright?"

"Yes!" Alcaius and I shouted in unison.

"Is this about Moirai? He told you about them, didn't he?"

I slowly turned my head to meet Alcaius's gaze. "What about her?"

"Oh, he didn't tell you. Oops. I'll just be going to breakfast."

"One of you tell me."

Ashern chewed on his lip for a second before shrugging. "All through school they were a thing. Even engaged."

My eyes widened as they pleaded with Alcaius to deny it. "Is it true?"

"Yes, but it was irrelevant. Neither of us talked about who we've been with because it didn't matter." Alcaius glowered at Ashern like he might take his scythe to Ashern's neck

Ashern ducked out of the room. "I'll let you two talk this out."

"It matters because she's a part of my quest which you knew because we talked about how Mistral had located Moirai and Moderatus to send them a message. That was the time to tell me, so I wasn't caught off guard."

"It still didn't matter."

"Fine!" I threw all my items into my bag, closed it up, and hurried to the door. "How easily our love dies by your mouth."

"Where are you going?"

"Away from you. We no longer have a reason to share a room. Feel free to leave to clear your name all on your own whenever you want. Oh and..." I unzipped the front of my bag and threw the ownership certificate at him. "Why don't you give that to Moirai when you see her next?" I slammed the door behind me before he could see my lip tremble.

Mistral stood at the end of the hall. "You need a different room?"

I nodded and accepted the blue rag she handed me to dab my nose and eyes. "Yes."

She led me back to a room two doors beyond Alcaius's room, and I locked the door to keep him out. The warm water of the bath I drew myself caught my tears, but it was for the best. Alcaius and I were realms apart. It made no sense that we even got together in the first place. He was a gods damned prince. Moirai was a much better fit for him in every way. She grew up in his world and was stunning. The dragon quest had to continue, but it had to continue without Alcaius. I knew him well enough to know he'd still want to accompany me, even with us no longer together.

I crawled into bed with the plan of resting up and leaving before the first morning's light. The first thing would be to free the familiars and then confront the Nightmare King about releasing them from whatever source he'd bound them to. My tracker sense would keep Alcaius from me, and he wouldn't be able to watch me in the looking globe anymore as he'd explained the Valkyrie had taken it when they captured him but didn't have the ability to use it because it was attached only to his use.

A knock hit my door a short time later and a quick mental scan told me what my heart already knew. Alcaius regretted his words and wanted to fix things. He eventually stopped and left, and I closed my eyes to sleep but set a sapphire in an incense bowl. It would heat up and rattle after allowing me four hours of sleep.

The sapphire worked and I packed up after pinning up my hair, concentrating to make sure Alcaius was sleeping. The sun hadn't yet risen, but I still had the extra light Ashern had given me. I spotted his dice flying up and down before I found him.

He stood up when I moved toward the door. "The dice told me you'd be leaving."

"You don't have to go, but I guess you should since the dragons assigned you. We have a side mission we need to do first. If you don't want to participate, feel free to stay behind." I left a note for Mistral by her teapot and exited through the front door.

Ashern closed the door and put on his wool, green hat to help against the chill that had formed in the air. "Where are we headed, master?"

"I didn't win you in a tournament, so you can drop the master."

He chuckled and took out a light stick from his bag. "What's this plan of yours?"

"We have to go into the sleeping forest."

He cleared his throat and stared off. "We have to go into the sleeping forest where sandmen lurk?"

"Yes, it's important."

"Not as important as you saving all the dragons. If the sandmen eat you, that brings that to an end."

"I have no intentions of being eaten. This will be a quick thing." I walked behind the house and stopped at the tree line. "It'll be fine."

"Probably as quick a thing as the arena was an easy thing."

The horror on Ashern's face grew as I stepped into the trees.

Chapter Nineteen
Fertilizer
Azora

O n the outside of the forest, it looked typical, with ordinary oak trees growing closely together. How drastically the scenery changed after we stepped inside made me think a cloak shielded the true reality from anything outside the trees. The true forest had ground fog that reached my knees and dull yellow leaves that clung to pale trees. Even the dirt had a muted look, as though someone had zapped all the color from anything that lived there. The silence boomed so apparent that I cringed. Nothing stirred anywhere close that my sense could pick up, but I pulled out the knowledge Mistral had given me when we connected and headed toward the middle of the forest to find the small shed.

"You know where we're going?" Ashern said it so quietly I barely caught his words. He stepped with caution, and it was clear he believed much more lurked here than petrified trees and silence.

I raised an eyebrow and stared at him.

"Right. Of course, you know where we're going."

The farther we stepped into the forest, the more energy built under our feet. It created discomfort, but I kept going with the shed in view for motivation. It appeared over a small hill with rotted wood that had holes in random places. The roof looked disheveled, with several shingles missing and moss growing like a patchy quilt throughout the structure. The door had a lock that I easily turned to dust when I went to unlock it. That wasn't something I'd done before, but it made me think the components had aged so thoroughly that the slightest pressure placed by my key sense made them crumble. The boxes lined shelves, the length of which extended much farther than the shed looked like it should hold.

Ashern frowned and lifted his finger within an inch of a box before he pulled back. "What exactly are we doing in this creepy shack in the middle of the sleeping forest?"

"Freeing all the familiars."

"We're what?"

"Me. I am freeing them all with my key sense," I said.

"Here I thought you learned the lesson of not opening magical things."

"Not quite yet." I chose a random one and placed my hand on it.

Now that I'd released Amir, the lock was familiar, and with each new one I opened, it became easier. Illuminated swirls of colors flew from the boxes each time I opened them. The hue varied with each familiar I set free. They all gravitated to the ceiling before finding their true animal forms and escaping out the door and other cracks in the old walls. After dozens, I tired, and my work took longer or only opened them halfway before I had to rest. So many were left to be freed, and I had to keep going.

Ashern put his hand on my shoulder. "Maybe we should stop. This is releasing a lot of magic."

"Only a few more." My chest heaved, and I had to fight the urge to slump onto the ground for a nap.

"You're wearing yourself out. That can't be good for us getting out of here quickly should something attack."

"You're free to leave before anything does."

"I'm not leaving you."

"You should." I let two more out and rested my forehead on the edge of a shelf. "Only a few more to go."

"More like a hundred."

"That's not helpful."

"Come on, Pandora. You've done enough good." He tried to tug me away from my task.

"Did you just call me Pandora?"

"Someone else who got in trouble for opening something she shouldn't have," he said.

"Yes, but she also opened hope." I struggled to open another. "My key sense is tiring."

"I've noticed. You're going to make it so I have to carry you out of here."

"If you're so lazy, take your exit, as I have suggested many times." I slid to the ground. "I just need a break."

"Hope stayed in the box, Azora. Nothing good came of her opening the box."

"She got to keep it," I mumbled.

The energy in the ground moved under my legs and took hold.

"Sleeeep!" the hypnotic voice whispered until I obeyed.

"Did you enjoy the present?" Belphagor's voice broke through to my hazy mind.

I kept my eyes closed and relaxed into my steady breathing. "What present was that?"

"The Oblivion dragon. The most powerful kind placed at your feet and ready to bond with you."

"He is nowhere near my feet now."

"He will be, and you'll need him for times to come. It's why I sent him."

I opened my eyes to find myself back in the colorless forest with no Ashern or shed anywhere to be seen, but my exhaustion sat so deep it forced me not to question or care. "Why are you so generous? That you commanded the most powerful dragon to create an eternal bond with me? Who are you that such a great dragon would listen to your orders?"

"You welcome trouble so often that I needed something to guard you at times I can't protect you. And I convinced him, not command-ed. You intrigued him, and a dragon must sate that curiosity."

My back scraped against bark, making me realize I rested against a tree. I only spoke with Belphagor in sleep, but this felt like no rest. "What do you want from me?"

"Everything, kitten."

"I will puke right here on the ground if you call me kitten again. Everything is such a broad statement. Narrowing it down would be appreciated."

"The familiars have been good practice. It's a thing I thought would be helpful for you to improve your skills. The witch was thrilled to ac-commodate when I told her all about you. The opportunity presented itself when I realized Alcaius would take you to her house."

I opened my eyes and stared into the darkness where barely visible shadow men bobbed in the air between the trees. Their red-rimmed glowing turquoise bodies provided an eerie light across the forest floor. "Who are they?"

"Sandmen."

"Why did you want me to practice my ability so badly? Why are you doing this?"

"In time, I will give you all the answers you need, but for now, there is something you want."

"I want many things." The way none of the sandmen blinked their glowing yellow eyes sent shivers across my arms as the floating phantoms surrounded me and made me realize we were in a perfect circle of trees. I jumped up. "You brought me to a fairy circle."

"Nothing like misinformation on myths to animate you into useless fright."

"I've experienced them before and informed myself. Fright is useful to get the brain awake and thinking."

He disappeared from across the circle and appeared in front of me. The fire on his shoulders burned bright, and he lowered it when he noticed me squinting. "Here, I thought you were a fearless one."

"Shows how little you know about me. Why did you want me to practice my ability?"

"Because I have much bigger things for you to open. Alcaius always believed my father was the one he should watch. My father, the moron, who did terrible things for his own foolish ideals. He was so easily killed because he was nothing in the end."

I kept my eyes on the sandmen, waiting for them to move. If they all moved at once, we couldn't take them. I felt in my pockets to find my daggers gone. Could they even be stabbed? "You're saying you're the real threat? That Alcaius misjudged the true villain?"

"Villains are a matter of perspective. In the eyes of many, that title belongs to Alcaius himself. I think even to you."

"He has some confused morals, but he's hardly a villain."

"He'd burn a village for you."

"But he'd save all the innocent from the flames."

"Only if your life wasn't the price of their salvation." He grinned, probably because he knew he'd arrived at a conclusion I agreed with.

"It doesn't matter much now. We're broken up, and he can move on from me."

"You know little about him if you are unaware of the obsession you've created in him." He brought his shimmering bronze hand to my face. His golden rings nipped my skin with their chill, like his body had no warmth for them. "Pretty little thing that you are. You have many significant tasks upon you."

"And what exactly are those?"

"You want to speak with the Nightmare King to free the familiars from the forest. I can get you an audience with him, but he will have a price, and that's something I can't help you with."

I jerked my cheek away and stepped back for air void of his smoky scent. "You'll send me to the wolf with no assistance?"

"How badly do you want to save those precious apparitions?"

"You can't give any clues at all about what might get me what I want from him?"

He took out a golden dagger and slid it up my throat, stopping at my chin. "Negotiations are what he loves. He'll ask you to do something for him rather than give him something. It's how he operates." He moved the dagger back down my neck to my shoulder, like my blood dripping to the floor would give him pleasure, but something kept him from cutting me.

I shivered at the sharp touch of the blade moving to my cheek. "So another quest. Great. It seems one quest after the other before I can finish what I started." I grabbed his blade. "If you could get this out of my face, I'd appreciate it."

"Such a beautiful woman you grew to become." He lowered the blade. "Does it not intimidate you?"

"Why would it? You gave me a dragon and have stated more than once how badly you want to use me. You're not going to kill me. And even if you were, you're welcome to try it."

"I could maim you without killing you."

"Again. You are welcome to try it."

He cackled, letting his voice echo into the misty night. "I'd love to spar with you at some point, but for now, we must line up with time."

"It must be exhausting trying to endlessly be on time."

"You would know. Using a sense all the way to exhaustion is something you seem to do well. Let's go to the castle of nightmares. "

"As lovely as that seems, I can't just yet. Where is my companion, Ashern?" I looked around to see if I could locate him, but all that surrounded us were trees and phantoms. My seer senses seemed tired and any small thing I tried to pull up revealed itself as confusing shadows.

"Yes, you have forgotten him, it seems. You may want to go that way." He pointed to the left. "Don't let them catch you."

"How?"

"Be faster than them."

My jaw dropped, and terror chilled me. "Where is he?"

"I told you. That way." He threw his pointer finger dramatically to the left. "He wasn't faster."

"No!" I looked for the widest opening to the left and shot for it.

Howls like rabid wolves struck my ears so sharply that hot liquid rolled down my cheeks, but there was no time to confirm it was blood. The ringing pulse beat at my skull, picking up pace each time the howls struck me again. I ran, refusing to let it disorient me. Ice prickled my back, but I didn't stop as I screamed for Ashern. The forest floor darkened, and I pulled out the light stick I'd left in my pocket.

"Use your sense, seer!" Belphagor appeared next to me.

"They won't work. I've burned them out," I shouted, trying to let my anxiety calm enough to think through a better plan, but there was no time with the phantoms surrounding us. Time was running out.

"Don't let the sand get in your eyes!" Belphagor kept pace with me but did nothing to stop the phantoms. Maybe he couldn't, but it all seemed one big game to him.

"Ashern!" I stumbled down an embankment but caught myself on a tree and fell back, gasping at the clear petrified face carved into the tree.

I ran until my side stabbed me, and each tree I saw had a face carved into it. "Ashern!"

The sheer will I forced into my seer sense brought forth a powerful image. He was close, and I only had to make it a little farther. I flew forward and landed flat on my stomach, keeping my eyes shut and only using my tracking abilities. The fourth time I tripped, I opened my eyes to see how I was messing up the terrain layout so badly.

A scream ripped from my mouth at the sight of people's faces sticking above the ground. Their mouths hung open, and their eyes remained still, like a terrible death had captured them. The vapor rising and falling from their mouths made it clear they'd been buried alive. A sandman flew at me, and I picked up a branch that went right through the creature when I swung at it. I hit it again and again until it broke up enough for me to take off running.

My screams tapered into wails as I dropped to my knees next to Ashern's face, poking barely above the ground. "No!"

He wheezed, and his mouth twitched like he tried to speak. I took the stick and scraped the ground to dig him free. The dirt didn't move in the slightest.

I dropped back next to him. "It's okay. I'll get you out. I'll figure it out! Belphagor! Help him!"

Belphagor yawned and leaned against one of the people trees. "Why?"

"I won't do anything else in your game until you do."

"That's not within my control, and what makes you think this is a game?"

I flung my thumb at the sandmen floating in a circle around us again. "They stop when you do. You're controlling them."

"No, they're afraid of me. Your friend has three days to live, and it's another thing you'll have to take up with the King of Nightmares. How derailed your original goal has become."

I swallowed as I watched Ashern. "In three days, he'll be dead?"

"Yes, in the ground, where he will eventually become a tree."

"The others have to be freshly planted, too. Can they be saved as well?"

"That's asking a lot. They are food for the forest. The sandmen lure travelers in to preserve their home."

I bent down to put myself in Ashern's view. "You're not being abandoned, and I'll be back to free you before the three days are up. I promise and am so very sorry." I stood up. "What now? My tracker sense won't lead me to a place I haven't been without me having a connection to someone who's been there, and since I'm guessing you won't let me connect with you, you're going to have to lead me."

"We go east to Misant. Sandmen wanting to feast on you is another reason I will accompany you."

"Yet, you let me run like my life depended on it just moments ago."

"Need to keep you in shape," he said.

My face heated with rage. "You're abhorrent."

"Yes, my little bunny."

I punched his arm, and he laughed, enraging me more.

We hiked through the forest, and I tried to keep my mind off Ashern's horrified face. If my mind wandered to his suffering for even a moment, I'd become useless on the ground. Belphagor's fiery shoulders lit up our path as we walked. The sandmen followed close behind until we exited into a hilly landscape. My legs cramped, but I kept going until the green grass changed to dirt and dead trees.

Finally, we made it to a courtyard that had tall pillars on each side of us. The second set of stone steps led to a garden full of various pink and purple flowers. Behind the garden was a black castle with red doors which gave it an ominous feel.

Four bulky trolls in blue metallic armor carried long axes as they marched back and forth across the main door. They stiffened and formed a straight row in front of the entrance. "State your business," the one on the left said with a gruff voice.

Belphagor stepped in front of me. "Tell King Strix the King of Oblivion has stopped by for a visit."

The first troll grunted something to the middle troll. "This better not be a trick."

"Fetch him, and we shall find out."

I stared off and pieced things together. "You're the King of Oblivion? But also a reaper. How can it be?"

"I'm a reaper on my mother's side. The Celestials have been messing with elemental matches for the last few generations. They have fated several outside their kind to increase power. The last one they tried to pair failed."

"Why is that?"

"Your reaper does what he wants."

I took a shaky breath and rubbed my arms. "Alcaius was fated to someone?"

"He didn't tell you? Interesting."

Nausea swirled in my stomach. "Lady Fate's daughter? Moirai."

"Yes, they are fated mates, but Alcaius rejected her."

"Why?"

"That is something no one seems to know but him, and maybe her."

I shook my head, thinking through everything Alcaius had told me. "He said that reapers had to marry within their own kind. It's one of their highest laws."

"That's true. Unless the gods decide otherwise."

The troll who'd left returned. "He will see you now." He and another troll pulled on chains on each side of the doors, and they opened wide for us to enter.

My head swirled with all the terrible events of the day, and I wanted nothing more than to crawl into a bed somewhere to sleep. We walked down a long empty black hallway until we arrived at the ceiling-high blue doors. Men in armor opened them to reveal a strange man sitting on a thorny silver throne. Strix, the King of Nightmares, twirled his hand, and the guards prodded me forward with a spear. We had a lot to discuss with his majesty.

CHAPTER TWENTY
GONE
Alcaius

I reached over to pull Azora to me and felt a cool sheet against my palm. That was right. I'd banished her from my room, not by force but by cruelty. Regrettable things had been said that I needed desperately to rectify. I'd chased her all the way across the realms just to blow it when I found her. I rushed to the room I'd seen her flee to earlier and knocked on the door. She didn't answer, and it ignited my anger. Not all of this was on me. How did I think we could ever be together if she couldn't accept my need to reap? I went back to my room to stew about it until sleep became the only option.

I sat at the breakfast table, eating the blueberry porridge the witch had made for us. "When did you say the others will be here?"

She stirred the pot on the stove. "Any time. Within the hour is my guess."

Fennec took his seat across from me. "You've looked better."

"Thanks. Are you packed up? Mistral thinks the others will be here soon, so we can get the rest of this quest over with."

He spooned some porridge from the green glass bowl. "I thought we'd be going home after that shouting match you had with Azora last night."

"I'm angry with her, but I won't let her face the Fates alone."

"She must not have wanted your company," he said.

"Why do you say that?"

He finished his current bite and sipped from his steaming teacup. "She already left without you. I saw her and Ashern leaving early this morning."

I jumped up, spilling my water all over the table. "You're sure?"

"Yeah, I figured you knew that would happen when you talked to her the way you did. I don't relate to feelings, but I've gotten good at predicting the reactions they cause."

"You shouldn't assume anything." I rushed to her room and found it empty, as well as Ashern's. For the hundredth time, I wished I had Azora's ability. I needed it more than her with how many times she disappeared. I returned to the kitchen and pleaded with Mistral for help. "Can you track where they've gone?"

"There's no need when I can tell you where she's gone. Would you like some eggs?" She lifted the plate next to her with eggs and pieces of red vegetables cut up on it.

"No, I'd like to know where Azora is."

"You really should wait for the others to arrive since I've gone to so much trouble to get them. I'll tell you as soon as they get here."

"They can follow. She needs no more time to get ahead."

She dished some of her food onto another plate and took it to Fennec. "You should have some. You look too thin."

Fennec thanked her and tried a bite of the eggs. "A few more hours won't make much difference. She was days ahead of you at the beginning, and we still caught up to her."

"Only because she let us."

"Maybe you shouldn't be following someone who doesn't want to be followed."

"Or maybe you shouldn't talk about something you don't understand."

He finished his eggs before he started talking again, like he had to mull everything over. "What do you even like about Azora? Why her? You have the perfect person assigned to you. Moirai is beautiful and raised in the same places as you. She knows all the rules, and combining the Fate and Death elementals was a smart move with talk of dark forces rising. You were the envy of all the kingdoms when she was on your arm. Azora is a human with a few gifts. Someone you most likely can't have an heir or acceptance with, since reaper and human pairings rarely produce offspring. Why would you so desperately chase after someone so clearly not compatible with you?"

I clenched my fist around my fork, letting the edges press into my palm. "Moirai would never free a dragon because it was the right thing to do. She would never risk her neck to fight for me in a tournament. Especially one with such terrible survival odds. She's shallow and cares more about being the envy of the kingdom when she's on my arm than actually caring about me. I felt nothing when I slept with her but fleeting pleasure that is empty. Moirai would not lift a finger for my benefit if it did not help her. Azora would travel to the end of the world if she thought it would spare me the smallest pain. And in that, I know I love Azora far more than I have ever loved anyone or anything because not only would I crawl to the end of the world to spare her pain. I would annihilate the source that inflicted it upon her. I feel that in the core of my being, and for Moirai, nothing."

"It's always feelings that get you in trouble. You would destroy everything all based on fickle feelings that do not last." He drank down the rest of his tea and pushed it away with the saucer to formally end his breakfast. "You know what I think you love most about Azora? It's also the thing you hate most."

"Hate is too strong a word for anything pertaining to her."

He put up his hand. "It isn't. Because your passion for her has always burned at both ends of the spectrum."

"Go on. Explain to me what this is that you claim I both worship and loathe about Azora."

"That is the problem. Isn't it? You worship her more than you have any god that might raise you up or strike you down. Maybe that's why you are struck down so often, brother."

I sat back in my chair and smirked. "Gods can try to smite me, but the only one who can rebuke me with any impact is Azora. Now tell me. What do I both hate and love most about her?"

"That she is your moral compass. She tells you when you've gone too far and pulls you back with words whose truth you can't stomach. You don't like how she puts the sun on your shadows and opens the wounds you have caused yourself through your transgressions. She sees that you're a monster and loves you anyway, but refuses to excuse it, demanding you become a better version of the person she loves most."

"Rubbish." My words had no conviction because my little brother, who couldn't feel, somehow understood the biggest thing I hadn't been able to put into words.

I went back to the room and cleaned up, readying everything for departure. The Valkyries had taken the one thing I desperately needed—the looking globe. I considered leaving and trying to find her on my own, but it was a ludicrous thought with no direction. Patience was the key to finding her in a reasonable time frame. The morning wore on with me watching the witch mix potions and placing them on her shelf. She also cut out patterns for four dolls.

Knocking stole the witch from her work, and she opened it to Moderatus, Moira, and a man with deep blue eyes I presumed to be Elisha. His eyes made it difficult to notice anything else about him, but

I could tell right away he had reaper blood. It felt diminished, like the ice-cold sensation in my veins didn't entirely chill to my bone. Moirai had her hair dyed purple and kept in various sized braids with beads and feathers mixed in. As a Fate, each braid had an important meaning from protection to housing curses for someone who'd pissed her off. Moderatus had more tattoos than the last time I'd seen him, and he always received two at a time to keep his body balanced.

Moirai pursed her lips and sat down on a wicker chair. "Alcaius."

I gave her a disinterested chin nod and ignored her growing pout.

Elisha looked around the room. His gaze became stiffer with each area he searched. "Where's Azora?"

"That's what we're waiting for the witch to tell us," I said.

Mistral returned to her sewing projects and unraveled the black threads she cut into strips. "She's gone to see Strix. The Nightmare King."

"Why would she do that?" I jumped up, ready to run out of the cabin and straight for Mistrant without stopping, but I needed more information.

"She wants to save all the familiars." The witch explained how Azora had saved her familiar and had wanted to help the others.

Moirai let out an exaggerated sigh. "She's taking saving the dragons so seriously. As much as I believe she needs to pay, it's time to just move forward without her. Time is running out, and she keeps taking on ridiculous side quests."

"Like freeing me from a lifetime of slavery." I kept my eyes pinned to hers.

"You would have figured that out on your own, and if not, you deserve to be enslaved. I clearly believe in you when she does not."

"Or you're not willing to do anything that doesn't have an advantage for you."

"Leaving you to rot would have definitely been an advantage for me." She fluttered her eyelids.

Moderatus moved toward the door. "We cannot complete this quest without Azora. The universe demands balance for what she has done. We will go after her even if it is irritating to do so. If she is not serious, we will have to force her to be."

I cleared my throat. "Want to rephrase that any?"

"I said the words that you heard."

"Force is something you won't do with Azora if you don't want me to force some things on you."

"If you had showed even a fraction of that enthusiasm toward me, we might have stood a chance of pleasing the Celestials," Moirai said.

"I would have had to care about pleasing them and you."

Moirai rolled her eyes and walked over to the table. "Is this lunch?"

The witch sewed long black hair into one of the dolls. "Yes, take whatever you want."

The three newcomers ate lunch before we set off toward Mistrant, the territory of the Nightmare King. We traveled between the mountain range and the sleeping forest, being careful not to step foot beyond the treeline. The sandmen stood at the edge of the forest in various forms to lure us in, but we all knew not to look too long toward the phantoms. It was a relief when we finally made it to the hills and set up camp for the night. The others had outvoted me on continuing until we got to the castle. They thought we needed proper sleep to face Strix.

Elisha started the campfire, and he cooked fish with Fennec's help. My brother had brought spices to prioritize flavorful food. I ate some of the meal and set up my tent early to escape Moirai's stares. The small tent reminded me of one of my first moments with Azora, where we'd shared a similar small space together. Her nose had crinkled out of frustration at being so close to me. She'd put blankets between us that didn't keep her scent or soft hums away from me. It was long before I realized sharing the tent had been one of the small moments that added to dozens that caused me to fall for her. Starlight broke through the flap in the tent as a figure slipped inside. I jumped up and had the intruder on the ground in less than a second.

"If only you had been that quick when the Valkyrie captured you." Moirai bit her lip and put her arms around my neck. "Fennec said you and Azora broke up. We should start where we left off."

I groaned and pushed away from her. "Get out of my tent."

"It doesn't have to be serious." She crawled over to where I'd pressed myself into the tent. "Just a little fun to relieve the stress."

"Out of my tent, Fate! Do not force me to remove you myself!"

She picked up a rock that had rolled into the tent and chucked it at me. "I hope they execute you slowly!" She hissed and threw another rock at me before leaving. All of it reminded me of how toxic we'd always been together.

I considered warding my tent even though she was probably done with me for the night. Instead, I closed my eyes and drifted to sleep. A chill woke me, and I could tell someone had entered my space again. "I told you to stay out!"

"Prince of Death, I am but a messenger." My dad's personal crow hopped onto my travel sack.

"I thought you were someone else."

"Where is the box, and why haven't you found it already?" He squawked. "Your father is growing impatient."

"We've run into a few bumps."

"What obstacles have prevented you from keeping your word to your father?"

"I gave him no oath. He could have better equipped me for this, since it's such a big deal for him. Right now, I'm still trying to find Azora. She's headed to Strix, and I need her to locate the box. It's where we're headed now."

"Samael says to hurry it up."

"Or he'll do what? What could he possibly do to me that he hasn't already?"

"Most would not ask that." He cawed and flew out of the tent, not zipping it behind him.

It took a while to get back to sleep after that, and I kept expecting everyone else to disturb me.

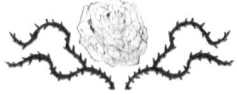

We made it to Mistrant by mid-afternoon and followed the view of the castle. Moirai had said nothing to me, and I welcomed the divine silence that came with her not speaking. The trolls led us to the throne room.

Strix had a thin, triangular face that gave him an abnormally point-ed chin. He looked made of black and white, with no color touching him or his clothes. "Is there a summit I'm supposed to host that someone didn't tell me about?" He picked his staff with the golden lion head and pointed it at me. "First Oblivion visits, now Death, Fate, and Balance." He turned his head when he spotted Elisha. "Your blood is the same as hers." Without clarifying who he meant, he returned his attention to me. "Why have you all graced my presence?"

I stepped forward and bowed. "We are here for a woman. Azora."

"Yes, she was here, but you just missed her."

I took deep breaths to calm my growing aggravation. "Where is she?"

"I sent her on a brief trip to do something for me." He clapped his hands. "What a rude host I am, and I am hungry. Why don't we discuss this over dinner?"

"At least tell me she's safe."

He giggled, a grating, high-pitched ruckus. "Most certainly she is not."

My scythe found its way to his throat. "If she's harmed, your kingdom will fall."

He halted his guards running toward us with the wave of his hand. "Perhaps we can make a deal."

"Or you could tell us where she is."

He shook his head, unconcerned with the way my very sharp blade was at his neck. "I want something first. You won't kill me because that won't help you know where she is."

"If you piss me off enough, I will and worry about the rest later."

He giggled in a way that induced the desire to stomp my ears. "Let's dine together, and we will both be happy with the results."

I tucked my blade back in its holster behind me and moved over to the others. "Fine, but if anything happens to her, your death won't be as easy as decapitation."

"Branching out from your father, I see. He cut off the heads of about three people the last time I visited." He rose from his throne and headed out a door to the side.

Fog blanketed the ground, and the only décor on the black walls was the red windows that gave a glow to light up the walkways. Each door blended with the walls except for blue swirls painted over them in random patterns.

A feast spread across a long table, and everything in the room looked drained of color as all else we'd seen in the place, including the occupants. The food possessed a dullness to it that matched everything else. We chose chairs and waited as servants loaded our plates with fruits, meat, cheese, and bread. Women in white dresses filled our glasses with red wine and teacups with a steaming cinnamon mixture. The smells of the liquids mixed with the strong savory meat scents. We ate while Strix rambled on about things in his kingdom that I mainly tuned out.

At the conclusion of dinner, Strix leaned back in his chair and clapped his hands. "Who is ready for what you can do for me?"

"I'm more interested in you telling us where Azora is." I pushed my plate back to let the servants know they could take it.

"Such impatience. Too much like your father, prince. The payment for that information is required from her." He flung his arm forward to point dramatically at Moirai.

She played with her pointer nail, running her thumb over it. "Let me guess. You want a fate thread read."

He clapped his hands for the sixth time since we'd entered the dining hall. "Yes! Yes! I need you to tell me if I have a thread line to someone. A relationship, and how strong it is if there is one."

"Readings are something for lesser Fates, and I really don't care to save Azora. But I do care to save the dragons. I will do this menial task for that reason alone." She walked over to Strix and grabbed the back of his wrist, turning his palm up. "Who is the thread you want me to search for?"

"The Queen of Dreams, Thalassa." His grin stretched to the bottom of his nose.

"You want a thread to your enemy? To see if you defeat her?"

"No, I have tired of feuding with her. While that will still be fun, I want more than that now. I want you to see if there are any possible threads toward coupling."

Moirai's face twisted and stayed that way as she closed her eyes. "You could have said romance."

"That too. Look for that too."

She took a while, slowly relaxing her face as she searched through the fate lines of Strix's soul. "Yes, there is one. It's small, but it looks like if it is linked to your soul, it'll hold and last. There are others that are short with her, and the most likely being that she continues to hate you and keeps far from you."

"How do I find the way to love?"

"It's difficult to trace the exact path, but I would brighten your realm a bit more. There is a sign that this thread may be close to taking. Like you already started that way, but it could unravel if you are too strange. My advice is to work on laughing and clapping less. Taper your excitement when you see her, but the thread is slowly taking as we speak, but it is not a sure thing yet."

"She must be doing well. I sent Azora to Bloree to invite Thalassa to my ball. I throw one each week in hopes she will grace me with a dance. She never has." He frowned at the floor before lifting his head and smiling at us. "You are all invited as a thank you for this good news. I will have my servants give you accommodations while we await Azora's return."

Chapter Twenty-One
Invitation
Azora

S trix looked human, like the other elementals I'd seen. They all had things that looked a little off, but at first glance, they looked ordinary. He wore all black and his skin had a grey hue with a slightly bluish tint, and the most peculiar thing about him was his head appeared to be an upside-down thin pyramid. He had long black hair to his shoulders, and he blended with the lack of vibrancy around him.

"Greetings, guests. It's wonderful to see you. Few people seek out nightmares, but I have a few chambers you can visit if you're here for frightening entertainment."

I walked to the steps that led up to the platform his throne was on. "You and I need to speak about a grave deed you have committed that needs redeemed."

He leaned forward. "A human here to accuse and demand of me. Having the King of Oblivion next to you must fuel your foolish boldness. Do you not know what I am capable of?"

"Yes, you are capable of causing torment to hundreds of familiars, their mages, and anyone who enters your woods."

His jaw dropped, and he stared at Belphagor like he couldn't believe I'd dare to chastise him in his throne room. "Will you do anything about her mouth?"

"There is not much anyone can do about that." A hint of a smile displayed on Belphagor's face.

"I am waiting for an answer as to why you think it's okay to cause such harm," I said.

Strix's attention returned to studying me. "The people are food for my sandmen. They deserve treats for serving me so well. If people are dumb enough to invade my territory, then they deserve it for trespassing. As far as the familiars and mages, they were something I long forgot about. Thank you for reminding me of that amusement."

I took one step up and then another. "If you have forgotten about the familiars, you won't mind taking down whatever keeps them in the forest, so they can return to their masters."

"I long ago lost the keys to open their boxes. Sorry."

"I can deal with that, but you need to take down the ward that traps them."

He yawned and tapped his mouth a few times. "Why would I ever put forth any effort into that?"

"Because it's the right thing to do."

Belphagor's shoulders lit up the stairs as he floated next to me. "We are willing to make exchanges."

Strix's head bobbed on his thin neck, and the upper portion of his head looked like it might topple from the weight. "I have no use for anything you could give me. You'd need to do something for me. I'm having a ball and have been inviting the Queen of Dreams for the last several months, and everything I send her is returned broken. She also puts any messengers I send into an eternal sleep. It's a peaceful one which makes it tremendously boring. My poor little nightmare imps are suffering in blissful slumber."

"You want us to wake them," I said.

"No, I want you to deliver the final gift I have for her before the ball. Your timing makes this an opportune moment for you and me to mutually benefit. But that is of little surprise for you, Belphagor."

"We have to deliver a gift to her? That's it? How long will this take? Because your sandmen are currently feasting on one of my friends, and I would very much like him back before he becomes a tree."

"You want a lot from me. The familiars set free and your friend back. For our deal, you are to not only get her the present but also convince Thalassa to come to the ball."

"I will need to connect with someone who knows the way to her so that I can track her with my seer sense."

He held his hand out. "You may see only that. I can tell if you try to peek."

"Hide anything you don't want me to see and all will be fine." I climbed the rest of the steps and took his hand.

He had solid walls around most of his mind and had probably learned to guard his thoughts over centuries. A small light trickled in from the back of his mind, and I focused on it until the information I needed transferred to me. A map to the Queen of Dreams opened up for me to follow.

I released his hand and joined Belpahgor at the bottom of the stairs. "How do you expect me to convince the queen to come to your ball? If it were an easy thing to do, you would have done it rather than calling in a big favor from me."

"I have a present that I want you to give her, and I think it will change her mind. No messenger I have sent has gotten close, but you're traveling with the King of Oblivion, and your unique abilities should get you to her for an audience. You must be careful because anyone she is unhappy with, she puts into an eternal sleep. You'll dream sweetly until you turn old and decay where you are."

"There could be worse fates. Like burying people alive until they slowly become trees."

"I never said she delivers the worst fates. Only that you should be careful so you can make it back."

"I want a written agreement. Simple with no fine print. I want that stated that no fine print counts, and you will not trick me in any way."

He snapped his fingers and yellowed paper and a black feather pen appeared in his hand. He handed it to one of his servants to bring it to me. "There you go. Just as you wish, and I can assure you that if you accomplish Thalassa coming to the ball, I will have no trouble keeping my end of the bargain."

King Strix had trolls bring out a box the size of an arm chair, and he undid the brass latches. The sides dropped, and a golden harp shone as the brightest thing in the room. "When this is played, it turns nightmares into dreams. It is my white flag."

"How will we take it?"

"I will have horses prepared for you with a cart for it to ride in. It'll get you to her in enough time to spare your friend."

"That will work. Thank you."

He gave his trolls orders and had two of them take us to the side of the castle where we found two black horses hooked to a wooden cart with a cream canvas over the back and a bench in the front to fit around three people. Under the canopy was the wooden box with a harp and dozens of wrapped gifts.

A troll handed me a sack. "For you to eat on your journey." He handed me another sack. "For you to drink."

Belphagor floated up to the top, and I used the bars to pull myself to the high seat. I was grateful the bench was wide enough to keep space between us. Belphagor wanted to use me for something, so I knew he wouldn't kill me, but there were other things he could do. He steered the horses, and I watched the scenery change from the black and grey of the nightmare kingdom to the green rolling hills at the base of the Greock mountains. The sleeping forest dotted the background, and I sent thoughts to Ashern to hold on. Guilt overwhelmed me that I'd brought him with me, and he'd paid the price.

Colorful pastel trees appeared. The pink and blue leaves looked lovely over the turquoise grass. Yellow birds danced in the air, singing a pleasant tune to serenade our journey. The water next to our path shimmered violet, and red fish jumped in the air, seeming to dance with the tiny songbirds overhead. We'd entered a paradise that I knew likely held hidden horrors.

I rifled through a bag of food from the back and pulled out small cheese sandwiches and two jugs of water. "Would you like some?"

Belphagor kept his eyes focused ahead in the stiff way he seemed to do everything, like he had a force around him that kept him from relaxing. "No."

"Do you ever eat?"

"Rarely. It's not needed often and is otherwise a chore."

I took a bite of the sandwich and savored the sharp taste in my mouth. It had a creamy sauce that complimented the type of cheese well. The bread had a garlic butter taste that was delicious, and I was grateful for the mint candies that someone had placed in the bag. I drank several swigs of water and finished the meal with the candy. The trees grew closer together as the grove turned into woods. The sunlight adequately bathing the ground through the trees provided clear visibility. Purple flowers grew at the base of each tree trunk and released a mist that smelled like roses and vanilla.

My shoulders slumped, and I blinked to keep my leaden eyelids open. "Do you mind if I slip into the back and sleep?" I yawned with every word.

Belphagor's head turned slowly to look at me like someone had turned down time. He said something I couldn't make out and blurred. His image rippled, and it took all my willpower to try to figure out what he said. I briefly felt the pain of falling out of the wagon before the sweet floral scent carried me into dreams.

Fairies fluttered everywhere in white glowing dresses like tiny stars underneath a bright morning. Tall, blue grass tickled my cheeks, and I sat up in time to see a rainbow of butterflies rising and falling like a ribbon whipping on command. Wildflowers broke up the grass in as many varied colors as the butterflies. I yawned and stretched, standing up to figure out where I was.

My tracker sense didn't pull forward no matter how hard I tried to force it, but panic didn't overtake me like it normally would have. All emotions sat irretrievable, pressed down by a sense of serenity. Any conflict of shame, anger, guilt, or sadness didn't belong to me in that place. It felt as though blindness had struck me, but there was no way to feel bad about it.

"Azora!" Alcaius said behind me.

I leaped into his arms and relished him spinning me around. He kissed me, moving his lips over mine with a desperate hunger that he further fueled with his hands slipping under my dress. We found ourselves buried in flowers. There was no room for the argument we'd had, and it was unclear why I'd ever felt bad about any of it. Only bliss lived in this place. Nothing else mattered but breathing in everything with Alcaius beside me.

"Get up!" The angry voice pulled me from my reaper.

Alcaius disappeared as Belphagor stood over me. "Weak, foolish human. It's basic magic skills to ward yourself from the effects of poppies when entering the land of dreams."

"Why would anyone ever want to leave this place?" I tried to sit up and failed.

Belphagor blew blue dust into my eyes. "Snap out of it!" The fire on his shoulders rose above his head and flailed around like he'd lost control of it. "Wake up! Human!" He blew more dust into my eyes until I opened them.

It took an unspecified amount of time to realize I'd woken up. It took several more heartbeats of blinking to sit up, and the dizziness almost sent me back to the ground. "You could have warned me about the poppies and what to do about them. This isn't a place I've ever been."

"King Strix told you that Queen Thalassa put people into an eternal sleep. That's poppies. Common knowledge that you would have learned early in school."

"You realize I am human, and they don't teach us a lot about magical properties unless we are royal and allowed to enter the magic fields."

"Knowing the ways of magic is a gods-given right," he said.

"Not for us. Our ruling class keeps it from us because they say we can't handle it and wouldn't know what to do with it."

"They have to know you are capable of learning basic magic to protect yourself. That's common sense." He held out his hand and helped me to my feet.

"They believe if we have equal power, they would lose theirs, so they diminish our rights and call it safety."

"That's a greedy way to live."

"Precisely," I said.

He climbed onto the cart and stretched across the bench to pull me up next to him, handing me a small jar of potent ointment. It had a sharp medicine scent to it, and even the lid didn't conceal its nip.

"Put this over your face and cover yourself with blankets in the back. It should help lessen the effects of the poppies." He faced his palm up and out. "Show me the directions to Thalassa's castle first."

I placed my palm over his and sent the needed information to him. "I would have thought you'd know the way."

"I am not all-knowing."

"Good to know." I climbed into the back and did as he'd told me to.

The wagon bobbed back and forth as I pressed my face into the wooden bed, keeping the blankets over me. A thud hit the canvas covers, followed by another and another. The patters sped up until they happened so quickly I couldn't count them. I tried to figure out their shape, using my seer sense to track the other side of the wagon. The scenery changed, so I couldn't quite grab an entire picture, but they looked like shadow pixies ramming into our wagon cover.

A ripping sound broke up the thwaps, and I peeked out to see a tear ripping apart the canvas. Massive talons poked through the fabric and lifted us off the ground. Tiny faces popped through the holes created by the talons. Their creepy appearance had childish cutesy features with disturbing black eyes. They wiggled and shoved themselves all the way in. Their tattered white dresses sat on their thin bodies and dragonfly wings fluttered on their back so rapidly they were difficult to see clearly.

They hissed and stabbed at me with tiny swords the size of a daisy stem. I flung them away with my forearm as they continued to fly in and overwhelm my abilities to keep them away. Dozens poured inside, and I used the blanket as a shield as I crawled out onto the bench where Belphagor sat, casually staring at the ground far beneath us.

I held onto the side as I got myself situated next to him. "There's an invasion happening in there, and you're sitting here like it's a great day for a causal stroll through the air."

"If there was something to worry about, you would see me acting like there was."

"Fairies were stabbing me, and a giant..." I leaned over the side to see the giant eagle carrying us into the sky. "A giant eagle is carrying us away."

"It's your dream."

"What?"

"You're the one dreaming all of this. If you don't like it, change it."

He pointed to the back of the wagon. "If we were truly being attacked by pixies, why didn't they follow you out here?"

"That's a good point." I turned my head slowly to figure out what was an illusion. "Are you real?"

"The only real thing besides you."

"How long have I been sleeping?" I feared he'd tell me always, and I'd wake up long before I'd even gone on the quest with Alcaius. My entire life would unravel into nothing in front of me.

"Since you climbed back in the wagon less than an hour ago. You fell asleep even though I told you not to. Nothing around us is real. Your imagination made it up because we are in the land of dreams. He's not real." His gaze locked on the eagle.

The moment he said it and I looked at the bird, it vanished, and we plummeted to the ground. I screamed and clawed at the tarp, trying to spare myself from the hard landing. We glided to a halt on black stones as glowing blue liquid flowed through cracks in the ground.

A stunning woman with black curls to her waist stood on a platform by our wagon. Her heart shaped face, delicate features, and crystal blue eyes gave her a unique beauty. "Welcome to my kingdom,

Azora. Do you want to tell me the reason you have trespassed on my lands, and why I shouldn't leave you in eternal sleep?"

"How do I know you're real and not part of my dream?"

She spread her arms out. "Everything here is your creation. You are the goddess of this world, and everything obeys your command. You should want to stay here. Escape the disappointment of reality."

"That sounds like a lot of fun, but I have friends and dragons to save. I have a proposal for you."

Her eyes burned with blue flames, and that somehow made her even more beautiful. "Speak quickly."

Chapter Twenty-Two
Gift
Azora

I searched for the harp for three seconds before not having my tracker sense reminded me all of this was a dream. "Strix, the King of Nightmares—"

The flames in her eyes grew larger, overtaking the sockets and rising to her hairline. "I want nothing to do with that bastard! He is a mindless moron who thinks of nothing but himself. He traps people in eternal nightmares for disagreeing with him."

"Like you put them into dreams?"

The flames receded to the size of normal irises as she seemed to take in my words. "Who wouldn't want to stay trapped in pleasant dreams where they are the ruler of their existence? They never want for anything. Unlike Strix, I make sure they are physically cared for in an ethical way, and it keeps them from being a threat to my kingdom. It protects my people and gives them a better life. Nothing like what Strix has done."

"You take away their life and give them something artificial. Some, if not most, probably have families grieving them. If you keep me in eternal sleep, dragons will end and my family will miss me."

"That doesn't seem my problem." She crossed her arms and turned her head to the side.

"It would be because you'd be responsible for that happening. It would be your fault."

"No, it would be yours for coming here. What is your proposal? You said you had one."

"Yes." I pictured the box with the harp in it, and the illusion of it appeared next to me. "In the waking world, what's inside this box is a present that King Strix believes will change your mind enough about him that you will attend his ball."

"That would have to be a gift unlike all others."

"Would you allow me to wake up and bring it to you?"

She pursed her lips, and her flames grew. "Fine, but if I am unhappy with it, you shall sleep until death claims you."

"That's not something that scares me, so I will take the risk." I opened my eyes to Belphagor's glare.

"You were told not to sleep!" he snapped.

"I don't think I had much choice. The Queen of Dreams visited me while I slept, and she has agreed to let me present King Strix's gift to her." I sat up and rubbed my throbbing head, feeling like I'd drank too much wine during a wild party.

He helped me out of the back of the wagon and onto the bench in the front, and we continued our journey to the queen without further interruptions, and not even the elf guards stopped us at the entrance. They opened the main gate doors and let us go inside the pink castle that looked made from fluffy clouds. The lack of questioning solidified in my mind that it was really the queen I'd talked to in my dream.

A thin elf, who stood taller than Belphagor, directed us where to put our wagon. He ordered others to get a flat cart to carry all of Strix's gifts to the throne room by order of the queen.

After that, we were led into the castle. The sun lit up the pink walls and ceiling, adding a glow to each area we walked.

The throne room continued the pink cloudy theme but had added stained glass windows that moved. A unicorn slid down a rainbow on one while a knight fought a dragon on another. He held his sword clumsily, so it seemed the scaly beast would win the battle. Each scene differed.

"They play dreams. Random ones from all over existence." Thalassa, Queen of Dreams, stepped into view and sat down on her tall purple throne. She had on the same black dress as in my dream. Her features right down to the blue flame eyes stayed true to what I'd seen earlier as well.

"That's interesting and would entertain one for a long time."

"Yes, it often does. My guests will find chairs and watch the dreams unfold." She leaned her head to look around me. "Is that my gift?"

I turned around to see the box had been delivered and moved over to the brass fasteners. "Yes, this is the main one that King Strix hoped you would accept in exchange for doing him the blessing of your presence at his ball tonight."

She tipped her chin up and gave the crate a side glance. "We will see if this is worth my time. Endlessly, he sends people to me, and I spare them from his foolery by keeping them in my dream fields. I'm not sure I want any part of that."

I unlatched the door and swung it open. "This is your beautiful present."

"Pfft... I have no use for an instrument. I have an entire orchestra of them and that includes three harps. Much prettier than this one."

"This one is special. He gave you the key to his defeat with it. It's his surrender to your wishes."

She leaned forward, resting her chin on her hands and elbow on her knees. "Do go on."

"When the harp is played, it turns any nightmare into a dream."

Her eyes widened, and she sat up straight against the back of her throne. "No."

"Yes, I'm not sure how you could test it."

"Reginald! Bring me a gremlin and a sleeper!"

The guard at the back of the room bowed. "Yes, Your Majesty." He ran from the room, and when he returned, he had a wooden bird cage with a brown fluffy monster inside. It looked like a rabid mouse that had grown ten times its natural size.

Behind him, two men carried in a mat with poles attached to each corner. A woman rested on her back with her hands folded in front of her and her eyes shut. Her blonde curls shaped her peaceful oval face.

The queen stood up to get a better view of the entire scene. "Release the gremlin on her."

Reginald whispered something into the cage and opened the door. The fuzzy, cute creature opened its mouth to show lots of triangular teeth. It chomped over and over as it jumped onto the stretcher and bit the woman in the leg. She remained still until the gremlin quit biting and was put back in its cage. The woman's head moved back and forth until her movements became frantic and she screamed. She rolled off the mat and continued to scream.

The queen frowned. "Such vileness in nightmares. Play the harp, Azora."

"Me? I've never played a harp before and am merely delivering a message," I said.

"You brought a gift you don't know how to use?"

"I figured you probably had a harp player somewhere, since Strix didn't ask me if I could play. He seemed to assume I could handle the task."

The queen walked slowly to me and turned me by the shoulders to stare at the flailing woman. "And here you are failing it. That poor woman is suffering because of the claims you cannot prove. Play the harp or leave with it."

"Could you at least bring a harp player in here for me to connect with? It still won't be great, but it'll show me where to start."

"Play the harp, Azora!"

I thought of Ashern and how I couldn't afford to not to seal this deal, so I stepped to the harp and plucked the strings. It was a chaotic mess, no matter how hard I tried or what strings I plucked.

The queen stood over the woman, who had returned to her calm sleeping state. "Very nice. A gremlin bite should have left her in nightmares for months, and anyone can play it, it seems. You can stop your horrendous ruckus now. This is a great day for my people. Long have Strix's gremlins tormented my people."

I quit playing and mentally thanked Strix for having a harp that used magic with even terrible use. "You will go to the ball with me, then?"

"Yes, I will go with. Let me get ready. Come with me. You need much better dressed." She stopped and pointed at Belphagor. "You stay here. Ladies only." She went through a door behind her throne and led me through more pink cloud hallways.

We entered a room with a lot of vanities and mirror sets. Most looked ordinary brown with simple oval mirrors. She took the middle one at the back of the room. It was painted purple with red roses, and ivy wrapped around the vanity legs and round mirror. She plopped down in the chair and removed a knife from a small drawer. I gasped as she ran the blade up her arm, but instead of blood pouring out, sapphires shimmered under her cut. She did the same thing to her other arm, and the jewels glimmered as they reflected the flames in her eyes.

Servants helped her put on an elaborate dress that started a dark purple and changed to a light blue at the waist and slowly changed back to purple. Tiny yellow stones created a look of stars over the fabric, and a fancy jeweled cape attached to the sleeves. The last thing done was to pin up her dark hair into a fancy braided bun. Jewelry with stones that matched her slit open arms decorated her neck and ears. She hurried me along without addressing my attire that she'd complained about earlier.

We stopped in the throne room to collect Belphagor, but he was nowhere to be seen. He'd vanished on me, and I concentrated on his location only to be unable to pull him up. He'd find me if wanted to, that I was sure of. Thalassa and I went to a stable where I figured we would ride our wagon back, but she insisted we ride flying horses. That shortened the journey significantly, and we made it back to the nightmare kingdom long before sunset.

Strix sat sideways on his throne like the first time I'd met him. He straightened himself forward and took a moment to gape at Thalassa. "My lady, you have come to my ball."

Thalassa gave him a brief curtsy. "Yes, but this is promise of nothing. Remember that."

"No pressure. The ball doesn't start for a couple more hours. Would you like to go for a stroll in my garden?"

I waved my hand in front of Strix to stop him. "Before you go on your walk, I'd appreciate you freeing my friend and the familiars of their suffering."

His smile dropped. "Yes, let's get that out of the way. My servants will take you to my head mage, who will make that happen. Tell him who you are, and he knows he is to help you." His smile returned when his attention returned to Thalassa. He hooked arms with her and left through a side door. I stood in the empty throne room for a few minutes before a troll came and took me to the magic wing of Strix's castle.

A basin of lava flowed around the entire mage's room. It stayed contained by stones with strange markings on the side. Above the lava were shelves cut into the walls that resembled Mistral's house. Decorative boxes, potions, powders, and jars all filled dozens of shelves on three of the walls. The fourth had rows of leather books.

The greying man wore all green, including his large floppy hat. He appeared ancient, with wrinkles inside wrinkles and age spots all over his skin. "How may I help you today?" He kept his eyes on the enormous book on a pedestal in front of him.

"I am Azora. King Strix sent me to you and said he told you what to do."

"Oh, yes, he did. Shall we begin our journey to your friend first? I'm guessing that is the order you would like to do things in?"

"Yes, it is."

He grabbed a bag sitting on his desk by the bookshelf and handed me a vial of blue liquid. "Drink this to protect yourself from the effects of sandmen."

I eyed the concoction skeptically. "There is this habit I have, to not really drink things I don't understand the ingredients for."

He got out a cup and poured half the liquid into a cup, drinking it down. "See, nothing to it. If you want to save your friend, I suggest you get to drinking."

"Fine." I drank the bitter substance that brought nausea for a moment before my stomach settled.

We rode black horses to the sleeping forest. Once again, the trees looked lush and beautiful until we stepped across the border, and everything took on a petrified appearance of smooth dead tree trunks.

"Strix said you can track your friend's location. Would you do so?"

I focused on Ashern, and his face poking above the dirt flashed into my head. His closed eyes made it unclear how he was. I nudged my horse forward and led the way to Ashern. The sandmen followed us with only their yellow glowing eyes making them visible. A steep hill took some effort to climb, and closely spaced trees thinned the path enough that we had to look for places to slip through. Finally, we made it to Ashern.

I leaped off my horse and crashed next to him, running my fingers through his hair. "We're here. We made it. Only a few moments longer."

He groaned and didn't open his eyes.

The mage adjusted his green hat and kneeled beside Ashern, removing several potions from his bag. His fingers went into a pink ointment that smelled of cinnamon and flowers. He caked it on Ashern's forehead, which had become a mixture of skin and bark.

Ashern gasped a few times before taking steady breaths and opening his eyes. He seemed to go in and out of consciousness as the dirt around him rumbled and pushed upward. The ground quaked, and Ashern's body emerged like a flower bursting from the ground in spring. He curled on his side and shook.

I wrapped him in a blanket from my bag. "It's okay. Everything is going to be okay. You're alright now." I picked up the jar of ointment from the ground and gave it back to the mage. Can you save some of the others while we're waiting for him to wake up?"

"Sorry. But I only have orders for the friend and the familiars," the mage said.

"I should have been more specific. Can you handle the familiars on your own, or do you need me to show you where they are?"

"I know where they are. Removing the barrier keeping them here will be a little tricky but stay with your friend, and I will return when finished." He gave me some of the blue liquid I'd drank earlier. "Give this to your friend as soon as he is fully awake, so we have no issues with the sandmen when we're ready to leave. It'll be important since I feel they will be angry about losing several sources that they feed on."

"I thought the sandmen fed the forest the tree people?"

"The tree people feed all that lives in the sleeping forest, including the sandmen. The sandmen also eat the familiars from time to time by breaking open a box and feasting on them between people entering the forest. They aren't as appetizing, so they try to ignore them, but sometimes it's all there is."

"We're basically taking their food storage. Probably would anger anyone." I put Ashern's head in my lap and brushed the hair from his eyes. "Are you awake yet, friend?"

"If I admit I'm awake, you'll make me do something," Ashern mumbled.

"Yes, something that makes it so you don't become a tree again."

He opened one eye halfway. "That sounds important."

"It's vital to your survival, and I went to a lot of trouble to make sure you stay an elemental and not a plant."

"Fine. You've convinced me."

"Can you sit up any?" I helped him lean against my chest and held the vial to his lips. "Drink this, and it'll keep the sandmen away from you."

He slowly sipped all of it down. "Thank you. I would have been miserable, stuck as a tree."

"You shouldn't thank me. I'm the reason you were stuck at all. If I hadn't gotten the notion of saving familiars in my head, you'd have stayed safe at Mistral's."

"Did you hold a knife to my throat?"

"No, but you weren't going to leave me when you need me to save the dragons."

"My feet moved by my will alone. You don't get to claim my foolishness as your own even if you instigated it." He reached into his pocket, sat all the way up, and tossed his dice in the air. "Thank Tyche, my dice are fine." He kissed the two small cubes and put them back in his pocket.

The red returned to Ashern's pale cheeks. Other than his cheeks, he was normally as white as a cloud on a sunny day, but he'd looked almost transparent when he'd first risen from the ground. Blue animal figures shot past us like a supernatural stampede. Slowly, they lessened until one or two at a time flew by.

The mage appeared over the hill. "It's done."

"There are several I need to go back and open that are stuck in the shed."

"I pried them open with special magic that Strix gave me. They are all free, but if you wish, you can go back and check yourself."

I closed my eyes and thought of the shed. My tracker sense showed me it was empty. "No, you did well. Thank you."

We climbed onto the horses, and Ashern had to share mine, but I made him sit in front of me so I could watch his balance. Jugglers greeted us right inside the castle gate as they threw fire sticks in the air. Another man pedaled on a massive wheel, and other people flew on ropes. The mage got us through the growing crowd with no issues. Humans, trolls, and elves all wore fancy clothes into the castle.

The mage took us in a back way and stopped at a blue door. "This is your stop, Azora. King Strix has requested I leave you here. Ashern, you're to be somewhere else."

Ashern tossed his dice in the air three times and stared down at the mage. "I don't think I should leave Azora."

I shooed him with my hand. "Go. Don't offend our host. I'm pretty sure I've proven I'll be just fine."

"Fine. But I'm not going far."

"Deal. Go." I smiled and watched them leave down the hall.

Once I entered the room, servants demanded I bathe. When I finished, they placed a fluffy dress over my head. The skirt was a shimmering silver to complement the deep blue of the bodice. It sparkled in random places as Thalassa's dress had. Both dresses looked like a night sky in their own unique ways. The bodice fit tightly against my upper body but wasn't uncomfortable.

It showed each one of my curves, and gold stitching crossed over the fabric to leave diamond shapes from my hips to between my breasts. A thin strap landed at the start of my collarbone, leaving a gap in the sleeves until at my upper arms long flowing sleeves started, leaving my shoulder bare.

I expected them to pin up my hair, but they magnified my curls and took a great deal of time weaving tiny blue flowers into my locks. The last thing was the shimmering powders they put on my face. I swished in front of the mirror, barely recognizing myself. Pain stung my chest as I thought of Alcaius, and how much I missed him. He'd have loved the dress extensively and removing it even more. I frowned and closed my eyes to keep tears from destroying my face. We weren't together anymore, so it wouldn't have mattered if he saw me in the dress. My lip quivered, and I bit it. The mission was too important to give into the grief of losing him.

A troll woman entered the room and bowed. "Miss, the king requests your presence in the ballroom."

"Alright. I will be right there."

She backed out of the room and gave one final bow. I closed my eyes and took slow, deep breaths. Lingering in my heartbreak had to wait until I saved the dragons and the reaper who'd broken my heart. I stepped out of the room and focused on Strix to find my way to the ballroom. I stopped at the end of the hall to take in the abundance of people who'd joined the event.

"Azora," the deep voice I'd know anywhere said behind me.

CHAPTER TWENTY-THREE
WILLOW TREE
Azora

My heart fluttered because it wanted so badly to run to Alcaius. It proved worse when I turned around to see his dark hair sitting wildly on his head in the way he purposely made it chaotic. His golden eyes lit up above his blue leather armor. His gorgeous face stared back at me as he took two steps toward me.

He released a small gasp as his eyes took me in. "Never seen anything more beautiful in the entirety of my existence. This life or all the ones before it."

"You couldn't possibly know that."

"I do because there is no way anything could look more stunning than you."

"Flattery won't grant you forgiveness."

"Maybe I want an apology instead." His grin grew as the outrage growing in my chest probably spilled onto my face.

"Your skull is hollower than I imagined if you think that statement will help you."

He took more steps toward me. "You're acting pretty slighted for someone who moved on from us so quickly."

"Did you get your head bashed on a tree?"

"Sharing a horse with another man is an apparent sign you've moved on." His grin fell, and anger flashed through his eyes that he quickly suppressed.

I stepped back to put more distance between us. "That was because we didn't have a horse for Ashern, and he had just suffered a severe medical trauma that he needed to be watched for. What would have been better is if you had not assumed."

"The old man could have watched him on his horse."

"What does it matter, anyway? You're the one who said we were through, so if I want to share a horse with another man, that is my right." I spun around and marched into the crowd, using my sense to put greater distance between me and the charming asshole. Every once in a while, I caught him pushing through the crowd to get to me. I ran faster until I squeezed through enough people to make it into the ballroom. What I expected to be lots of people dancing was instead everyone on the edge of the dance floor, and Strix in the middle of the room, holding Thalassa's hand.

He stopped talking when he spotted me stumbling into the room. "Our honored guest has arrived! The human Azora brought the beautiful Queen of Dreams to our court."

Everyone cheered, and the attention on my clumsiness caused the room to spin, and I gripped the wall to steady myself. Strix started dancing with Thalassa, and that cued everyone else to grab their partner's hand as the fairy orchestra played a beautiful melody. I dashed into the dancers to blend in and avoid Alcaius. I bumped right into a firm leather body and looked up to see Ashern.

His gaped as I pulled away from him. "You make it difficult to breathe looking like that. It's irresponsible to slay as many men as you will tonight. You clean up nicely. Damn!"

"She does, so I suggest you find someone else to dance with before I send you off the balcony." Alcaius had found me in the few minutes I'd forgotten to track him.

His arms went around my waist, and I ducked away from him and back into the crowd.

"Can we just talk?"

"What's there to talk about? You made where you stand on us perfectly clear." I dodged spinning couples and tried to anticipate their movements.

"Let's talk about how much of an idiot I've been."

"I'm listening."

"I figured that would pique your interest." He grabbed my wrist. "Dance with me."

"Maybe I should go dance with Ashern." I charged toward where I sensed the Lord of Luck.

Alcaius growled like he'd become a beast. "You must not value his life." He shifted into a reaper.

"And you must not value having me in yours."

He turned back into his human form. "Talk to me!"

"All we've done is talk, and it's one big shouting match. You were right. Everything about us is incompatible. Lord of Death with a weak human seer."

He glared at the fourth couple who bumped into us like they were terrible for dancing on a dance floor. "Weak is the farthest thing from what you are."

"Yes, that's why it's one of your highest laws that we can't be together. We're so incompatible, but you chase me all across the lands while you have someone as perfect for you as Moirai ordained to be with you. I can list all the reasons she's a better match for you, and yet you still chase after me. The only explanation is you've gone mad!"

The room spun as the heat of all the bodies around me increased the dizziness that had started when I entered the room.

The tension on his face softened. "What is it?"

"Nothing. I need to get out of here. The room is too hot." I tried to push through the crowd that pushed back, slid to the ground, and buried my face in my knees as panic set in. "I can't breathe with all these people."

He picked me up and threw me over his shoulder. I could have kicked him and set myself free, but the giddy flutters in my chest threw my mind far from me. Not only that, but my need for cool air let him carry me into the garden courtyard.

He set me down on a stone bench next to a bunch of lilac bushes. "Are you alright?"

"I'm fine. It's suffocating with all those people. You didn't have to go all savage on me."

"You wanted out of the room, so I got you out of the room the quickest way possible."

"Well, thank you. I'll be on my way then." I hopped up and hurried into the garden as my sense told me it was the fastest way back to the room Strix had given me.

"Azora! I don't want any part of not being with you."

"Then why did you say it?"

"Because I'm a fool. You split me open and see everything about me, and that should make you run, but it doesn't."

"I've been running all night."

His face fell. "You're done with me, then? If you really want me gone, say it, and I'll leave."

"Why me? Explain that to me. How you can defy deities to reject your perfect mate, only to chase after me? Explain how that makes sense, and while you're at it, tell me how our lives can ever be compatible." I shoved aside the branches of a weeping willow to hide from all the other people who strolled through the garden. The branches did well to conceal us from any prying eyes.

Alcaius rushed forward and put one hand on my waist, reaching his other arm above my head and resting it on the tree. "All my life I have chased after feeling alive. The pull to death is so strong that my soul craved it, but I hated it. Early I learned the hold the darkness had on me like it turned me into someone I hated. The bleak depths of death were so easy to give into, but all I wanted was to feel alive. To feel something, to take away the weight of my depravity. I chased so many thrills and relationships, and all of them brought highs but none brought me close to the euphoria that reaping did. None until you."

I slowed my breathing to calm my heartbeat. "You can't mean that."

"The gods created me to desire reaping above everything else, but the high it brought left me empty far too soon after each assignment. When I found you, it started slow. Small moments that you amused me. Your indignation at something I said made me want more time with you, and before I knew it, I'd fallen into something with you I never expected. For the first time, I truly felt I understood what living meant. The Heir to Death is alive because a human seer showed him what it means. If we are so incompatible, Azora, why do we gravitate toward each other, like you and not death, are the purpose of my creation?"

I yanked him by the collar to meet my lips, and he responded with a greedy kiss, tugging me to him and pressing me against the tree like he desperately needed to merge with me. He hiked me onto his hips, pushing my dress up my leg and kissing and sucking on my neck. He smelled so good, like the forest and home. I undid his pants to free his hard length.

He grabbed my cheek and placed a deliciously harsh kiss. "Tell me if you want this to stop."

I kicked my dainty shoes off and used my feet to lower his pants. "Why would I ever want that?"

He rammed into me with small fast thrusts, like he needed to stay as deep as possible. Pain shot through my back as it scraped against the bark, and it mixed with each wave of pleasure surging and falling. His form twisted in shape until he transformed into the skeletal form that told me I was about to have his primal instincts take over the pleasure.

The thrill of it pulsed between my thighs, and I threw my head back. He teased me with his fangs against my shoulder. He slowed his thrusts but slammed as deep as he could go. I clawed at his back as he sent me over an edge that left me writhing in his arms and clenching around his cock. He bit into my shoulder as he came with me, and it elevated my orgasm through my entire body until I had no working muscles. Everything he did filled my body with an addictive bliss that made me forget why we'd been fighting.

I went limp, and he fixed my dress to cover me again. He held me against the tree as he adjusted his pants and positioned me against his chest, pushing aside the willow branches that had hidden our passion as he carried me through the garden and into a side door of the castle. The hall to the sleeping wing was mainly empty and lit only by dim lights on the ceiling. Alcaius opened the door to his room and placed me on the bed. He removed his pants before helping me out of my dress and brought me to the top of the bed with him, where he removed his shirt so we could sleep skin to skin.

He kissed my temple. "I love you."

I snuggled into his chest with a ferocious need to feel his heart beating against my cheek. "I love you."

We both fell into sleep.

I woke up the next morning with Alcaius still holding tight to me the way he always did after he thought he'd lost me. A strange feeling swirled in my mind that I had issues figuring out. It wasn't regret over what we'd done under the willow tree, but it was close. It hadn't fixed any of our problems. I maneuvered out of his arms with creative twists that I thought were sneaky enough.

He groaned and pulled me back to him. "Don't go."

"I need a bath."

"I'll join you?"

I pushed out of his arms and sat at the end of the bed and shivered at the cooler air hitting my naked body. "We still have a lot to talk about."

He sighed and said nothing for a few seconds. "I know. It's too much to think everything could be fixed now."

"It is too much."

"Right. We have a lot to talk about. Could we do so in the bath?"

I walked across the room, and he rumbled a small growl like he always did when I turned him hard. The bathtub was huge with four seats poking above the ground-level sides, and it made me wonder what kind of kinks everyone was into at Strix's castle. Not that I could judge when I'd screwed a full skeletal reaper on a Ferris wheel and under a willow tree. After seeing the tub's size, I told Alcaius he could join me after all, since we had adequate space to talk. I used the railing and steps to climb in the already warm water like they used natural hot springs to keep the tub filtered and warm. Soaps and oil sat on little shelves next to each of the chairs.

Alcaius climbed into the water with his cock looking clearly ready to repeat last night. "This is tepid."

"You can leave if it's too much. There is a shower behind that curtain, and it looks like the temperature may be adjustable." I looked through the different oils and chose rose and vanilla to pour into the water.

Reapers hated heat, and it often surprised me that Alcaius wanted to cuddle so closely to my human warmth.

"I'm fine. Just didn't expect it to be this hot." He slid over to the seat next to me. "Do you want me to wash your back?"

I wanted to say no out of principle of still feuding with him, but Alcaius washing me in the bath was one of my favorite things. I decided he should benefit as well. "Let me wash you."

He leaned over and locked his fingers with mine to pull me across the tub and onto his lap. I reached behind him for the white cloths and chose the cedar soap, since it already complemented his natural scent. He closed his eyes as I scrubbed the back of his neck and moved lower. His cock grew against me as I worked on his body. I scrubbed it, and he threw his head back, groaning as he became as hard as the surrounding granite. Alcaius grabbed my wrist and took the rag from me.

He chose a floral, citrus scent for me and ran the lathered cloth gently over my body. He only made it to my breasts when he started kissing and sucking on my neck. I tilted my neck to the side to give him full access. I moaned as he took the cloth lower and worked between my legs. We needed to talk. The why fled my mind as he circled my clit with his fingers. My body went rigid as it locked up, ready to orgasm. Just as I was about to let go by his fingers alone, he stopped.

He lifted my breast from the water and sucked on the nipple, spreading that pleasurable warmth through me. He pulled back with a smirk. "We should probably talk."

"Later," I gasped out as he shoved his fingers inside me and returned to my breasts, alternating his attention to them. I grinded against his lap. "More. Inside me. Now!"

"Are you sure? Maybe we should talk first."

"Alcaius!" I gasped his name.

He lifted me onto his cock while not removing his mouth from my breasts, and I bounced up and down, reveling in the friction his length inside me caused in pleasurable places. I cried as my orgasm hit, rocking my entire body with surges of pleasure. He kept the high flowing through me with the way he took over moving. He didn't release any venom this time, but still took me to floating, unaware of anything but the way his body brought mine to the Celestial Realm.

He lifted me from the water and bent me over the side of the rub, thrusting deep. He rolled his hips as he curled over my back while still holding my breast and working the nipple. The position pushed him so far inside me that I cried out as the sharp pains split me in a way that mixed with the pressure growing from my clit into my abdomen. Warmth spread everywhere until I burst, and he rode through my orgasm, slamming me into the granite until my vision blackened. The pleasure wouldn't stop as he kept it surging in shuddered blissful bursts. He took me there three more times before he came with me on the final time.

He finished washing me before wrapping me in a towel and carrying me from the washroom. He always rendered my legs useless and tucked me in bed when his body destroyed mine so thoroughly that I lived in rapture long after we'd finished. My muscles continued to fire, and I curled around him to ride through the lessening sensations. I couldn't stay with him for the sex alone, though I greatly wanted to.

"You're perfection personified," he whispered in my ear and kissed it.

I hummed in reply and fell back to sleep.

Chapter Twenty-Four
Fated Bonds
Alcaius

I woke up with Azora in my arms, and everything felt right again. Once again, I was reminded of how quickly she could slip away from me, whether by death or by her choosing to live life away from me. Life was frighteningly fragile, and something until Azora, I didn't know I could have. Her legs entangled with mine as she rested against my chest, and I ran my fingers down her spine. If we could pretend nothing existed outside the room, we could live there forever and never want for anything.

She broke up that wish by lifting her head and rolling off me. "We really need to talk. Our extreme attraction to each other won't build a solid relationship."

"It's a good foundation." I ran my hand over her silky shoulder.

The way she sat up and held the blanket just high enough to cover her nipples drove me insane.

She shoved my hand off. "Quit touching me. I really want you to touch me." The way her breathing quickened at my touch also drove me insane. Everything about her did in good and bad ways.

"If you want me to touch you, what is the issue?"

"We need to talk. You know this, but you distract by how perfectly you touch me. It will not fix things to keep having sex."

"It feels like a pretty good fix."

"If all we had to do was live in the bedroom, then maybe it would be enough. The world will tear us out of here sooner than we're ready for." She pointed to the window where the pink and orange of sunlight peeked in. "It's almost morning, and I have an important quest to complete. You can return to Zaire's house if you so choose."

"There's no way I chased you across two realms to leave you now."

"The dragons told me you couldn't be on this quest. That it would cause issues, but they changed their minds after Belphagor spoke with them. For some reason, he says you should be on this quest. However, you are a mighty distraction."

"A mighty one? That sounds serious."

"It is. You make it difficult to think sometimes with the looks you send me. They make me want to melt into your arms and ignore all the threats around us. They make me want to ignore what you are."

"A reaper." My eyes shifted away from her to the ground.

"Yes, and trust me when I say that I love you for everything you are. That's not the issue. You're so easy to love and reaping is who you are. That's not something that you can separate from, and it was something I thought I could live with until I saw you kill that man in the alley. The look of joy in your eyes at his demise chilled me." She moved to the edge of the bed and picked up my shirt from the floor to swim over her perfectly curved figure. "You're right though. That I killed too, in the arena." The shaking in her voice undid me.

"No, that was the dumbest thing I could have said to you. As soon as I said it, I regretted the words. In the arena, it was self-defense. You didn't enjoy it like I do when I kill." My chest and face burned hot with the familiar shame I usually escaped by killing someone who deserved it.

"This is what I mean. You deserve someone who isn't conflicted by what you were made to do. You aren't responsible for how I feel, and I can't separate my morals from you loving murder."

"Shouldn't I decide what I deserve? And it seems strange to me you are discussing how you see me as a monster, but you think feeling conflicted about that makes you unworthy of me." I moved away from her and leaned against the mahogany headboard.

"You're not a monster. You've convinced yourself that you are, but you are what you were designed to be."

"I was designed to be a monster, Azora. By every definition across cultures, that's what I am."

She climbed back under the covers and rolled over to face me. "You're what you tell yourself you are because it dictates your actions."

"And my actions also make me one. " I slid down, so we could talk face to face.

She ran her leg gently over mine. "I think maybe I need more time to think about us."

Twinges of fear hit my gut at the thought of not convincing her to stay with me. She scooted over and snuggled against me. I lifted her chin with two fingers, and she pushed up to meet my lips. I kissed her gently, moving over lips in slow sensual movements to show her I loved her. She returned my kiss and pressed closer, and my hand hands explored her body with no rush. Emotions and not lust fueled each way I kissed her and moved with her. I eased inside her, giving her time to adjust. I kept my thrusts deep and slow, simply wanting to feel her around me.

I kissed the tears from her face. "I love you, and I'm sorry."

She moved in rhythm with me and moaned, rolling her eyes back as she let go and rode out her orgasm. "I love you. Don't apologize for who you are. I need time to think it all through."

"That's fair. Take all the time you need. If I have to wait years for you, I will. Whatever it takes to have you in my arms like this again." I kept myself deep inside her, keeping my movements shallow to stay as intertwined with her for as long as possible.

"You shouldn't have to wait," she panted.

"There's nothing without you."

She placed her leg between mine and moved with me, kissing my lips, my ear, and then my neck. "If only this is all we had to be all the time, but you're a prince, and I'm a peasant."

"You're the woman I love more than my soul. The woman I eagerly damned myself for and would for the rest of eternity."

She sobbed into my chest, still keeping a gentle pace with me. My own tears joined hers as we came together, and I held onto her like a violent river wanted to rip her from me. When we fell still, I stayed inside her, and we slept.

When I woke again, the sun had clearly risen, and I reluctantly pulled myself away from Azora. By the look of the sun, we'd nearly slept all morning, and she needed to eat. I showered and put on my black leathers. I smiled at our pile of blue clothes and how Strix had matched us. My threats of violence every time he spoke of her had probably given my feelings for her away.

He'd placed us in the royal wing, so it wasn't a complete surprise when he exited a room down the hall. King Strix beamed and shot toward me with his arms outstretched, forcing me into a hug as he vigorously smacked my back. "Son of Death, your woman is everything."

I tensed. "Yes, she is *my* woman."

He released me and beat my back while guffawing. "Yes, yes, I would not fuck your queen. No worries there. I have my own now. That's what we were doing all night long, thanks to your woman. Tell her thank you."

"I will. Thank you for the accommodations."

"Not a big deal at all. It's the least I could do for gaining the best night of my life. I have something to discuss with you if you would follow me." He put his arm over my shoulder and pushed me down the hall. "Let's discuss over breakfast."

It took all my willpower not to shove him away, but I'd play nice because we still needed to safely leave his kingdom. "That's what I was searching for, but I need to bring it back to Azora. She needs to eat before we depart."

"Your departure is what we need to discuss. There is a slight uprising on the border of my lands. Angry sandmen."

"Should we be concerned?"

He shoved me through the dining room door in front of him. "Your woman started a war, but all is well because she brought me Thalassa. It rids me of any malice I'd otherwise feel over it. Take any seat you'd like, though I recommend one close to the head to hear me speak."

The black table extended all the way across the extensive room, with a small walking space on either side. The chairs, also black, were heavy and plain, with only the grey cushions giving them any kind of distinction. If it hadn't been for my mother, I imagined my father's castle would have looked much the same, but with an added touch of gore. I chose the seat next to his large one at the head of the table, next to a grand stone fireplace.

Strix took his seat, and food was rushed to us. "My sandmen are unhappy with my decision to grant Azora's requests."

"Her requests?"

"She didn't tell you?" He snickered and reached over to smack my chest. "I suppose you had other things to occupy yourselves last night, but she required payment to convince Thalassa to come to my ball. I would have paid any price, mind you."

"What did she want?"

He gulped down his wine and slammed his cup on the table. "To save her friend from being eaten and to free the familiars from the mage wars. It was something that wasn't a big deal to me. My sandmen thought differently, so I suggest you take the sea to the north. I will provide you with a ship and crew to take you on the next leg of your journey. To the east, I believe Azora said." He broke a loaf of bread and dipped a piece into butter before gnawing on it and sending crumbs everywhere.

"Yes, we need to go southeast. Is there anything we should worry about traveling that way?"

"No, it should be pretty peaceful until you circle around into Drien's Gulf. A few sea monsters and sirens live there, but it shouldn't be terrible."

We continued our breakfast, and he sent me back to my room with a large plate, juice, and a sealed bottle of wine. I pushed the cart into our room to find Azora finishing her shower. As tempting as it was to join her, I'd give her the space she'd requested as we'd made love.

She emerged from the bathroom in her traveling leathers, pinning up her brown curly hair in a bun. "That smells delightful. You brought me breakfast?"

"Yes, at almost noon. It was intended to be in bed, but King Strix caught me in the hall and told me some dire things about our travels."

"What kind of things?"

I told her the news of the sandman war. "It's not a big deal. King Strix is giving us a ship and crew for the journey."

"I caused quite a bit of problems, it seems. Can't say that I care much. Those sandmen do terrible things." She grabbed a silver plate and piled fruit and scones on it. "We should save the wine for a time we are bored."

"Probably best, as it seems a pretty strong blend."

She grinned and stuck it in her bag. "Maybe while we are traveling across the sea without much else to do."

"I could go for that."

She took the plate over to the bed and rested against the headboard, crossing her legs at the ankle. "There are more things we need to talk about."

"Yes, I know. Like where we stand. Are we together still, and you only need space, or are we still separated?" I took some of the meat and poured tea into a porcelain floral cup to join her. Once I was next to her, I finished my first bite of meat and anxiously waited for her reply.

She sipped on her juice and set it on the bedside table. "You're the one that said we were no longer together." She held up her finger when I opened my mouth. "Here me out. Yes, you said that in anger, but I think you meant some of it, too."

My heart fell into my stomach at her interpretation. "I didn't. Some people might believe all things said in a heated moment are deep down what a person thinks or wants, but it isn't for me. I say a lot of dumb things when angry. My impulsive nature is an idiot."

"Maybe. However, I think we both have some things to sort, and we should take time apart to think everything through and decide what we want."

"There's no thinking anything through for me. I've had way too much time away from you lately. You're everything I want. My future. All of it."

Her lip trembled, and she bit it, turning away from me. "There is something I need to tell you, and it will most likely change your mind."

Heat flowed through my cheeks as I felt the reaper bursting through. "Do I need to kill Ashern?"

"Jealous temper chill. You have nothing to worry about with Ashern, no matter how cute you are when you're jealous."

"Cute? You find my rage cute?"

"Yes." She giggled. "Yes, I do. Let's move on from that. Do you know how it works at the fate gate?"

"Yeah, I went through the fate gate. You have to give up a thread to something you might have had. It's usually insignificant. This time I didn't have to because my brother went crazy and killed all the guardians there."

"He did?"

"Yes, and collected all the stolen fates for whatever reason. What did you give up?"

She nibbled on her toast for several seconds as the tension heightened in the room. "All three choices were big things. The whole thing got me thinking more about how we don't belong together."

"That's strange. They made you choose between large threads of your fate?"

"I'm not sure. To me, they were all things I wanted for my future and all had to do with you. There wasn't a single choice that didn't mean losing something with you."

I squinted, trying to make sense of what she said. "What did you give up with me?"

"The chance to live a hundred years with you and give you an heir."

Something I'd never thought of before hit me like a boulder cata-pulted into my chest. "Humans rarely live even a hundred years. That's something I guess I should have realized and makes little sense how you would have even had a thread to that."

"That's what you're concerned about? That I'm not going to live a hundred years. Not the heir part?"

"I'd give up any chance of an heir if it meant I wouldn't live cen-turies after you."

She blinked and scratched her eye. "You're such a beautiful fool."

"What were the other two that you didn't give up?"

"Simple moments with you. Peaceful, perfect moments of just ex-isting together. The last is confusing to me, and I don't know how it's possible. Maybe it should have been the one I chose, but I thought there was no future with you if I threw it out. It was me as your queen, and your people happy about it."

"I like that one. I like it a lot." I slipped my hand into hers and squeezed. "Something isn't right. You should have had a variety of choices."

"The Fates are angry about the rift and the dragons. I messed up so bad, and it was all for selfish reasons. Belial was about to give me everything I wanted if I opened it. Big fates were probably another punishment."

I ran my thumb over the back of her hand. "Anyone would have done the same when presented with everything they wanted. What most people wouldn't have done is stop when they realized how badly getting everything would hurt others."

"I don't think that's true."

"It is. Most people would let the world unravel to get what they wanted. I would have."

"You wouldn't have."

"Yes, Azora, I would have. I'd let the world become dust for you."

She leaned her head on my shoulder. "Like I said, you make it very easy to love you."

"And very difficult."

"That's what you tell yourself to be true." She took a deep breath and kissed my shoulder. "There's something else."

"Great. Go ahead."

She lifted her shirt and sat up on her knees to show me opal shining diamond scales right under her ribs, below her heart. It rested flat on her skin like a tattoo. "This happened in the arena."

"How did I miss this with how naked we've been?"

"It disappeared right after the arena fight, and then in the shower this morning it came back. It's a—"

"Dragon marking. A dragon claimed you?"

"Yeah, I don't know exactly what that means. The dragon said he needed to go to sleep for the bond to take."

I touched it again, and it spread ice into my joints. "He must be awake and has fully gone through with the bond. What kind was he?"

"All he told me was his name is Eiro, and he's an Oblivion dragon."

My eyes darted to hers. "That's impossible."

"Why? Why do you look so horrified?"

"He had to have told you wrong. I'll be back." I marched from the room and didn't stop until I found an empty room. "Belphagor!" I yelled his name over and over, demanding his presence.

"No need to shout. What do you want, son of Death?" He sounded irritated, but his small shoulder flames showed it as a minor reaction.

"Since when do your dragons bond with people?"

"Since Azora became valuable to me."

"Whatever you have planned, figure it out without her."

"No, there is no other way."

I charged him, slamming him against the wall and placing my forearm on his throat. "You will find another way!"

"I've told you, it will be her choice to go with me."

"How will you force her to think she has no choice?"

"It will be her choice. Just because you can't fathom that doesn't mean she won't of her own free will. Do you not know her? How many times has she run from you for something she believes in?"

"A bond with an Oblivion dragon will kill her if it uses too much power while connected to her. You know this."

"Not Azora. I told you from the very beginning of your relationship with her that she is a lot more than she seems. What I have also told you is she is valuable to me, and I would never do anything to kill her. That should tell you something."

I shoved him away from me. "Find a different way to fulfill whatever you're chasing, or I'll kill you with my own two hands."

"You say that like it would be a bad thing." He disappeared.

I paced the room and jumped as a hand touched my arm.

Moirai put her hands up. "You were shouting. I'd know your voice anywhere."

"Stop acting like we had such a fantastic connection." The anger I'd directed at Belphagor was still loud, and Moirai wasn't helping it diminish.

She stuck her lower lip out. "But we had a great bond throughout school."

"We're not in school anymore. I know what you did."

"Which thing is that?" She puffed out her chest to show off her cleavage.

"You changed Azora's fate threads at the gate. Gave her no choice but to lose something with me."

"It was deserved. Because of that whore—"

"Watch your mouth when it comes to her!"

"I only state the truth. Because of your pretty human toy, I had to give up a fate too, and it doesn't matter how big or small it was. As the daughter of Destiny, I'm always exempt until this stupid quest with her. If it wasn't for the dragons, for you, I wouldn't be here. All of this is on Azora." She lunged forward and kissed me.

I took hold of her wrist and pried her away from me. "Never touch me again! And if you harm Azora in any capacity, I have no trouble sending you to the executioners for judgment."

"Didn't our relationship mean anything to you?" She pressed her lips, and tears welled in her eyes.

"At which point should it have meant something to me?"

"Because the Celestials said it should. We're destined to be together, and you defy it. That makes no sense. How can you deny us when we are perfect for each other?"

I grabbed her wrist again as she went to touch my chest. "I said don't touch me. All the Celestials did was force a match I never wanted on me. You cared more about image than you ever did about me. You're still pushing boundaries."

"They should have held you accountable for breaking the betrothal. For you not making me your mate. Your father shouldn't have stepped in."

"It was the one time he did something for my benefit, and the fact you want me punished for wanting a choice is a big reason we aren't together. It sums up a large portion of our toxicity." I stormed out of the room and nearly bumped into Ashern in the hall.

"Azora is my friend, Alcaius," he said.

"It's not a good time for you to talk about what Azora is to you."

"You and Moirai?" He threw his thumb toward the room she hadn't left.

"Are not friends." I continued down the hall before I punched someone into their next life.

Chapter Twenty-Five
Restless Travels
Azora

S omeone knocked at Alcaius's door, and I opened it, expecting it to be anyone but Moderatus. He was the elemental I'd least talked to on our quest.

"Alcaius just left. I'm not sure where he went, but you're welcome to wait for him." I opened the door for him to step inside.

Moderatus accepted my invitation and sat in a chair close to the window. His posture was the straightest I'd ever seen a person hold, and he looked even taller than his large stature already did. "I'm here to speak with you. Moirai saw you entering this room with Alcaius last night. When I went to check your room, it was vacant of you."

My cheeks burned at the thought of Moirai seeing Alcaius and me entering a room full of lust, and then the thought made me smile. "Yeah, I've been here. What did you need?"

"King Strix wants us to meet in the eastern courtyard within the next hour. He has sent me as the messenger like I am a servant."

"I'm sorry he's diminished your status."

"Only I can do that. He is lucky I agreed to this."

"He is. I will be there. Moderatus, while you are here, I have a couple of questions."

He bowed his head. "You, I am here to serve."

"I feel honored."

"It is the wish of the dragons," he said.

"Oh, right. Ummm... You're a scholar. Ashern mentioned that, and I have a couple of questions. What do you know about Oblivion dragons?"

"They are the most mysterious dragon. Not a lot is known about them as they keep to their own kind and don't appreciate the alliances of other dragons."

"Do you know anything about what they can do?"

"Not entirely. It is probably similar to other dragon types that are connected to elementals. They can do things similar to what their connected elemental tribes can do. Possibly other things as well."

"What can Oblivions do?"

He stood and clasped his hands in front of him as if to serve as a warning that he tired of my questions. "They also hide, but less than their dragons. It varies, but what is known is they can teleport, change their size, see through time and manipulate it, and send people to voids."

"That's frightening."

"Yes, they are dangerous and only kept in line by the Accounters and Celestials." He stepped to the door, facing me at all times and reaching for the doorknob.

"Moderatus, what would happen if an Oblivion dragon bonded a human?"

His hand dropped. "They don't bond at all, let alone humans. A human would be far beneath them. It wouldn't be done. Their pride would see to that."

"But what if they did?"

"I don't enjoy operating in theories, but they hold great power. The human couldn't handle it. It's the same reason Death dragons don't bond with humans. Every human they do is obliterated. Oblivion dragons are even more powerful. I imagine they know this. Maybe tried it long ago."

"Maybe humans die when they bond Death dragons because death is in the name."

"No. I must be going." He opened the door and walked down the hall with his perfect posture, using small strides that looked swift for his calm demeanor.

I shut the door behind him and went over to the mirror. "Did you bond with me just to kill me, Eiro?"

I thought maybe he'd answer me in my head or out loud but no reply arrived.

Alcaius burst back into the room and slammed the door, looking as angry as when he'd left. He threw things in his bag as quickly yet organized as he could for someone looking like they wanted to start a century-long war.

I hopped off the bed, ready to go to my room, which had only ended up being storage space for my belongings. "What is it?"

"What interactions have you had with Belphagor? You mentioned him earlier. He's been talking to you?"

"Yes, he helped me in the dream realm when I had to speak with Thalassa. He also told me the dragon was a gift to me. That was pretty intrusive on his part to assume I'd want a dragon bond, but all the elementals seem to think they are entitled to things."

He stopped packing and looked over at me. "I'm an elemental."

"Yes, exactly." I kept a straight face for only a second before I broke into laughter.

The anger melted from his face, and he strode across the room and wrapped his arms around my waist. "What exactly do you think I feel I am entitled to that I am not?"

"Me."

"Maybe it's that I don't care if I'm entitled to you or not. I want you so deep in my bones that I will crawl over hell's fire to reach you."

"You're oh so dramatic, my reaper."

"Only when it comes to you." He swooped me back and kissed me until I wanted to forget our quest and return to the bed.

When we finally came up for air, I pressed my ear to his chest, letting his heartbeat lull me into a near trance. "Your temper is most dramatic when it concerns me. You can't commit violence on any minor threat to me."

"Sure I can."

"The guard looking at me sternly doesn't always mean anything. His thoughts could simply be wandering."

"And that will never happen again in your direction," he said.

"You're ridiculous. We need to get going on the quest. We're already so far behind, but first, tell me, what has you so angry?"

"Belphagor says you're going to go willingly with him into the rift. He can see threads in time the way the Fates see them with destinies, but he's also an Oblivion elemental. They are manipulative, and he knows we are aware he can see the future, so he could be saying all of it to make us think it's a firm prediction."

"There's no way I'm going near that rift again. The horrors I saw escaping it are burned into my mind." I shuddered. "There's no way I would."

"That's what he keeps saying, that you'll go by choice. Something about the way he insists is disturbing. There's no way you can go into the rift with him."

"I leaked terrible things from it without realizing it. There's no way I'd risk it again after everything we're doing to remedy it." I hugged him and gave him a quick kiss. "Trust me, and don't worry so much."

"You aren't the one I don't trust."

"Fair. I have to go pack and will meet you in the eastern courtyard. While you were gone, Moderatus stopped by and told me that's where Strix would like us to be in about an hour." I left to finish preparations and returned to my room.

The courtyard was surrounded by a beautiful garden that gave the only color in the entire nightmare realm. My mother lived to garden and kept a pretty one outside our house until grief over Lowan consumed her too much and she had to go live with the fae for recovery. Alcaius had paid enough money for her to stay with them indefinitely. I often missed her and wondered if I'd ever see her again. The fae traveled in flying cities and were not easily found. She'd most likely have to search for me and my siblings if we were ever to be reunited. She had, in the time I'd had with her, taught me a lot about plants. That was how I knew the deadly ones that grew all around King Strix's garden. It seemed fitting that the only color he allowed to live in his land carried a fatal bite.

Red rosary peas with their black eyes and white hemlock grew next to the less colorful nightshade. Dire thorns and troll thistle stood out the brightest with their blues and purples. Many I didn't recognize, and it was easy to guess the entire garden was a botanical sanctuary for potent beauty. The courtyard had dark grey stones that spiraled in like a nautilus shell, and white stones spread out everywhere else.

Moderatus stood in front of Moirai, who was leaning forward as they discussed something. I held back until Elisha showed up, and they stepped away from each other. I went to enter to circle until Ashern called my name.

He jogged to catch up and put his hands on his upper thighs. "We need to talk."

"Can it wait? We're supposed to meet everyone right now," I said.

"No, it can't" His eyes darted to Alcaius walking up behind us, and he bolted for the circle.

Fennec walked beside his brother, and we entered the circle together. Moirai, who I hadn't seen since the storm separated us, scowled at me, but I had a better understanding of her attitude. All her lavender braids were down, and she'd added a few new items to them. Alcaius met her gaze and wrapped his arms around me, which deepened Moirai's glare. We waited in silence until it was disturbed by King Strix's laughter and clapping. He had a group of about ten Oblivions with him. Their bald heads and shoulder flames gave what they truly were away.

Strix twirled and clapped, spreading his arms out to all of us. "Everyone is here! Wonderful! These men behind me have been gifted to you by the Oblivion King. They are to protect you on your journey. He said you're going to need them where you're heading. Don't let that unsettle you."

"We don't need them." Alcaius pulled me closer to him like he wanted to protect me from the Oblivions.

Ashern threw his hands up. "If they want to sacrifice themselves for our well-being, we should take it."

"Coward," Alcaius said.

"Okay." I wiggled out of Alcaius's lung-crushing hold. "It can't hurt to have extra help. The important thing is to make it the elders."

Ashern raised his hand. "How many vote to let the Oblivion protectors stay?"

Everyone but Alcaius raised their hand, and we followed Strix and his mercenary party down to the northern docks, where a massive black ship was waiting for us. An abundance of red sails fluttered in the wind above the ship's deck. The ship appeared to have several levels below the main one and halfway across had a level that looked good for stargazing with several tables and chairs throughout the upper section. Men at the top lowered the ramp and let us all on board. The bottom of the ship had lots of suites that we were assigned. They gave Alcaius and me separate rooms. Odds were we'd share one by the end of the journey. He insisted our rooms touched, so it would be easy to slip from one to the other. Each suite had a shower, toilet, and sink, along with the normal bedroom features and a table and two chairs.

The captain gave us a tour around the ship and told us the times meals were served. The kitchen stayed open for in-between snacks, as Strix had stocked everything well for our departure. We ate dinner together in the main dining area as the ship left the port. King Strix and Thalassa waved from the shore. It didn't take long for my prediction to prove true. Alcaius knocked on my door only minutes after I entered my room.

He popped his head in when I answered him. "I thought we could shower together."

"They aren't the biggest showers. You can come in."

He shut the door behind him and set his fresh clothes and towel on the table. "We don't need much space, do we?"

"No, I guess not, but I thought we were taking a break?" I stared at his bare chest with its perfectly defined muscles and wondered why I'd even agreed to such a thing as a break for us.

"Who says anything has to happen?" His eyes smiled, and he leaned back with his palms resting on the bed behind him, giving an even better view of his abs.

"You know we can't be naked in a shower together without doing something. It goes against all universal laws."

"That shows exactly how much chemistry we have and proves we belong together." He got up and put his arms around me, resting his forehead on mine. "Do you feel the same electricity rolling across your skin as I do?" He used his low voice and enunciated each word in a way that stopped my breathing until he finished speaking.

I gripped his wrist. "A break doesn't mean we can't enjoy ourselves in the place with not much to do."

"Exactly."

I crossed my arms and lifted my shirt, freeing my breasts. He licked his lips but stopped moving toward me when I smiled and shook my head. I removed the rest of my outfit and stood naked in front of him. A low rumble escaped his throat, and his eyes filled with hunger. I sashayed to the shower, turned on the water, and started washing my hair and body. His eyes stayed on me like a wolf about to pounce on a deer. I washed between my legs, dropping the rag and circling my fingers over my clit. I bent forward, bracing myself with my free hand on the wall.

He couldn't stand it anymore and charged forward. "That's mine to touch." He replaced my fingers with his and pushed me into the icy wall. His cock played at my entrance while his fingers kneaded, flapped, and circled in a pattern that had me squirming and pleading for him to take me further.

He went still and nibbled and sucked on my ear, and I nearly screamed at the pleasure that ripped through my body. "Don't you dare let go yet!"

I threw my head back against his shoulder. "Stop torturing me."

"As you wish." He slammed into my entrance as deep as he could go as he returned to worshiping my clit. He thrust so fast the climbing sensations seemed to rip me in two as everything locked up and released. Stars swirled in my vision, and I shook as he took me into an orgasm that wouldn't let up. I rode it out, screaming, and he did nothing to stop me as he slammed into me over and over. The entirety of the ship most likely heard my cries of elation. The pleasure felt like it carried on for hours and didn't leave any part of me untouched. I didn't even know if I existed at the point he destroyed me for anything else for the night.

He finished his shower while holding me upright. "All spent, my love?"

I moaned and rolled my eyes back as more orgasmic aftershocks rocked my body.

He turned his head and kissed my temple. "I'll take that as a yes. Let's get you to bed." He dried us off and tucked us both under the covers. My exhausted body slowly eased down from the high and allowed me peaceful sleep.

Over the next few days, we traveled on the ocean, and Alcaius and I found new places to entertain ourselves, including a supply closet and under the stairs. When we'd stayed in my house for all those weeks, we were each other's greatest distraction. The biggest problem was I knew none of our issues had been resolved, and we only ignored them. I sat on Alcaius's lap after our latest session. He had his back against the wall behind my bed. My legs wrapped around him, and we kissed, drawing things out in no hurry. It was a simple way to enjoy each other.

He pulled back. "Do you hear that?"

"What?"

"The tapping."

I listened for a bit, and sure enough, something rapidly tapped. "The window, I think." I crawled off his lap and peeked out our small window, jumping back as the blackbird fluttered at the glass. "I believe one of your father's messengers has come to say hello."

"Yes, he has. That reminds me of something I forgot to mention. Can you give me a minute?"

I scooped his shirt from the ground and put it on, followed by my soft blue sleeping pants. "The stars look nice, and I haven't been on the deck at night. I'll head up there." I reached into my bag to grab a light stick, but something cold brushed my fingers that I took from the bag. "Our wine. We should enjoy this tonight. The captain says we have a few more boring days."

The bird tapped the window more rapidly.

"Go ahead, and I'll join you later."

I slipped out the door and went up to the top deck that had green cushioned seating and a hammock that Ashern occupied with his hands behind his head.

He removed his eyes from the stars to glance at me. "Hey! I've been needing to talk to you."

"Yeah, I remember in the courtyard." I took a chair across from him and set the bottle on a small table.

ELAIA CROWE

"You've grown on me, so I say what I'm about to from the best place."

"A disclaimer is never a good way to start a conversation."

"That's because it's not exactly the best thing." He swung his legs over the edge of the hammock, so he was facing me. "The morning after the ball, I was heading to go pack after breakfast. As I strolled past a room, I saw Alcaius and Moirai kissing."

I laughed and forced down the anger that wanted to boil from my gut. "There has to be an explanation. How long did you watch? What kind of kiss was it?"

"Does it matter? It was on the lips. I didn't watch long because it felt awkward."

"I appreciate you telling me this because it's what a loyal friend would do. However, I trust my reaper and will hear his side through before judgment."

"That's why you'll last."

I studied the sea-stained deck. "I hope so. There are many things we have to overcome."

"Trust and communication are barriers most can't deal with. But now that I can rest with you knowing, let's have some fun." He jerked his head toward the wine as he rolled out of the hammock and studied the bottle. "This is the good stuff. Probably a bit on the strong side. Will get you drunk pretty fast."

"Are you saying I can't hold my liquor?"

"I'm assuming so, since you are a human. Let me go get us some glasses." Ashern left and returned with two small cups. He pried the bottle open, poured us each a glass, and brought out his dice. "Every time one of us rolls doubles, the other has to take a drink. You get to keep rolling until you do." He tossed the little cubes to me. "You go first."

"Simple enough." It took me six rolls to finally roll two threes.

Ashern downed a big gulp of the wine and rolled twice to get double ones.

I swallowed nearly half my glass. "This is delicious."

"Slow down or this won't last very long."

We went back and forth, and he rolled doubles faster than me.

The entire bottle emptied, and I tipped it to get every drop. "No more." My lower lip plopped out.

"You've had enough." Ashern sounded completely sober as far as I could tell with how drunk I clearly was.

"We didn't save any for Alcaius." I blinked slowly several times. "Everything spins." I tried to stand up and plopped back on my butt."

"Did you get her drunk?" Two Alcaisuses stood at the edge of the stairs.

I lifted my finger and attempted to point. "Which one of you is real?"

Chapter Twenty-Six
Siren's Call
Alcaius

Azora carried the wine from the room, and I waited until the door shut to zip up my pants and let the crow inside.

He flew over to the table. "Your father says you are too slow. Have you located the box yet?"

"Not yet. There have been a few bumps. Nothing too terrible, but they have caused delays. Tell him there is nothing wrong."

He stretched out his long wings and cawed. "If there are bumps, something is wrong."

"It's only delayed things and is no longer any concern."

"He is also unhappy you have taken Fennec with you."

"He just noticed Fennec is gone?" I shook my head and rolled my eyes. "Figures it took him that long notice."

"Fennec often goes where he wants, and it was not abnormal for him to be missing for some time. However, I saw him the last time I brought you a message and informed your father of the development. He wants you to send him back."

"Fennec does what he wants, and nothing I say will convince him to leave. You're welcome to talk to him yourself if you think your persuasion skills are superior. Also, how you expect him to head home on the open ocean is a little baffling."

"The next time you are on shore. He needs to strongly consider it."
He flew back to the window ledge.

"I'll give him a stern lecture on the matter. Tell my father he'll have his box soon enough."

"Let's hope for the seer's sake that he does."

I lunged for the window and slammed it on his tail feathers. "Is that a threat against Azora?"

He fought to free himself and let out a stream of frantic caws. "Let me go!"

"Stop any thought of harm to Azora or next time It'll be your neck smashed." I opened the window, freeing him back in the sky to whine to my father.

I stopped at my room since Azora had stolen my shirt from the floor. It did things to me to see my shirt on her, and I'd let her steal a hundred of my shirts if she wanted. I took a shower and left to see Fennec, knocking on his door.

He opened it and yawned. "Been a while since I've seen you with how occupied you've kept yourself screwing like it's a new amusement for you. With my room right next to hers, it's been a disturbing few days."

"You can always tell me how jealous you are."

"Jealousy does nothing and therefore is a nonsense emotion that causes more harm than good. What do you need?"

"Father sent Darren. He wanted me to tell you Father knows you came with me and wants you to return home," I said.

"No, I've come this far that it would make little sense to turn around so close to the end. He has no say on my choices. The Determiners approved my leave."

"You used your one and only leave to go on this quest with me? Why would you do that?" Reapers were allowed to ask for one leave of absence with no questions asked. All other leave had to fall into a very strict category like a wedding or the birth of a child. It surprised me he'd give that up to come with me.

"There was nothing else I'd use it for. Reaping is my favorite thing, and therefore, I only want to leave for something I care about more. Is that all you need?"

"Yeah, that was it. I don't know what to say."

"Nothing needs to be said." He shut his door.

Azora was waiting for me at the top deck, and I guessed she'd probably fallen asleep waiting for me to join her for wine and stargazing. I heard her slurred words before I made it to the top of the stairs. I ran the rest of the way up, and my body loosened like it did when it was about to shift into a reaper. "Did you get her drunk?" I stood ready to pummel the son of Luck.

Azora lifted her hand that plopped quickly back to her side." Which one of you is real?"

"What were you thinking, letting her drink that much?"

Ashern picked at his fingernail, looking undisturbed by my outrage. "Last time I checked, she can make her own decisions."

"She doesn't know how dangerous it is to drink that much elemental wine. She's a mortal!"

"I warned her, but she wanted to play a game. You should loosen up if you want to keep her in your life."

"You think you can get her drunk and make a move? That's what this was. You couldn't get her to do anything with you sober."

"Woah! Slow down there. What exactly are you accusing me of?"

"You heard exactly what I'm accusing you of." My reaper rippled under my skin, urging me to release it.

"I'm not the one letting another woman enter my tent or kiss me. Playing both of them while accusing me of the worst sort of ethics."

I launched at him, and he caught my fall with a punch to my jaw. His chair tipped, and we crashed to the floor, beating on each other. Blood burst from his nose as I broke it, and he slammed his forehead into mine. He kneed my stomach, knocking the wind out of me, but I powered through to crack his jaw.

"Alcaius!" Fennec, yelling my name, jolted me from my blind rage.

I stopped beating Ashern to look over at him, and Ashern took that distraction to land a hard blow on my temple. Everything spun, and I landed one last punch between his eyes.

"Alcaius! Azora!" Fennec kicked me, and it cleared my thoughts and gathered Ashern's attention, so that we both stopped fighting to see Azora balancing poorly on the side of the ship. She wobbled, ready to plunge into the ocean.

I jumped up in one swift movement. "Baby! Come down from there!"

She put one foot in front of the other, nearly losing her footing each time. "I fwing!"

"Come down from there and we'll find other ways for you to fly." I shot toward her, but before I could reach her, a massive cavity full of triangular teeth leaped from the water and yanked her into the ocean with it.

It took way too long for me to process what had happened. When I got to the edge, I searched for anything moving in the water. Once again, I needed Azora's ability more than she did. Sheer panic turned everything in me to ice. She was going to die with no body for recovery this time. No chance of getting her back, even though I knew her soul couldn't be returned a third time.

Ashern stood next to me on the edge of the ship, and it took all my willpower not to shove him into the waves. Blood ran down his nose and two black rings had formed around his eyes. That left enough satisfaction that I restrained myself.

He spread his arms out. "I know what to do. Give me a moment. Sea monsters are something I know. Let me speak with this one."

"You can speak to them?"

"When I am of the utmost need, my luck shifts to positive with skills I've practiced."

The wind picked up, and Ashern teetered on the edge. I held onto his arm to steady him with my superior balance, that did not falter. He glowed blue as his lips moved, but nothing audible exited them. His expression grew as intense as my impatience, and I wanted to demand an update. Not wanting to break his trance, I tried to focus on the rolling waves instead.

He hopped off the edge and sunk into a chair, running his fingers through his rusty red hair. "He's taken her to the sirens."

"Why would he do that and not just eat her?"

"You'd rather her be eaten?"

"No, but you could have asked him to spit her back out."

He touched his face and stared at the blood on his fingers. "It's something he does as part of a deal he made with them. He brings them sailors and maidens in exchange for them sending the fish he loves most his way."

"What happened to them patiently waiting on the rocks and singing?"

"Laziness has entered their mix."

"Or efficiency," Fennec said. He'd taken a chair close by without me noticing him.

I pointed toward the lower deck. "Fennec, go tell the captain we have to take a brief detour. How do we get to the sirens? We have a kingdom to rip to shreds."

"We need to plan that doesn't involve starting a war."

"A war they already initiated by taking Azora.

Ashern hopped back onto the deck. "They live in this cove quite a bit out of our way. He already dropped her off because of how swiftly he swims. He can open small portals for short distances that make him even faster. There's no way we could have caught him. It'll be grueling. There's no other choice. We have to get her back."

"We will." I stood up to gather the others and form a good plan for rescuing her.

"Look, Alcaius. I'm sorry about all of this. Let's not start a feud over this." Ashern stuck his hand out for me to shake.

I stepped around him. "I'll consider it when she's back in my arms."

The captain turned the ship toward the cove, and all of us sat in his office discussing how dangerous yet necessary the quest would be. He had large fish mounted on his walls attached to wooden planks. Dozens covered an entire wall behind his desk, and the other walls displayed maps of several realms. He stroked his long white beard as the rest of us spoke.

"They're tricky folk. The sirens have slaughtered many of my men," the captain said.

I studied the map on the wall. "Are you not wanting to risk it? We could take the lifeboats and go after her ourselves."

He slammed a large curved knife into his desk. "I never run from a fight, boy!"

"I didn't imply that. It would make sense if you wanted to look out for your own first."

"King Strix has commanded we take you wherever you need and paid us, and we will follow through with that duty. It will not be easy and many lives will probably be lost as the sirens are a difficult foe. They need battled or they will continue their destruction."

We spent the next few hours methodically working out all the details of our plan. As the sun rose, we all tired. We returned to our cabins to rest until we reached the cove. The closer we got, the more my rage grew at the audacity of the sirens to steal the woman I loved.

I never slept much as it was, and with Azora gone, it was nearly impossible. We traveled for the next few days, and the captain informed us we'd reach the sirens in the next two hours. Moderatus, Elisha, Moirai, Ashern, and Fennec were all in the captain's office when I arrived for the final briefing of the plan. We discussed everyone's roles, and it seemed we were set. We'd planned everything down to the smallest detail over the last few days, and I obsessed over it because we couldn't risk losing Azora. I couldn't. Nothing would remain of me with her gone. If she was lost to us, I'd slaughter the sirens and turn myself in to the executioners, hoping they sent me to the same place as her. If they did not, my soul would spend eternity finding a way to hers.

Someone knocked, and the captain swung open the door. "I told you not to disturb us!"

The sailor removed his hat and held it at his chest. "Sorry, sir, but the woman is back and asking for the reaper."

"Azora? Azora is back?"

"Y-yeah, the sea monster set her on the deck."

I shoved past them to the main deck, where Azora sat with her face buried in her knees.

"Azora!" I kneeled in front of her. "Baby?"

She sniffled as her puffy, worn eyes met mine. A lifetime had been lived in those eyes since I'd last seen her was exactly what her expression conveyed. I scooped her up and headed for her room.

"Do we still fight the sirens?" the captain shouted.

"No, return to the original destination."

"Blast it! I wanted to kill me some sirens! Men turn the sails back to the east."

I got her into the room and out of drenched clothes that smelled of sea and fish. "Shower?"

She nodded and let her tears fall freely. I'd missed them at first because water droplets covered her. She was frigid to the touch, like ice had spread to her bones. A chair from the dining set fit well in the shower to keep her stable as I made sure the water reached the right temperature to not shock her body. She shook, nearing convulsions as I set her under the flow. I lathered a rag with her favorite soap that smelled of roses and cleaned all the sand and seaweed from her skin, slowly adjusting the water to warm her. I wrapped her in towels and got her under the covers. My skin heated to an uncomfortable level, and I kept it that way for her sake.

Once we settled in bed, she sobbed into my chest, and it would be much later before I would ask her what had happened. She trembled, and I focused on stabilizing her temperature. Even as she slept, the shivers continued. Finally, by morning her body calmed, and I was able to lower my heat.

She opened her eyes and brushed the scruff on my face. "I missed you." She scooted closer, entangling our legs together and resting her forehead on my chest.

"I missed you. I was terrified. Terrified you were gone too far from me this time."

"That might not have been a bad thing for you. Less trouble."

"Less everything but trouble. Less happiness. Less life. Less of everything that makes my heart want to beat."

Her hand cupped my cheek, and she kissed me softly. "I'm sorry I drank the wine without you. It was stupid and selfish. I wanted to cut loose with you and got caught up in a game."

"The imbecile Ashern was why. He knew better. The realms have lots of other wine we can indulge in together. Don't think about it anymore."

"You can't blame Ashern for my actions."

"I'm not. I'm blaming him for his," I said.

"Ridiculous reaper."

"You scared me, Azora."

"I know, and I'm so sorry." Her fingers massaged my scalp, varying the pressure.

I closed my eyes to savor the way her touch always branded itself into my memory for later times, when I needed to dwell on her when we were apart. "Let me know when you're ready to talk about what happened."

"Everyone will probably want me to talk about it." She played with the front of my hair, watching it like it might do something amusing.

"You don't have to share anything that makes you uncomfortable. I'll make sure of that."

"You can't protect me from everyone all the time. It leads you to terrible places, and you should have realized that by now." Her hand fell to her side. "I am definitely a killer like you now."

"You could have slaughtered all the sirens and not be a killer like me." I slipped my hand under her shirt to rub her back.

"I gutted the siren queen tail fin to breastbone, and it was like when my father took me fishing, and we had to clean all the fish. Except her upper half was much more disturbing when her entrails fell out."

"You gutted the Queen of Sirens like a trout?"

She rolled away from me to face the walls. "It's not a good thing. Not something anyone should rejoice over. For a moment, I did not regret it, and I felt how you must feel when you slaughter someone evil. There was a satisfaction to knowing she could do no more evil.

At that moment, I was truly a hypocrite for telling you how terrible you loving killing is."

I wrapped my arms around her and kissed down the back of her neck. "What made her evil?"

"I suppose I should start at the beginning." Her shoulders rose as she took a deep breath. "I don't remember much from shortly after Ashern and I started playing the wine game. I woke up with the sirens after the alcohol had left my system, and there were many other women and even some girls that couldn't have been much more than ten. All human. We were in a cage above the water, but that was no match for my key seer abilities."

"That would have made for an easy escape."

"It did, but before I fled, I talked to some of the women, and they told me that the queen came in each night and removed one of them from the cage. She'd put a breathing star on their face like she wanted them to live, but they never returned. The women told me the queen chose anyone who caused problems first, and so they all tried to stay quiet and not cause any issues. Naturally, I caused some trouble to get her attention, and she chose me as I expected." She scooted back against me and laced our fingers together.

"Not too happy you put yourself in danger like that, but not sure what else I'd expect."

"I lived in danger long before you, and I had a good reason. I needed information. The moment she touched me, I entered her mind and saw the horrible atrocities she committed. They feasted on men and did much worse to the women and girls. She drained them to add years to her life and keep her beautiful. It drained their life from them painfully. She'd done it for centuries, and the most horrific part was that she had to dissolve their soul into herself, so her victims no longer existed after she tormented them in their final moments."

"Terrible way to die." I curled as much around her as I could.

"It was, and I knew I couldn't leave anyone to suffer that fate. The other thing I saw made me hesitant." She trembled like she'd returned to last night.

"If it's too much, we can save it for another time."

"No, it's okay. I saw I had to gut her because it was the only way her kind could die. Their organs had to fall from their bodies. Anything else, and they would heal. They placed the breathing star over my face, and since I'd already experienced one, it wasn't shocking. I connected to the guards that led me to a shipwreck. It told me the reason they couldn't drown us was because the queen had to be the one to stop our hearts for the ceremony to work." She sniffled and squeezed my hand. "Sorry. Everything is fuzzy and difficult to sort."

"Take all the time you need." I kissed her shoulder and rested my chin on her head.

After several minutes, she cleared her throat. "They tied me to a statue on the bow of the ship using chains and locks. I unlocked them all when they swam away but held them in place while I waited for the queen to approach. She lifted her large dagger in line with my heart, and I knew as soon as it pierced me, she would siphon my soul into her. I whipped the chain into her head and took control of the dagger while shock froze her. That's when I gutted her top to bottom." Her breathing stuttered. "And I liked she was dead. Same as you when you kill evil people."

I breathed in the soft floral scent of her hair, which always eased me into peace. "It was something to be happy about. A monster that has destroyed souls for centuries can no longer cause harm. I'm proud of you."

Her body shook as her tears started up again, and I held her for as long as she needed me to be still and silent.

She rolled back to face me again, looking up with watery eyes. "I used to think morality was black and white. Wrong was wrong and right was right. Now I'm all mixed up about everything because it was good she died. It was good I killed her, and that's me doing what you've always done."

"I don't think every situation fits into a concrete mold. Most people probably believe it's fine to kill when it is to protect but not for mere desire. Ethics change with circumstances, and we behave with what we personally believe is right and wrong at that moment. I didn't always kill bad people. When I first started reaping, I did each assignment with no questions."

"What changed?"

I wiped her tears away with my thumbs. "A child."

Chapter Twenty-Seven
Trudging
Azora

A lcaius wiped my tears and kissed my wrist. "The first time reaping ever bothered me was my first child assignment."

"You had to kill a child?" Pain beat at my chest as I thought of losing Lowan and what losing a child did to any family.

"No, it's like I told you before that some assignments are different. We don't kill children. They pass because of things outside of the control of the Determiners and their fate fabric. I'd always reaped adults. Mainly elderly. It was like I was eased into it, and I collected or killed, as I was told." He sat up, leaning against the wall. "I was sent to a house, and a woman was asleep in the chair, and I was confused because when I approached her my scythe stayed silent."

I pushed myself up next to him and took his hand, resting our arms on his leg. "Your scythe knows who you're sent to kill?"

"Yes, we're given names and ages, but I had missed the age for whatever reason. Normally, a scythe only reacts to who you're assigned to. I changed mine after this. That's a story for another time. The woman was asleep sitting up, and I looked around the room and realized it wasn't her I was sent for. I concealed myself in my hood since I couldn't reap in my human form and held the child close to me, rocking them. It was peaceful, and I made sure they had a slow transition, so the experience wasn't jarring for the child."

I studied his distant eyes that filled with sadness at the memory. "That would have been so heartbreaking."

He nodded. "It changed my entire perspective on what I did, and I no longer looked forward to assignments. They filled me with a dread that seeped in whenever I went to see where the Determiners wanted to send me. It fed into everything, and I became obsessed with possibly being sent to another child. Then it increased to worrying about if the people I reaped, and especially those I was sent to kill, were good and kind. People that didn't deserve to die. I followed my targets around and that made it worse because most didn't deserve it."

I rested my head on his shoulder and squeezed his hand. "That's why you started to stalk your targets?"

"Yeah, and then I started switching mine with other reapers. Rook helped me because chaos wielders can mess with the fate fabric to some degree. Everything became elaborate after that, and instead of simply switching with other reapers, I picked who I wanted to kill to keep my reaping count accurate, and Rook had to move things around a lot more. He could have been caught and executed for it, but Zaire covered things up for him, which he couldn't do for me because I was discovered first."

"Why do you think Rook agreed to put himself at risk like that?"

"Loyalty, and he agreed with me. He also saw how not changing fate was eating at me."

"You defied everything you were told to be because it was the right thing. Because you're good and not a monster."

He studied the black blanket over us. "I'm still a monster, Azora. I still crave ending life. The only thing that makes me happier than slaughter is you. I'm not good. Don't mistake me soothing my conscience as good."

"So then I am a monster because I killed too and was happy about it."

"It wasn't the same. You killed to protect."

"And so do you."

"Most of the time." He got out of bed and placed his hand on the doorknob. "Are you hungry?"

"Not really, but I should probably try to eat something."

"I agree." He left and came back with a tray of fruits, bread, and chicken broth.

We fed each other strawberries and blueberries and split the bread in half.

He slid the broth my way. "To ease your stomach."

"Thank you."

He knew me well enough to know everything that happened with the sirens had made me ill.

I finished my latest bite of strawberry. "What happened with the crow?"

"My father helped me leave through a portal because he wanted me with you to find the box for the objects."

"Yes, he visited me a while ago and told me to find it or you would suffer."

He tossed two blueberries into my mouth. "Of course he did. Have you tracked it?"

"Yes, it's in the same direction we are going, and we could get it on the way."

"Is there anything guarding it like the others?"

I held a strawberry to his lips and waited for him to take a bite. "Not that I could tell. That doesn't mean there isn't. It is a concern that it just happens to be the same way we are going, like someone wants us to think it's an easy thing to get."

"We'll keep our guard up."

"There's something I need to ask you about to clear the air."

He looked up from dipping his bread in butter." What's that?"

"I'm told you kissed Moirai the night after the ball. It seems crazy you'd have the energy for that after how our night went."

He stiffened. "I didn't kiss Moirai. She kissed me, and I stopped it immediately. I swear it." He held out his hand. "See the truth in my mind. Everything is yours to take."

"No need. I believe you." I popped a blueberry in my mouth.

"I should have told you sooner."

I shrugged. "We've had a lot of other things to deal with. Emotions were high that morning because of my dragon bond and like I said I believe you. I only wanted your side."

"Good because all others next to you are as tempting as a mountain troll."

I laughed. "Moirai would love to know you thought that about her."

After breakfast, we took another nap until a sailor woke us to let us know we approached land. The crisp air had a light breeze that cooled the heat. I held onto the railing on the side of the ship that faced the sand beaches we approached. Thin trees with an abundance of leaves and vines covered everything beyond a small stretch of sand, and I wondered if there was even a path to walk. My tracker sense struggled to make sense of the area, and that happened for a few reasons. The person I connected to in order the find the way to the Celestial Realm must not have had much experience with a particular area. It was either that or some creature or magic hindered my abilities.

The captain lowered the ramp, and I threw my bag over my shoulder as I exited the ship. I bent down and let the warm sand fall through my fingers, hoping it would help me connect better. Before landing, I'd thought I had a straight path to Death's box and the Celestial Realm. A sizeable gap that I guessed was the jungle ahead filled the path anytime I tried to locate the way. It didn't matter how hard I concentrated; it didn't improve.

I went back up the ramp and found the captain talking with Alcaius and Ashern. "Excuse me, sir, I need to know if you or any of your men have any experience with this stretch of land? Anyone that would be willing to connect with me and give me a better grasp of our path."

He stroked his long white beard. "Can't say that I do. We don't really venture over to this part. Little is known about it, so I would be cautious. Let me check with my men to make sure." He left and returned to let me know no one had ever been close to here.

It left me unsettled. Enough that I attempted to ask the Oblivions with us, but none of them ever talked. Our main group all said they hadn't been there either.

Elisha pulled out his map collection. "There's not really anything mentioned about inside this jungle, and it doesn't look like there is a way around on either side. The foliage appears to extend the entire length." He held his silver compass out in front of him. "The best we can do is head east and hope for the best."

Four of the Oblivions surrounded me on all sides and the rest created a circle.

Alcaius pushed his way through them to stand next to me. "I got this."

A couple of their shoulder flames grew, but they didn't respond to him beyond that.

"You need to let all my friends in the circle so we can speak better," I said to the one on my right.

They parted and made space for the others to get in the middle of the protection circle.

Ashern leaned his head to the side and looked in between our protectors. "Does it bother anyone else that Azora sees nothing here and that the Lord of Oblivion, who can see time threads, thinks we need this many people to get us through this?"

"We have all thought of that. It is a prominent thought in the minds of everyone here. There is a great unbalance in the air as well," Moderatus said.

My skin burned to an almost painful degree before it eased up and burned again. My tracker sense often did this to a lesser degree when someone I had a connection to that I hadn't seen in a while got close. The strength of it confused me because the only person I felt that close to was Alcaius, but not even he produced a reaction from my sense to that magnitude. Then it hit me that it resembled when Eiro bit me, and I looked to the skies to see a speck of red zipping through the clouds. I concentrated on it and knew I'd guessed correctly.

Alcaius held my hand and pulled me closer, and the scythe on his back crackled like even it was worried about where we were going. It took a little while for us to find a pathway large enough for us to walk through, and it required us moving through in a straight line. Everyone placed me in the middle like they really didn't think they could save the dragons without me when they clearly could. The lengths all of them but Alcaius and probably Fennec went to make me pay retribution seemed too extreme. Alcaius stayed in front of me, acting as a shield against whatever might meet us on our journey. He kept his grip tight on my hand and insisted I stay close to his back. My other hand curled around a dagger that I'd protect myself and him with.

Elisha held the compass out, directing us each time we needed to alter our trajectory. The humid hot air beat on us and not even my armor that regulated my temperature helped the misery of it. Alcaius shifted into a reaper to make himself more comfortable, and the chill of his bony hand in mine cooled my blood. The path opened up, so we could walk side by side again, and he looked back to see me a sweaty mess. He placed his free palm on my neck and turned it to ice.

"I could use a turn, lover boy." Ashern smirked.

Alcaius elbowed him. "Find your own reaper to love."

"Why when my comfort is at stake right now? I'm sure Azora doesn't mind sharing?"

"No, go right ahead and let my reaper put his hand so close to your throat as he cools the back of your neck," I said.

"On second thought, I'll just endure."

We set up camp as the sunlight faded. It had already been diminished by all the trees and plant life. Rain pattered on the leaves, leaving only a few drops to make it to the ground. It cooled everything a lot, and I had to put my cloak back on. The air chilled even more as it got closer to night, and Moirai created a fire while Ashern and Moderatus left to fish in a nearby stream. Alcaius left to walk around the parameter to ensure nothing lurked that could harm us while we slept. He bossed the Oblivions around like the future king he was. Moirai's nostrils twitched as I walked over and sat on a log in front of the fire. Fennec was there too, writing in a book. Moirai looked like she wanted to shove me into the fire as she retreated to her tent.

"She hates you," Fennec said with no inflection in his voice.

"I know."

"She wants my brother back, and that is why she left just now."

"I know that too."

"She would be the better choice for him. Keep him more emotionally stable. More like a reaper should be."

I rubbed my chest to ease the sting of his blunt words. "What do you mean, more like what a reaper should be?"

"Reapers were meant to have lesser emotions to keep us from developing morals around killing. In the fabric of who we are, we feel nothing too strongly, except sometimes anger. Alcaius is broken because he not only feels emotions at the level of a human, but he is often extreme for even a normal human. He's the worst when it comes to you. You most of all make him an abnormal reaper."

"That was a lot of words to tell me Alcaius loves me and you don't like me."

He picked up a stick and drew lines in the black dirt. "I feel nothing for you and therefore neither like nor dislike you. I am what a reaper should be, and I only deal with logic and facts. I am only sharing information pertinent to you."

"Is that why your father is so harsh with him?"

"Partly. Father has tried all our lives to get Alcaius to feel less. It never worked and only caused Alcaius to become superb at hiding his emotions from our father. The emotions were still there to cause him to do foolish, impulsive things outside our father's presence. This is all our father's fault, and he knows it. He takes his guilt out on Alcaius as well."

"Why is Alcaius having emotions your father's fault? Your father seems to feel nothing except anger, which you said was normal for a reaper."

"My father was never supposed to be the King of Death. He craved power, and he knew the Celestials would choose a new royal line because the last one couldn't produce an heir, so he made a deal with the King of Oblivion to make sure he was selected. He would get all the power from the last Death and all the other perks that came with ruling over the Death elementals."

"Your father made a deal with Belial?"

"Yes, he would ensure my father took over the throne and gain the Grim Reaper's power, but at a price. He had to be willing to give Belial four parts of his essence. His kingdom, his power, his line, and his soul. They would be placed into objects as a safety measure for Samael to never betray Belial. What Belial actually wanted in the deal was eternal life. Samael as the new Death would ensure that no reapers ever reaped Belial. The objects were to be destroyed upon Belial's death if Samael went back on his word and Belial was reaped. He tied his heartbeat to three dragons and a sea beast that would ensure the objects were destroyed if Samael went back on his word."

I took in everything he told me and took a moment to think it all through. "If Belial's life was tied to the objects, why didn't he protect them better after he realized we were going after the objects?"

"My assumption is Belphagor told him not to worry about them because you were a key seer, and if he could raise the dark armies, he could take over all the elemental kingdoms, and not even Death himself could reap him. Belphagor told him to do everything the way it was done to get you to agree to open the rift."

"Why would Belphagor do that to his father?"

"Because he hates him." He drew a sun in the dirt and quickly erased it with his stick.

Alcaius walked up. "Everything looks cleared. The Oblivions are patrolling all around us."

"You enjoy having them here all of a sudden," I said.

"They have their purposes. I just don't like that their leader wants to use you for some obsessive purpose he has."

Ashern and Moderatus brought back ten fish, and we cooked them all to make sure even the Oblivions could eat if they wanted. We shared a night of storytelling, and I enjoyed hearing about Alcaius when he was younger. Once night fell, we retired to our tents.

Alcaius and I shared his tent with Fennec for safety reasons. Fennec slept at the back of the tent, and I slept in the middle while Alcaius took the spot by the tent flap. At first, I thought he was being an overly protective of his little brother until I realized he was surrounding me with protection. He wanted me alive for a different reason than everyone else on the quest. The sky above the jungle must have broken as the rain grew so heavy that it pattered rapidly on the tent, and not even the botanical barrier hindered it.

Silhouettes of the Oblivions guarding our camp appeared any time I turned on my light stick to find something. Even with all the guardians around me, I felt for my daggers to make sure I had clear access to them. Alcaius slept with the staff of his scythe in his hand. Eiro was close, somewhere on the ground, and I had yet to tell anyone, even Alcaius, about his presence. The idea of me having a dragon bond had bothered him greatly, and I didn't want him hunting my dragon down to have a word with him. The rain brought the familiarity of Aresgan, and I drifted to sleep.

Nothing happened for the next two nights, and I could feel a dim light in my tracker sense, the feeling that we'd reached the end of the jungle with no incident. I told everyone it felt as though we should break through to the other side by the end of the day, so when we came to a paradise, we took a break rather than making camp by the glistening water source. Five waterfalls cascaded down the cliffside between large orange and pink flower patches.

Vines hung over the water from several tree branches that grew beside the riverbank. The water was clear, which showed tiny fish swimming above blue and purple pebbles. Alcaius grabbed my hips and directed me toward the edge of the river where he reached out for my hand and yanked me onto the vine with him, climbing up with one hand and keeping his other arm around me. We swung together until we made it far out into the water.

He kissed my neck. "Ready, love? Let go."

We spiraled down, separating as we fell. When we both surfaced, he splashed me, and I returned the favor by shoving all the water I could at him with both my arms giving full effort.

We ducked under the water to swim and explore the fish and tiny yellow crabs digging holes between the rocks and sand. Something knocked into me, jarring me from watching a small turtle waddle on the river floor. I covered my mouth as I realized it was the body of one of our Oblivions. It had on their dark robes, and the water sizzled by their shoulders, but he looked drained of everything, like a skeleton covered in only skin. Arms grabbed me, and I resisted until I realized it was Alcaius.

"Seraphim! Stay behind me. One bite will kill a human. I can handle many of them." He pulled me under and through the water, keeping us close to the bottom.

My chest burned from lack of oxygen, and panic set in as it reminded me of the time I'd drowned. I fought to get to the surface, twisting out of Alcaius's hold. I needed air. I needed air, or I was going to die like the last time. Alcaius tried to pull me back down, and my heart knew he'd never hurt me, but it couldn't convince my anxiety the water wouldn't end me.

I made it to the surface and sucked in the air while whipping my head around to figure out what was happening. My heart pounded like it would beat itself out of my chest. I couldn't see the others, so I concentrated on Ashern and swam in the direction I knew he was. Alcaius grabbed me again and pulled me down, and I screamed, fighting against him.

"Azora! Stop! We have to hide in the water! Stop!" He held me tighter. "You're safe. I won't let you drown. I promise."

I couldn't slow my breathing to take in the air storage I required to hide with him. "I can't!"

"You can. You're the strongest person I know." His eyes shot to the sky, and he jumped on top of me."Take a deep breath now!"

I did as he said, and it still felt inadequate. He cried out as he shoved me under him, and I rolled over to see what was happening. His flesh was dissolving, but not like when he shifted into a reaper. He twisted around, hooking his scythe on the neck of his attacker and yanking. He kept shielding me with his body as he ripped into one after the other. Feathers and blood filled the water, bathing everything in crimson. Three attacked him at once, biting him as he shriveled more each time they stuck their fangs in. He brought his scythe across all their necks to remove their heads. He butchered dozens, taking bites and scratches as he stopped them from reaching me. His precision for slaughter annihilated the mass threat that far outnumbered us.

Another horde approached, and he tired as venom from many bites surged through him. I withdrew my dagger from my thigh and swam up and out of the water. A white-winged man had his mouth latched onto my reaper. I brought my knife into the angel's neck and stabbed it four times before it let Alcaius go. The creature grabbed my wrist and brought it to his open mouth, lowering his two-inch fangs to rip into my skin as he knocked my dagger into the water. I inched the other dagger from my other thigh and penetrated his eye with my blade.

I withdrew it and stabbed it around his face twice more. He hissed and withered into scarlet foam that floated in the water. Another attacked me from behind and a nearly unrecognizable Alcaius tugged off my attacker's head before going limp. I screamed when I realized Alcaius had sunk to the bottom.

I fished him out and turned him over to see his still eyes, but his rattled breathing told me still lived. He blinked and reanimated yet remained the drained husk I prayed was reversible. More winged creatures filled the sky, and we hid in an area surrounded by vines and trees. He turned us so that his back was to the exit and pressed me into the wall. Even though he was dying, he insisted on protecting me.

CHAPTER TWENTY-EIGHT
INTENTIONS
Azora

Alcaius pushed me back farther and covered the only open spot with plants. We had to wait them out. I held my breath as shadows crossed our hiding place. I held onto Alcaius's hand, even though the wrinkled leathery feel of it startled me. We had to find him help. The vines flew apart and an eerily beautiful angel hissed, ready to tear us apart. Blood splattered everywhere as a massive red scaly mouth bit our attacker in half. Eiro flung vampire angels in all directions, ripping off limbs and splitting torsos in two.

The enormous red dragon heaved and growled as he looked around to make sure he got them all. "Why do you foolishly play in the territory of the Seraphim?"

"We were on a break from the quest and needed some time alone." I held Alcaius close to me, not liking how limp he'd become. "I need you to get us to safety."

"You. I will take you to safety. He should have taken better care of you." He puffed smoke over Alcaius.

"He killed dozens of them before they overwhelmed us, and I'd be dead right now without his fierce protection. I am not going anywhere until you agree to take him. We need to get him back to the closest person we have to a healer on this trip."

Eiro grumbled but carefully placed us both on his back before taking to the air to return to the others. We found the camp ripped apart, and I slid off Eiro to track the rest of our party. Husks of six Oblivions scattered across the camp. I located my team hiding in a small cave where they had used a boulder to block the entrance. Eiro moved it, and we found almost all the Oblivions had been drained giving the others time to get away. They all used their powers to fend the seraphim off but had bite marks.

I looked around. "Where's Ashern?" I closed my eyes and realized he was there. Something was wrong. I found him behind a stalagmite and covered my mouth. He, like Alcaius, was a barely breathing husk. "Elisha! Help him!"

Elisha came over to me and showed me a blue potion. "I tried, but it's not enough. It'll only hold the venom off a few hours, so we have time to get them somewhere more equipped. We need to get them to the Fates as quickly as possible."

"I have a dragon for us. If I can convince him to give everyone a ride, that is. He doesn't have any ropes or poles to help us stay on. That might be a problem."

"How did you get a dragon?"

"It's a long story. Can you and Moderatus carry Ashern?"

Elisha rubbed his arm. "I'm not able to move my arm well."

I noticed a gash in his white shirt with red seeping through. "Were you bitten?"

"No, just scratched. I'll be fine."

Moderatus picked up Alcaius and awkwardly held him out like he was cradling a diseased child. "I can alone."

Eiro clawed the ground, rumbling his complaints about my request. "This is not what I was told I'd have to do if I bonded with a human."

"What were you told you'd have to do?" My eyes shifted to Alcaius and Ashern. "You know what? It doesn't matter. We can talk about what this arrangement means after we get our injured to help."

"It matters. I am a dragon, not a courier." He lifted his chin and straightened his body to make himself even taller."

"Yes, but if they die, I will not be okay. I may follow them into the afterlife from grief."

"That's ridiculous."

"It's the truth."

"Fine! I will lower my worth for only you." He lowered his head to the ground to make it easier for everyone to climb onto his back. "I will not save anyone who falls off."

"Fly reasonably then. If you hadn't put Alcaius on the ground after we landed, it would be less effort."

"I was determined to be done with him, but you can't be reasoned with."

"So I've been told."

He lifted Alcaius and Ashern onto his back for us without me asking him to which felt like progress.

Elisha stood between two trees, staring at something. "I think that Oblivion is alive. I've checked the others, and they are clearly not."

Moderatus helped him bring the fallen guardian over to Eiro, who placed him on his back. We carried all the bodies to an open area and buried them with branches and vines until we could tell Belphagor where to collect the dead for a proper ceremony. I held Alcaius's head in my lap as we flew out of the jungle toward the Fate kingdom's border.

I brushed his hair away from his eyes and kissed his forehead, softly singing to him. "I love you."

He squeezed my hand but kept his eyes closed, saying nothing in return.

Fennec sat at his feet to assist me in keeping his brother on the dragon. "I will fight any reaper that comes for him. Know that."

"Thank you. He wouldn't want you to jeopardize yourself for him, though," I said.

"He is the heir to my people's throne, and I will save him out of loyalty to my father and people."

"Nothing to do with him being your brother and not wanting him to die?"

Fennec looked away and shut his eyes. As unfeeling as he came across, it was clear he cared about his brother. "He was hurt protecting you." He stated it like it was a fact, not him asking me.

"Yes."

"That makes sense. Most of his trouble is to protect you." Fennec's bluntness seemed more of him stating facts than actual rudeness or an attempt to be cruel. He spoke to the world honestly, with no room for politeness or formalities.

"You're right. It is. He feels strongly for me as I do him."

"He has cost you a lot as well. Neither of you looks after yourself when you sacrifice for the other."

"Yes, that's what love does."

"Love is illogical and goes against self-preservation," he said.

"Experiencing love and keeping it makes it so life is worth preserving."

"Yet you throw it to the wind at the first sign a person you love is in danger."

I kissed Alcaius's forehead again. "Because love makes you want the other person to survive more than you."

"That is a foolish concept."

"Would you not sacrifice your life for anyone? Not even your brothers?"

He seemed to mull it over for a second as he studied Eiro's scarlet scales. "Yes, if it would make sense to do so. I do not fear death or damnation, for I have done an excellent job as a reaper, and they are my blood."

"Then I think you understand where Alcaius is coming from when he fights to protect me. Love and protection always go together."

"Not long ago, you were a stranger to him. It gives him no advantage to save you. If I sacrificed my life for my brothers, it would prevent pain for my mother and keep my father from anger."

The wind picked up and loosened my hair, so I quickly re-pinned it. "Wouldn't your death anger your father?"

"No, he pretends like he will let me ascend because Alcaius is too emotional to be even the lowest-level reaper. If Alcaius were not the son of the Grim Reaper, he would have either been chosen for lesser work or executed at his tests before his abilities were awakened. We all go through the tests, and they can't be forged or cheated on. Alcaius passed, but there's no way he did. My father altered the results. My father is cruel to Alcaius because he wants him as his heir but wants to break the emotions out of him. He would not care if I died. He'd even reap me himself."

"Emotions can't be taken from a person through cruelty. It will only magnify them or turn them dark," I said.

"Alcaius turned dark and volatile until you. You magnified his emotions in a way that caused him to smile again."

"That's beautiful."

"It's dangerous for a reaper to smile. It is fatal. Not beautiful." His face remained still during our entire conversation. Not even a sliver of emotion crept into his voice or eyes.

"The fact he smiles over me even though it could get him executed makes it more beautiful."

Fennec's brows narrowed for the briefest of seconds before he returned to his baseline of stoic.

I scanned the area hoping to spot the gate close, but only endless trees spanned in front of us. They appeared shrouded in dense fog that could have been hiding behind the gate.

Elisha slumped against one of Eiro's back spikes and caught my eye. "Let me see your scratch," I said.

He opened his eyes. "Nothing the Fates won't be able to fix. It's a minor thing."

Eiro tilted his head back. "We have arrived at the gate. Brace yourselves for landing. If you fall, that is of your own doing." Smoke flowed from his nostrils at his declaration.

His four oak tree-sized legs slammed to the ground, and I curled myself over Alcaius to keep him from rolling to the ground. Fennec helped me as well before assisting Moderatus in getting his brother to the ground. Fog flowed everywhere, creating low visibility and wrapping itself around a small black gate that looked like it led to a little garden and could be easily hopped.

The fog thickened the farther it traveled from the gate, and I walked over to it, looking for a wall. Nothing expanded out on either side like I could step around the gate and into the new realm. "This really can't be the gate to the Fates kingdom."

Eiro puffed out smoke, filling the air with ashes. "Are you saying I took you to the wrong location as though that is even possible?"

I pulled up the location the dragons had given me in my mind and realized it was the gate. "It's so anti-climatic."

"The less elaborate it looks, the fewer people want to get in." Moira held her chin up. "It's a spectacular place inside. The best you'll ever see. A place worthy of a king to sit beside his queen and rule."

"A king who has his own realm to rule?"

Her lips pursed so tightly I thought they'd crumble. "I will most likely get my throne hundreds of years before Alcaius gets his. Fates retire long before reapers do. The weight of holding destinies is much heavier than holding death."

Moderatus removed his hood from his bald, tattooed head. "Neither is as heavy as keeping all of you in balance. The arrangement would have shattered, anyway. Everyone knew it, and it was foolish from the moment your relationship with Alcaius was decreed. Everyone knew it."

"It wasn't! If we had been mated, it would have been fine!"

"You screaming it does not make it so. There are many others who desire you that you overlook out of pride."

I stepped next to the gate. "So, how does this work? Do we just walk in?" I touched next to the gate to feel for the invisible wall my tracker sense said was present as several of them shouted for me to stop. Pain shot from my palm to my wrist as the skin on my arm shriveled and blackened. I sunk to the ground as agony rocked me like I was paper writhing in a flame.

Eiro jerked me away and a cool mist poured from his snout as he blew tiny ice shards over my burning arm. The pain lessened until it numbed completely. Tiny crystals grew over my burns, and I shook from the shock.

"Who dares to disturb the gate?" A howling whisper drifted out from the fog. "It's impolite not to knock." Emerging into view galloped a purplish blue unicorn creature with a narrow sloped snout. Its horn rose slightly above and between its glowing red eyes. The horn had ringed grooves like a ram's horn and bent backward, becoming a tiny sharp spear that ended halfway over its back. Wispy spikes created its mane and tail, and its hooves, each divided into four leaf-like sections it balanced on the tips of. The creature stretched out feather wings for a few seconds before tucking them right against its back. "Explain yourselves."

I attempted to stand up, and Eiro yanked me against him and held me in place with one of his paws. "Don't be a fool!" He hissed. "I didn't bond with you for you to be an idiot and get yourself killed immediately."

"This is my quest, and I must explain myself."

"Explain yourself from here."

Moirai lifted her braid that had blue crystals woven in. "I am Gomarala's daughter. Moirai, Lady Fate."

The creature scraped the dirt with its hoof. "Why would you use the common gate?"

"My mother disapproves of me helping with the quest I am on. She said since I insisted on doing this, I must receive no shortcuts."

It sniffed the air, bending toward Moirai. "Hmm..."

I ducked away from Eiro, and he grabbed the back of my shirt with his teeth, pulling me back. "No," he said as he flooded my vision with steam.

"And here I thought Alcaius was aggressive about my safety."

"Myik always says no one can out stubborn a dragon," Fennec said.

I cupped my hands to my mouth and shouted at the creature. "What must we do to be let into the gate? We have an urgent need to get treatment for our friends and to speak with the elders."

"The price is your blood." The beast jabbed its head forward as though to demonstrate impaling us. "You will prick your finger on my horn and drip it into the pool. If your intentions are pure, the gate will open for you. It will only allow one person through at a time, so don't rush the gate. It also can't tell who the one person is, but if anyone cheats, I will drag them back through and slaughter them. Do you agree to the terms?"

Moirai flung her hand at the creature. "Get it over with."

Its horn twisted on its head until the sharp end faced the other direction, allowing it to pierce Moirai's finger. The unicorn's red eyes changed to deep royal blue, and the gate creaked open for her to enter. Moderatus and Elisha moved our three wounded over to the gate.

The unicorn stared down at them and nudged the Oblivion with one of his hooves. "The creatures who bit them corrupt their blood, and that will taint the test."

I sunk down to Alcaius and squeezed his hand. "We don't have a choice but to take them with us. Can you try the test?"

"Not unless you want me to judge them and find them lacking. If that happens, I will purge them."

Alcaius's rattly breathing urged me forward. "We don't have time to wait, and we can't leave them. The dragons have arranged for us to meet the elders, and it's important that we do so quickly. Are there any other options for us?"

"No, they will have to die here. If you aren't happy with it, you can die with them." It hovered its hoof over Alcaius's chest.

A flash of silver moved so quickly that I missed what had happened until the unicorn's head rested at my feet.

Fennec's scythe dripped with blood, and he bent down, pricking his finger on the horn and squeezing his own blood into the pool. Rather than going through himself, he pushed Alcaius through. "Go with him, Azora."

"What about you? How did it even let you pass with what you just did?"

"My intentions were pure to save my brother, and there's no guardian here to determine it wasn't Alcaius's blood in the pool. It only knew to let one person in.".

Moderatus copied what Fennec did and pushed Ashern through the gate. "I will take care of the reaper heir's brother. Go with Alcaius."

I pointed to the Oblivion shivering on a blanket on the ground. "We can't leave him to die just because we don't know him that well."

"There is no other choice. You must save them. This is your quest."

Elisha bent down and stuck his finger with the horn. The gate remained closed, and the beast's body rose from the mist, driving its jagged hoof into Elish's upper chest. "You are not pure of intention," its bodyless head roared.

Elisha flopped to the ground with his brilliant blue eyes fixed on nothing.

CHAPTER TWENTY-NINE
REQUEST
Azora

My eyes wildly went from Elisha to the unicorn. "You killed him!"

The unicorn's head still rested on the ground, but its mouth moved. "He was unworthy of passing through the gate. He has hidden intentions I cannot see." The unicorn's body stomped the ground.

"You killed him for that?" Rage crept into my chest. I stared at Elisha's arm. "The scratch! You killed him for no reason. The creatures had scratched him, and it was their venom you detected. You killed an innocent!"

"I warned you not to let your infected test the pool."

"We didn't think it was the same!"

"You did not think."

I felt for the dagger strapped to my thigh. "He didn't think because he was so eager to save a stranger! His intentions were beyond pure."

Before I could deliver my retribution, Fennec hacked his scythe into the creature's skull and dug out its horn, sticking it in his bag. The body collapsed to the ground. The horn was so large it stuck out the top. He continued to dig at the head, scraping out pieces of bone and brain matter until it was a shredded mess. "He won't be able to come back without his horn now."

Elisha released a gurgled sound, and I dropped beside him. "We'll get you help. Eiro! Fly him to the witch as fast as you can."

Eiro shook his head. "I can't leave you."

"It's not like you can go through the gate."

"I can." The dragon rippled and shrunk. His enormous body diminished to the size of a bear.

"Right. Oblivions can change size. Your large size is needed more. I need you to get him to the witch, Eiro!"

He brought a claw up to my cheek to catch a tear. "It's too late, Azora,"

"Elisha, you're going to be fine."

Elisha's eyes slowly turned to mine. "He's right. Nothing can be done for me. My injuries are too great. Along with the vampire venom. There's nothing to be done. I have a gift for you since rules no longer matter." He lifted his hand to my cheek and warmth seeped into my veins, traveling around my head. Then it stopped. Elisha's hand dropped and his ragged breathing ceased. Nothing felt different, and I wondered if, like my memories returning, whatever he gave me would take time to manifest. I closed his eyes and sobbed as yet another person I'd failed died.

Moderatus placed his hand on my shoulder. "We will return him to his scythe and care for his ashes. The quest must continue, and grief reserved for later."

I let Moderatus take him from me and stood up. He was right. I had to get the others safe. "How do I enter the gate now?"

Fennec took out the horn. "It should still work."

"What about the Oblivion? Can't we just poke one of your fingers again?"

"No, these types of gates only allow one blood drop per person until the blood evaporates from the pool after several days. It can't tell whose blood it is, but it can tell if it's the same as it already has. You don't have a choice but to leave him. Finishing the quest is more important than anything. We will try to find him help elsewhere." Moderatus picked up the Oblivion and threw him over his shoulder. Fennec took Elisha's scythe and touched the fallen reaper's shoulder. The scythe lit up in all the decorative etchings, and Elisha's body became dust. Fennec collected all the dust in a container and stuck it in his bag.

My lip trembled, and I bit it. Moderatus was right. Grief would come later. It lived in me always simply because death existed at all, magnified by all those I loved who had died long before they should have.

A miniature Eiro the size of my palm fluttered in front of me. "Open your bag and tell no one I have accompanied you. If they know an Oblivion dragon has entered the Realm of Fates, it could cause war."

"Why even come then? You could stay here and help them," I said.

"You will need me at the end of this quest to return you quickly to your lands."

"You could have shown up at the start of this quest. That would have helped." I opened my bag for him and moved things around, fluffing a few rags to give him a comfortable spot.

"There was nothing I could have done any sooner. Timing is everything."

I pricked my finger on the unicorn horn and dripped it into the pool. The gate swung open, and I stepped into the Fate kingdom.

Everything turned into pastel yellow, orange, and pink clouds like the heaven I'd seen in picture books as a child. The legendary place appeared as described by all the philosophers, only there was no white gate creating another barrier for us to be judged.

Moirai sat with her legs tucked under her next to Alcaius. "Took you an eternity. Good thing I am immortal or I'd have withered to old age by now. Where are the others?"

"Elisha is dead." I swallowed and didn't meet her eyes.

"How?"

I rubbed my upper arm. "His scratch had seraphim venom that the unicorn misread it as him being evil. It was why Fennec and Moderatus can't come through. They gave up their turn for our injured. Elisha tried to do the same for the Oblivion."

"Moron. He was so much more important than a lowly Oblivion guard."

'It was my fault. I said it wouldn't be right to leave an injured person behind simply because we didn't know them well."

She gawked as though I'd rendered her speechless for the first time ever. "You sacrificed a reaper and memory seer for a soldier? Fool. More so than I ever imagined. You get to live with killing your uncle."

"What?"

"Your uncle. Elisha." She squinted one eye and turned her head a tick to the side. "You didn't know? Not that it matters now. We need to get these two to help. Somehow."

"What's worse is I had this?" I pulled the god stone from my pocket that Phyrix had given me in the library. "If I had known Elisha would be stabbed in the heart, I would have given it to him."

"Instead, you selfishly kept it for yourself."

I let guilt sting so deeply I could barely breathe. "It was forgotten about until I saw him pierced through the heart, and it is now a terrible regret."

"One day we will teach you to use your instincts better. How are we going to move the men?"

I removed two blankets from my pack. "We place them on these and then tie our rope around them. Then we can pull them wherever we need to go. The ground is smooth enough they should slide easily."

I laid out the blue blanket and rolled Alcaius onto it, binding one rope around his thighs and then another around his chest and under his arms several times. The rope also went under the blanket to keep it attached to him. Moirai did the same to Ashern, and we set off into endless stunning clouds. The blankets moved effortlessly over the almost slick surface.

I adjusted the ropes in my hands to get a better hold. "How do you know Elisha was my uncle?"

"I'm surprised you didn't. Fate ties. I can see fate ties, and I saw a thread between the two of you the moment you stood close enough. It was orange, and that told me he was a relative but not an immediate relation like a parent or sibling. I became bored as we walked and touched the thread at one point when you were walking close enough to him. It told me he was your uncle." She shrugged. "I assumed you knew."

"I didn't."

"That's clear now."

I squinted and placed my hand above my eyes, keeping the rope in one hand while taking a break from pulling. "How much farther?"

"Not much longer. Once we are in range of my mother's castle, I can call the spiders to help."

"Did you say spiders?" I shuddered.

"Don't tell me you fear such beautiful creatures."

"They are not what I would have called anything close to beautiful."

She snickered and rolled her eyes. "The only thing you have good taste in is men."

"Yes, but apparently he liked my taste over yours."

Her upper lip twitched, and a fang slipped out. "You're lucky I am doing all of this for him." She stepped into a wall of clouds and disappeared.

I followed, telling myself not to panic because she wouldn't leave Alcaius to rot. The clouds thickened so much my lungs spasmed as they attempted to suck in air that seemed to be in limited quantities. That feeling pressed me forward as fast as I could pull Alcaius with me. We burst through into a beautiful city with opal shimmering buildings that had colorful jewel crowns at the top. Clouds continued to create the ground and no plant life could be seen anywhere I looked. People flew in the sky with feathered wings. A few glided about a foot off the ground through the cluster of towering structures. The air smelled sweet, like apples and lilies, and my nostrils flared to take in the scent that expanded my lungs so I could breathe again.

Moirai tapped her foot as she waited for me to get over the impressive view. "It's like you want Alcaius to die."

"Why would you say that?"

"Your speed is that of a Corittian sea slug crawling up the Greock Mountains during an ice storm."

"Let's hurry then. Where is the best and closest healer?"

"Those two words do not go together here." She brought out a blue cylinder and whispered into it.

Up from the clouds shot several furry little blue spiders with several round, glossy eyes. They waved their two front legs in the air in greeting. They looked almost cute, but I stepped away from them just the same.

Moirai bent down and held out her hand, and one spider climbed onto her palm. "Cleome, I need you to get us help as quickly as you can. We need to get two people to the healers immediately."

Cleome twirled her fuzzy hand, and a sparkling string shot from it that she used to climb into a mini black portal above her head.

Moirai shooed the others away. "You all may leave."

The tiny arachnid horde vanished into the cloud blanket beneath our feet.

"That wasn't so bad." I took a deep breath as the last one disappeared. "They weren't as terrifying as I'd envisioned."

"That's because you're a very judgmental person."

I side-eyed Moirai and sighed. "Yes, I'm the most judgmental one here."

"Self-awareness is an important step."

"How long do they usually take to do tasks?" I studied Alcaius and then Ashern's breathing to make sure they both still lived.

"Not long. She will bring the best healers, and you will meet with my mother and convince her to recommend you an audience with the elders."

"Why can't you do that since she's your mother?"

"Because it is you who wants an audience. If you haven't noticed from all the times I've made sacrifices on this quest, she isn't happy I'm even helping you at all, but I knew you wouldn't make it without me. Not when you got to this realm."

I watched ribbons of color flutter over our heads, and it took a few moments for it to become distinguishable as a massive colony of butterflies. They swirled around us as a tunnel, tightening more and more like a cyclone gaining stability. Everything went black, slowly opening again into bursts of butterfly wings and sunlight. The light brightened, and we landed in a garden courtyard with bushes cut into animals and neat rows of yellow and red rose bushes. Pink and cream stones formed a checkered pathway that led to multiple junctions.

I twirled around and relief loosened my muscles at Alcaius and Ashern still with us and alive. Figures robbed in blue silk walked in rows of two, branching off into various pathways. A group adorned in red approached and placed our injured on wooden beds. They started back down the path they came from with Alcaius and Ashern, and I followed them.

Moirai grabbed my wrist and yanked me in the other direction. "There's no time to mope at his side with dragons at stake. You've already taken too much time with the random side quests you kept assigning yourself. One would think you didn't care at all about the plight you caused."

"I have jumped through so many obstacles to get here and keep everyone alive."

"And yet you failed at even that." She pressed her lips into a snide grin.

"You're vile."

"Honey, you have no idea."

"It's not that difficult to fathom the depths of your malevolence," I said.

Moirai didn't slow down and refused to release my wrist until we made it to the top of the massive ivory steps. At the top, enormous jade doors with animals carved into them rose all the way to the top of a castle that looked made of sapphire. The windows shimmered red like rubies, with gold around them. The same gold wove through cracks in the walls. Guards opened the door and let us inside. Everything sparkled with pastels and white, and at the ceiling was a dome that swirled blue and gold together in a churning vortex of vibrancy.

Belphagor appeared in front of us, snapped his fingers, and transported me to a plain white room with a table and four chairs. A painting of a lion eating honey from a hive hung on the wall as the only decor.

I searched for a door or window and found none. "Take me back now."

"And have you fail this? No."

"You're here to give me advice?"

"I'm here to give you orders."

I crossed my arms and sunk into a chair. "In that case, you're wasting my time."

"Saving Alcaius's soul is wasting your time?"

"I'm listening."

"The Queen of Fates will ask something from you, and you must be prepared to give it to her."

"What is it?"

"Something she will want."

"That clears that up."

"She will ask for your soul, and you must be prepared to hand it over. I'm preparing you now, so there is no hesitation. You can offer it before she even asks or realizes she wants it."

"It's not like I would give her my soul," I said.

"Not even in the place of Alcaius's?"

"Why would she have access to that? "

"He's here, isn't he?"

"Yes, but he's not here to make a deal with her, and souls can only be infused and given to another by the owner's choice. Alcaius explained that to me when we went on our quest."

"And what would make Alcaius give up his soul?"

I took in a sharp breath, like I was back in the thick clouds again. "Me. He'd give up his soul for me."

"Precisely. If you hesitate too long, it'll give Alcaius time to offer his, and she will want that more. I believe you would have eventually chosen to accept her request, but in the time I see you pondering it, Alcaius will reach you and stop it."

"She would want the son of Death's soul more, I suppose. Is it to give as a birthday gift to Moirai?"

The smallest hint of a smile twitched on his lips. "Fate cannot see death. It is the one elemental she cannot rule over because not even she sees when death is coming to seal fates. It was a big reason she asked the Celestials to match Alcaius to her daughter."

"I thought deaths were placed on the fate fabric and literally bound by fate?"

"They are, but too late for her to do anything about it. She can only see the threads of fate for the living and move them around within the rules. Death can burn the plans she has, and she hates it. If she owns Death's soul, that will change. The soul will have to show her what it knows."

I thought through everything, giving myself time to sort through his words to make sense of them. "So taking Alcaius's soul would be for the future when he became Death himself. Why doesn't she bargain for the souls of the Determiners?"

"Because only Death has the power to tie deaths to fates. They are carrying out his orders. That's what they are watching on the fabric and making connections, he dictates to them."

My eyes slowly went from the floor to his. "So if Alcaius was Death, he'd get to interfere with fate and determine who dies?"

"Yes, within the bounds of balance. There are rules, but Death has a lot of power. When a new Death is crowned, the power of the old Death is fused to him. The reaper given that power goes from simply reaping by orders to handing out the orders."

"Does Alcaius know this? If you do, surely, he does, but he told me the Determiners tied the deaths on the fabric, and he hated them because they have no accountability."

"Not everyone knows. It is something that is kept secret, maybe even from Alcaius until he is given power in case his father in the end does not choose him as his heir. It is Death's choice unless he is killed suddenly, then it is given to his firstborn son without dispute."

"How do you know about it, then?"

He sat in the chair across from me and folded his hands on the table. "My father made a deal with Samael. Samael wanted to be the next Grim Reaper because the one before had passed with no heir. There was no chance the council who had been called to decide would choose Samael because he was a weaker reaper."

"Fennec told me that Myik and Alcaius are not normal reapers because his father was weak when he gained Death's power."

"Yes, Samael was not a good choice, but my father was hungry for power. If he could hold the soul, the flame, of the next Death, he could also have that power. He'd tried other ways by marrying my mother, who was a reaper."

"Okay. So that makes sense why Belial had Samael's soul, but why the extra objects?"

He leaned back in the chair in the most informal pose I'd seen from him. "My father was greedy. He wanted to own everything in case Samael betrayed him, he could thoroughly destroy him. But it took several times of my father manipulating Samael with the objects for the Grim Reaper to decide to get them back. It became an obsession he couldn't quell until you."

"Why did he let me find them? Alcaius and I felt like he was letting us get them."

"He wasn't entirely. That was me," he said.

"Why?"

"Because I needed you and still do, so I convinced him he wanted you more than the objects." He looked at a clock on the wall that hadn't been there earlier. "We are out of time for explanations. You must be satisfied with the answers you have for now. Do not hesitate to offer your soul." The chair scraped on the stone floor as he stood up.

"Why are you helping me?"

"This is a favor. One you will return to me soon."

"Do I at least get a break before having to venture off to satisfy this favor for you?"

"A short one." He snapped his fingers and put me back with Moirai, who didn't seem to notice I'd left at all.

A stout woman in a lilac dress opened a door to our right. "The Queen of Fates will see you now."

I feared what would happen if she didn't accept my soul and took Alcaius's instead. Belphagor wouldn't have guessed she'd accept the present without it being true. I thought so anyway, but how infallible were Oblivion elementals? If this went wrong, I needed to know where the silencing box was that Death sent me for.

If she took his soul, I'd get it back, and I'd need the box to return it to him safely. I concentrated on the object and stopped myself from screaming. The trail had gone cold again. The box to destroy essence objects without harming the essence owners had vanished once more, and I wondered if the entire thing was an elaborate illusion. Death or someone else taunted my seer sense with some powerful object to lure me into their will.

Unease crept in that I had no backup plan as I followed the woman into a room dimly lit by two torches on the wall. The door shut, leaving Moirai outside with me stuck inside. It all felt very much like a trap.

CHAPTER THIRTY
OFFER
Azora

I opened my bag a crack and peeked in on a sleeping Eiro. Tiny streams of smoke fogged up my hand mirror next to him. He looked cute with his paws tucked under his chin, and I didn't mind miniature him so much. I focused back on the room I was in and looked around for a direction to go.

Splashes of red popped against the shiny black walls and ceiling. The floor rippled with each step I took, but I stayed level and never sunk into the firm surface. It was as though I walked on glass and disturbed a pool each time I took a step. The room had no apparent end, and I walked until three silver pillars appeared. Each one had a dragon that looked made of stars with purple and blue glowing swirls that contrasted the black that filled in the rest of their scales.

"Fate dragons," I whispered. I'd known they existed, but nothing I'd ever read had mentioned what they looked like. Maybe because no one outside of the Fates had ever seen one.

A woman with black flowing hair descended from the ceiling. Her blue dress fluttered around her and covered nearly every inch of her body but her hands and face. "Azora, I was told you were coming days ago. You are late."

I bowed and kept my head lowered. "Yes, for that, I am sorry. Our quest hit several bumps."

"Was this not your most important task?"

"It was, but some things could not be helped."

She landed gently on her feet and twirled her hand in the air. Red ribbons grew from the ground and wrapped around her arms. She let them fall and disappear, repeating the exercise three more times like she needed to fidget. "Like competing in Valkyrie tournaments and setting familiars free. Yes, those had to happen before you saved the realms from folly."

I straightened myself out, no longer willing to bow to her. "No, they couldn't wait."

"And now we all will pay for that."

"What do you mean?"

"The rift is unstable and has the potential to burst at any moment unless you seal it with things only the Celestial elders can provide."

"So, you agree I need to speak with the elders? I'm told it is your choice to bring the case forward," I said.

"Walk with me Azora." She turned her back on me and drifted up a wide staircase I hadn't seen before. "Yes, I screen the cases and decide based on several things if they line up with the fate of the requestor. There are other factors, but that is the first screening I give each request. Normally I am given parchment with a small amount of information, and I take it to the fate fabric first. After that, I decide if they have anything of value to offer the elders or if there is a great need for what they want to be fulfilled."

"Why are you speaking with me personally, then?"

"My daughter, I believe you know her."

I kept the disdain out of my voice. "Yes, Moirai. We've been questing together."

We walked between the columns of dragons, and I stared at the magnificent beasts. Their scales swirled and shifted like galaxies changing over millenniums.

"Moirai has a soft spot for dragons and the son of Death." She held out her arm and a silver bird with red-tinged feathers landed near her elbow. "My daughter asked me to hear your request. The one thing I need to hear from you is what you want. You must be precise. There is no time for saying you misspoke or left something out later. Second, what will you pay in return for your desires being granted?"

Had Belphagor not prepared me, I wasn't sure I'd have had the answers. The dragons warned me of sacrifices and seemed to think I'd know what to give up. It definitely wouldn't have been my soul. "What I need are three things, and one is in two parts."

She ran her silk-gloved finger across her chin. "That is a lot to ask of us."

"Yes, for this reason, I will give you the most valuable thing I own. My soul."

Her eyes shifted to the right. "Hmm... Tell me why we would want such a thing? What could you possibly do for us that we would want to control?"

"Do you know what I can do? Do you know the reason I was expected to fix mistakes the dragons said I made?"

"I didn't look into it much and probably wouldn't have paid it any mind if it hadn't been for Moirai. She's long cared for the dragons and spent a good portion of her academics choosing dragon studies as a secondary focus to learning to be a Fate. I know you opened some rift in the human realm that is killing all the hatchlings."

"Do you know how I was able to open the rift?" When she shook her head, I held out my hand to her. "Can I show you what controlling me would offer you?"

She removed her glove and let me connect with her mind, which was foggy with many blocks. It didn't matter because I was there to give information, not take it.

When I finished, her eyes widened. "You're a key seer. We have missed your kind," she said.

"I am a tracker too."

She flung her hand dismissively. "Two seer senses are unusual. However, the key is the only one of use to the elders. You could open the gate to the gods."

"I'm not sure. That I can't promise. I could try."

"You'd do more than try with your soul in our grasps. Tell me now. What do you want in exchange for your soul?"

"I want the son of Samael, Alcaius's name, cleared of all wrongdoing, and he will not receive punishment for anything he has done ever at any point. Second, I have a wisp, and she needs her wisping abilities back, and the dragons told me you could help with that as well."

"Such minor things to give a soul over."

I was giving my soul to save Alcaius's, and that was the most important thing I could fight for. It was the most important thing to give everything up for. "Yes, it would be if it weren't for my final request. I need something to close the rift and remove its effect on anything it's harmed. Even the dragon eggs."

"Yes, that is a much bigger thing. Saving an entire species that is doomed is a huge event to shift on the fate fabric. This deal sounds fair. I will take it to the elders, and we will let you know within two hours. In the meantime, exit where you entered, and I will have a servant there to take you to a room to clean yourself. You need to be more presentable to meet the elders."

I gave her a small bow and walked toward the exit. A bath, while I waited, would help remove all the grime from the travel and seraphim battle. It would also give me time to check on Alcaius and Ashern. My fear had ebbed when I'd spoken to Belphagor because Alcaius had to have lived if he was well enough to offer his soul. A small wood elf with a green hood met me at the exit and led me back through the castle. Moirai had completely disappeared, and it didn't matter to me if I saw her again. If I did, I owed her a thank you for speaking with her mother on my behalf, even though I knew her reasons were her own.

The elf dropped me off at a room where I showered and changed into fresh leathers. I chose my blue ones with gold stitching, as they were the fanciest thing I'd brought with me. I scrunched my curls and let them air dry. I tracked my way to Alcaius's room first and found him still sleeping. His skin had filled in and smoothed back into its usual gorgeous state. I'd have loved him as a shriveled husk as long as he breathed, but I wouldn't mind having him fully back.

I resisted the urge to climb into bed and wrap myself around him until he woke up. We'd pretended for the last part of the quest that we had no issues to resolve. That was far from the truth. I didn't know if we'd even have a future after I gave the elders my soul.

I brushed Alcaius's wild hair from his eyes and kissed his forehead. "I love you. Heal and wake up soon."

The next person I searched for was Ashern, and I found him a few rooms over from Alcaius. His door was open enough I could see him reading in bed.

I knocked on his door. "You've looked better. Even after being a tree."

He put his book down. "Hello, darling, I'm glad to see you made it through our fancy bird battle."

"Fancy bird battle? Interesting interpretation of angelic vampires."

"Only terms to give them more power than they deserve. You look like you have a lot on your mind. Want to talk about it?" He pointed to the chair by his bed. "Have a seat if you'd like, unless you have to get back to the reaper."

I accepted his invitation. "He's still sleeping. The healers think he'll recover."

"Why the troubled face, then?"

I looked at the wooden clock on the wall. "I have about another hour of worry. The elders have my request to save the dragons and clear Alcaius's name. Queen of Fates is presenting it to them, and they will decide."

"It'll all be fine. All your work getting here will pay off."

"All of yours to save your sister will, too."

"Thanks to you," he said.

"Couldn't have come close without you."

He shrugged. "You would have kept going until you did."

"Until I died is more like it." I stared at my hands clasped in my lap. "Like Elisha."

Ashern sat up straighter. "Your uncle is dead?"

"Did everyone but me know he was my uncle?"

"I'm not sure, but when we were at Mistral's cottage, I heard her mention he was your uncle. She said something to Fennec about how your Uncle Elisha should give back what he had stolen from you."

I rubbed my temple where Elisha had touched me as he'd died. "He gave me something right before his last breath. I'm not sure what it was because I feel no different. Maybe he gave whatever he stole back to me and it'll eventually find its way to my thoughts." I stood up and stretched. "Recover, so you can come with me to save your sister."

He spread his arms out. "Come here. You've grown on me."

"I'm glad I could weasel my way into your affection to take root."

He laughed, and his arms wrapped me into a hug. "You've definitely rooted yourself into a permanent place as my friend."

"Same." I told him goodbye and walked toward the fate door.

A room with an opened door appeared empty, and I slipped inside. "Belphagor!" I called his name a few times before he appeared.

"Are you aware the Queen of Fates wants to use my seer sense to open the gateway to the gods?"

His shoulder flames stayed small and blue, giving no reaction to my question. "Yes, that's why I knew she would accept your offer."

"And you don't have a problem with that? If the gods wanted us with them, they'd open the gate themselves. How much control will the elders have over me if they own my soul?"

"Total control. That's what it means to give them your soul. Your soul still stays in you but allows you to be controlled by the one who posses your flame. You stay the same person, but have only the autonomy granted to you by them. They will whisper to your flame, and you will do whatever they ask without hesitation." He brought his hands to his mouth and lowered his voice with each word.

"That's why Samael was so desperate to get the objects back."

"My father didn't use his control often. It was mainly leverage for him if Samael got out of hand."

"There's no other way but for me to give up my soul?"

"No, unless you want it to be Alcaius instead."

I shook my head and buried my face in my hands. "You're sure you have all of this right? There's no way for us both to keep ownership of our souls?"

"More than I am on most things. Without me saying anything at all, what could you possibly give the elders that they could want?"

"I could offer to open the god gate while keeping my soul," I said.

"It won't be enough. They will not only be dramatic about it, but they will want the assurance they will have you around to unlock things for them. There is no other way."

Belphagor had a secretive angle to all of this, and it made me uneasy. He disappeared, and I continued on my way to the fate door where I would give up the most sacred thing I owned for the reaper I loved.

"Azora from the human realm, the elders will see you now," said a small elf at a little desk next to the door.

My heart slammed my ribs, and I forced my feet forward.

Chapter Thirty-One
Fate Fabric
Alcaius

I felt around the bed for Azora and found it empty and cold. When I finally opened my eyes, my reflection stared back from the long mirror on the wall across from me. I touched under my sunken eyes and wondered if I'd drank too much for my reaper abilities to work through fast enough. It had happened a few times at the academy. Haze pressed on my brain, and I sat up to get a better view of my surroundings.

My scythe rested against the wall next to me, and I grabbed it to recharge myself and dispel any lingering toxins I might have had from my irresponsibility. The heat and power surged through me, electrifying my fingertips. Blue lightning zipped across the floor and up the walls as it recharged me and returned my strength. It took me longer than usual to feel like I'd gotten enough energy. As the scythe replenished me, the memories of the seraphim returned.

I jumped up and ran to the bathroom to see if Azora possibly was in there. Panic climbed in my chest as I ran out of the room, desperate to know if she'd survived the attack. A crow squawked on the windowsill, and I considered leaving him outside. I opened the window and walked out of the room.

He flapped his wings next to me. "We must discuss things. It's urgent."

"Talk while we're walking."

"It's private. Not for the Realm of Fates to know."

"Then you will have to wait because there's something a lot more important I need to know than anything my father needs to tell me."

Round stone windows gave a view to the outside land, and it was clear from the opal buildings and cloud landscape that we'd made it to the Queen of Fate's kingdom. On the opposite side of the windows were doors and several looked into rooms with sleeping or groaning people. Fate healers in red robes attended to them.

"Nothing is more important than this. An army is growing from the darker realms in anticipation of the rift bursting. It is bulging and boiling at an increasingly alarming degree. You're needed back home to help with the war effort," the crow said.

"As soon as I find Azora and Fennec, and we complete what we came here for, I'll be right on that."

He landed on the window and panted. "You must slow down and talk to me. Your brother isn't even in this realm."

My scythe crackled on my back, and I turned toward the crow. "What do you mean Fennec isn't here?"

"Your father said you entered another realm than Fennec. He sent a second crow to find him and bring him home. He's furious you left him."

"I got attacked by a horde of seraphim and was unconscious. I'm not the one who left Fennec. Do you know if he's okay?"

"He's alive. That's all your father knows."

I spotted a woman in a blue robe who was pushing a cart of glass potions and red rags. "Excuse me. I need to know where someone is."

She looked over my loose white pants and shirt. "You're a patient and need to get back in bed."

I removed my shirt and pulled one out of my bag to replace it. "No need. You do great work. I need to know if you've seen a woman. The most gorgeous woman you could ever possibly see with stunning silver eyes. A head full of thick brown beautiful curls. A face straight out of the highest ethereal realm. Smells of roses and rain."

Her nose crinkled. "A name would be more helpful than that description."

"Her name is Azora, and she's a human."

"A human? That is quite unusual. I would have remembered one of those."

Fear ate at my chest that she'd died before entering the Fate Realm. I ran my fingers through my hair, holding on as panic took hold. "Azora! Has anyone seen the human Azora?"

Darkness surrounded me, and only a quick snap could be heard as torches illuminated the darkness.

Belphagor stepped forward and ignited his shoulders. "You really need to stay calm when it comes to her, or one day you will mess up more than you already have. Your emotions are your greatest weakness, but you know that because you feel them and see what they do to your life."

"I'll calm when I find her. Put me back."

"She's fine. I was just with her."

"Then take me to her." I pulled the scythe from my back and powered it up to provide light to locate an exit.

"She's occupied, waiting for an answer from the elders."

"Take me there." I stalked all around the room, but he'd taken me to a place with no exits made strictly for teleporters and wall-walkers.

"Soon. You have a task to complete, and I'm here to make sure you do it at just the right time."

I punched the wall but only received bruised knuckles that I soothed by morphing them skeletal. "What task is that?"

"You need to give the elders your soul. Alcaius's Flame, as they will call it."

"Why would I do that? That caused nothing but trouble for my father. I'm wise enough to learn from his mistakes."

"Because if you don't, Azora will give them hers as payment to cure the rift and dragon hatchlings. And mostly to clear your name. She wants to pay penance for your sins."

I took my scythe to the wall, and it merely bounced off. "Get me to her now, Belphagor!"

"Tsk. Tsk. Timing is everything, Alcaius, you know that."

"Timing is everything for you. For me, it's the sooner I can get to my woman, the better."

"The only thing they will accept over a key and tracker seer's soul is that of the heir to Death's soul."

I tried my scythe in several places and contemplated taking it to Belphagor's head to make myself feel better. "Get me to her now! Or I'll break our laws again and reap you."

"And be stuck in here forever? That sounds counterproductive when you only need to be patient a short time longer."

My scythe sent lightning into the ceiling, and his scythe caught it and let it fizzle.

"As soon as you can calm down, I will take you to the elders to request registration."

"It's not like they are going to give me an audience out of nowhere. The dragons already petitioned for Azora, and she has to speak to the queen to see if it'll even be granted."

"If you put you are the son of Death and here to offer your soul, they will listen. You will have to pass through the door where it'll see if you're lying. Since you are not, that will grant you an audience."

"Take me then." I holstered my scythe behind me.

"Your sparking fingers suggest you need to calm down a little more."

"That's not going to happen until I have her in my arms. This is the best you're going to get." I closed my eyes to cool the charge. When I opened them again, I was in front of a green door decorated with painted golden leaves.

A wood elf sat next to the door at a desk small enough to accommodate her tiny size. "Can I help you?"

"I need to petition to see the elders as soon as possible. Within the next hour."

"What makes you think they're even in session? It would take a great deal for them to squeeze you into the schedule." She tapped her green furry fingers on her desk,

"I know they're in session, and I have something better to offer them than the person they are about to see now."

She grabbed forms from the bin behind her and slid them to me with ink and quill. "You are probably wasting both our time but fill out that paper in its entirety."

"Thank you." I took everything over to a little table.

Several others, of various races, sat on a bench, waiting to probably be seen or at least have their requests approved. I filled out everything, including what Belphagor had told me to announce, and handed it back to the elf. If they did not grant me access, I'd grant it myself. Azora giving her soul to the Fates had consequences far-reaching beyond anything she probably realized. The Fates weren't known for their transparency when making deals, and Azora was quick to accept things to save others. If they owned her soul, they could not only control her but wipe her from existence.

The elf sighed as she sent the form up a tube. "Have a seat. We will see if you even get a response."

I tapped my knee up and down before pacing and studying ways I could break in.

The green door swung open, and a Fates male stood in formal lavender robes with his hands clasped in front of him. "Alcaius, son of Samael, the elders will see you now."

I ignored the eruption of disbelief and anger over me just arriving and gaining an audience in front of those who had waited hours. The elders didn't care about fairness, only getting what they wanted. This time, it was to my advantage. The vast room spread out to bridges with deadly bottomless drops that led to more rooms, and to the left, covering an entire wall, was the bane of my existence—the fate fabric.

Small dots lit up various colors, and I didn't know what all of them meant. The white ones with yellow rings around them represented living beings. The fabric reached without end as the Determiners floated with scrolls in hand, determining who would live and who would die. I hated them for their choices because they often chose wrong. Chaos wielders worked beside them, recognizable by their brass armor and wild hair that flopped in chaotic directions.

They created the orders for disasters for the Mothmen to warn about. Some worked on that, while others orchestrated events that caused loss to land and property without casualties. The Determiners and chaos wielders worked together at rapid speed, connecting different color threads to lights that barely flickered among the trillions up for determination.

Among the bigger players were other entities that dealt with weather and other natural happenings. Every tiny faucet of fate had some entity sewing it together to manipulate events to what the gods and Celestials determined it should be. I hated the entire organized system that purposely bred catastrophe in its order to ensure balance. Balance elementals stood inspecting the fabric on their ladders that moved up and across the fabric as they had the final checks to the stitches before approving it as final with their stamps. Their final decisions sent it off as law for the movers of the realms to carry out the wishes of the fate fabric. Orders were sent out to each of the elementals assigned to carry out duty. That's what reapers were. We ensured the orders of the Determiners moved the living to the afterlife.

The Fate took me beyond the fate fabric to a small white room with hooded blue chairs and another door across from the one we entered. He advised me to wait, and I took a seat. The room remained empty, and I'd almost knocked on the other door right before it opened wide for me to enter. The room lit up, blinding with light shining on all the white surfaces, like a sun against a mirror. I shielded my eyes and looked at the Fate's heels to continue to follow him.

Through another large door, that bright light shined through blue glass with a scene of angels with white and black wings fighting each other. In the center was a queen with brown, almost golden, feathered wings on her back, firing an arrow. Behind her marched an army of creatures, including zombies, crawling out of the soil. Purple jewels in her crown drew my eyes to her over all the others. Next to her was a fallen angel, stretching his sword out to the army of white-winged warriors. Something about it mesmerized me, like I could jump into it and be transported to the depicted event, like it happened and wasn't mere artwork.

On fourteen slate thrones sat the fourteen elders. Twelve to represent each of the elementals, one for the humans, and another for the fae. Each throne at the top had a symbol that coincided with the race they represented. In the middle, behind all the thrones, sat a silver dragon with orange eyes. His diamond pupils dilated into circles as he took me in. He had his front legs crossed in front of him and his black wings tucked against his back.

The reaper counterpart, the elemental of birth and life, stepped forward. She had moss hair dropping to her waist, and her skin looked made of bark, like a dryad. Green leaves created a corset that reached her collarbone, and vines with red flowers created her long skirt. "Alcaius, son of Death, we have read your request and ask you to tell us what you want in return for such a large gesture. The elders also need to know that you understand the consequences of such a decision. We are unsure you do as we could have you tried right here for your crimes. We were told you were in hiding and sent many to search for you. And here you have walked right into our midst. What do you have to say for yourself?"

I stepped forward into the blue square that gave all of them the best view to hear me speak. "You could subject me to trial and execution and condemn me to eternal hellfire, but you can't take my soul from me. That is something only I can give you willingly. I also understand the gravity of my decision. You will be able to control me for the rest of my days or extinguish me from existence."

"So why would you offer us such a gift? Why would you allow us to see the things forbidden to us by the gods?"

"I am not Death yet, and therefore, you wouldn't see anything more than you already do until I take his power at my father's death."

"We have eons and are patient. Why are you willing to give such a great sacrifice?"

"There is a human woman, Azora. She is here to correct wrongs the dragons claim she has committed against them. I ask that everything she desires is given to her, and at that, I will bow to the elders and become your property until the end of time."

"He's only here to save himself!" Rook's father, the King of Chaos, stood from the third chair on the left. His twisted beard nearly reached his knees as he spouted his protest.

Life glanced at the king and back at me. "His punishment would have merely been his life, and he'd have kept his soul for the afterlife and even possibly had the chance for reincarnation at some point after serving his sentence dealt by the executioners. We will discuss your offer and see if we are in agreement to give the human Azora what she desires. You will wait here while we deliberate."

They left the room, and I waited for their answer. If they denied my request, I'd have to consider something more drastic.

A squawk echoed around as my father's crow landed on a pillar. "Do you know how difficult it was to track you down?"

"How did you even get in here?"

"I have my ways. You know I can't leave until I fulfill all your father asked of me."

"And what did he ask?"

"For you to return with the box and prepare for war. Can I tell him you located it?"

"You can tell him whatever you want." I shooed him away. "Tell him I'll be home soon."

The crow flew back out the way he came, and I watched the door for the elders to return and tell me my fate.

Chapter Thirty-Two
Flames
Azora

We walked into a room that appeared to extend to infinity, where beings flew all around it, moving threads to dots of light. It looked like organized chaos, like there was no obvious order to it, but they all knew what they were supposed to be doing. We walked so long that I thought I'd embarked on another quest just to talk to the elders. The next set of doors led to a smaller yet still enormous room with a dais that held Fourteen thrones occupied by people in various colored robes. At the top of the thrones were symbols I recognized from the dragon library, and I was able to piece together that twelve represented the different elementals. The last two I couldn't place their meaning. A silver dragon sat behind all the thrones, staring at me with not even the smallest blink from his flame eyes.

A woman who appeared made of plants stood and walked to the edge of the platform. "Azora of the humans, we have discussed your request in great detail and have arrived at a decision. Another has offered us payment for the things you desire. We had to weigh both options and decide which would serve us best."

She held out her half-closed palm, and vines grew from the floor, lifting two objects onto pedestals at the bottom of the stage. Both looked chiseled from white stone. One was a rose and the other a butterfly. I squinted and leaned forward to get a better look. No, it was a moth.

She picked them up, holding one in each hand. "The Fates made these essence holders for us, so there would be no delay when we arrived at a decision. The rose is for your soul and what the Fates believe is a good representation of your inner self." Her gaze went to the back of the room. "Nice that you have finally arrived, Alcaius."

I spun around and swallowed as my legs threatened to buckle. Belphagor had said if I offered my soul, Alcaius would be safe. They had to pick mine. Flutters filled my stomach as he sent me his crooked smile. He stood next to me and slipped his hand into mine, not caring in the slightest that he was displaying our love in front of some of the most powerful beings in the universe. He didn't care they'd see our love as highly forbidden and could prosecute us for it.

The plant woman stared at our hands for a few heartbeats before recovering and continuing her announcement. "After weighing both choices, we have accepted Alcaius's offer."

I slowly turned my head to face him as chill ran down my arms. "What offer?"

"He has offered his soul as you have yours, and we have chosen his over yours."

I gasped and jerked my hand away from his to approach the stage. "There's some kind of mistake. I came here to save him. Not bind him to you. It's my punishment! The dragons sent me for punishment. Take my soul! Please!" Fear ripped apart my lungs in agonizing waves, and I fell to my knees. "Please!"

"The decision of the council is firm. All your requests shall be granted. You will be sent home with everything you need to spare the dragons, return your fairy her wisping abilities, and Alcaius has been cleared of all his crimes."

"What good is it that I save his life for you to take his soul?" Anger simmered, ready to burst out at the elders until I tore through as many as I could. I'd come all that way to save my reaper for him to be placed in a worse situation.

Strong familiar arms wrapped around me, and Alcaius turned me around to let me cry against his chest. "It's alright. Things will be fine."

"They won't! How could you give your soul in place of mine? It was my punishment!"

"No, it was mine. You were giving yours to spare me from the consequences I brought on myself. I know you well enough to know that was it."

An invisible force pried us apart. "There will be no discussion!" The plant woman pointed a finger at each of us as her arms shook from the force of separating us. "Alcaius, step forward and give payment."

I tried to run between him and the moth, but she held me back with her power. I sobbed as Alcaius pricked his finger with a special dagger. The blood dripped on the moth as he gave his oath to give his soul to the control of the elders. His head whipped back, and light burst from his mouth and shot into the moth. I wailed, paralyzed to do anything as he became completely tied to their mercy.

The fourteen members of the elders rose and exited the room, all except Life and Existence.

Existence handed me two small bottles, and Life finally allowed me to move and take them. "Have your fairy drink these one after the other, and her wisping abilities will return to her within one moon cycle." Next, she handed me two wooden boxes. "The blue one is for the dragon eggs. Rub the ointment on every egg. It will replenish itself, so you will have plenty for all of them. Once the ointment is on an egg, it will not only repair any damage done to them, but also create a protective barrier, so any more of the rift leaking on them will not

cause harm. The green one is for the rift. You will be able to pour it
from the outside on all but the origin of the tear. That will have to be
sealed from the inside."

I paused, putting all of it in my bag. "Someone has to stay stuck in
the rift?"

"Yes, choose wisely who it is."

I caught Alcaius's eyes then, and he shook his head, already insisting
it shouldn't be me. Of course, it was me who needed to seal the rift
from the inside. The entire quest I went on was to rectify my mistake
of opening it in the first place. Not only that, but he'd just sacrificed
something massive and had no room to talk. They dismissed us, and I
didn't run to him. Instead, I bolted for the door to process what he'd
done.

"Azora!" he called behind me several times, but I didn't stop.

I dashed through the doors and back to the room with blinking
lights and the scramble of so many beings working on a massive pro-
ject. When I made it outside the second set of doors, Ashern was
waiting.

"Azora?" He followed me too.

I ran through the palace of fate, wanting so badly to run from
whatever destiny had planned for me. I made it back to my room
and locked myself inside, sinking into a warm bath to calm the storm
swirling inside me. Not even closing my eyes and sinking against the
cold porcelain took away the tumultuous pain in my head and stomach.

I fell asleep in the tub, and the water had gone cold when I finally
woke up again and got dressed. Night had also fallen, and the wooden
clock on the wall told me I'd slept only a couple of hours. I focused
on Alcaius's location, and the familiar buzz of my reaper landed right
outside my door. I opened it to see him sleeping sitting up and grabbed

his hand to tug him to me. He blinked open his eyes and let me lead him into the room. My anger toward him seethed for reasons and at a level I didn't fully understand, but I needed him until morning. I was pretty sure he needed me.

We climbed into the large bed, under blue silk sheets, and I buried my face in his chest, in his scent that I craved on all difficult and easy nights. I wanted to wrap myself up in him until the end of time and defy the upheaval that fate continued to vow for our hearts. He kissed the top of my head and relaxed against me like all had been put right with me next to him.

When I woke again, he was watching me with sunlight splashing all around us. "Morning, love."

I kissed him, moving my lips against his with a desperation to tell him how much my soul loved his. How angry I was he'd given it away, and I needed him to ask for it back. "You shouldn't have done that, Alcaius. You shouldn't have given the elders your soul!" The last part released as a stuttered cry.

"Like you were going to do?"

"That's different. It was my price to pay, and you keep paying my prices. You keep offering yourself as a sacrificial lamb on my behalf."

"And I always will. I will bleed for you until I have nothing left to pump my heart because I desire no life where harm finds you. I will annihilate realms to get to you and destroy any threat that even whispers in your direction. I will always pay any price necessary to keep you safe, including giving up my soul." He wrapped the blanket around me tighter as I shook, despite the warmth diminishing his comfort.

"Don't you think it was my turn to do that for you?"

He lifted my chin, so I'd meet his eyes. "No, never will it be your turn to suffer to relieve my pain."

"That's just it. Isn't it? Your suffering is so deeply intertwined with mine as mine is with yours that anything terrible that happens to you is etched into me as well. I will suffer because I see you suffering. The pain of that is much greater than if it were me bearing all of it."

He held me while I cried, and we didn't move for a long time. How could I ever live or even exist without the peace of his heart against mine? I feared for the future because of the wholeness the present brought, and all I wanted more than anything in all the realms was to have that with him until my body gave in to old age.

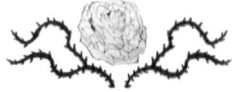

Eiro stared at me, sitting on my nightstand. "It is time to return to your realm and save my kind."

I rolled over to see Alcaius had already left. "If we must, it seems my reaper has already left."

"He went to gather his belongings, and I told him I'd watch over you."

"Well, I've never needed a babysitter, so if you'll excuse me, I need to get ready in the washroom myself."

"There's no shame in having others look out for you, so you can fully rest sometimes. Long have you insisted you had to do everything yourself. That is no longer the case."

I grabbed a new outfit from my bag and headed toward the bathroom. "Relying on myself has helped me survive just fine until now."

"Maybe one day, you will wish to do more than survive."

"Maybe one day the Fates will let me." I disappeared into the bathroom, dressing and pinning my waist-length curly hair into a braided bun. My boots were by my bed, so I returned to the room with the mouthy dragon and put them on.

Eiro insisted I find breakfast like he thought he had to parent me. My stomach rumbling agreed with him, and for that reason alone, I complied with his request to find the guest kitchen. I ate toast, eggs, and fruit, tucking extra away to make sure Alcaius also had something. I tracked him to a room where I found Ashern as well. The frowns on their faces lifted into smiles when I entered the room.

My eyes bounced back and forth between their forced expressions. "What is it?"

"War has descended upon the realm and dark forces are leaking from the rift," Ashern said.

"I was too late."

Alcaius shot Ashern a stern look. "It's a small leak, but it's invited other things already in the realm to rise and join what is emerging. There's still time to stop it, but we have to hurry."

Eiro's wings brushed my cheek from where he sat on my shoulder. "I shall fly you back to the realm quickly. A dragon should help your plight."

"Yes, after Alcaius has breakfast." I pulled out the bundle of food I'd saved and handed it to him.

"What about me?" Ashern set his lower lip in a pout.

"The kitchen is down the hall. Fourth door on the right. Besides, can't you eat after we leave?"

Alcaius smirked at my response as he popped a strawberry into his mouth.

Ashern pushed off the wall. "Not when I'm coming with you to help. You already invited me to save the dragons with you, and I signed up for this quest. I'm seeing it through to the last dragon egg finding salvation."

"Very well. We can leave from the eastern doors by the kitchen."

Outside, we found an extensive field for Eiro to grow back to his typical size of nearly reaching the height of a castle. He stretched out his leg to help us climb on easily, and we settled into a spot that would help us stay on during any aerial stunts. Alcaius asked me to track Fennec, and his signal was so hazy that it made me think he'd already returned to our realm. He didn't appear to be anywhere reachable by anything but a portal. We flew over the next few days and slept by tying rope around Eiro's neck and then tying it to our feet while also tucking ourselves into his wings. Once we made it back to the gates, we strolled through both with no issues. No one guarded the portals to leave, and they apparently only wanted to keep stragglers from entering too close to the Fates and Celestials.

From there, we had to travel to the hatching grounds to save the babies. Eiro knew the way, as he claimed most dragons did. They had a natural pull to their place of origin. Black rocks with veins of lava covered the hatching grounds that could only be accessed through a cave that most dragons struggled to squeeze inside. Eiro shrunk down to a few feet taller than Alcaius for us all to fit better while still staying a sizeable threat.

He approached the wooden gate that blocked every inch of the entryway. "Keep your hands on me and be ready to run. My dragon's blood will allow me to enter without consequences. If we move quickly and stay touching, it should let all of you through with me."

Alcaius, Ashern, and I all grabbed onto his scales, locking our hands underneath them. The gate opened for him, and we all slid through into a tropical paradise. The sun baked anything it touched, like we'd walked into a massive incubator. Scaled eggs in all colors rested in nests lined up on dirt shelves, with thick blue grass surrounding the bottom half of each egg.

As I approached the first set of eggs, I noticed black splotches in spots, and when I lifted an egg to place the ointment, a luminescent silvery liquid dripped into a small pool under the egg. "The Rift. Can we move all the eggs? I know the elders said the ointment will prevent further harm, but I think we should move them out of it to be sure."

Eiro shoved dirt over the spot I'd removed the egg from. "Yes, I think we should cover up the spots before placing them back in the dirt."

Alcaius stood back and leaned from side to side. "This is going to take years. We need help. I have a portal key from Zaire. I'll go to the nearest city and bring back help."

"Eiro, you'll need to fly him if you want to save all these babies. We have war to worry about as well," I said.

Eiro puffed out smoke, and his chest and throat glowed with caged fire. "Only for the eggs will I allow this."

Alcaius and Eiro left to fly to the city of Hoffelim to find a public portal to cross the land quickly. Zaire had a portal chamber and could most likely send lots of help with them. Ashern and I set to work, spreading the ointment on eggs and using sticks to clean out as much of the rift as we could. We'd barely made a dent hours later when Alcaius and Eiro returned with dozens of people to help. My dragon had to lead a few through the gate at a time the same way he'd brought us in, and we divided everyone into teams. Most cleaned out the nests, and the group left took cups of the ointment that replenished as Life had said it would.

We worked long into the night, and Eiro lit torches for us to see on the new moon night. Each egg covered in ointment shined in the light, and the black spots had already begun to fade. Eiro claimed he could feel the baby dragons strengthening. He worked his energy across the area to look for any signs of us missing any, and we all cheered as he confirmed we'd rescued every egg. Zaire had given Alcaius another portal key, and we marched to the city to travel to Zaire's castle.

I entangled my fingers with Alcaius's as I studied his disturbed expression. "What is it?"

"War. Zaire says the forces are headed to Banloomis. If they make it that far, they could destroy all the channels to get souls to the afterlife. His castle is a beacon they'll head to first, so we have to do everything to contain them there."

"What will happen if the souls can't go where they need?"

"Depending on what stage of judgment they are in, they will become wandering souls or be destroyed."

Chapter Thirty-Three
Phantoms and Demons
Alcaius

We returned to Zaire's castle through the portal system that entered his house. It could only be accessed if he gave you a key. He'd sent as many servants as he could spare with me to save the baby dragons, and now that we'd accomplished that, I'd arrived to help him push back the tide of forces rising. All the dark creatures could feel the pull of the rift calling to them, and several of those inside had found small tears to slip through. It was believed something powerful had gotten through and was encouraging an uprising. The first thing Azora did when we arrived was to track Fennec, who she said was back at my father's castle.

Zaire's castle was known as a beacon. It drew the attention away from Banloomis, so that anything in the area threatening to attack would head there first, thinking it was the city of the dead. It wouldn't hold them off forever because if they managed to get inside, they would realize it was a facade. However, it served as a distraction from what everyone wanted to protect.

Zaire led us into his war room and shut the door. "We need to get the tears in the rift closed."

Azora placed her bag on the table and brought out a box. "This will do the trick, but someone has to seal it from the inside." She met my eyes. "I created this mess, so I will go."

I flinched and stepped in front of the door. "Like Hades, you will!"

"There's no other choice. You heard the elders. It should be me."

Zaire sat down on his white throne at the end of the table. "If you go into the rift and seal it, there will be no return."

"Which is exactly why she's not going. There are plenty of other expendable beings that can do it," I said.

She put the box back in her sack and flung it over her shoulder. "Do you hear yourself? My life isn't any more valuable than anyone else's."

"Yes, it is."

"You're so infuriating how you can spin your morals based on your feelings. I'm not more valuable simply because you love me and say I am."

I strode across the room and yanked her to me. "Your life is worth letting the realms fall for." I pointed at the door. "No one out there is worth that."

"Savage."

"When this is all over, I'll show you how true that is."

Zaire cleared his throat. "The rift needs closed. But so Alcaius doesn't tear everything to pieces, I will ask for a volunteer to go into the rift and seal it."

Azora waved her hand. "I already volunteered."

"And for everyone's sake, including the reaper, it's best we pick someone else to do the task. Or do you not believe Alcaius will rip the rift clean open just to get to you? It doesn't even matter that no one but you has been able to open it for centuries. He'd find a way."

She studied me and nodded. "Fine. Only if the volunteer truly understands the gravity of what they choose."

"I'd never send anyone who didn't know what they were sacrificing."

Zaire left to gather his troops and find a volunteer.

Azora's silver eyes looked ready to light me on fire. "You can't do that."

"Do what?"

"Expect that you can make sacrifices, but not allow me the same right. I'm just as scared of losing you. That didn't stop when you offered your soul on a platter."

"You mean exactly like you did."

She closed her mouth halfway through starting a rebuttal. "I opened the rift, and it's my responsibility to close it. Not some poor soldier who is after honor."

"The rift being open is no one's fault but Belial's. He manipulated you into opening it, and as soon as you figured out what it really meant, you tried to close it. The rift holds the darkest things in existence. You are the purest soul I know and belong nowhere near it. You marched across realms to make up for a mistake. That's enough."

"You're biased. There's nothing I could do you'd want me punished for."

"No, nothing. Not even destroying me with your key sense." I pulled her to me and rested my forearm on the wall above her head.

"You've already destroyed me over and over again."

"So what's one more time?" My lips moved over hers with the desperate need to kiss her goodbye before addressing the war approaching outside.

We broke the kiss, and her arms hugged me in a way that felt like she saw the dark things inside me and still loved me. She held me like she could piece me together whole and healed.

I lifted her chin and gave her one final kiss. "I love you. Close as much as you can of the rift with what the elders gave you and let Zaire's soldiers handle the other side."

She touched my leather battle armor with my ranking stitched in gold across my left shoulder. "Is that an order, General?"

My smile went crooked. "Would Azora of Aresgan, key and tracker seer, queen of obstinance, ever take orders from anyone?"

"No, I think not, so why waste your breath?"

"Because I hope you will choose to stay and live out the rest of our lives together. Not only that, but we've discussed Belphagor and how he told me he'd get you to go into the rift with him willingly. It's one reason I'm strongly against it. You can't go with him for any reason."

"That won't happen. He lied to me about something big, and I no longer trust him. There's no way he can get me to go with him now."

My shoulders dropped in relief. "Good."

She pushed up on her tiptoes and kissed me again. "I will see you when this battle ends, so stay alive."

"That I ask of you as well." I walked her to her dragon and kissed her goodbye.

Her dragon was something I didn't particularly like for two main reasons. The first being it had bonded to her without her consent. Even though that was the way most dragons operated, I didn't like anyone forcing anything upon her, most of all something as intimate as a dragon bond. The second reason was that he was a present from Belphagor. It was another reason I'd reacted so strongly to her mentioning sealing the rift from the inside. Belphagor wanted to use her for something. The Oblivion elemental could manipulate timelines with practiced precision, and for some reason, he'd been altering Azora's for years. The gift of the dragon was another one of his chess moves, with Azora as the pawn.

I met Zaire and Rook back in the war room, where he sat back on his throne. Zaire had gotten all his troops set up to defend the castle, and we left to discuss strategy while we waited for the threat that could arrive by nightfall. We were the last defense before Banloomis where the dead were judged.

Zaire had a map of his property and another of the realm spread across the table. "The troops all have weapons and moon dust. We had enough to give each soldier two pouches." He tossed me three small leather bags that I strapped to my pants. "It should be enough to hold back any onslaught of phantoms." He went over more of the strategies and everything he thought we should know, answering any questions we had.

Rook leaned against the wall with his thumbs tucked under his arms. "There's a rumor that the son of Death has given his soul to the elders."

"I heard the same rumor," Zaire said.

"It's true. They put my soul essence into a stone moth. Found that interesting that the Fates pulled that up as representing me. That's more your thing, Zaire." I took a seat a few chairs down from his and ran my palms over the cool marble table.

"That's not how it works. It pulls out who you are, not who everyone else sees you as."

"Tell me then. What does a moth say about me?"

Zaire stared out the window at his troops spread across his lawn. "Moths symbolize death."

"I thought it didn't make who everyone else thought you were."

He held up a finger. "I wasn't finished. They represent darkness always trying to reach for the light, even to their own demise. They desire to be immersed in it but never fully belong to it as they are creatures of the darkness."

Rook smacked my back. "Pegged you just right."

Shouts tore our attention from our conversation. Phantoms, shifters, and other netherworld creatures had reached the gate in the masses. We ran to join the battle, to keep it from ending the afterlife for millions.

Zaire stood on a boulder at the top of the hill that rose above his fence line. He'd shifted into Mothman form as I shifted into a reaper to prevent vulnerabilities. His black wings twitched on his back, ready to rain terror from the sky. His massive red eyes glowed as the only part of him not blending into the shadows. Mothmen were created by the gods to drive fear into anyone who saw them.

I leaped into the battle, ripping off heads with the hook of my scythe. My greedy weapon sated its appetite with each creature it dismembered. It crackled with excitement, and I used that to increase the electricity surging in me until it burst free and fired into at least ten enemies at once. I killed with precision, sensing exactly where to strike to stop hearts. I became a blur as the thrill of battle surged through me. Phantoms were the trickiest to kill with their lack of a body. I sprinkled moon dust on them until they writhed enough for my scythe to extract their souls.

Rook tore through any of the enemy darting for Banloomis. He kept the edges of the battlefield to make sure none snuck past. Zaire dropped onto enemies and ripped out their throats with his claws. He released potent steam from his mouth that dropped many within close vicinity of his targets. Smoke bloomed in the distance at the same moment the ground shook.

A high demon rose over the hill at the horizon, stomping the ground with his colossal legs. Lava flowed through cracks in his skin like he'd pried himself from a volcano. Smoke streamed from his charcoal eyes. Zaire flew toward him, throwing moon dust into the demon's eyes. It swatted at him, missing a few times before landing a strike and sending my friend spiraling to the ground. Zaire's body remained still, and I charged toward the scene as I yelled orders for everyone else to keep fighting the lesser foe. I ran up the creature's leg. Heat blasted from him, but in my reaper form, it couldn't harm me.

I dodged his palms slamming down to smash me and pierced my scythe into cracks in his rocky flesh. I tugged the blade back out and flung pieces of his obsidian hide to the ground. Lava leaked from him, and he roared. Once I'd torn a large enough hole in his chest, I filled it with most of my moon dust. He screeched as it sizzled his insides, and I drove my scythe into his neck like an ax until his head rolled off his shoulders. I flew as the ground rumbled at his collapse. He squashed several of his comrades, and I quickly hacked any that escaped from under him.

Zaire had recovered and was back in the air, diving to attack any enemy that still moved. When all went still, he sent his scouts to be sure the threat had ceased. I walked with him through the battlefield to ensure we'd ended all enemies and none would be allowed to enter Banloomis and threaten the afterlife of anyone.

Zaire prodded a walker with his sword. "As long as Azora succeeds in closing the rift, we should have time."

"You found a volunteer to do the final closure?" I stabbed my scythe into a twitching goblin.

"Yes, an older soldier who didn't hesitate. I sent a few mages with him to make sure he closes it."

I touched the tip of my scythe to collect any souls still loitering in their bodies. "You don't trust him?"

"I do, but anyone can do the wrong thing, given the right circumstances. I have no reason to doubt his loyalty, but it's best to confirm things like this."

We walked the entire field three times and found none living. Rook took care of all the areas around with his scouts, watching for any signs of missed enemy. I took a shower to wash away the battle and changed into my typical black leather. I retrieved a horse from Zaire's stables, choosing a silver stallion and riding toward the rift that was within a couple of hours of Zaire's castle. The setup was so he could monitor anything unusual around Grimheldin, the dark forest that surrounded the rift.

I rode through the barren trees, watching for phantoms and ghouls as I rode. Other than the occasional shadow movement, nothing approached me. My scythe had gone quiet, satisfied for the first time in a while with the bloodshed it had committed. Its thirst would return before too long and pester me to seek sources to take life from. Its desire mixed with my own took grand discipline to overcome.

The glow of the rift peeked through the trees as I drew closer, and as I reached it, I could see things had changed with black marks scarring up the silver opal liquid. It appeared Azora had closed the leaks, but the evidence of the damage lingered. I started at the edge of the rift and worked my way to the east, looking for Azora. My skin buzzed seconds before I spotted her on a stone platform between two pillars.

Relief over finding her lasted less than a minute when I saw Belphagor come into view. A visceral protectiveness for my woman surged rage at him being so close to her and the rift. His threats of taking her into it ignited my wrath. I charged him, knocking him onto the rift.

It was sealed, so he merely landed on the bouncy surface. The liquid rippled outward but remained contained.

He brushed himself off and hovered to solid ground. "So nice of you to join us, Alcaius."

I decked the smirk off his face.

CHAPTER THIRTY-FOUR
PROMISE
Azora

I checked everything I thought I'd need for the rift, and Eiro walked at my side as we headed out to a field for better take-off. Alcaius had left to talk war strategy.

Ashern strolled up with three men in grey cloaks. He pointed to the middle one. "This is Fredrick. He is here to seal the rift, and these other two are here to let Zaire know he did his job. They are energy seers."

I bowed my head quickly and handed my bag to Eiro's mouth. "Thank you, Fredrick. This is an unbelievably generous sacrifice."

He bowed and stayed lowered for several seconds. "My wife has left for the eternal plains and the glory of battle is long behind me." He pointed to his knee, which had a leather brace around it. "It's an honor to serve my lord and realm in such a way."

"When I return from this task, I will burn incense for safe eternal travels for you and your wife. That is a tiny thing compared to what you are about to do. Is there anything else I can do for you? Name it, and I shall do it."

"No, the incense is more than generous that someone would think to do that for my wife and me."

"All of Zaire's castle will burn it for you. I will see to it."

He brushed away a tear. "That is much appreciated."

My eyes watered. "This isn't something you have to do. I should be the one doing this. It's my fault the rift is opened."

Ashern shook his head and opened his mouth.

Fredrick raised his gloved hand. "Lady Azora, I know all about how the rift opened, and I ask you not to take this honor from me. Don't lengthen my time parted from my wife."

I closed my eyes to let my tears slip free and nodded. Eiro straightened out his leg and wing for us to climb on. Ashern and Fredrick offered me their hands to boost me to the top, and we all got situated, holding onto Eiro's back spikes for safety. It didn't take long to fly from Zaire's castle to the rift. The shimmering opal river was a beautiful sight that popped against the black and dead nature around it. Eiro landed next to the luminescent rift and lowered himself to help us off more easily.

I set to work pouring the potion from the elders on the seeping red and black gashes that had formed in the rift. We tried to pour some into another container like we had the elixir for the dragon eggs, but it dissolved into powder when it touched anything but the rift. Even though it extended my work, I insisted on being the one to carry out the duty. It was the least I could do for my transgressions. Once I believed all the rips were repaired, I asked the energy seers to sense anything still open. Energy seers could not only manipulate energy and sometimes matter, but they could also sense fluctuations in it. They found three more, and the main one I left open because it was the one Fredrick had to close from the inside.

A heavy weight pressed on my chest as Fredrick stepped onto the riverbank. "Thank you for allowing me this great honor." He slid into the original tear at the place where I had created the entire mess in the spot I'd died and Alcaius had sacrificed everything to bring me back. Fredrick disappeared inside the tear, and a few moments later, it closed. The energy seers placed their hands over it, and both agreed Frederick had succeeded.

Ashern put his arm around me and chanted something in a foreign dialect. "May the gods lead you to the heavens, where on the shores you find those who went before you and eternal peace." He squeezed me. "Think of him as happy with his wife right now."

"How do we know he's dead? If things can come out of there, then maybe he's alive and being tortured." I squinted to see if I could find him under the liquid barrier.

"No human would survive for long in an environment where dark creatures thrive in such mass numbers, with no one like me helping them. Why don't we—"

I pulled away from Ashern and waved my hand in front of his fixed eyes. "Ashern?" I glanced around me, and the stillness and quiet became tangible. The rift had no current and the bare branches of the trees no longer swished in the breeze. I also couldn't see Eiro anywhere.

"Azora, it's time for a chat." Belphagor stood on a platform that had a black and white checkered pattern, like we could play a life-sized game of chess.

"I closed the rift, and there is no way inside now." I waved my hand in front of Ashern again. "Restart time, and where is my dragon?"

"Your dragon will be back later. You could open it again. Give me the favor you owe me."

"Favor! You think I owe you a favor for getting me nothing? You said if I offered my soul, it would save Alcaius from giving his. That's not what happened! They took his." I marched up the steps and pulled my dagger from my thigh. "I should kill you instead!"

"That's a little extreme."

My eyes grew while the rest of me tightened. "You think killing you for manipulating me for reasons I don't understand and then expecting a favor for it is too extreme?"

"Yes, I do." He flicked his finger up under my chin and closed my gaping mouth. "Not that a small dagger would have any success at all."

"I'm willing to try it!"

"How about sparing Alcaius's soul instead?"

"No more tricks. I will definitely not trust you enough to reopen the rift. Especially after everything I went through to close it."

"Alcaius's soul will be housed at the gate of the gods. It's where the elders keep things like that, but we'll never successfully reach it up here. We have to pass through the netherworld for most of the journey. Once at the gate of the gods, I will pause time and let you retrieve it."

"There are issues with this. Why don't you just freeze time on our journey in places where we might get caught up here? And it would be better for Alcaius's soul to be with me, but it could still fall into worse hands after we got it."

"It has to be done this way. I've made all the calculations millions of times." He snapped his fingers, and a wooden box with strange writing appeared in his hands. "It would be given back to him with this."

I covered my mouth. "The silencer box! You know how long I've been looking for that, and it keeps vanishing."

"I saved it for you, pet."

I socked him in the arm. "Call me pet again, and I will find a way to make my dagger work on you."

"I used the box to lure you to places I wanted you to be. It was a beacon that I didn't have to put much effort into. Go with me into the rift, and I will give you the box and help you retrieve Alcaius's soul."

"What makes you think I'll believe anything you say?"

He shifted from one leg to the other. "I have sent many tests your way to see how you reacted to circumstances in which you would not benefit from doing something for someone else. I tested you to see how valuable Alcaius's soul was to you. How willing you were to give up everything for it. The familiars and the sea monster were tests for other things. You reacted as I'd hoped each time. You reacted as I saw was your most probable timeline."

"You traumatized me to test me?"

"Yes, for so long I searched for the child who would be both a key and a tracker seer. It was the answer I got when I asked the timeline for a way to do the one thing I needed to do. Long ago, before I knew I needed you, King Samael had asked me what his downfall would be. I told him a tracker seer and a key seer but did not tell him they would be one and the same. He became obsessed with it and made deals with human kings to kill them all. Your father and your uncle spared you."

"Elisha." Pain struck my chest like tiny needles jabbing in sharp waves.

"Yes. Ironically, by the time I realized I needed a key seer to go into the rift, Samael had wiped nearly all of them out. I searched through time and space and found you. Still so young and still not fully manifesting your seer senses. I tracked your uncle down and knew that out of all memory seers, he would help me and not tell what you could do to anyone. We made several deals. Your father and Elisha had been estranged, but your uncle agreed. He traveled with me and convinced your father to wipe your memory of your abilities. For some reason, it didn't take on your tracker sense. So your father trained you to keep it a secret, and I saw that would be enough to keep you safe."

"But he gave me an old lock to practice on without telling me I was a key seer." I pulled it from my pocket. "It's something I carry with me everywhere."

"Yes, it was a way to get you to practice your key sense without putting you in danger, because someday I would need you to use it. But we had warned your father early enough about your abilities that he was able to train you before you accidentally revealed what you could do. If anyone else had seen you, you would have been executed and your soul bound for Death's collection. For the rest of your life, I guided all the events around you to line you up exactly where and when I needed you to be." He snapped his fingers and held a small jar. "I have a tiny amount of the potion needed to close the rift. If you open it, we will be able to go inside and close it again."

My eyes shifted to where Fredrick had disappeared. "So a poor man sacrificed everything when this could have been our plan from the start?"

"I did him a mercy by waiting. He went into the rift for his wife. To be with her again, and for that reason, I relate to him. But it had to happen this way with Frederick doing what he did, and us going in later. It is vitally important that the plan I've worked on for so long happens the way it should." He twirled a silver decorative pen in his hand. "I offer you two assurances about this."

"I won't give you a fae ink promise."

A fae ink promise had killed my father and me. He'd broken one to save me, and I'd broken one to stop the invasion from the rift. A person tattooed a vow on their skin, and if they broke the vow, the ink would kill them.

He spun the pen between his middle and pointer fingers. "This will be a one sided promise. Only I will make the oath to you. I will vow that if you follow me into the rift and help me with tasks you are capable of until I say you are done, I will help you get Alcaius's soul back and give you the silencer box. I will also return you to the reaper whole with an added surprise that will bring you both great happiness."

"No, surprises. What do you think will bring me happiness?"

"No, it will remain a surprise. Those are the terms. In case your sacrificial heart needs another reason. Do we have an agreement?"

"Can I touch the pen? I need to feel that it has the same essence as the other fae ink I've connected to." I closed my palm around it when he handed it to me and knew he was telling the truth. "Vow all you have promised, and I will do as you wish, but you must promise me one last thing."

He rolled his eyes. "Haven't I been generous enough?"

"Promise me your plan will not unleash anything that will harm innocent people. That nothing you have me do will harm them, either."

"Done." He lifted the pen. "Do you want to do the honors, or should I?"

"I can't draw to save the realm."

"The pen does the work. It only needs a willing vessel."

"Feel free to mark yourself."

He hovered the pen above his wrist. "I hereby vow to you, Azora of Aresgan, mate to Alcaius, son of Death."

"We're not mates. We've thought about it, but we aren't."

He blinked. "Could you not interrupt?"

"Proceed."

"I hereby vow to you Azora of Aresgan that if you go into the rift with me and help me, I will help you get Alcaius's soul back and give you the silencer box, so you can safely return his soul to him. The things I intend for you to do and the things I intend to do will not harm the innocent or destroy the realm. Is that sufficient of a vow for you?"

"How long will these tasks take? You could keep me down there for decades."

"It will take less than two moon cycles by my best estimation of the timelines I see."

"Okay. Then yes, it's a sufficient vow."

He held the pen to his skin, and it drew a rose that looked similar to the stone one in the Realm of Fates. "It is done" He looked over his shoulder. "Your reaper is coming."

"How?" I stared at a still frozen Ashern.

"I have only frozen him. It's much easier to do while having a conversation."

"The trees stopped blowing too."

"That's because he was causing the breeze."

I wanted to ask why, but let it go. Curiosity had no place in this moment. "Should we hurry into the rift?"

"No, Alcaius is too close, and we need the rift sealed for hours before he tries to find a way in. I can freeze him too, but it'll end as soon as I'm in the rift. Tell him goodbye while telling him nothing and meet me here once you are sure he sleeps." He turned and waited for my lover's approach.

Belphagor went flying off the platform at Alcaius's shove and landed with a thud on the rift. He floated and smiled. "So nice of you to join us, Alcaius."

Alcaius punched him so hard Belphagor's head whipped to the side, and his jaw made a cracking sound. All Belphagor did was laugh and disappear. Ashern vanished at the same moment too, which was a concern I'd have to address with Belphagor another time.

Alcaius ran for me and searched my body for injury. "Are you alright?"

"I'm fine and had it handled. There was no need for violence."

"There was when he's been manipulating both of us and putting it in my head that he's taking you into the rift. Violence was justified."

"Can we go to the castle now? I promised a man I'd burn incense for him and his wife?"

"Sure. We have to share a horse on the ride back."

"Perfect."

He climbed onto his horse and pulled me in front of him. I relaxed, and he kissed down my neck.

I closed my eyes to savor the time with him. "Tell me how the battle went."

He told me everything that had happened, and I told him about Fredrick and all that had occurred on my end, being careful to leave out any details of my deal with Belphagor.

CHAPTER THIRTY-FIVE
CHOICES
Azora

Z aire agreed to have everyone burn incense for Fredrick and his wife to have the best possible eternity. Alcaius and I went straight to our room after the ceremony. Fireworks boomed outside our window. Alcaius led me into the bathroom and started the shower. I dropped my clothes to the ground, and he swallowed as his eyes moved over my body. "Perfection, he said,

He stripped down and rushed toward the shower, pulling me with him under the water. The warm water flowed over my skin at the same moment he pressed me into the cool wall. He worshiped my body, kissing, touching, and teasing me with his fangs.

I tilted my head to give him better access to my neck. "Do you think we'll ever be mates?"

"The moment you want that with me is the moment we are."

"What would it feel like?"

His fingers moved to my clit as he kneaded it until I moaned. "At first, it would feel like the other times I've bitten you. You'd feel extreme pleasure. Orgasms all over your body, and then I would dig deeper than I have, and there would be pain that would burn through you, but as the bond took, the pain would diminish into warmth, and the pleasure would return with greater force than ever. We'd both be engulfed in bliss and intertwined for hours as our souls fused together."

"We can't do that now. With your soul belonging to the elders."

"My soul is still in my body, and I'm the same person. They own control of it when they want to use it, which they most likely won't do until I take over for my father. At that point, I'll be at their mercy and be forced to do whatever they want with no agency. They can also destroy my soul anytime they wish. They have mages powerful enough to do it." He held my arms above my head as he sucked on my nipple and slipped his fingers inside me.

My eyes rolled back as I shuddered against his fingers, on the edge of bursting. "It would be foolish to mate with me."

"It would be everything. All I want. Something I in no way deserve but yearn for it the way spring is craved after the harshest winter." He spun me around until my nipples hit the chilled wall. He thrust inside me, rolling his hips in slow movements, and giving me time to adjust to him.

My head fell back against his shoulder as he moved in and out. His arms caged me in and his palms rested on the wall. He slammed into me, forsaking the gentle lovemaking until waves of euphoric pleasure rocked me. He sucked on my ear and twisted my nipple, easing his pace and then ramming me hard against the tile. I screamed and crumbled in his arms as my orgasm clenched over his cock. He kept my body surging and surging until I was a floating puddle around him. He'd unraveled me without even an ounce of venom in my blood. On my fourth release, he came with me, and it was then that he bit me just enough to leave me convulsing for a few minutes more. He cleaned me up and carried me to bed.

I rolled over and kissed him as my love for him shook me. "All I want from you is a life, son of Death. The simple moments like we had in Aresgan, but you're destined to be a king. I'm a peasant."

"With a fate thread to be a queen. You saw it yourself. Neither of us may understand how certain threads are possible, but that doesn't mean they aren't. If they exist, there is a way to them. The only thing between us now is if you can make peace with my thirst to kill."

I rolled onto my back and studied the intricate painting of angels on the ceiling. "I think I may struggle with it from time to time. That the aversion to it is something that doesn't fade away all at once. But I understand it better, and I realize what you were created to be. I also understand what you are is needed, and you reaping the people you have has helped many others. Like when I had to kill the siren queen to free the other women and girls. You will always crave slaughter. That's something that can't be helped as a reaper. But I love you for not just blindly accepting what they demanded of you. I love that more than insisting your need to kill is something black and white."

His fingers brushed my skin, awakening the nerves that were still alert from my orgasm. "You would be okay being my mate, then? For all time?"

I hummed at the bliss he sent everywhere. "Yes, forever. I could be yours and you mine. That would be the happiest fate thread."

"But?"

I opened my eyes halfway, drowsy from everything he'd done to me. "I cut the thread to give you an heir, and I will die long before you do. Old age will wrap around my throat and choke my beauty, while you will look like perfection for millennia."

He cupped my face. "My brothers' sons can rule on the throne after I have left it. For I have no need for an heir, only days of watching the sun on your face and dancing with you in the rain. Days of you on my chest, horseback rides through the wildflowers, and adventures to see all the realms together as we live an abundant life. Old age will greet you as a soft wind for the life I promise you, and even as decades pass, your beauty will only magnify, as will my love for you. And when death comes for you the third and final time, I will carry you into the next life so we may meet again and again until the universe itself ceases and our souls find eternal peace."

I held his face and kissed him, running my fingers through his scalp in the way he loved. We made love yet again, and this time it was the same as the last time we'd slept together in Aresgan, right before I left to confront dragons. It was a goodbye. I waited until his breathing evened out, indicating he'd reached a deep sleep. "I love you," I whispered as I slipped out of bed and dressed in the bathroom. After gathering everything I needed, I slipped through the castle, allowing my seer sense to lead me to an exit that felt empty.

I expected to walk all the way to the rift. Taking a horse would have been too risky, but there in the yellow grass field to the south of the castle stood a dragon. I ran to him and used his scales like a ladder to his back. If I was to have a dragon, I needed to learn to get on his back quickly.

He flew me to the rift. "Are you sure about this?"

"It's what your master wants. Why would you question it?"

"He's not my master. We may be newly bonded, but you are the only living creature I care anything for. That will grow fiercer as time goes on."

"Then why do you always listen to him?"

"I don't. Everything he asks of me, I do because I see the benefit to either you or me. I ask again, are you sure about this?" His wings beat the air at a rapid pace.

"I am," I said.

"Alright. I will be coming with you in your bag."

"I would like that. We can get to know each other better."

"It is a necessity. The closer we stay together in the first few months, the stronger the bond will take."

He landed right outside Grimheldin and shrunk himself so he could fit inside the forest, but stayed big enough for me to ride him like a horse. Before we reached the next open area, he shrunk to fit in my bag. Belphagor was waiting at the rift, holding a long golden staff with a large sapphire at the top. His scythe was tucked behind him like Alcaius's always was, and he had a sword holstered at his side.

He spread his hand out to the rift. "Go ahead."

"What do I do?"

"The same as you did last time. Unlock it, but only a little. As soon as we are inside, we will seal it, so there will be no leaks this time."

I dropped to my knees and placed my hand on the surface. A tingling energy tiptoed around my fingers. A flood of terrible images flashed through my head. Belphagor had promised no one would be harmed, and if he had lied, he'd die. That caused me to push through. An angry, swirling gash opened under me, and I fell, landing on solid black rock. Belphagor reached up with the potion and spread the contents over the tear. It sizzled and sewed itself whole again.

I didn't know if I'd survive the rift or what Belphagor had planned for me. I only had to get Alcaius's soul and release it back to him. If I returned to my reaper and he still wanted me, I would become his mate, and we'd defy all the fate threads the elders devised by creating the ones we stitched by choice.

FOLLOW THE AUTHOR

For the latest updates on Elaia Crowe, Follow the link below.

https://linktr.ee/authorelaiacrowe